Beauty Bites

A Biting Love novel

Beauty Bites

A Biting Love novel

Mary Hughes

This book is a work of fiction. Names, characters, places, and incidents are the product of the author's imagination or are used fictitiously. Any resemblance to actual events, locales, or persons, living or dead, is coincidental.

Entangled Publishing, LLC
2614 South Timberline Road
Suite 109
Fort Collins, CO 80525
Visit our website at www.entangledpublishing.com.

Select Otherworld is an imprint of Entangled Publishing, LLC.

Edited by Christa Soule
Cover design by Fiona Jayde
Cover art from iStock

Manufactured in the United States of America

First Edition August 2013

To Christa Soule, whose brilliant editing makes my other author friends jealous. :)

To Jessica Mittendorf for the perfect balance of critiquing, cheering and gentle pushing to soar into new skies.

To Gregg Hughes for everything else. And body heat.

Chapter One

Life is like brain surgery: it's smooth and pretty until you have to open it to fix something. Then you see the wrinkled, slimy mess. The surprise reversal is, that mess creates poetry and music and seeks to understand the universe.

Well, some brains do, at any rate.

"Hey, Sugar Babe. Yeah, you. The classy blonde." The squeal was male, barely. "Where you going?"

I'd merry-go-rounded through a heavy revolving door into the Luxe Indulgence Condo Community of Minneapolis. The door whoosh-whooshed behind me as I searched for the speaker.

A young man leaned negligently against the wall, leering at me.

Lovely. I didn't care for the leer, but I understood it. Even in medical scrubs and a messy ponytail, when I walked by heads turned. Decked out in my cousin's skyscraper heels, short skirt and low cut blouse, I regret to say necks snapped. I guess I cleaned up good.

He let out a wolf whistle, eye-stripping me of the few

clothes I wore.

Dammit. All I had to do was get to Holiday's penthouse to be safe. I swept a recon. Luxe Indulgence was one of those all-in-one communities, condos stacked above a cavernous concrete market bazaar. No signs saying "This Way To Penthouse". No elevator, escalator, or stairwell, not even a really long rope. The signs which marked stalls were mostly dark.

No other people were in sight.

Cold shafted my belly. Clutching my tiny evening shoulder bag and crunching my foil-wrapped package to my side, I gave the young man a no-nonsense glare, doing my best to radiate *not a victim* vibes.

He was radiating tough guy vibes, undermined by the stink of trendy, cheap cologne, the kind a kid would wear, like Eau de Boy Band.

I peered closer. Pink face, curly straw-colored hair, broad pug nose and squealing…he reminded me of something, maybe an animal. I couldn't quite put my finger on it.

"C'mon, Sugar Babe. Talk to me." He stroked the sparse hairs on his chinny-chin-chin…

Oh yeah. Little Straw Piggy from the Three Little Pigs.

I clamped my eyes against the image. During my surgical rotation I'd started reading *The Big Red Book of Fairy Tales* to a young patient. Apparently the stories had crawled into my brain and nested.

I consciously relaxed and opened my eyes in a friendly smile. "I'm trying to find the penthouse. Is there an elevator in this retail cave?"

His eyes lit up. "You lost, little girl? Let me help you." He pushed away from the wall and grabbed my arm.

Didn't it figure? I'd driven safely all the way from Illinois to Minneapolis, over four hundred miles, but Google Maps didn't cover this part of the route.

I slid out of his grasp. "On second thought, I'll find it on my own."

Two shop signs were lit—La Liquor and Zeki Sandalli's Turkish Coffee House. Maybe I could get directions at one of them. La Liquor was closer, so I shifted the package under my arm and headed that way.

He trotted after me in a wavering line. "Wait for me, Sugar Babe. Why the penthouse? Do you know Ric Holiday?" His tones were tinted with awe. "C'mon wait. You're classy, I'm rich. Not as rich as Holiday, but who is? You and me, we were made for each other. Let me show you my assets."

"Haywood, you idiot," a second male voice rasped. "She's not interested in your flat ass-ets."

My eyes snapped front. Reeling out of La Liquor were a brunet and a redhead. Clinking bags dangled from their arms.

I veered toward the coffee shop, pretending I'd been headed that way all along. Pretending nonchalance, but my heart beat faster and the air began to saw through my nostrils.

"Apple Bottom, wait." The scruffy brunet was on the porky side, like Little Twig Piggy. Trotting beside him, the redhead was built like a brick outhouse—yeah, Brick Piggy.

Straw Pig, Twig Pig, Brick Pig...the rushing adrenaline had surely eaten my brains.

They cut me off from the coffee shop.

My heart kicked up a notch and my grip tightened on package and purse. *The Three Little Pigs gone to the dark side*. My eyes cut left and right for an escape route. Come on, stairs or escalator or even a clue. Or at least a store that sold jet packs. All this money, and not even a sign?

Apparently, like a pricey restaurant, if you had to ask, you didn't belong. Nothing resembling a "You Are Here", so I picked a non-Piggy direction and pushed into a power walk. If the fates were kind, I'd find a way to Ric Holiday's luxe penthouse before they could catch me.

"Fates" and "kind" in the same sentence? Virtually inviting a cosmic wedgie.

I stumbled, nearly breaking a heel. My cousin's very expensive shoes were four-inch spikes, originals from famous designer MB. Cousin Twyla had tried to tell me angular was sexy, but I think they were the original Cruel Shoes. I could have gotten the same effect by smashing my toes into beetle carapaces and cranking my arches with a winch.

I caught myself but not in time. Twig Piggy reached sausage-like fingers for me. I ducked, dodged and spun out of there so fast my nylons smoked. Well, in my skyscraper shoes, more rolled out, to keep from twisting an ankle or busting a heel.

Piggy trotters rang behind me. "Honey Nips," Brick Piggy bellowed. "Don't run—we'll have some fun!"

Ah, the flower of male poetic expression. True, my nipples *were* unhappily poking up—I wore my cousin's bra too, and Twyla's penchant for whisper thin lace, while perfect for her Ds, was somewhat abrasive for my doubles.

A set of silver doors sprang into sight. An elevator! I sprinted for it, churning my hips like an oil rig. I careened inside so fast I hit the rail in back, bounced like a ball through the car's bright, mirrored expanse and found myself at the panel. I blinked. Okay, roll with it. I hit the close button.

The doors huffed and began to shut. I pumped the button like I was rubbing a genie's lamp, scrunching my eyes and wishing really hard. If there were any fairness in this world, I'd escape now.

Right. Why not give myself that wedgie and be done with it?

Thunk. My eyes popped open. A hand was jammed between the parting doors. Stupid safety bumpers. I backed from the panel.

With a toothy grin, Straw Piggy sauntered in, Twig Piggy and Brick Piggy behind him.

A fourth man strutted in after them like a chicken. A yellow claw of bangs, beaklike hatchet nose, sallow skin and red wrinkled wattle of a neck added to the image.

Straw Piggy said, "How's it hanging, Little?" *Chicken Little?*

Briefly, I scrunched my eyes. Don't do Fairy Tales, kids. It's ugly.

"It's hanging low, Haywood." Chicken Little grinned at me as the doors closed behind him. "Hey, bay-bee. Going my way?"

Lovely. Four of them and one of me, stuck in a small metal box—porn setup number nine, cue the wacka-chew-wacka music.

What to do, what to do? If I were Dr. House, I'd say, "Give me a differential, people."

Chase would say *Run*. Foreman would say *Attack*. Cuddy would say *Wait*. The one whose name I never remembered would say *Lupus*.

Nah, it never ended up being lupus. Besides, there were twenty-five minutes left minus commercials and someone had to spew gouts of blood first.

I smacked myself discreetly on the forehead. C'mon neurons. Gotta fire faster than this.

Run? Not with these heels; they maxed out at a brisk strut. Attack? Nah. They'd harassed me, but as I've mentioned, my looks arouse guys who then expect me to be horny because they are. Not my fault, but it's not theirs either.

If they actually assaulted me, I'd take action. But for now, I decided to wait. I only had to make it to the penthouse.

"Hey, Apple Bottom." Twig Piggy licked his forefinger and drew slow circles around a white floor number button. "Which one you want pushed?"

Brick Piggy leered.

"Let's get one thing straight," I said. "The name is *Synnove*, not Sugar Babe or Apple Bottom or Honey *anything*. Sin-no-vah. And I push my own buttons." I strode past Twig Piggy to hit the top floor. Crossing my arms, I glared. I'd made my point. In a few floors I'd be at Holiday's penthouse. No need to go nuclear.

The elevator started moving.

So did Straw Piggy, who stumbled over. "Cindy's a nice name. What's in the pretty box?" His breath released a cloud of Irish cream, which had been a favorite of mine up until now.

"Synnove. Not Cindy. Could you back off?" I tried to ignore the alcoholic weather system. Twenty-seven stories to the penthouse. This could be a long ride. "It's Toys for Tots, for the party." My cousin had gotten me the invite. My cousin's artistry had also plumped my DDs into rather dramatic mounds, the better to lure Holiday into helping us. But as a drop of drool from Straw Piggy's mouth barely missed me, I made a mental note to kick her artistic ass.

"Party?" Brick Piggy sidled to my other side. "Party with me, Honey Nips."

Sure, that would happen. Right after I discovered the cure for chronic hemorrhoids and male pattern stupidity.

"Toy?" Stick Piggy leaned across my body and ran a finger suggestively along the gift's foil edge. "I like toys. Especially the buzzy kind." He waggled his eyebrows.

In case I, you know, didn't get it. As pickup lines went it ranked up there with "Hey, bay-bee." I pinched the bridge of my nose. Above the door, five went out. Six lit. Definitely a long ride.

Piggies sidled around me, packing tighter and tighter until I reconsidered the nuclear option. At the very least I could whack Piggy skull with my cousin's heels to give them more open minds.

Open minds. Of course. I hunted in my evening bag for my wallet. "Guys, listen up. I may look, um, tempting but that's because I have some persuading to do and my cousin thought it would help. I'm not really like this."

All four men blinked at me.

Got their attention, now to drag their brains up out of their boxers. I pulled my wallet and flipped it open to my pictures. The one I wanted was on top, ready to remind me who I really was. I waved it under their noses. "See?"

Twig Piggy took the snapshot. "Yuck. Who's the scrawny kid?"

Brick Piggy snatched it from him. "Lumpy boobs, hair like straw, teeth like a horse...and those glasses, *ugh.* I've seen more attractive spectacles on a geek. Is this your ugly stepsister, Honey Nips?"

"That's *me.*" Age fourteen, lost and alone. Before my sister set me on the path to medicine.

They stared at me, then at the picture. Then they stared at me again. Their faces lost the glazed lust and acquired a sort of shocked intelligence.

I sighed in relief. Finally, they were taking me seriously. Just in time too. The elevator slowed as we reached the top floor.

Then, with a laugh, Straw Piggy handed me the picture. The rest joined in. I smiled and tucked the photo away, wondering what the joke was.

"You had us going, Sugar Babe." Straw Piggy grabbed me in a tight hug. "That scrawny kid, you. Ha!"

It was just a hug. Despite his cloud of bad breath and boa constrictor arms, everything would have been fine.

But he gave me a hard slap on the butt, a whack that hurt.

I'd taken self-defense. Good self-defense courses teach you what to do if harassed or threatened. Great self-defense makes those actions ingrained. Mr. Miyagi's training had become part of my very cells' mitochondria.

At the whack, my knee jerked sharply into Straw Piggy's groin. I didn't quite sock him in the 'nads but his sucked-in breath said *this is not a drill.*

His hands dropped and he made a sort of sick moo.

I stiffened, horrified. "I'm so sorry. But really, you'll be okay. I pulled it."

"Not...okay," Straw Piggy squeaked.

"Well, you may bruise. There's a lot of blood down there, the pampiniform plexus and the testicular...well, a lot of blood. But really, it's okay."

With a moan, Straw Piggy curled over and slid to the floor.

"What the fuck?" Chicken Little got in my face, his spaghetti claw of bangs shuddering with emotion. "What did you do to him?"

"Nothing." I clutched my gift and purse and, heart hammering, edged toward the still-closed doors. *C'mon open, open.* "He grabbed me and I reacted, that's all. It's fine. He'll be fine."

Chicken Little stalked me nose to nose. "He is *not* fine."

My vision zoomed. My internal doctor kicked in. *Bad breath. Small, purplish acne. Thinning hair under the hair gel but a whole swarm of chest hair escaping the neck of his shirt.* "You should stop those steroids, Mr. Little. They don't make you look any healthier and they can lead to high blood pressure and testicular atrophy—"

"You witch," he snarled. "Don't try to weasel out of this. Haywood's hurt and it's *your* fault."

My warning congealed into a lump in my throat.

"Why are you really here, Sin-no-vah?" He poked a threatening finger in my face. "Who invited you to Ric Holiday's *private party*?"

I leaped back to escape the finger, expecting door but hitting air. My heart skydived into my stomach. I stumbled, sunk my spiked heel into the gap—my cousin was so getting a "Kick Me" slapped on her back when I saw her next—but I managed, barely, to turn it into a floundering spin.

I blundered into a plush lobby of red textured walls and well-oiled lustrous wood. A single alcove, lit by mellow lamps, housed the only door.

The penthouse. My salvation. I sprinted for it.

"Oh no, you don't." Chicken Little seized my arm.

I executed a simple twist, popped loose and skied on the balls of my feet across the thick red carpet. I didn't stop so much as splat palm-first against the door. Panting, I cranked the knob.

The door was locked.

My heart kicked into race. A thrown glance showed Chicken Little rolling toward me, arms waving like a Dalek, expression set to exterminate.

I hammered the door with the heel of my hand, getting in a couple good *bams* before he grabbed my arm and yanked me away.

"Holiday Buzz is most definitely my business." His eyes cracked with bloody lightning strokes.

"Oh, crap. Are you Ric Holiday?" Sick dread thickened my throat. Had I offended the guy I'd come to impress? One of the Piggies called him Little but it might be a nickname. My cousin said Holiday was good-looking in a blond business-y way, attractive enough to be a playboy, but it wasn't clear if the attraction was looks or money. She hadn't acted particularly impressed, but she liked her men a little darker and a lot more dangerously dominant.

Dammit, if Chicken Little was Ric Holiday, I'd royally fucked up.

Snatching both my wrists, he cinched me in until his sour

breath cascaded over my face. "Would you like that? Would meeting a filthy rich ad man make you so hot you'd melt into a puddle of come?"

Eew. I gave up trying to be subtle and punched both hands down. He resisted, yanking up. I reversed with him, adding my own velocity, and swept my arms up and out. My wrists tore from his grip with such force that he stumbled back. For good measure, I gave him a chest pop, smacking his pec with the heel of my hand, putting my shoulder behind it. With an *oof* he hit the Piggies behind him. I noted with relief that Straw Piggy was standing again. Mostly.

I glared at Chicken Little. "Hands off."

"Bitch." He pushed away from the Piggies and came at me like Frankenstein, slow-slow-slow. I pivoted away, too scornful to block.

Mistake. He grabbed for me and managed to get his fingers hooked on the edge of my cousin's low cut blouse.

I went one way. The blouse, in Chicken Little's fingers, went the other. It tore, revealing Twyla's red lace push-up bra underneath. I stared down in shock.

Click. Pine-scented air flowed over me. My eyes lifted. The penthouse door had opened.

A man filled the doorway.

Everything—the scuffling, arguing, *time itself*—stopped. Even seeing extreme trauma during my ER rotation didn't freeze me like that. At first I only saw a broad chest in a tailored navy suit and snowy white shirt, a blue-black tie lining the valley between mountainous pecs. Eventually I'd have to get around to looking at his face. Eventually I'd have to start breathing again too.

"What's going on here?" The male voice was soft but the anger in it carried.

The Piggies shuffled their feet and stuttered.

"We were kidding around." Chicken Little's tone was

pleading, almost whiny. "Just playing, honest. Roughhousing."

"Your roughhousing went too far, Charles." The chest peeled out of the suit coat, spinning it off with ethereal grace, revealing shoulders wide as a four-lane highway and a body exuding enough power to run the CTA train system.

I fell back a step. My gaze landed on his face and I finally sucked in that breath. Strangely, all the oxygen had been siphoned out of the air.

Razor-straight nose. Sensual mouth, now the slash of an uncompromising line. Carved jaw, cheeks like knife blades. Spiky, tousled blond hair. He was good-looking like an F-22 Raptor. That face made my eyes hurt.

My lovely cousin, who'd done the research and so must have known what he looked like, had sucker-punched me, a ha-ha-gotcha-back ten years after that high school incident with the cat and the water balloons in the principal's office that wasn't my fault exactly.

Naturally that's when I caught sight of his eyes. My lungs imploded.

Ever been in a dark movie theater contentedly munching popcorn, and suddenly there's a close-up of an actor's eyes so blue they spike you straight in the brain?

Ric Holiday's eyes were blue like that. Azure, spelled s-a-b-e-r. He was glaring at Chicken Little—or actually Holiday Buzz VP Charles Little if I'd heard the name right—or I'd have had a complete meltdown. Once he'd drilled through Little's skull he bored into Piggy brains. "You three. I don't tolerate drunken rowdies. Didn't I make myself clear when I tossed you out?"

Trotters shuffled. Little said, "But Ric, they're my posse… er, my friends."

"I'm not impressed with your choice of friends. My word is final. They're not welcome until they sober up. Why do you think the door is locked?"

Then those azure eyes switched to me.

My breath stopped again. My hand landed on my throat. Beneath my fingertips my pulse was drumming *Stars and Stripes*, thundering away at 120 beats per minute or more. I scrabbled for something, anything, to say to those *eyes*. "Did you know the average resting heart rate is between sixty and one hundred and blood pressure is normally 120/80 although mine has skyrocketed to maybe 170/110…um, yeah."

Who needed the brain surgery now? *Focus*.

The glare warmed to an amused, appreciative gleam. I braced myself for a snide comment or a drop of drool on hastily and inadequately covered DDs.

But to my surprise, he draped his suit coat over me. For as big as it was, it was feather light, falling around my shoulders like a gentle hug. The fine fabric of the lining slid along my skin like butterfly wings.

"You must be Synnove." He pronounced my name with a Scandinavian lilt, S'*noehh*-veh. "I know what you're here for, and while I'm sorry I can't help you, that's no reason you can't enjoy the party—after we find you something to wear. Come in."

I opened my mouth to ask how he knew who I was. He waved me inside with the effortless grace of one strong hand. The force of his personality was such that I stepped inside at the gesture, the question dropping from my head. Chicken Little, minus his sidekick bacon, slunk through behind me.

A spacious living room pulsed with colored lights, music and glittering people. Holiday, head and shoulders above the crowd, glided through with the same effortless grace. The man was even sexier walking away.

Arousal is marked by increased heart rate and genital swelling as blood rushes to erectile tissue… I groaned and ground to a halt, pinching his coat closed at my neck. *Blood-rushing idiot*. I was here to negotiate, which meant getting him to take me seriously. Lust would only get in the way.

Holiday half turned, cocked a smile at me and gestured that I should come along. Again the force of his personality towed me along.

I tripped after him like a happy puppy.

What was going on? I was never instantly attracted to a man's mere looks. Substance drove me, not image. Although in my defense, I'd never met anyone whose image made as much of an impact as Holiday's.

As I followed him I stirred air filled with exotic perfumes, intensified by the heat of packed bodies. Tangy notes underlay the perfume, strawberry and chocolate and shrimp sauce. Long buffet tables were visible to my right through gaps in the glittering men and women enjoying champagne in crystal flutes and nibbling exotic canapés from molecule-thin gold-rimmed china in every shape but round. The central buffet table was lit by a bubbling fountain sparkling with both seasonal lights and cheer, and the tables were draped with expensive, brightly colored cloth.

Even the tables were wearing silk. And here I'd thought my cousin had overdressed me.

Only one woman wore anything like my simple skirt and top, a round-faced twenty-something in an unsophisticated A-line, her hair a sleek auburn bob.

But for the rest? Talk about conspicuous consumption. Holiday must have one heck of a credit card bill. I'm not unused to money—I had some very rich classmates. I just didn't grow up rich nor did I expect to get that way, because a medical degree without three years of residency and a license was only a title.

Holiday led me to the head of a hallway, where he stopped and turned. Beyond him was a knot of people whose smiles and nods for Holiday cooled into stares for me. I pulled his coat tighter.

As if he could see my thoughts, my trepidation, he smiled reassuringly. Those azure eyes said that, despite the stares, I was safe here. "My study is down that hall, first door to the right. Why don't you wait there while I find you something to wear?"

"Take this first?" I offered him the wrapped present, awkwardly clutching his coat to keep it from slipping off my shoulders.

"Ah, yes. Thank you for the shelter gift. I'll send someone along with a fresh blouse." He considered me, his gaze filled with warm appreciation touched with a hint of concern. "And perhaps a glass of champagne. Relax in my study. Then—shall we take a few moments to chat, you and I?" His smile heated.

Chapter Two

A shiver hit me at that hot, promising smile. *Testosterone plays a starring role in sexual arousal in males, but in women its purpose is less clear...*

Argh. What was wrong with me? No lusting, especially after the opposition. My cousin had charged me with a job, and while I wasn't against sex overlapping with work per se, I'd seen it cause aggravated stupidity too often. Extended bathroom breaks and three-hour lunches, sneaking around like nobody knows when in fact *everybody* does and resents the extra work.

Holiday's smile sharpened, a wicked glint of teeth edging it like a knife. Pure lust shimmered through me. *Oh yeah. Lubrication is followed by vasocongestion of the vaginal walls...*fuck.

I had to escape that promising smile, stat.

But the path to the study was clogged with people. I was screwed, and not in the good way.

Then Ric "Moses" Holiday extended one elegant hand toward his study. The sea of black, gold and silver miraculously parted. "Off you go now."

All that, with just the force of his personality. *Ooh.*

Before I got too girly over it, I paused to wonder if he had any real character to back it up. I heard sizzle. Didn't mean he had the steak.

His smile broadened. His eyes twinkled with an *I have all the steak you need.*

I gasped and escaped into Holiday's study.

It was an upscale man cave—walnut wainscoting, leather couches and recliners, a leather-and-oak wet bar, and a seventy-inch smart TV, the ultimate in flickering fires. Its impressiveness was kicked stratospheric by the 7.1 surround sound, eight speakers' worth of movie-quality goodness.

But an upscale man cave is still a man cave, and I'm not much into sitting on skinned cow. I crossed the room to a set of French doors cracked open to an evening breeze.

My breasts tightened. Not arousal but simple chill; I'd let go of the suit coat. I pulled it closed. Maybe Holiday made a habit of loaning articles of clothing to women. None of my business, but strangely, the thought bothered me. As if, for some reason, I wanted to be special to him. Had to be hormones making my brain mushier than normal. Stupid norepinephrine. I shook it off.

Nudging the French doors wider, I inhaled. The air, lightly scented with petunias, reminded me of home, back before my mother and father sold the house to travel the world, currently in Turkey or Abu Dhabi or something. Under the floral odor was a darker scent, mellow wood smoke with the tang of something spicy, elusive but mouthwatering. Unconsciously I turned my head to take the scent deeper—and buried my nose in the shoulder of Holiday's suit jacket.

My cheeks burned. The cooler outside air seemed less a treat and more a necessity now—nothing to do with Mr. Flamingly Handsome Holiday. But of course I was lying to myself.

Didn't matter. Uncomfortable was uncomfortable. I slipped outside. And stopped when my mandible hit the floor.

The terrace—it was too large and elegant to be a simple porch—was the size of my whole student apartment. Its black basalt surface was swept clean. An artful scattering of potted trees and graceful, discreet statuary merely enhanced the terrace's stark elegance.

I crossed to the far side.

The edge was safeguarded by a heavily lacquered oak railing supported by worked iron spindles. I ran one hand along the rail's silky smooth surface. This wasn't conspicuous consumption supported by a maxed-out credit card. This was a sign of solid wealth. Advertising sizzle apparently paid better than I knew.

The cooler air, combined with the railing's smooth feel, soothed me. Tensions I'd carried since even before the elevator incident drained out of my muscles. What a mess my life had become, that even that obnoxious incident seemed mostly an annoyance.

Leaning elbows on the railing, I looked out onto the Minneapolis-St. Paul night. Holiday's penthouse was high enough that the view was rooftops and stars instead of the sides of buildings. Random fireworks burst in the air. Below me, streetlights blazed. The lamps were so distant they might have been stars.

What the heck was I doing here in Rich Man's Canyon? Despite my runway looks, I was a hometown girl, raised in the small German-immigrant-settled city of Meiers Corners, Illinois. Ric Holiday's rich penthouse and vast terrace made my tummy shimmy. If I hadn't heard the desperation in Twyla's voice, I'd have thought she'd reverted to another of her endless childhood pranks on me.

But she *had* been desperate, and I loved her like a sister.

Besides, she invoked *You Owe Me A Favor*, calling due everything from when I'd borrowed her best suit for my med school interviews to covering for me the time I'd broken her Grandma Tafel's reading glasses using them to magnify bugs. Although I put my foot down when Twyla added twenty years of interest. Favor interest, really. Everyone knows you have to call "Bank" or it doesn't count.

Twyla was actually my second cousin, our grandmothers being sisters, although Meiers Corners was so insular I was related to half the population. If my father had been a native too, that percentage would have been higher.

But Twyla had a problem. Meiers Corners's local economy was too local; the city was in danger of going bankrupt. The solution? Tourism. The single benefit of straitjacket insularity is that we're steeped in local flavor. We have Quaint Local Shoppes coming out Ye Olde Sphincter.

So tourism seemed a natural fit, and was indeed working great, except for getting the word out. After all, tourism without tourists was, um…*M*.

Which was where Ric Holiday came in. Holiday Buzz International was the *Número Uno* ad shop for innovative campaigns. Holiday thought so outside the box that even circles were too square. Meiers Corners needed that desperately. We're hard workers but tend to think right angles are the epitome of chic.

So Twyla, wearing her city admin hat, called Holiday. But he said no.

So the mayor called him. Holiday said no. Our chief of police called him. Holiday said no. The mayor's secretary Heidi called, cracking her whip. Holiday said something unprintable that translated to no. Then our top lawyer and prime negotiator Julian Emerson called.

Holiday wouldn't even speak to him.

Twyla said *enough*. Time to meet Holiday face to face,

to find out what the sticking point was. Then she could apply either carrot (the mayor) or stick (Heidi) as necessary.

Time, Twyla said, to confront the lion in his den.

If she'd met lithe, tawny, forceful Ric Holiday in person, she couldn't have gotten that any more right.

I fingered the expensive material of his suit coat. There was something untamed about him, sinewy strength barely civilized by suit and tie.

A bolt of lust sheared through me, so long and hard that I shuddered.

Which was of course when the French doors behind me opened.

"Here you are. Escaping the heat? I knew you were beautiful, but now I see you're smart too."

I spun to behold the owner of that deep voice. He'd changed into another suit, this one a charcoal gray that contrasted sharply with his azure eyes. In even those few moments I'd forgotten how handsome he was—so gorgeous he made my eyes hurt, my only excuse for blurting, "Did you know that seeing a good-looking person of the opposite sex makes the brain release dopamine which triggers pupil dilation?"

I slammed my stupid dopamine-dilated eyes shut. This was my *opponent.* I tugged his coat tighter, thought constricting thoughts, opened my eyes and tried again. "If I were smart, I wouldn't have gotten my blouse torn."

He glided closer. "The smartest move of all. Not your fault and yet effective, since you're here to ask a favor. Visual aids are always useful in negotiations." His eyes, sparkling with sensual intent, dipped to where his coat covered my cleavage. A smile, full of promise, curved his lips.

That wicked smile was a pilot light to the broiler of my body, igniting every cell, *whoosh.* I flushed hot, shivered with it.

But my brain wasn't all that charmed. "Visual aids? Implying I should use sex to negotiate? That was beneath you."

His smile pursed. "The bra isn't a Temptress Siren Special? Retail $199. A thirty-six D unless I miss my guess, but a bit too small for you." His eyebrows rose. "It's not yours, is it?"

"I find it disturbing that you observed all that in a glance." I'd thought his gaze had been on my face in the lobby.

"Good peripheral vision." He quirked a grin. Devastatingly handsome morphed to boyishly attractive, actually even more devastating.

I squashed a groan. "Then what were you suggesting with the 'visual aids' crack?"

"My dear Synnove, I wasn't suggesting anything. Merely observing." He handed me a champagne flute. "Housekeeping is bringing you another blouse."

I clamped the coat with one hand to accept the cut crystal with the other.

"And in observing, I find myself curious." He sipped his champagne. "A beautiful woman from out of state attends my third annual Christmas-in-July house party, bearing a gift no less, but not because she wants something? I'm not sure I quite believe that."

I sipped champagne too, ended up with my lips in my esophagus. The stuff was dry. "You invited me." The words rasped like sandpaper. I coughed and tried again. "Do you always invite strangers to your house party?" Better.

"I'm in advertising. Even the people I know are strangers. But in this case, my admin handled the invites."

Which reminded me that, though we were strangers, he'd named me on sight. I again opened my mouth to ask how the hell he knew, when he hit me with those startlingly blue eyes and drilled both question and oxygen from me.

He wedged his own question into the gap. "Why go to so much trouble to see me?"

It took a few quick breaths to pump up air for an incautious answer. "You're a hard man to see." *Hard.* I clutched my champagne and dredged my brain up from the gutter of my hormones. "You're something of an enigma, Mr. Holiday. We want to negotiate, so we want to get to know you better."

"We? I'm disappointed. I was so hoping this was about *you.*" Lean fingers slid under my chin, raising my face.

Our eyes collided. His sparkled with intelligence and confidence and a sexuality so blistering I couldn't breathe. My body flooded with begging-for-sex estrogen. "M…me?"

"Yes. Your partners have sent the perfect leverage. The perfect female." His voice deepened, husky. "You."

"I'm…I'm not…" I cleared my throat.

He bent closer until his mouth hovered over mine. "You're not perfect?" His breath heated my lips.

Desire arrowed straight through me, sudden and splashing and hot.

I jerked back, hitting railing. "Not female."

"No?" Lips quirking, he straightened, giving me some space. "My mistake."

I covered one hot cheek with a hand. "I mean… Of course I'm female. But I'm not generally this…" I waved the hand at my short skirt and high heels, "…feminine." I forced myself to meet his eyes. "And I'm definitely not here in that capacity."

His gaze held an amused twinkle. "The clothes are a bit at odds with your trimmed nails." He caught my hand and held it in his. His thumb caressed the back of my hand.

The friction of his feather light stroking paralyzed me. But deep within me fires roused, as if I'd been asleep all my life and was waking at his touch. Heavens, was this what Sleeping Beauty felt at the Prince's kiss? The fairy tales I'd been reading Teddy seemed anything but innocent now.

"You have competent hands. Strong but refined." His thumb continued to stroke. "Are you a musician? Ah, no. A physician."

He was pretty damned smart. Or he'd lied and his admin had vetted me. Which, come to think, was much more likely than his knowing the truth by touching my hand.

His thumb moved down, caressing my wrist. My paralysis dissolved into trembling.

A discreet knock at the French doors saved me from crumbling into a pile of Synnove-shaped dust.

Bonus, I got to see Holiday walk again. Mmm-hmm.

He spoke briefly with someone at the door and returned with a scrap of red cloth in his hand. "My apologies. This was all that could be found. Apparently the nearby stores are closed. I'll hold your champagne and the coat."

He exchanged the cloth for my glass and turned discreetly away. When I shook out the scrap it proved to be a cropped cami too small to cover one breast, much less all of me.

On the plus side it had a darling little teddy bear appliqué.

I snorted mentally in disgust. I was a doctor, wanting desperately to be taken seriously in spite of my looks. Yet here I was, contemplating donning spandex because some primordial feminine mote in me thought it was cute. Life will play its little jokes. "You expect me to wear this?"

Over his shoulder, he gave me yet another version of his smile, a self-deprecating quirk, before turning again. "I don't expect you to wear anything. Pardon the double-entendre. But remember, you're here to ask a favor of me. It might be easier for you if you're clothed."

"I'm not sure this counts as clothing." I considered the charming yet far too small camisole. Holiday was right, this sexy little scrap might be our best bet to get him to agree to take us on as a client.

But despite Twyla's costume high jinks, I don't like using my looks to get my way. Life is unfair enough. I stuffed the top into a pocket. "The coat works for now. Look, Meiers Corners needs a creative ad firm. We need *you*."

"Me." He shook his head slowly. The back of his yellow head gleamed silver in the moonlight. "That's what your associate said. The delightful Twyla Tafel."

He turned, clasping both his glass and mine—in one big hand.

I swallowed a sudden flood of saliva.

His ever-changing smile was now regretful. "I'm sorry you made this trip for nothing, Synnove." Again that Scandinavian lilt made my tummy shimmer. "I have to say no."

"That's what you said to Twyla. But *why*?"

His smile tilted. "You're direct, aren't you? I'm not. I prefer to say no and leave it at that."

"I prefer to know the full story. Why?"

"Persistent too." His smile subtly altered, as if, for the first time, his real interest had been engaged. "All right, then. Your charming executive Ms. Tafel is not simply asking me to create an ad campaign for your fair city. She's determined that I visit in person."

"There's a reason for that." I extended both hands in a gesture of appeal.

I'd forgotten the coat. I had to scramble to grab it before it did the inevitable before-sex towel-drop.

He raised an eyebrow. My cheeks heated. I half-shrugged and bobbed my head, a nonverbal *I didn't do that on purpose*.

His eyebrow lowered and he handed me my champagne flute, nodding as if he'd understood.

Whoa. Twyla and her significant other did the silent communication thing, but I never had. It was scary and disturbing and frankly a bit exhilarating.

I took a slug of champagne, regretting it immediately when my eyes started watering. Sec means dry; it's also the sound of your epiglottis being sucked down your windpipe. I rasped, "Meiers Corners is not your usual Chicago bedroom community." Another, more careful sip helped clear my throat. "We're a small city with our own unique flavor." I thought of our stick-straight streets, broom swept sidewalks, ruthlessly weeded gardens. "Beyond unique. Mr. Holiday, you need to visit, get a feel for us, to get the campaign right."

"Call me Ric, please. I'm sure your city is delightful. But it's too far away."

"I drove it in seven hours. It's a day trip, two at most. You don't have time for a couple days?"

He pursed his lips thoughtfully. His gaze slid down my body, heating as it went, caressing the length of my legs. A twinkle in his eyes turned it from ogling into appreciation. "Would you drive with me? Just the two of us?"

Yikes. All that male alone with me in my little hybrid scared the crap out of me. His big body filling my car, me in that scrap of a red top, or worse yet, nude but for Twyla's too-small bra...

His lips curved into a smile so hotly ripe with promise that it went beyond sexy and shot into screaming orgasm territory.

Stab me with a 20G needle. I opened my mouth to tell him where he could stuff his hot, eat-me smile...*between my thighs...* "Many people think the quad muscles raise the thigh but actually the iliopsoas are the prime movers, whereas the muscles which pull the legs apart are..." I groaned. Years of medical school discipline, and his mere smile reduced me to a babbling idiot. "Please, if you just listen to my arguments, I'm sure you'll see why it's in your best interests to accept Meiers Corners as a client."

"Tempting." His eyes began to glow with a feral heat. He

took a step closer.

I clutched the coat tighter.

"But no." The glow cooled. "It really won't work. I have too many trips scheduled already. You'll see yourself out? Keep the coat and the camisole. You can mail them back if convenient." He spun and stode off the terrace.

"Wait!" I trotted after his broad shoulders into the study.

The room was empty.

I slowed. None of this had gone the way I'd expected, from the moment I'd whoosh-whooshed into Holiday's store-footed building. I felt off-balance, like I'd been clumping downstairs and landed on a missing step.

But I'd fought off-balance before and won. Both Mr. Miyagi and med school had taught me the value of persistence. Well, Mr. Miyagi also tried to teach me not to telegraph my kicks so much. But if Ric Holiday expected me to give up and leave, he didn't know me as well as he thought.

I found the only cloth chair in the whole man cave and sat.

He'd said no. But he hadn't said *why*. He'd smiled and twinkled and talked but he hadn't told me anything, nothing real at any rate. Typical ad man.

No, wait. He'd said one important thing, one *real* thing, about Twyla being determined that he visit in person.

But what was the problem with that? As head of an international business he must travel all the time. Right?

Maybe Twyla had come across something in her research that could help. I pulled my cell phone from my purse and called.

She answered on the fifth ring, out of breath. "H…hello?"

Pump me full of Novocain. She'd been doing it *again* with her Happily-For-Now fella, Nikos. Nikos was big and Greek, a human Mount Olympus.

Maybe a little more than human.

Sometimes Nikos's eyes turned a funky shade of brown. Like red. And sometimes his canines sprouted a mite too long. And he and Twyla giggled a bit too much about neckties when they thought they were alone. Okay, that probably wasn't supernatural.

Upshot was, I suspected Nikos was a vampire.

Yes, I know vampires don't exist. And I behave like they don't—pending independent confirmation. Call it waiting for a second opinion.

Besides, Nikos doted on Twyla and she was happy. That's what counts, right? I greeted her with, "I need help."

"Synnove? Aren't you supposed to be at Holiday's party? Are you okay?"

"I'm fine. I made it to the party. But..." I realized her voice had echoed, electronically, like she was going through lots of relays. "Where are *you*?"

"Me? Oh, the cabin."

"What cabin?"

"Chipmunk Lake. Wisconsin north woods? I told you Julian is thinking of buying a summer vacation spot for his househol...I mean his townhouse residents. Nikos and I are trying it out."

Julian Emerson owned the set of townhouses where Twyla and Nikos lived. But it was little stutters like "househol..." that made me think there was more to the story than that. "Where are you in relation to Minneapolis?"

"By car? A little over an hour away."

"*What*? Why in the name of my pert gluteus maximi did you send me, if you were going to be so close?" Although now I understood why she'd been in such a hurry to take off after getting me ready for the party.

"It's a vacation." Twyla's tone was defensive. "My first since New Year's, which didn't turn out to be a vacation at all."

"Hon, I'm sorry, I didn't mean to grouch at you. I'm happy you're getting a break. I'm a little touchy because I have a situation here. Holiday said no, which we figured. Didn't say why, but he did leak one thing—"

"What? You asked him already? Synnove, it's only ten o'clock. You must have just gotten there."

"So?"

"For heaven's sake, it's a party. You were supposed to connect with him first. Relax a bit, socialize. That's why we picked the *party*. Dressed you up."

I peeked under Holiday's coat at my torn blouse. "Yeah, that last part didn't work so well."

"Knowing you, I won't ask." Twyla sighed. "So you struck out. We all did, no shame in it. We'll find a way. Okay, if you haven't taken a motel room for the night, why don't you head over here? Turns out this cabin has three bedrooms. The big guy and I are only sharing it with Bo and Elena."

"I haven't given up yet. The sticking point is him coming to Meiers Corners in person. Any ideas why?"

"Hmm. Not offhand. I'll look into it." Twyla paused, her silence exposing suspicious smacking sounds. "Um, first chance I get."

"Uh-huh. Well, before you get too distracted, answer me one more question. Do we absolutely need Holiday? Can't we ask another ad agency?"

The smacking stopped. Nikos's dark growl sounded in the background.

"I know, lover." To me, Twyla said, "Unfortunately, it has to be Holiday. He's, um, the best."

Um, the best. Like the whole glinting canines and stuttered "househol…", there was more.

Like maybe Ric was a vampire too.

I smacked my forehead. *Not having that thought.* I was a med student. I'd seen my share of dead people and *none* of them had risen at the stroke of midnight. Until I got that independent proof, I was not filling my world with vampires. *Repeat after me, Synnove. There is no such thing.*

The door's click brought my head around.

No such thing as a…

An impossibly svelte, exotically beautiful woman in black eye shadow and blood red lipstick glided into the study, her clinging gown the exact blue-black of her hip-length hair.

…vampire.

Chapter Three

"I don't see why you had to zap my guards, darling," Vampersella said. "They wouldn't have hurt anyone. Much."

Ric glided into the study after the woman. Seated as I was, he didn't see me right away. He turned to close the door with a decisive click. "I told you when you called not to mess with us, Camille. We're protected. Your goons got what they deserved. Now, I've honored your pax and let you in. What do you…" His head tipped to the side as if sensing something. As if sensing *me*.

He turned from the door, color flagging his cheeks. "Excuse me, Synnove. I wasn't aware you were still recuperating."

I said to Twyla, "Call you back," and stowed my phone.

The woman, if she was one, glided between Ric and me and put red-nailed hands flat on his gray lapels. "Yes, yes, darling, you can have fun with her later. Right now you need to pay attention to me."

From behind, the plunge of Camille's dress revealed back cleavage too. As I stared at the shadow—was that blusher along the curves?—it all came together in my head, Ric's red cheeks, him with an impossibly sexy female in the study he thought was deserted. He'd brought her here for a tête-à-tête.

Whoops. My own cheeks heated and I rose to leave.

Ric glanced at me over Camille's head. She was tall, maybe my height, but he was so much taller that his eyes met mine. Something in their blue depths said he'd explain if I would just wait.

Maybe I imagined it. Only married people talked with their eyes, or, like Twyla and Nikos, those who were married but didn't admit it to themselves.

But I still had business with him, so I sat down.

"Stop looking at her, darling. That's not very flattering. Look at me." Camille slid her palms onto his cheeks and turned his face toward her.

His eyes clung to mine a moment longer, then shifted down. "What do you want?"

"To make you a very happy man." She clamped hands on his hips and ground herself against his slacks.

I popped to my feet again. I had business with Holiday but I didn't have to sit here while he did *his* business. Or got the business.

His gaze flicked back to me. Surprisingly, especially having seen the embers glow, they were stone cold, almost gray. "Not interested, Camille." He spoke to her but it seemed his words were for me.

Slowly, I sat back down.

"Oh, pooh." She backed off. "We both know it would be good. Why not mix business with pleasure?"

"It makes for poor business and worse pleasure. You're trying my patience. What do you want?"

She sauntered away from him, toward the wet bar in the corner, cutting me a glance on the way. "I'd almost think you were Alliance, darling. They're all enamored of their little human whores—"

"Watch it." His tone was flat, dangerous.

She twirled, giving him a quick smirk. "Their little playthings." Completing the spin she leaned over the bar and helped herself to a glass, poured amber liquid from a crystal decanter then took a delicate sniff. "Nothing but the best for you. I like." With a satisfied smile she sipped.

"I can afford a few luxuries. You've taken what patience I had. I know you're Nosferatu's lieut—" He glanced at me. "VP. Cut the crap. What does he want?"

The fine hairs rose on the back of my neck. Those significant pauses, the careful word choices. The strange words, cut off, like household and lieutenant.

This wasn't my independent v-guy confirmation, but to paraphrase Ian Fleming's character Auric Goldfinger, Twyla and Nikos were happenstance, Ric and Camille were coincidence. We were getting close to enemy action.

"Not simply what Nosferatu wants, darling." Camille smiled at Ric over her glass. "I'm an independent businesswoman. It just so happens I have my own *wants*." She licked slowly around the glass's rim. It would have been sensuous if not for the snake-like flicking of her tongue.

Ric's broad shoulders twitched. "If you want my advertising expertise, I'll save you some time. The answer is no."

"But darling, you haven't heard my offer." Her tongue retreated to caress her full scarlet lips.

He crossed his arms. "You haven't delivered it."

"Well, let me fix that." She set the glass down and sauntered back to him. From my perspective I saw red-nailed hands digging into his hair, prelude to an act I didn't want to see. I jumped up, this time determined to leave.

Ric threw an exasperated glance over his shoulder at me. "*Synnove*." His voice was richer than usual. It echoed in my head. "*Sit down*."

My knees buckled at the command. Vampire mind control? Not happening. Gathering my willpower I shook the compulsion away, and straightened. "No."

He whipped fully around, surprise clear on his face. Camille peeked around him, her own pencil-slim brows high.

"She's immune?" She started to laugh. "Not another one! Where do you Alliance boys find these little treats?"

"I'm *not* Alliance." Ric ran an agitated hand through his hair. The mussing only made him appear more boyish, more sweetly desirable. In a softer tone he said, "Synnove, I don't want you to leave before I've had a chance to explain."

"You don't owe me any explanations."

"Please? Just give me a few moments."

Wow, a "please". I got the feeling Ric Holiday didn't say that word very often. Besides, I wanted to hear her offer too. I let myself be mollified and sat.

"Good girl." Camille smirked.

"Camille." Ric took her by the arms and physically turned her attention from me. "Leave Synnove alone." He sounded tired.

She snuggled into him, fusing like iron-on tape. "I will, if you work up a campaign for my amazing new business." She puckered.

"Last time, Camille. *What* business?"

She stepped back with a pout. Seeing me watching, she turned it instantly into a brilliant smile. "Picture this." She swept her hands in a "wow" gesture. "High stakes gambling. Glittering showgirls. Anything and everything seductive and electrifying, 24/7."

"You want me to promote a new casino in Las Vegas?"

"Not just a casino, and not Vegas. I want you to promote a whole city."

"I see." His doubtful tone made it clear he didn't see at

all. Neither did I.

"The New Vegas." She painted the air with a broad sweep of the hand. "The Vegas of the Midwest. The new den of exotic pleasures. Ta-da!" Her grin turned sharp, almost fanged. "Meiers Corners."

I blinked. She was proposing to market my hometown, all that was traditional oom-pa-pah, jolly *gemütlichkeit* and wholesome fun, as gambling, glitter and girls-girls-girls? It was the polar opposite of what Twyla wanted. Picturesque becomes Burlesque. Stark incredulity bubbled up inside me with reason-choking adrenaline, and I opened my mouth to blurt *Please don't do that.*

A switch clicked in my brain. Emotion cut off. I was a doctor. I could handle anything. Or, as my sister Alexis put it, there was Miller Time and there was Crisis Time.

Problem: Camille wanted Ric to kill the spirit of Meiers Corners. Solution: Block Ric from taking her offer. Problem: Patients with bad habits actively resisted good advice. Blocking Ric might only force him to her side. Solution: Motivate Ric to my side instead. Problem: How? Solution: My nipples tingled as my breasts raised a suggestion or two.

Fuck. Somehow Ric Holiday derailed even doctor mode.

"Come with me to Meiers Corners, darling." Camille's lush red lips were only inches from Ric's. "We'll remake it together."

He stiffened. "No way in hell."

"Pooh. Don't say no yet." She wrapped an arm around his shoulders—and a leg around his hips, clinging like CD plastic. "Let me show you the benefits." Then she stepped back, reached behind her neck and tugged. Her gown slithered to the floor—hell.

She wasn't wearing a stitch underneath.

I slapped a hand over my eyes, but it was burned into my brain. Full, high breasts tipped with rouged nipples.

Flat belly, vertical navel pierced with a glittering gold ring. Adorning her mound was a single black curl tied with a tiny pink ribbon. Red lips glistened, not the ones under her nose.

She was most men's wet dream. When Holiday made a choked noise, I leaped to my feet. I did not want to be here when all his sizzling sexuality burst into flames for *her.*

He took two steps to my chair and grabbed me instead.

"Wha—?"

His mouth, landing on mine, cut me off. His hand tangled in my hair and his lips started moving, and I was suddenly immersed in male heat and gliding pressure.

It occurred to me in the first millisecond that he was doing it for show, still for her. But then he sighed and his tongue coaxed my lips open, and my heart started thudding in excitement and I forgot everything but the scent of him, the heat of him.

And the taste of him. As he deepened the kiss, it hit me in layers, like expensive wine. Fresh. Spicy. Male. And, at the edge, a darker, more complex note of danger.

His hands opened on my back in a firm caress. I melted into his embrace. In the depths of his arms it was even hotter.

"Synnove, *mmm.* You taste wonderful. Sweet. Hot. Bright."

"Hey. I'm right here." Camille's tone was pouty.

"Pure sunshine." His voice slid like silk over my lips.

"Right here." There was the sound of strings being tied, testily. "Fine. You've made your point. For now."

A skirt swished sharply to the door. The door opened then slammed shut.

With a sigh, Ric lifted his head. I lay in his arms, my lips throbbing pleasantly, wondering what had just happened.

"I'm sorry," he said.

I wasn't.

"I wouldn't have kissed you like that, but she'd never have

believed it with anyone less beautiful than you."

I snapped straight. Now I was sorry too, very sorry. Dammit, my first impression was right. He'd kissed me for show.

It didn't help that *I'd* kissed him because I was stupidly turned on.

"No problem." I pulled out of his arms. My tone of voice left no doubt that, hey, *huge* problem. But he himself had handed me the stick to motivate him to our side. "You needed my help, I helped."

His eyes narrowed. He nodded cautiously. "Thanks. I appreciate—"

"And Now You Owe Me." I made sure he heard the capital letters.

His eyes glinted like blue fire opals. "Do I." It wasn't a question.

"Quid pro quo, Holiday. I did you a favor, you do me one."

"I am not, under any circumstances, going to Meiers Corners." His teeth glinted as he spoke, canines extra-long.

The problem with a barely civilized male is that, when you corner him, the talons come out. His tone was so deadly, my insides spasmed. I held the advantage, but it was time to beat a strategic retreat. "We'll see about that." Mouth still throbbing from that kiss, I stalked out.

Yes, maybe I should have pressed. Ric Holiday owed me and there was only one thing I wanted in return.

My swollen lips reminded me there were actually two things. But I didn't *want* to want the second. So I left, at least until I could press my advantage in the proper way.

Annoyed that I wanted the second thing more.

As I stalked through the glittering partyrazzi, my irritation translated into motion. Ric's—*Holiday's* suit coat snapped behind me like a cape, exposing my fluffed bosom, but I didn't care. I stuck both chest and jaw out, making more like Wonder-Woman than Wonder-bra, elbowing through the crowd until the front door was in sight.

A claw-banged blond blocked my way. Charles Little grabbed for me.

As Synnove slammed out of his sanctum, Ric's eyes snapped involuntarily to the sway of her hips, so fast that he got ocular whiplash. His heart stopped beating for a moment at the sheer beauty of her backside, its lushness evident even under his tightly pulled coat.

Literally. His heart stopped pumping. Fortunately any such physical ailments were quickly remedied. He flexed the muscle with a thought and it kicked back into rhythm.

Turning away, Ric palmed his nape, wondering what the hell had happened. He kept a tight leash on his life, since he hadn't had any control of his death. A simple kiss shouldn't have hit him this hard. He'd indulged in decades of no-limits sex, the endless variety almost hiding the glaring fact that it was meaningless. Almost, but not quite.

Maybe that was it. He was tired of the trivial, shallow connections. Tired of sex without substance.

Synnove was a breath of fresh air. No, brighter, more life-giving. She was sunshine.

Oh God, he missed sunshine.

He shook himself. He didn't need sunshine. He had his work, his home and his freedom. He calmed himself by touching the things that made his existence worthwhile. The warm, hand-buffed golden oak, the cool glass of graceful vases. His touch and gaze lingered longest over the faces in framed pictures, decades' worth of friends.

Reminders of all he stood to lose.

A click spun him around. Had Synnove returned...?

But a tall shadow filtered through the doorway, unseen except Ric knew what to look for.

The assassin had come to visit him.

Shadowy hands raised in pax. Wouldn't stop the assassin if he wanted to kill. Ric knew that because the assassin had already beat the crap out of him a few dozen times.

Ah, the good old days.

Ric smiled. "Hello, Aiden."

"Nice party." The shadow moved into the light, but it never seemed to make a difference with Aiden. Black hair, black eyes, black stubble on his square jaw, he was shadows from head to toe. Even his clothes, sleeveless T-shirt revealing dark bronze muscles, loose pants and soft-soled shoes, were all black to ensure that no matter what the lighting, he was as deep as the darkness from which he emerged. Hell, even a sense of dark menace clung to him like a shadow.

All black. Including his near-permanent scowl.

It was Ric's mission in life to make Aiden smile. So far Ric had managed that feat twenty-two times over the decades. Only full smiles counted. "Thanks for patrolling the party in person. Sorry to make more work for you."

"You should be sorry, leaving your guests like that. Where have you—" Aiden's nostrils flared. "No, you smell like you took a bath in estrogen. The question isn't where, it's what? What have you been up to?"

"Kissing one woman to annoy another."

"You're lying."

Ric wondered what gave him away. He'd lose less money to Aiden at poker. Of course the reason Ric had given Synnove, that he'd kissed her to make a statement to Camille, was a lie. He'd said that automatically to protect the real reason, the unacceptable reason—he *wanted* to kiss her. "How do you know?"

"Your words say one thing, but your eyes another."

"And *your* words say you're a pain in the ass, but your eyes say…wait, they say the same thing."

Those deadly lips quirked, but it wasn't a full smile, so it didn't count. "You're very good at manipulation, my friend. But sometimes you wield lies like a sword. Beware lest the wrong people get cut."

"Good advice." Ric scrubbed a hand over his face. He'd hurt Synnove, and was sorry for that. "Although in this case, maybe it's for the best." Dropping his hand, he began to pace. "The last thing a beautiful human female with her whole life ahead of her needs is to be in thrall to a vampire."

"Beautiful?" Black brows rose. "That's the first time I've heard you apply that term to a female. In fact, I think it's the first time I've heard you apply *any* term to a female other than 'convenient'."

Ric stopped pacing to scowl. "You think you're so funny."

"Just honest." The eyebrows lowered. "You enthralled her?"

Ric started moving again, slower, wandering around his sanctum, touching things. The velvety petals of fresh-cut flowers, as soft as Synnove's skin. The freshly laundered bar towels, smelling of sunshine, like Synnove… "No, actually. She managed to turn my mental suggestion aside. Coupled with her—" luscious body, fiery-sweet taste, "—personality, it makes her quite compelling."

"Compelling. I see." Though Aiden's face was absolutely straight, Ric could hear the sarcasm.

And the unspoken question. *Compelling enough for Ric to care again?*

It was the last question Ric wanted to answer. He didn't have a great track record when it came to young, beautiful females needing him. Especially the ones he wanted to protect most.

So instead, he stopped behind his wet bar. "Want a drink?"

"If you're buying, sure."

Buying. Ric considered his well-stocked bar as he set out two heavy whiskey glasses. These were riches he'd never known as a child, growing up an orphan near Fort Dearborn. Even a single scrawny chicken would have been riches then.

"Do you ever stop remembering it?" Aiden's cool tones broke into Ric's thoughts.

Ric cocked his head. "Do you ever get tired of being omniscient?"

"I'm not omniscient. I just read people very, very well."

"I'm not people."

"You know what I mean. You're not that boy anymore, Ric. Not sleeping in whatever stable you can hide in, doing whatever menial chore you can to get food, not fighting dogs for table scraps."

Ric rubbed a thoughtful thumb over the deceptively plain bottle of fifty-year-old whiskey from the Isle of Islay. "I'll always be that boy. Can we talk about something else?"

"All right." Aiden glided soundlessly to his side and accepted the glass he poured. "The testing of our boundaries has begun again. I was hoping Nosferatu's last wave was the final one."

"Would've been nice. It's Camille."

"Fuck me." Aiden downed his drink in two large gulps.

"Show a little more respect for the whiskey. But well said." Ric grimaced. Two years ago they'd decided to stop hiding from Nosferatu, the unofficial vampire king of Chicago. They'd had a plan, but it didn't include confronting Nosferatu's best. Should have picked a different path.

"Damned right we should have done it differently." Aiden held his glass out for a refill.

"Asshat mind-reader." Ric poured a generous three

fingers. "We had no choice. Nosferatu was onto us. You discovered that." The assassin had expanded his repertoire over the years, taking to spying like a hawk took to hunting.

"We could have run." Aiden sipped this time.

"Impossible. He'd have taken his revenge on my household. My humans are my friends. My family. I could never stand by while they were abused."

Aiden grunted. "The old fart *does* have an awful sort of creativity when it comes to torture. But I'm not sure we picked the right way to fight." He shook his head. "Marketing and mirrors."

"Again, what choice did we have? The head of a veritable vampire mob versus two vampires? Besides, nobody's better than me when it comes to image."

"Marketing and mirrors," Aiden said again.

"It lured them onto our turf, didn't it? Gave us the advantage?" Ric had created an image to entice the vampire out of his power base in Chicago. Then Ric and Aiden set booby traps and mindfucks on all possible routes to Minnesota, triggered by vampires only. Unfortunately Nosferatu hadn't bothered to show up himself—the old vampire did like to sit in the middle of his web—but his exploratory waves had all run home crying. Until Camille. "And now we know the new electrified windows work. Camille's crew got zapped."

One corner of Aiden's mouth crooked up. "They did indeed. Screamed like a bunch of prissy little girls." The half-smile died. "Why'd you let *her* through?"

"She declared pax. Said she wanted to talk about advertising. Since that involves the agency, I thought I'd better hear what she had to say."

Holiday Buzz was a public business so he and Aiden hadn't electrified it. But they'd installed silver fixtures, lots of running water and garlic booby traps to make any invading vamps nice and sick.

Now Camille, a top lieutenant, was here. The game had turned deadly.

"So..." Aiden drank off his whiskey. "What did Nosferatu's bitch want?"

"Bitch?" Ric pursed his lips. "What do you call people you don't like?"

"Dead."

"Ah. She wanted marketing advice, if you can believe it. She didn't mention my past—didn't even seem to know you exist." Ric paused. "Maybe Nosferatu didn't send her."

"Please. He doesn't let any of his puppets off their strings. He sent her, all right. But he hasn't trusted her with the full story." Aiden held out his glass.

Ric covered the glass with a palm and leaned closer to his friend. "What's eating you?"

Aiden's eyes held Ric's. "I have a bad feeling about this."

Ric's shoulders tightened. Aiden's bad feelings were never inconsequential, and never wrong. "Damn it." He picked up the bottle and poured. "I don't suppose it's telling you anything specific?"

"No."

"Well then. Shut the fuck up. I have enough to worry about."

"Your wish is my command." Aiden sipped, seemingly nonchalant, but Ric's shoulders tensed even more. With the assassin you never saw the killing stroke coming. Sure enough, Aiden said, "So, you kissed Camille to annoy Beautiful?"

"Other way around. But you knew that."

"Hmm." A mischievous almost-smile flirted with Aiden's lips. "Then aren't you worried Camille will do a Wicked Queen on Sleeping Beauty?"

"Fuck me." Ric threw his glass into a paneled wall. He took a couple controlled breaths before turning back to Aiden. "Camille's too self-absorbed to consider any woman could measure up to her, much less beat her. Still…well."

"Do you want me to make sure Beautiful is all right?"

"Her name's Synnove. It means sun gift." Ric took another controlled breath. "Like your name means annoying wiseass. If she's threatened, it's my fault. I'll take care of it." It wouldn't hurt to make sure that Synnove had made it out of his building all right. That she was safe.

The thought of going after her, of *seeing her again*, blew all his careful breaths out the window. He inhaled sharply, oxygen drilling his chest.

"Okay, then," Aiden said with a chuckle. "See you later."

Ric was already out the door.

Chapter Four

I ducked Little's grab—only to get snared by his second. His hands cinched a tourniquet on my arm, his eyes were daggers and his wattle was shaking. If that weren't clue enough to his mood, his teeth were grinding so hard he was doing his own root canals.

I wanted to leave, but I wanted to do it without triggering Chickengeddon. "Excuse me," I said politely. "Please let me by." I tried to edge past him.

He stalked off, dragging me with him.

I could have twisted out of his hold, but my body was still trembling from Holiday's kiss and I wanted to resolve this civilly. Besides, the skyscraper shoes and clutching at Holiday's jacket hobbled my technique.

Chicken Little yanked me into a small room with washer, dryer and wire wall racks. He spun me inside and released me to slam the door shut, then leaned against it.

Briefly I pinched the bridge of my nose. Trying to help my cousin, I'd gotten this. Yep. No good deed goes unpunished.

"I can get you what you want, baby." Little's snarl rasped

with a disturbing lecherousness. "You want Ric, I can get him."

Hard to believe. Holiday didn't seem like a man to bow to pressure. "You don't even know what I need him to do."

Little laughed, not nice. "Women only want two things from Ric, advertising or sex. Usually both."

My face heated. "I came for the advertising." What else I'd gotten, well, Little didn't need to hear. "Why would Holiday do what you want?"

Little puffed out his scrawny chest. "I'm his partner."

"Please." I barely managed to keep my disbelief from extending the word into a derogatory two syllables. "Holiday Buzz isn't a partnership."

"Not in the papers of incorporation sense, but I'm Ric's senior VP. I'm in on all the decisions. I'll be CEO soon. I already run the company when he's away."

"He doesn't seem to be away a lot."

"What are you talking about? Ric travels all over the world for clients."

My turn to stare. "Then why won't he come to Meiers Corners?"

"My-ers what?"

I shook my head impatiently. "A city near Chicago."

"Oh, that." Little rolled his eyes. "He has a thing about Chicago. Won't go within a hundred miles of the place."

"Really? Why not?"

"Who knows? Who cares?"

"I do, because that's the job. Since you can't make him do it, I might as well leave." I reached past him for the knob.

He grabbed my wrist and used it to push me back three steps. I barely kept myself from responding sharply—with a knee. Hadn't he learned anything from the incident with the Piggies? He said, "Not so fast, baby. I can get him to take you on, don't you worry about that. Worry about how you'll pay me."

"Money? That's the usual way." I shook my wrist gently, trying to make him let go. I really didn't want to turn the guy's testicles black and blue.

"When the other person looks like you? Please. You've got other things of much greater value."

I searched his face and did not like what I saw. I said softly, "Don't go there."

He smirked. "You want Ric to take your job. I'll get him to. *If*." He raised himself on the balls of his feet, until we were nose-to-nose, the wash of alcohol breath almost overpowering. "You and I do the horizontal boogie."

Well. I guess that was better than the horizontal line dance.

In case the alcohol fumes were as bad inside his skull as on the outside, I spelled it out. "I don't sleep with every man I meet. I'm not that kind of woman."

He laughed. "Of course you are. Look at you!"

I huffed. Dammit, there it was again. "Appearances can be deceiving."

"Sure they can. But not in your case, baby. You're built for lovin'. How about a down payment?"

He thrust fingers into my hair and laid one on me.

My lips were still tingling from Ric's, and at first the pressure and heat revved an already idling motor.

Then he thrust his whiskey-saturated tongue down my throat. My motor cut off like a switch, *click*.

"Stop," I said, or more like "shlah" because he was a sloppy kisser and really getting into it. I let go of Holiday's coat and wedged my hand between our mouths. "I said *stop*."

He nibbled my hand, with enough tongue to slime my fingers. Yuck. I yanked away and wiped my hand on my skirt; the instant I got it home, it was going into hot water and bleach.

"You want it, baby." He shoved the coat off my shoulders. "And I'm the man who can give it to you." He snatched at my breast, thumbing the nipple through the thin lace of Twyla's bra. Shocked, the poor thing leaped to attention.

I was shocked too. But I was also trained, and enough was enough. I needed him to stop, and not start up again. Which meant significantly altering his impression of my "wanting it, baby". But his fingers were still tangled in my hair, so I couldn't yank bodily away without tearing out a chunk.

My brain went into overdrive, ala Downey's Sherlock Holmes.

Grab Little's wrist to control distance.

Fake a groin shot to open a gap.

Make my point.

Go. Grab, fake. He hopped back, still hanging onto my hair. It raised his upper arm, giving me the opening. I jabbed a spear hand into a pressure point in his armpit. The armpit shot was dangerous (don't try this at home!) but I'd done it soft to minimize damage.

He yelped and let go instantly. "What the fuck?"

I snatched up Holiday's coat and whipped it around me. "I said, I'm not that kind of woman. Whatever you think I'm built for, it isn't *you*."

"You think it's Ric?" Little sneered it, but he cupped his pit protectively. "Ric already screws tons of sluts like you every day. You're nothing special, baby."

I hadn't done anything to bring this on except exist. Not fair, but being achingly plain until puberty hadn't been fair either. I ratcheted myself to my full height and glared down at him. "Let me make this crystal clear. If you can influence Ric I'm open to talking terms. But sex isn't part of the offer."

"This isn't over." Glaring, Little flung open the door and stalked out.

My neck tightened. I didn't like making enemies and

Charles Little struck me as the worst kind—backstabbing. I pinched Holiday's coat closed and left as quickly as my cousin's high heels let me, hyperaware all the way to the elevator. I punched the down button. A trilling ring from below said I'd have a wait; the elevator was being held.

While I waited, I stewed. Dress up, Twyla said. Flirt a little, get us some information. Easy. Yeah, right. I took out my phone and hit redial.

Twyla panted, "Hello?"

"I don't care what the mayor thinks. We can get someone else for the advertising campaign. *Anyone* other than Holiday." I may have spit the name.

"Whoa, wait. Calm down and tell me what happened."

"I am calm," I said through teeth grinding their way to a dental appointment every bit as expensive as Charles Little's. The elevator finally dinged its arrival. I ignored it. "I talked to Holiday. He said no. I talked to you. You said Holiday or nothing. Then in waltzes Naughty Vamprietta in a spaghetti noodle's idea of a dress. Honestly, there was more material in that teeny top Holiday gave me."

"The top Holiday gave—Wait, what?"

"Nothing." My cheeks heated. I plowed on. "Holiday glides in after her and shuts the door with a very I-want-to-be-alone click. She's all *dahling* this and *dahling* that, but I was there first so it wasn't my fault Camille's two's company became a crowd."

Twyla hissed. "Camille? Skewer me with a palette knife."

"You know her?"

"She's a rat in a people's suit. What did she want?"

"To make us the Midwest's Vegas." I outlined Camille's plan.

Twyla started swearing—in Greek. She once told me Nikos was so taciturn she had to speak for both of them. At the time I'd thought it was exaggeration. Apparently not. Underneath her cussing was a low, ominous growl, more animal than human. Nikos got a little feral when his protective side came out, another thing that made me think v-thoughts.

"This changes things," Twyla said when she'd finally run out of cuss words. "We can't let Camille get her red-nailed hookers into Holiday. This isn't the first time she's tried to ruin Meiers Corners, but while she's only semi-competent on her own, Holiday is frighteningly good. With him as her tool, she could do it."

I pictured Holiday as a tool…a long and thick one…and tamped down a lusty shudder. "How are you going to keep her from hooking him?"

There was a telling silence on her end.

"No. Oh, no."

"Synnove, we're desperate here."

"No, I tell you. I do not live by the accident of genetics and nutrition that makes my body. I am not saving Ric Holiday's skin from Camille's hookers by sinking my own short and sassies in. And in case that's not plain enough—I am not sleeping with him!"

"You don't have to sleep with him. Just…seduce him a little."

"Seduce him a *little*? Is that like being a little bit pregnant? Dammit, Twyla, I'm a doctor, not a hooker!"

She sighed. "You've changed since The Incident. Become all mistrusting."

"The Incident only clarified the truth."

"You say potato, I say mistrusting. Tell you what. Drive to the cabin and we'll talk. Together we'll think of something else."

Tension released. "Thanks. Especially if thinking includes alcohol." I hit the down button with less force. The elevator dinged and started to open, not having gone anywhere. "How do I get there?"

"Take I-94 east. Exit 24, turn north, then follow the signs for Chipmunk Lake Cabins. Call me if you get lost."

I tucked away my phone, stepped forward—and bounced, breasts-first, off a powerful, dark-suited arm barring my way.

"What is The Incident?" Ric Holiday said.

My mouth hung open but no words came out. My DDs tingled from where they'd air-bagged against his arm. Either he worked out a lot or he was built of granite. My nipples poked up for a look-see; yep, granite, mmm-mmm. "Did you know breasts are composed of terminal duct lobular units covered in subcutaneous adipose tissue?"

I slapped a hand over my mouth.

A tiny smile warmed his face. "Do you always quote *Gray's Anatomy* when you're nervous?"

"I'm not n…nervous." Damn. "Let me pass."

"It's cute, you know." He dropped his arm and schooled his face into an expression of serious inquiry. "What is The Incident, please?"

"Direct, persistent and polite. You're a trifecta of virtues, aren't you?"

"Why do I get the feeling that was sarcasm?"

"Because you have a good ear?"

"That's not the only organ on me that's good." His lids lowered with lazy suggestion.

I snorted. "You need work on your pickup lines."

That got a genuine smile out of him. Damn, still edible. I escaped into the elevator. "Goodbye, Holiday." I hit door close.

He slid through the gap with one effortless step. "Is The Incident why you gave up your residency berth?"

My head jerked up. "How did you know that?" I hit the G button with more force than necessary. Hitting the G-spot… damn, what was it about Holiday that put sex on my brain?

"That's not common knowledge. Spying?"

"Facebook. Same thing. Not your page, your cousin's."

"Why me?" I glanced up, but no answer was written on ceiling or wall, unless the answer was Max Cap 15. "I have the only cousin in all of Meiers Corners who's made it into the twenty-first century."

"Not her fault. She's running a city trying to pull in tourists. Social media updates are part of her job. The Incident?"

"It's a long story."

"I have time. Buy you coffee?"

Damn, he was smart and persistent and sexy as hell, and the only male *not* trying to grope me in recent memory. Plus he wanted me to talk about myself.

I blew a resigned breath. "All right. But we go Dutch."

As a young girl, I was plain and shy. Puberty added a patina of ugly, with lumpy breasts, frizzy hair and terminal acne. Before puberty I'd had a few girl friends. After, well, they were all interested in boys. I was interested too, but no boy would be caught dead with me.

My friends drifted away and I found myself alone.

Then, the weekend of my first homecoming, when all my friends had dates and I was alone again (naturally), my older sister Alexis took pity on me. We'd never connected much—I was fourteen and she was twenty-two—but she collected me that weekend and showed me college life, or the tamer parts of it.

A first-year med student, she really didn't have time for me. But she took time anyway, cheering me up, showing me that at least someone cared. Only one thing didn't center around me that weekend—finishing her biology lab.

As a prerequisite she hadn't completed, she was taking advanced bio independent study. The lab had to be done or she'd fall hopelessly behind. She gave me the option to join her or not.

I nearly didn't. But she'd spent so much time cheering me up, the least I could do was make the effort. I went, sat down and prepared to be bored.

But as she got absorbed in the work, well, it absorbed me too. As the afternoon progressed, she let me help. It was so engrossing I forgot my troubles, my loneliness. Forgot I was awkward and ugly.

I discovered a new Synnove that day. One who was smart, who was capable. Who was wanted, even needed.

Medicine was my salvation. I never looked back.

Until The Incident.

We got our coffees—I tried to pay for mine but Ric nudged a twenty into the barista's hand before I even ordered—and made our way to a small café table. He didn't confront me immediately about The Incident. I wasn't reassured. It only meant he'd blindside me later. We sat.

He leaned forward. "So. Why did you leave medicine?"

I was his entire focus—my face, not my boobs. It was thrilling, him taking me seriously, looking directly into my eyes, into *me*. Maybe actually seeing me, seeing the human being inside the golden five-nine fashion doll.

But while sexy, his intense gaze was also unnerving. I blurted, "The iris has two layers and both fibrovascular and epithelial are pigmented which is why some men have such startling eyes…uh, I mean…"

He was smiling again. I sipped coffee to cover my confusion. Damn it, he was right; I did spout *Gray's* when flustered. I didn't remember doing that before meeting him. Maybe it was some special new disease he'd given me, Stupidous Vomitous or Synnutcase or Holidayammeritis.

Foam tickled my upper lip. The coffee was Turkish, the good kind, the kind that you had to chew and that chewed right back. The heat was reassuring, the bite energizing. My neurons finally started firing and I recalled what he'd actually asked. "I haven't exactly left medicine. Or, not yet."

"You withdrew from your residency. No residency, no specialty training, no MLE-3, no state exam, no license. You may be a doctor but you can't practice."

"You know your medical education."

"I do my research."

"Or your spy does."

He smiled slightly. I was coming to see that he was a lot like Nikos in that his words didn't communicate much content. But his smiles made up for it, as varied as snowflakes. This smile said he was enjoying our banter.

Strangely, I was enjoying it too.

He tore a packet of sugar into his coffee. "Your problem isn't academic. You're top of your class."

"No." I sighed. "But it started in school."

"Explain."

And because he was looking at me and not my breasts, and because we were both enjoying this, I did. "It's a long story, so I'll give you just a few examples. My first year of med school, not one, not two, but five pairs of my panties were stolen from my dorm room. I put it down to freshman high jinks."

"I see," Ric said.

"Do you? Second year, in my organic chem lab, I isolated semen in my unknown. I put that down to kids under pressure, blowing off steam, screwing with other kids' experiments."

"And the plot thickens."

"Not just the plot. That year my reproductive anatomy study group wanted hands-on experience. As in, wanting me to strip for a thorough exam. A third of us were women so I attributed that to high hormones and not enough sleep."

"Well," Ric said doubtfully, "you're certainly forgiving."

"Dense, you mean? A few sides short of a bedpan? Pumpkin positive?"

"I haven't heard that one."

"Shine a flashlight in her ear to light her eyes. That was just pre-clinical. During clinical, I'd give instructions to male patients staring south of my neck, who called back to ask for the same information from other doctors. I'd give instructions to women, who did the opposite of what I told them."

"Out of spite?"

"At the time I thought it was stress and trauma making them forget what I said. And before sheer volume and repetition told me otherwise, it'd be time to move on to another specialty. But yeah. Probably they weren't taking me seriously. Or hated me because of my looks."

When I grew silent, Ric said, "Their loss."

My heart warmed. "That's when I started rethinking my career choice. What does a doctor have if she doesn't have respect?"

"Oh, I don't know. Competency? So general discontent made you give up your residency?"

Something in his tone told me he already knew me better. That possibility of being known, of *connecting*, made me share something I'd never told anyone except Twyla. "No, there's more."

I took a deep breath, cut my eyes away and started slow. "When Match Day came, I got the residency of my dreams. I was set to start this fall. But a few weeks ago at the clinic, the guy who'd put the semen in my lab experiment confessed. I laughed about how he'd tried to screw up my experiment.

And he said he'd done it because he thought I was the sexiest thing he'd ever seen, and that my lab equipment was better than any girly magazine for jacking off."

"That was The Incident?"

"No. But it woke me up. The semen, the panties theft, the constant sexual innuendo wasn't accidental, none of it. There were no excuses."

No excuses.

"My whole perspective shifted. Even stuff from before medical school, stuff I'd always thought was high jinks—it was because of my damned looks." I looked up then, braced to see his eyes on my cleavage.

His azure gaze, locked on mine, said *I understand.* He took my cold hands in his, warming them. His simple kindness freed something inside me for the first time since The Incident. Anger, frustration, fear…it all came pouring out. "Damn it, Holiday, I spent years honing my brain, dreaming of being a doctor and helping people. Of making life a little less unfair for the hurt, the sick, the injured. But now I knew—I *knew* no one took me seriously. I couldn't help people because I looked like a damned porn star instead of a doctor."

"I'm so sorry." He rubbed my hands. I realized I was trembling only after the shaking slowed.

I took a deep breath, pressed it out and continued more calmly. "Once it clicked, I saw evidence everywhere. Or maybe I was raw and hadn't built up the skin again. But everything set it off. I didn't think it could be worse."

Ric's thumb caressed the back of my hand, silent support.

I took strength from his understanding and spilled it. "Last week during a surgery—during the entire surgery—the doctor stared at my breasts. I felt violated and angry. But worse, because he wasn't paying enough attention, he screwed up the surgery. He caused permanent damage to the patient."

My eyes prickled. "All because of my damned body."

Gently, Ric said, "He isn't much of a doctor then."

I shook my head, not willing to let myself off so easy. "Maybe. But it still happened because I was there." I retrieved my hands and drank off my coffee. "Well, now you've had my whole sorry story."

He tilted his head. "There's more."

I flushed. I hadn't even told Twyla the horrific rest. How the hell could he know? "Isn't that enough?" I crushed the coffee cup in one hand, wishing I could crush my pain. "I have to go. Better get back to your party. Your guests will be wondering where you are." I started to stand.

To my surprise he caught my hands and tugged me back down. "My guests can wait. I'm sorry you had to experience that harassment, but your looks are part of who you are. You shouldn't leave medical school because other people can't handle your appearance."

I warmed at that.

"Especially when you can put your beauty to use."

Abruptly I chilled. "What do you mean?"

His head tilted; he'd heard my tone shift. Carefully he said, "Attractiveness is important. It's what gets politicians votes. Pulls customers into stores."

"Bullshit. Political issues get votes. Product quality gets customers."

Men don't like being told they're wrong but amazingly, a smile flashed over Ric's lips. "Yes and no. Quality *keeps* the customers. But even there, appearance plays a role. We keep coming back to that which attracts us."

"What are you suggesting?"

He leaned forward, engaged, amused and determined to win. I realized he thought this was more banter between us, a light argument as meaningful as an exercise in point-counterpoint. "I'm suggesting that you can use your looks to help people. To attract patients who need you—"

"No." I pulled my hands from his, stung. What he was saying went against everything I believed in.

"I'm only trying to help you." All amusement disappeared. Frustration furrowed his brow. "Brains are fine, but you've got more arrows in your quiver. Why not use them?"

"Why not...?" I gaped at him. He'd seen the real, inner me? I was so gullible. I'd wanted to believe that, but he was a salesman at heart. "Sorry, it's not your fault. Of course you'd say those things. You're in the business of trying to make things look better than they are. It's your business to lie."

He opened his mouth, closed it. Studied my face before saying, "I don't lie."

"Spin the truth." I waved my hand. "Whatever. It's sizzle versus steak, and you're on the side of sizzle and I'm on the side of steak. Although in my favor, eating sizzle isn't very filling."

"Without sizzle, how do you even know there's a steak to eat?" His half-smile said he knew we weren't playing anymore, but he was still enjoying it at some level. "Plus, the sizzle adds to the pleasure of eating."

"That may be true of food, but medicine isn't about pleasure." I stood again, determined not to let him seduce me into staying. "It's about helping people."

"Is this about your cousin? Please know that I'd help her if there wasn't more to the matter. There are aspects I can't share with you, but please be assured, I'm not helping Camille either."

"Who are you helping then?" Letting anger hide my pain, I leaned knuckles on the table. "That surgeon got away with his butchery because of someone like you, Holiday. An ad campaign—billboards, magazine ads, even robocalls—pushing 'Dr. Bearsylls Cares'. But a slogan doesn't make it true." I turned away.

Spun back. He wasn't smiling now, in any of his variations. I said, "I think the reason you won't help us is that you're afraid. I think that once you blow away all Ric Holiday's razzle-dazzle, there's nothing underneath."

I left.

He didn't try to stop me again.

Chapter Five

Driving east, I breathed through the tightness in my chest. At the first clear stretch of traffic I fumbled in my purse and pulled out my freshman picture, staring at it without seeing it.

I'd thought Ric had seen past my pretty image, had understood the real me.

My heart felt like it was shrinking.

No. I slapped the picture on the dashboard, stinging my fingers, pain which distracted from my hurt inside. *This* was my reality. I'd been ugly, which hadn't been fair. Now I was beautiful, which wasn't fair either.

Life wasn't fair for a lot of people. My job—my crusade—was to fix that for others, one reason "The Beauty and the Beast" resonated so strongly for me. I'd read the old French tale to Teddy in the hospital right before driving to Minneapolis.

The story started with a prince being a jackass to a wicked fairy, or in some versions a witch. Now, even the veriest noob knows never to screw with a fairy and especially not a *wicked* fairy, so in my humble opinion, the prince deserved what he got—which was the fairy turning him as ugly on the outside as he was on the inside.

Too bad real people weren't like that. If only you could see what you were getting and didn't have to guess.

Anyway, Beauty saw past the Beast's appearance and redeemed him with her true love. There are different morals to the story—true love saves all, be kind to strangers. My favorite? "Don't judge people by their looks."

And yeah, the parallels between the Beast and Ric Holiday were only too obvious. The prince of advertising, who, like the Beast, was really just a jerk.

Until love made the Beast live up to his royalty.

Damn it. Not thinking about love or princes or Ric damned Holiday. I put my reality-check picture away. Tonight I'd stay over at Twyla's cabin and try to avoid her guilting. Tomorrow I'd head back to my apartment and get on with my life, my future. Whatever that was. But it wouldn't include Ric Holiday.

I squeezed itchy eyes and drove on.

When Twyla said "cabin", I thought of the raw, cold bunkhouses I'd suffered at various summer camps as a girl, the kind with ten narrow beds, no heating and no plumbing.

So when I saw "Chipmunk Lake Supplies" over a split-log exterior shop by the side of the road with the lights still on, I stopped. A sign midwall said, "Fireworks Here!! Open Till Midnight July 4&5". There were two doors and no other signs, so, picking the right door at random, I went in.

A jumble of trinkets and knickknacks confronted me, a souvenir shop stocked by a tornado. Instead of regular shelves, wooden crates were turned on their sides and stacked in squares and pyramids to form random cubical farms.

A beefy man with long nose, red lips and a head like a basketball covered in curly blond hair—crown to chin—was setting shot glasses in a pyramid. He turned to me. "Kinaye 'elpya?"

I stopped. "I'm sorry?"

He pointed to his nametag, which read "I'm Roy Your Friendly Shop Owner". "Kenaye 'elpya?"

Can I help you? my brain finally translated. "Oh. Yes. I'm looking for blankets."

"Een back, dontchaknow."

I made my way into the store. Sure enough, along the back wall was a set of crates holding everything from snowshoes to blaze orange trapper hats. The blankets were in the middle. I picked two and brought them to the front where Roy the Friendly was waiting behind a counter. "Do you take credit cards?"

"Shur." He pointed at a surprisingly modern self-swipe. "D'ya went wirms wih dat?"

I stopped midswipe. "Wirms?"

"Yah. Wirm." He made squiggly motions with his forefinger. "Wirms." He waved them all.

"Um, no. Just the blankets. Oh. Do you sell milk?" Twyla would have cereal, but I like skim and she's a two-percent girl.

"Nix dur." He bagged the blankets and the receipt.

"Nix dur?"

He jerked his head to the right, then handed me the bag.

Oh, the other door. "It's late. Are they open too?"

He gave me a look like I'd grown a second head. "Ferth o' July? Yah, nix dur's opin."

"Thanks." As I turned to leave, clear as a bell, he called, "Have a nice day!"

Shaking my head, I exited the souvenir shop to go into the grocery "nix dur". The door opened to a space similar in size to the souvenir shop but crammed with shelves and coolers.

The sixteen-year-old at the register was a long-nosed

scruffy dishwater blond. If he hadn't been thin as a rail he could have doubled for the souvenir store owner. "Kinaye 'elpya?"

Hmm. Must be a local dialect. "Milk?"

He pointed to a bunker-style cooler just inside the door. I went to it and peered through the glass to see a bunch of half-pint cartons packed like Tetris. I slid open the glass, reached in and snagged a red one. Whole milk. I put it back and tried purple. Two percent. I put it back and was about to pull out a light blue when I saw the round Styrofoam containers stacked next to the milk. Curious, I pulled one out.

It was labeled "Earth Worms".

Revulsion shot through me like an electric shock. I dropped the container.

Luckily it landed on the bunker's glass. I don't know what I would have done if the lid had popped off. I took a deep breath. Using my fingernails, I picked up the Styrofoam container and put it back in place *next to the milk cartons*. "On second thought, I'll take powdered milk."

He pointed to aisle one. I found a small box of powdered milk and brought it to the register. He rang me up, and as I swiped my card he said, "Dontcha went wirms wih dat?"

Again? What was with these people? "Why would I want worms?"

"Fer feeshin'." He looked at me like I was two neurons shy of a synapse.

"Um, thanks, but no." I took my milk and blankets and went back to my car.

A short time later, a hand-painted sign at the mouth of a long gravel drive announced "Chipmunk Lake Cabins—Fishing, Swimming, Boating". I turned in, gravel crunching under my tires.

Twyla's "cabin" turned out to be part of a summerhouse complex. About a hundred feet in was a big two-story house.

There, the drive hooked left, running parallel to a small lake for another three hundred feet or so.

Six log-faced bungalows dotted a line between the driveway and the lake.

I crunched gravel past two dark cabins, one lit one, and two more dark before my headlights picked out a quaint one-lane wooden bridge. I slowed to a crawl. I'm a city girl. Concrete and girders is my idea of a bridge. My car weighs one and a half *tons.* Wood for a bridge? Just wrong. Still, there was no other way to get to the last cabin, so I released the brake and let the car inch over. I admit I was holding my breath. The matchstick bridge creaked like I was killing it.

But finally I was on the other side and pulling onto sandy soil in back of the final cabin, where I cut the engine.

The screen door banged open. Twyla ran out, a big smile lighting her face. She's brainy, artistic and can make any organization run like a Ferrari. But what most people notice when they meet her is she's curvy, well-dressed—and black.

Well, so am I. A quarter compared to her half, but it's another example that appearances can be deceiving. Twyla's parents are an African diplomat and a famous surgeon. Our grandmothers were sisters. Twyla's married a Ngozi while mine married a Brandt, though in the Corners, everyone is half-German, whatever your color, creed or actual genetics. I'd always thought people reacting to my looks was about me, something I could change. It wasn't until Twyla and I double dated for senior prom and we went for ice cream outside the Corners, and Twyla got snubbed for being black while I didn't that I understood that it was them not me, and that people who judge on looks alone are idiots.

"Synnove! You made it." Twyla greeted me with a hug. Her sig-o Nikos silently filtered out behind her, silently pulled my bag out of the back seat and silently toted it into the cabin. Nikos does everything silently, putting the tacet in taciturn.

But when he does talk, people listen. He's big, moves like a cat and was something significant in the military. Twyla calls him her Spartan general and that nails him so well I sometimes wonder if it isn't the truth.

I hugged her tightly in return. "I had good directions. Nice 'cabin'."

"Wait until you see inside." She led me into a rustic, pine-paneled interior. A spacious kitchen opened onto a large living room. "There's a deluxe bath with whirlpool tub." She pointed to a short hallway off the kitchen. Two doors were open, a big double bed in one room and a narrow twin in the other.

A third door was closed. Suspicious noises were coming from behind it.

I raised an eyebrow. "With four empty cabins and a big house, you've got roommates?"

"The owners live in the house," Twyla said. "And we're only trying this up north thing, to see if it works. Why spend double the money? It might end up a bust. Want some coffee?"

"Thanks, but I'm caffeined out. I'll take some of that, though." I pointed at a corked bottle on the red Formica counter top. "Burgundy?"

"Merlot. Nikos, honey, pour us some of that grape nerve tonic, will you?"

He grunted, which Twyla says is him being eloquent, and proceeded to competently decork the bottle and pour three glasses, ending each with a professional swirl.

While he was pouring, a particularly loud squeal came from the closed bedroom. I winced. "That's Elena O'Rourke? She sounds...different." An understatement. The Elena I knew was tougher than most WWE wrestlers. That little girly squeal would have been anathema to her, although I'd been out of the Meiers Corners's gossip loop for a few years.

"Strongwell, now." Twyla handed me my full glass.

"Oh yeah. Sometimes it's hard to keep up." I sniffed the wine appreciatively. Fruity, with a hint of oak. "I can't believe Elena married Bo. Isn't he the Viking who owns the luxe apartment building on the upper east side?"

"That's the one." As Twyla reached for her wine Nikos tapped the back of her hand. "What?"

He took her fingers, kissed them. "Breathe."

"You want her to breathe?" I said.

"He means we should let the wine breathe." Twyla was apparently good at translating Gruntese. "After our nerves are calmed, right Synnove?" With a grin at her big dark SO, she clinked glasses with me and knocked back a healthy swallow.

Nikos only sighed.

Twyla waved her half-empty glass toward the living room. "Sit. Over there, by the fireplace. Night's cooled us off enough that Nikos can make us a pretty fire with apple logs and we can get drunk and toast marshmallows and have s'mores, not necessarily in that order. Why are we getting drunk, by the way? And does it have to do with that very expensive Italian suit coat you're wearing? Hand-tailored, unless I miss my guess. Athletic cut, hubba-hubba."

I laughed. "Curious much? Thanks for not starting in on me the moment I arrived." I tucked myself into a big chair by the fireplace and sipped merlot. It had a bite, like that Turkish coffee…a flash of regret hit me. No. Ric wanted me to use my looks to win patients. "I had a bit of trouble getting to the party. Holiday loaned me his jacket to cover it."

"Road accident? Are you okay?"

"Not an accident, at least not on the road." I flipped back the coat to show her the torn blouse. "Sorry about this. I'll buy you a new one."

She sucked in an angry breath. "Who did that? I'm gonna kick his ass."

I looked down. My breast was bruised, a souvenir of Little's "proposal". "Don't worry, I took care of it. But it did put a damper on my making rational and convincing arguments to Holiday. As I told you, he said no."

"Good grief, if you think I care about Holiday after seeing that—"

"I took care of it, Twyla. And I'd like to put it behind me. Now let me debrief so I can enjoy the treat of upcoming s'mores and pretty fire in peace."

"Not the wine?"

"That's medicine."

"Says the almost-a-doctor."

"Emphasis on almost."

While the wine warmed my belly, Nikos efficiently stacked kindling and logs in the fireplace, then lit it with one match. If you've never built a fire, let me tell you it's a skill to get it going that fast. I reflected on the luck of some cousins, finding such a catch. Not to mention he was almost eerily in love with her. He said it, not with words, which could lie, but with his actions: his tender yet protective hovering, the softness in his eyes when he looked at her, the only softness about him. Although if anyone deserved such a great guy, Twyla did.

"Are you enjoying your vacation here?" I asked. "Since New Year's was a bust?"

"Yeah." Her eyes sought out Nikos and softened, confirming if I needed it how she felt about him. "I'm sorry everything toileted at the party. It was supposed to have been some fun for you."

"It wasn't a total epic fail." I held my glass up to the firelight; it gave the wine a warm, ruby glow. "Holiday said no, but he said no to Camille too. And he gave me a clue as to *why* his answer was no. He won't come to Meiers Corners. He travels all over the world, so it must be something to do with us particularly."

"Or something near us," Nikos said.

Twyla beamed at him. "Honey! Four words. You're improving every day."

He stared at her, deadly black eyes that made me blanch, but she just laughed. Jumping up, she hugged him then goosed him. "You know I'm teasing. I love you, however you talk."

"But only for now."

"For a whole bunch of nows, lover. In fact—why don't you go get the bed warmed up? Synnove and I want a little girl time, but then I'll be in to show you how much love happy-for-now can bring you."

His lips curved, a small reflection of the giant smile that lit his eyes. We watched him glide off, our minds on all ten muscular acres of him warming up Twyla's bed.

The door shut behind him.

I shook my head. "I have to say, Twyla, I don't understand. You get a hunk like that, money and looks and brains, and loves you besides, and you don't get a ring on his finger?"

Her smile disappeared. She sat. "What's wrong with happily for now?"

"Nothing, if you're not sure. But I've seen you two together. You click. That's rare, and I'd think you'd grab onto it for as long as you could. Forever, if possible."

She leveled me with a steady brown stare. "That decision is mine to make."

I leaned over and touched her shoulder. "I'm sorry, hon. It's your life. I only want you to be happy."

"Thanks." She set down her glass and smiled briefly. "We were talking about Holiday. You have to go back."

"Go back? I can't."

"We need Holiday. He's the best."

"What part of 'he said no' are you missing, the *nicht* or the *nein*? I'm telling you, it'd be an exercise in futility. I might as well try to herd chickens or avoid chocolate over the holidays. Ric's not the kind of guy who changes his mind."

"Ric? You know him that well?" The implications were hot in her voice.

"No! Well yes, but not how you're thinking." I remembered his kiss and flushed. "Well, sort of how you're thinking."

"Progress!" Her delighted smile said she meant more than snaring Holiday for ad campaigns. "Synnove, you've got to go back. You owe me."

"I *owed* you. I tried; it didn't work. Favor done. Besides, what you're asking is so much bigger than lending me a suit."

"Problem is, Camille's entered the picture. Shit got real. I need your help, and I need it all, everything you have to give. If you haven't used every weapon in your arsenal, you haven't tried hard enough."

"All my *weapons*? What is this, an advertising jihad?" It echoed Holiday's "you've got more arrows in your quiver," which made me a little sharp. I winced, contrite. "Hon, I don't want us to fight." Though we were solid; we could fight passionately and still be okay after. Fighting with Ric Holiday would be like that, passionately hot but okay after—and passionately hot after too... Crap. "I learned to sum up people quickly to get an accurate medical history. My doctor sense tells me Holiday's made up his mind. We'll find another advertising firm—"

"No. It's *got* to be Holiday."

So much for the olive branch. Exasperated, I said, "Why?"

Her cheekbones darkened. "He's the best."

The blush and the broken record. She did the same thing around Nikos's aversion to sunlight, or his amazing strength. My psych rotation said she was resisting something. My intuition said it had to do with Holiday and Nikos being of the *vin rouge* persuasion. "I see. And that's the only reason?"

She stared at the fire for a long while. A big snap, sparking red, broke her trance. As the logs resettled she sat forward. "I'd better be honest with you."

At last. She was going to come clean about v-guys.

"If this gets out it might cause a panic, but you need to know—the Meiers Corners bank is under a consent decree."

Not v-guys. But the tightness in her tone said she was honestly worried. I needed to listen up. "What's a consent decree?"

"It's when the feds take a closer look at how a bank's being run. If the Sparkasse Bank doesn't get more capital soon, or repayment on enough loans to rebalance their portfolio, well, they may get put up for sale."

"And that's bad, why?"

"Some very nasty people would like a toehold in our city." Twyla rose and snagged the wine bottle from the kitchen. "Buying our main source of business loans would give them that and more."

"But a white knight—"

"Synnove, I can't go into it, but we're being targeted, and all our defense eggs are in the tourism basket. Seemed like a sure thing at the time." Returning with the wine, she topped off my glass, refilled her own and sat, curling her legs under her. Her dark eyes were serious. "We need to draw warm bodies with our Kinkadesque local color before our picture turns Gorey."

"Hey. I like the drawings he did for MYSTERY!"

"You like cutting people open with a knife and digging through their guts. I question your grasp on charming and touristy."

"Viscera."

"What?"

"Viscera, not guts. Sounds better. Less slimy. See? I can do charming."

"Lovely. The point is, after our great start with the off-Broadway musical, we need to get the word out or we'll backslide. Which means Holiday."

"Why can't we tout our own fudge shoppes and luncheon nooks?"

She heaved a big sigh that said clearer than words that I was being a stubborn, short-sighted ass. "It's not simply about pushing quainte shite. Research told me tourists are looking for walkability and multiday potential and 'vibe', whatever the hell that means. More than advertising, we need someone who *understands* advertising. We need Ric Holiday."

"Okay, got it." I tapped my glass against my lips, thinking. Twyla wanted Ric Holiday. I wanted to avoid Ric Holiday. How could I get both? Hey, sometimes doctors did the impossible. They were called miracles.

And I thought I might just have one. "This is more than wine can handle." I set my glass down. "Where's your chocolate?"

"S'mores?"

"No. Straight up."

"You're going to do it." She smiled. "You're going back."

"Don't sound so happy. You're going to owe me so bad you'll be my Favors Bitch for the rest of your life." I rummaged around in the cupboards, caught the sting of cacao and found the giant extra-dark bars between a box of graham crackers and a bag of marshmallows. I cracked one in half without opening it, tore the paper in two and handed one to Twyla.

"Favors Bitch?" She took her half, unwrapped a corner and bit into it appreciatively. "Aren't you forgetting the time I bailed you out of the principal's office after you greased Anna Versnobt's 'back' vibrator with heat rub?"

Should have kept the whole bar. "Not my fault. She went on and on about how she used it for sore muscles. I was only trying to help her."

She ticked up fingers. "Your student loan paperwork, the tax returns I did for you, the time you 'helped' me with my new car by filling the tires with air except you'd only ever pumped 90-psi bicycle tires before—"

"Enough." I sat and snapped off chocolate with my teeth. "Do you want to hear my idea or not?"

"Sure." She smirked. She knew she'd won.

"Some day you'll regret that smirk," I grumbled. "You won't know where or when, but it'll involve bubble gum and hair curlers. I'm just sayin'."

The smirk widened. "Why don't you tell me your idea before I expire of ooh-I'm-scareds?"

"Nice one." I chewed and swallowed. Ah, the healing properties of chocolate. "Holiday Buzz is one of those prestige firms where clients are 'hired' instead of the other way around. All I have to do is get the *agency* to take us on. Holiday has his touch on everything his firm does. I convince any account rep and *voilà*."

"Once the firm takes the job, he'll become involved?" She raised a brow. "You're banking an awful lot on your assessment of his character. You're sure?"

"My entire hometown's fate rests on this. More—my Favor Balance rests on this. Of course I'm sure."

Chapter Six

Ft. Dearborn on the Chicago River, 1812

The scrawny chicken scuttled across the settlement's dirt road. Ric darted after it, ten-year-old arms stretched. He was scrawnier than the chicken. If he could catch the beast, he'd eat like a king, filling his belly for the first time since his parents died.

The chicken ducked around a wooden building—straight between a set of pants-covered legs.

Ric piled up short at the sight of two men arguing. One man wore a military uniform, and the other the costume of a prosperous trader. Both looked angry and concerned. Ric's meal dashed away, forgotten.

The uniformed man's eyes were narrowed against the bright morning sun. "I won't go against orders, and we've been ordered to evacuate this fort."

"It's suicide to leave." The second man kept to the building's shadow. "Where are we supposed to go?"

"East. To Fort Wayne."

Ric perked his ears. He seemed to remember his parents came from "out east". That his grandparents lived there.

"I don't like the idea of leaving the safety of the block-houses," the trader said.

"The danger isn't imminent. And I have my orders."

"Always orders," the trader muttered.

"My duty is clear. We will leave the fifteenth, at nine a.m.. You can come with us, or you can try to defend this place by yourself."

Days went by. Anxiously, Ric watched the preparations in and around the fort. The uniformed men were given ammunition and supplies. Baggage wagons were made ready for the sick, and the women and children.

On the morning of the fifteenth, Ric slipped into one of the wagons, his sweating not all due to the August heat. Outside a band played martial music. He tried to feel brave and optimistic as the wagons rolled out.

But as they rode along, the temperature dropped. Ric's sweat chilled. He could smell the lake when suddenly a shout went up, and another. The curtain was ripped aside and a man leaped into their midst. He looked like the trader, only something was wrong with his face. It looked like a living mask hacked out of wood, with red fire for eyes. Women screamed, children cried. Blood flew.

The last thing Ric remembered was the man smiling at him—with gleaming fangs.

The official report said twelve children were tomahawked in one wagon alone by a single savage. The truth was darker, more complex. The single killer was a white man, and the bodies were mutilated to cover the true atrocity.

Ric woke in the cool dark. He felt completely relaxed. Good. Strong. And starving.

No, he was *thirsty.* His mouth worked with a deep, abiding need to suck. His teeth ached to bite. He reached up to massage his throbbing gums but his arm was restricted. He wrestled against cloth bindings until they tore. He rubbed a thumb over his gums and nicked his skin on a sharp new fang.

The smell of his own blood kicked him into overdrive. He thrust hands through the windings, into soft dirt. It was easier than he expected, cloth tearing on his sharp little claws, arms digging powerfully. He was stronger than he'd ever known. He scrabbled up through the earth and burst from his grave into the bright light.

And promptly fell on his face.

His limbs, so potent in the ground, didn't work properly in the air. He felt like a newborn, bursting from the womb only to find himself in a place where he was uncoordinated and unprepared. He lay there, blinking against the bright light, shocked when it resolved into the moon and stars burning like lamps.

A face wavered in his vision. Instinct took over. His claws snapped out toward the prey…who was gone.

"You look like a baby bird flopping around." The face reappeared. Black hair, black eyes, straight nose. Red slash of a mouth, slightly curved in amusement. An older boy, maybe twelve.

Don't stand there like a jerk, Ric said. *Help me up.*

Or at least, those were the words in his head. What came out was, "Whuh wa wa."

Surprisingly, the boy understood him. He snared Ric's hand. "You bite me and I twist your head off." The boy yanked Ric to his feet. Ric's legs wobbled like milk-soaked bread. The boy got an arm around him, and between the two of them Ric managed a stumbling walk. A succulent artery pulsed mere inches away in the boy's neck. Ric had to force himself not to bite into it.

"Good thing they didn't drain your blood," the boy remarked casually. "You'd have attacked anything that moved. Remember that, kid. Even stale blood in your veins is better than no blood at all."

The name is Ric, but what Ric said was "Ya wuh wih."

"I'm Aiden." The boy either knew what he was going to say or was almost omniscient. "The second thing to remember is never go out in the sun. You'll burn like dry tinder."

Aiden took Ric to a big house, the biggest he'd seen outside the fort. The cellar beneath the house was even bigger. It smelled of sweet bare earth. The older boy eased him to the ground with surprising gentleness. "This is your new home, kid. You're one of the lucky ones who made it. This far, at least."

Ric didn't find out what Aiden meant until he'd been given a dead body to drain (the blood was stale but still tasted so good) and slept a couple days in the rich soil, much better than the stuff he'd clawed up through. When he finally woke feeling almost himself, the thought came to him that the dirt of his current bed wasn't native. He opened his eyes to ask Aiden.

A man with a knife stood over him. The moment Ric's eyes opened, the man attacked. Ric screamed a ten-year-old's horror. The knife sliced through his arm. Blood fountained. He screamed louder. But when the knife slashed toward him again he snapped his mouth shut, leaped to his feet and ran until he blacked out.

He woke again. Same man, same knife. Same attack. This time Ric didn't bother screaming. He rolled aside. The knife *whumped* into dirt. Two-handed, Ric grabbed the knife. The man tried to pull it away. They wrestled until Ric yanked with all his strength. Bone snapped. The man screamed and the knife fell into Ric's hands. He jumped to his feet brandishing it, prepared to attack.

Aiden caught him before he did. "Good job, kid. The only one who figured it out faster was me. You're going to make it." And then, whispering in his ear for only him to hear, "I'll make sure of it."

Later Ric asked Aiden, "What is this place?"

Aiden said, "Training camp."

"Military?"

"Trackers. Spies. Assassins."

Later still, Ric saw Aiden filter out into the night. Ric followed, practicing some of the hiding techniques he'd learned.

The older boy stopped at an unmarked grave. "I know you're there," he said to the shadows where Ric hid. "You might as well come out."

Ric wasn't surprised. Aiden always seemed to know everything. Ric came out. "What are we waiting for?"

"A kid died three days ago, supposedly of an animal mauling. They buried him there."

"Was it really an animal?"

"You know better." Aiden turned to him then, and there was the barest gleam deep within those black eyes that told him Aiden was ferociously angry. "He does it on purpose. Turns children, young so he can control them, then waits to see if they survive. He calls it his first test. Doesn't sound so horrific that way."

Ric shivered, not knowing why. He was barely eleven then. "Who's 'he'?"

Aiden spat a name into his ear. "Nosferatu."

Ric shuddered.

"Don't ever say his name out loud." Aiden stared into the distance. "He has a long reach around Chicago."

Ric was confused. "He gives us shelter from the sun, blood when we don't catch enough. He trains us. Don't you trust him?"

"No." The word was flat. "He's turning us into murderers."

"I don't believe that. He cares about us—"

"You spend enough time standing here, watching, waiting to see if these massacred children rise. Watch frightened kids claw their way out of their graves, only to kill their first prey in blood lust. Or die in fiery pain if they're not smart enough to evade the knife. Then see what you think. It makes me sick."

Ric's brows went up. "Why did you rescue me then? Take me home?"

Aiden spun on him, nostrils flared, lips thin. "What else could I do? Where else is there to go?"

Ric was shocked at the emotion blazing from the boy who was his mentor, his protector. Anger and pain bled from Aiden, and a hopelessness so profound it tore at Ric's heart.

This boy had been Ric's salvation, safeguarding his life, his sanity. Ric couldn't let him suffer like this without doing something about it. If Ric's parents were still alive…but they weren't. Nobody but him and Aiden. It was up to him. Ric squared his shoulders. "I don't know where we go. But we'll find a place. We'll find a way to leave, to live a better life."

"You don't *understand*." Aiden slashed the air with one hand. "*He* isn't a vampire to take defection lightly; he'll kill us as an example to his other flunkies. And for the personal affront? He'll make it slow and painful."

"You'll let that stop you?" Ric challenged.

Aiden's black brows snapped together and his hand fisted. Then, slowly, both relaxed. "No. No, I won't let fear stop me. All right, I'm in."

They floundered with plan after plan, each one more desperate and less likely to succeed. Each day they lost a little more ground to the soul-killing training at Nosferatu's tender mercies, and those of his sadistic teachers.

They nearly succumbed and became pitiless killing machines.

A little human girl saved them.

Eloise was barely six years old when she came to live at the big house. Her father kept her apart from the vampires, but Ric and Aiden had long since learned the secret ways of the compound. They sneaked into the girl's room that first time because they could.

She captivated them with her innocence. She was lonely and thirsty for company, and she begged them to return when they could. The boys told themselves they kept visiting because they were bored. Little by little, each made the others' lives a little less lonely. A little less cruel. They pulled each other back bit by bit from the brink.

Then Ric saw Nosferatu standing against a sapling Ric measured his own growth on. It changed everything. Even then, Ric understood spin and image.

By this time escape itself was no longer a problem. Aiden had taught Ric how to lay down false trails, and Ric taught Aiden how to foster false images. They would cross the newly formed state line, run as far as they could, then hide.

The problem was keeping Nosferatu from coming after them. Ric now had the start of the solution. The final piece was provided by the little girl.

Ric was fourteen and Aiden sixteen when they finally ran away from Nosferatu. They asked their little human friend to escape with them, confident of their abilities to protect her.

Eloise didn't make it.

Now Nosferatu was after them again. And suddenly all Ric's mindfucks and razzle-dazzle didn't seem nearly good enough.

Chapter Seven

I went to bed but couldn't sleep. It was too dark in my room, and the noises, chirping and whoo-whooing, were all wrong.

I certainly wasn't bothered by thoughts of sexy Ric Holiday.

Skewer me with a scalpel. Yes I was. I *whumped* onto my other side and squeezed my eyes shut.

My phone went off, providing some much-needed electric light and manmade sounds. I snatched it up. The readout said *Hospital*. "Hello?"

"Doctor Synnove?" It was a boy's thin voice.

"Teddy, honey, why are you calling so late? Are you okay?"

"I miss you. Read me a story?"

The poor sweetie. He couldn't sleep either. I pulled out my ereader and thumbed open *The Big Purple Book of Fairy Tales*—there was a whole series of them including *Red*, *Purple* and *Blue*, but if you ask me, when they got to *Fulvous* and *Chartreuse* they jumped the shark—and read to him until he mumbled, "Good night." By then I was sleepy too.

I dreamed.

Such innocuous words. So very different than the hot, sweaty, sheet-twisting reality. I blame the naked image of Camille burned into my brain, and Ric's hot…everything. I don't normally have such vivid, carnal dreams; at least not that I can remember. And wouldn't both Freud and Jung have a field day with that?

I was a barbarian queen. My brave men had won a decisive victory against a rival clan chief and this was our victory celebration. My finest warriors and commanders stood at attention, awaiting their reward. Naked.

I paced before them, my white skirts swirling around my legs, my gown a suspicious cross between Princess Leia's and Camille's frontless/backless number. I gave a stirring speech. My warriors' oiled muscles gleamed in the sunlight. As I prepared to choose, the men grew hard in anticipation.

One brown-bearded warrior pleased me. I grabbed his head, my fingers sliding into silky hair, and kissed him. His beard bristled against my skin, his mouth hot and moist against my lips. He tasted of war. His hands cupped my face reverently and he kissed me back, his tongue teasing inside my mouth.

A third hand skimmed my back. I raised my head. The men circled close, surrounding me. Another callused hand found the soft skin of my shoulder. Yet another slid under my dress to touch my breast. As the men fondled me until I moaned, they kissed me, each deeper and harder, to gain my favor.

"Enough!" A deep, dark voice rang from beyond the circle. "I am your bravest champion, my queen. I claim exclusive rights. Any who denies my claim, let him face me now in single combat."

The men eased back as a tall warrior stepped forward. He was clean-shaven, with spiky blond hair and stunning blue eyes that captured my breath, even as his hands and mouth captured the rest of me.

He yanked me flush and kissed me. His mouth was fire; his hands were bolts of excitement. I arched into him as his tongue struck sparks that burst into flames.

I wrapped arms around his strong neck. "My tent. Now."

He lifted me effortlessly. His mouth claimed mine as he strode into the cool quiet of my private domain. All around us burned aromatic candles. My warrior laid me gently upon the silks and furs of my bed.

Then he stretched out on top of me with his huge, heavy body.

"No." I took him by his shoulders, his notched triceps like boulders under my fingers. "Beneath me." I turned him as I spoke. He went obligingly onto his back. I swung a leg over him, sat astride his thickly muscled thighs and took his fully unfurled cock in my hands. I caressed its sleek length, feeling it fatten between my palms. A drop of liquid desire glistened from its tip. His was the most beautiful erection I'd ever seen and rose so majestically that it made my lips throb. I had to do it.

I slid down his thighs and sucked him into my mouth.

He groaned. I slicked my tightened lips rhythmically over his cock. The large vein bumped under my lips, the sleek skin slid under my tongue. I scraped my teeth on the head. He shouted at that.

Outside, the cheers of my men urged me on.

I straightened and reached behind my neck. His eyes riveted to me. A tug, and the bodice of my dress fell to pool at my waist, leaving my breasts bare to his hungry gaze. His eyes burned red.

I cupped myself. My breasts filled my palms and overflowed. Under his fiery gaze, my nipples hardened. I plucked them and moaned softly.

He half-sat, his belly a turbulent sea of ridges, and grabbed the dress at my waist in his large, dark hands. A jerk of arm muscles, and he split the garment in two, tossing the strips aside. "My queen," he purred. "I am ready for my reward."

Naked, I gazed down at his hips. "So you are."

I slid up his body, flattening his throbbing erection under me. My palms landed on his heavy bronze pectorals. I pressed a kiss to his bulging chest, opening my kiss to wet his nipple. It pricked hard. I blew on it, then repeated my ministrations with the other.

"My queen." His voice was tight. "*My* queen."

"I like that." I rocked my hips, rubbing myself against the ridge of his cock. I was slick and hot and open for him, and a simple tilt of his hips lodged the head of his erection inside me. My breath caught. He groaned. He felt so hot, so good.

He grabbed my waist in his hard hands, the long fingers nearly meeting around my back, and prepared to thrust deep.

"Wait." I panted it. His hips stilled but his fingers, tightening spasmodically on my waist, shouted how hard he found it not to drive himself inside me to the hilt. "You shall have your reward. But on my terms."

He groaned softly but I would make it up to him. I raised myself —and drove down onto him.

His thick erection filled me with slick power. I moaned. He shouted. The men outside echoed him. Not only was this his reward for victory, but a token of luck for an abundant harvest. Clutching his shoulders for purchase I began to ride him like a stallion in full pounding gallop.

He clasped my hips and drove up into me with matching power. Need rose within me, began to overwhelm me. I cried out.

More. I needed more. I fell against his chest and pummeled my hips onto him. He released me to slide one hand between us.

He pressed his fingers against my clit.

I arched back with a gasp. He rubbed hard. I whimpered. He seized my nipple with his mouth and suckled.

Lava pleasure spilled through me, breasts, belly, pudendum. He suckled and rubbed me as I churned hips against him until I swelled with fire and need. I grabbed his head with both hands, pulled him from my breast and thrust my tongue desperately into his mouth, frantically beating against his hips.

He growled under me. His fine skin sheened with moisture. His hand worked me fiercely. I rose to dizzying heights of pleasure. Ecstasy beckoned.

Thrusting my tongue one last time into his mouth, I seized that rapture. Climax thundered through me as he found his own release. He shouted, barely heard over the pounding of my heart.

"Synnove," my warrior said. "My sunshine. My love."

Bliss flowered within me. The harvest would indeed be rich.

The next morning a stupidly exuberant sun streamed through the windows with all the subtlety of a middle-school brass section. I stumbled into the empty kitchen and blinked my way through a bowl of cereal and a cup of coffee. After showering, I found a new set of undies waiting. Twyla had come and gone like a little lingerie-spinning Rumpelstiltskin. Hopefully she wouldn't ask for my firstborn. She'd have a long wait coming, despite the dream.

All the sweaty fertility and hunky men cheering at first bothered me, not to mention the identity my subconscious gave to my dream lover. But when I boiled it down into a simple omen of good luck, deliberately ignoring the psychosexual overtones, I found I could push it from my mind. I had enough real trouble without having to worry about a little hot fantasy.

Today I was braving Holiday Buzz. I pulled on Twyla's sexy lingerie, the Prince girding to storm Sleeping Beauty's castle. Then I yawned, wishing I were the one sleeping, like Rip van Winkle…hmm, I'd have to get some different books to read Teddy.

As I started my car, a man slammed out of the other occupied cabin and ran to the bridge. By the time I reached the foot of the bridge he blocked it like a troll.

Definitely gotta twelve-step those fairy tales.

I braked and buzzed down my window. "Hi. Can I help you?"

He clomped to my side of the car and stuck his mug into the window opening. I reared back from a face that was thick ropes of modeling clay with two little black beads for eyes. Red ropes near the bottom moved, emitting a voice like a nail file. "Who the hell are you?"

Rude, yet annoying. I waved at the cabin. "I'm staying with my cousin."

His beady eyes narrowed. "Two women belong in that cabin, a black and a Hispanic. You're not either."

I might have argued the point, but I found it slightly creepy he knew who "belonged" in our cabin. "I'm sorry, but it's none of your business."

His face got uglier. "It's my business if I say it is."

"Okay," I said agreeably, and drove off.

He swore and tried to dash in front of me, but I'd gotten onto the narrow bridge first and he couldn't squeeze past. "I'd better not catch you in the woods," he shouted after me. "Stay out of the damned woods."

Well. That was disturbing. But I had work to do. I'd ask Twyla about it later. I left him swearing and shaking his fist in my rearview mirror.

A little over an hour later I pulled up in front of another tall Minneapolis building and cut the engine.

I didn't get out. Holiday's carefully folded suit coat lay on the seat next to me, reminding me this wasn't going to be easy. Forcing Ric Holiday's hand struck me as a shortcut to retaliation more lethal than even a cosmic wedgie. Maybe the Cosmic Backhand o' Doom.

A scent tickled my nose. Mellow, woody, like the apple logs last night. I found myself smiling.

Ric would never hurt me. I sighed and brushed a finger over the fine material of his coat, releasing a tang of spicy male. I picked it up and buried my nose in the fine fabric. *Mmm.* That sure was Holiday I was smelling.

My eyes opened on me grinning in the rearview mirror.

Bitch slap me with a bedpan. That was the same goofy grin Twyla wore when she'd been doing it again with Nikos... *Five primary branches of the facial nerve exist outside the skull, but the number of muscles used in expression depends on the person...*

Argh. No matter how many muscles it took to smile or frown, it didn't take any to feel like an idiot. I shoved the coat onto the passenger seat, started the car and drove around the block to cool off.

Which was how I found the entrance to the underground parking in the back. After a couple spins around the block I decided I was ready, or at least not so inclined to mental Tourette's, and parked. I gathered coat and purse, and a short elevator ride took me to the lobby.

Holiday Buzz's corporate headquarters was as posh and upscale as Holiday's penthouse. Elevator doors opened to a whole lot of sparkling glass, glossy gray-veined marble and a jungle of green plants. And chrome cladding. The silvery stuff was everywhere.

I checked a black felt directory with neat white letters beside a splashing waterfall. Holiday Buzz occupied two prime stories at the top. I started for the main elevator beyond a wide, curved oak reception desk.

"Ma'am." A burly man in crisp blue uniform sat behind the desk, his name tag reading "Hanner". "Your business?"

I stopped. "Holiday Buzz."

"And your business there? Who are you seeing?"

My brows lifted. Building security was surprisingly rigorous. I fudged with, "Ric Holiday."

"Mr. Holiday Himself?"

I didn't imagine the capital letters. I'd better have a good reason to visit Mr. Holiday Himself, and I'd better think it up quick. "Well, um, I need to return his suit coat."

The guard eyed me with disbelief, surprising me even more. Maybe Ric didn't routinely loan his clothes to underclad young women. Unless most simply didn't return them. I fingered the soft fabric in my hands. It *would* be a nice reminder, tucked in a dresser drawer where it could nestle with bras and panties, or under a pillow, to fall asleep to the delicious scent of well-heeled male, or, thinking about beds, do other things a bit more active…

I thrust the coat toward the guard and gave him a tentative smile. "It's from the Christmas-in-July party last night. I had a wardrobe malfunction."

He added a tapping pen to the glare. I was starting to sweat when he slapped a book on the top ledge. "Sign. I'll need to see two forms of ID."

I retracted the coat and scribbled before he changed his mind. When I dug out my driver's license, he actually checked the signature against the book. Finally he let me board the bullet elevator.

Whew. Done.

Remember the fate's wedgie? I stepped off the car on

thirty-two (with a slight case of jet lag), and was confronted by another security desk—with a doorway-style scanner.

The guard here identified every last bit of metal on me, including my fillings. Good grief, this was supposed to be the easy part. This was what airport security wanted to be when it grew up.

By the time I was escorted to the long curved pane of glass fronting the Holiday Buzz offices, I was wound tighter than an old-fashioned spring. I pushed open the door and stopped. More chrome and running water all over the place. Weird.

My first impression—after all the silvery stuff and water—was high-energy movement. Men and women marched, strode and segued to and fro in constant transition, the latest tablets and smart phones in hand. And the chatter! Arguing, explaining, expounding. It was worse than an episode of *The West Wing.*

The floor itself was a scramble of gold silkscreen partitions and curved chest-high walls. Wheeled workstations were scattered in haphazard groups, obviously according to personal style and need rather than any rigid plan. A bank of windows bright with morning sunlight lined the left wall. The only closed spaces were some offices way in the back, and conference and restrooms to my right.

Though advertising was style over substance at its worst, I was impressed.

"Hello, my name is Rosie," chirped a voice as cheery as the sunlight. "I'm the account manager on duty today. How may I help you?"

I dodged people to approach a wave-shaped reception desk. A six-foot HD screen hung on a false wall behind the desk, showing network news to test ads to kids' cartoons.

A young woman sat behind the reception wave. I hadn't seen her, lost in all the glass and gesticulating. Her auburn bob and white silk blouse were sleek, but not in that brittle overdone way. A blue and white handwritten nametag said "Rosie", a smiley face dotting the I. She was the woman at the Christmas-in-July party, the one as underdressed as me. I smiled at her, feeling more at ease.

But now I had a problem. Though I'd made my way up based on Ric's suit coat, I wasn't actually here to see Ric. I dropped the coat on the floor, stuffing it with one toe under the reception desk (which didn't cloak the alluring aroma *at all*), and launched my plan to acquire Holiday Buzz sans Holiday. "Hi, Rosie. I'm Synnove Byornsson. I'd like to be a client. How do I do that?"

She beamed at me—without dollar signs in her eyes. She was genuinely delighted to meet me. "That's easy. You tell us what your product or service is and why you consider it useful to people. We do the rest."

Useful? That was almost...philanthropic. "How do I do that? Talk with a rep or take a survey or something?"

"We have an online tool to help you write it up. We also have a paper survey. You can call or text or email or even act it out with hand puppets. Whatever mode of communication you're comfortable with, we aim to supply." She lowered her voice. "Actually, the hand puppets are very popular."

"Rosie," a gravely voice snarled. "Why are you still here?"

A big, beefy man stalked over. Shaggy dark hair, a sour expression and a low growl made him seem like a wounded bear. "You were supposed to go on break an hour ago. You need to take better care of yourself."

"Poor Harry. Do you still have that headache?" Rosie reached into her desk, pulled out a white bottle and popped the cover. She shook out a tablet, paused, eyed the man and shook out two more. "Take these. You'll feel better in no time."

His face softened, and he took the tablets meekly. "Then

you'll go on break?"

"After I help Ms. Byornsson, I promise."

"I'll hold you to that." He lumbered away.

A smile lifted my lips. That was sweet.

"Don't mind Harry. His headaches make him a little surly." Rosie was watching the man's big back with her own soft little smile. "He's assigned himself my keeper for some reason."

She was pretty and she'd been kind to Harry. I could guess why he was concerned about her, but simply said, "I'd like to talk to an account rep."

"Of course." Rosie was back to chirping. "If I weren't on reception I'd do it. I'll see who's available. Please have a seat."

"That won't be necessary." The deep voice came from behind me. "I'll help Synnove myself."

I whirled.

Ric Holiday glided in, all effortless grace and suited glory. Against the constant motion and chatter, he was a large fixed point, reassuring and solid. My heart skipped a beat, happy to see him, and my insides heated like a fireplace.

Then I remembered I'd been avoiding him.

Which, considering his name was Ric Holiday and this little ad shop was called *Holiday* Buzz, had been rather optimistic of me. It's a measure of how flustered he made me that that teensy-weensy fact hadn't occurred to me before.

Or maybe it was a Freudian slip. Yay, psych rotation. I couldn't avoid it but I could sure pin a label on it.

"Oh, Mr. Holiday!" Rosie's chirp was even brighter. "You're handling Ms. Byornsson's account personally? How lucky she is. Ms. Byornsson, why didn't you tell me you're a special client?"

I opened my mouth to say, *Because I'm not.* Or maybe to quote more *Gray's*, I don't know and I'll never know because the agency door swung open again.

Camille strutted in.

Her red power suit and crisp white blouse were very business-like—not counting the platform hooker heels, the skirt cut an inch shy of her crotch, or the neckline flirting with her navel.

Meow.

She latched onto Holiday's arm, rubbing sleekly against him. I shut my mouth with a snap.

"Ric," she cooed. "I've been trying to catch up with you since the parking structure. Didn't you hear me calling to you?"

"Sorry, no." He extracted himself smoothly. She tried to grab on again and when he evaded her nearly fell on her nose—although come to think of it, with her topography it wouldn't have been her nose hitting the floor first.

She pouted. "I almost didn't get in. It took a dozen of my Lestat foot soldiers to spring enough of your booby traps so that I could get through."

"I'll have to see those traps get reset," Ric muttered. In louder tone ruffled with annoyance, he said, "Why are you here, Camille? I told you yesterday I'm not interested."

"Oh, but that was yesterday, darling." She simpered at him. "Since then, my boss has helped me design a new offer."

Ric's stance changed, became wary. Dangerous. "Your boss."

"Yes, he wants Meiers Corners and I'm desperate for a certain promotion, so I came up with the Midwest Vegas idea. Anyway, last night I called him. It was very interesting." Her tone went sly. "I think Mr. Nosferatu knows you, and quite well."

Almost imperceptibly, Ric stiffened. He apparently didn't care for that idea at all. His stance shifted again, deliberately casual. "Arnaud Nosferatu runs CIC Mutual and is on the board of half a dozen other F500 companies. Every businessperson in the Midwest knows him."

"Possibly you better than most? I only ask because when I described you, Mr. Nosferatu said he'd known someone—Exactly. Like. You." With each word she poked one blood-red nail into the pristine white of his shirt. The cotton hardly dented at all, testimony to the rock solid muscle underneath.

But while she hadn't marred skin or shirt, she'd definitely drawn psychic blood. Ric's eyes glinted a furious violet, while a muscle pulsed in his jaw, shouting to me how hard he was working to keep his true reaction hidden.

I was reading him as if I knew him intimately...like a lover.

Twist me up a caduceus. *Which is actually the symbol for the U.S. Army Medical Corps with its two serpents twining a winged pole; the medical emblem is Asclepius' single snake around his rod...*

I waved the air in front of my hot face. Not *Gray's* but all the snakes and long hard *rods...* I was obviously flustered at the idea of being Ric's lover. And really, really turned on too.

"I thought it was my idea," Camille was saying. "Coming to Minnesota to snatch you up for my ad campaign. But now I'm wondering. Did Mr. Nosferatu mention you first? Well, either way, he wants me to bring you to him."

Ric's jaw continued to tic. "I'm not going anywhere."

"That won't do, darling." Her eyes narrowed. "Should I take one of your people instead? Maybe little Rosie here?"

Ric growled, low, barely audible. The sheer animal menace in that soft warning sent *frissons* up my spine. Classic vampire sound, and in front of the definitely non-vampire Rosie, a problem. I cleared my throat. "Holiday. Your slip is showing."

Camille swiveled her head to me, weirdly fluid. Something reptilian lit in her eyes. Talk about her vampire showing. "I've had an idea." She spoke to Ric but her lizard eyes were fastened to me. "I'll take Synnove instead. Mr. Nosferatu would love to meet Synnove." A threat iced her tone which I didn't understand. Nosferatu was a businessman. Why would meeting him be dangerous?

But Ric's growl stopped abruptly. "Damn you, Camille." He cut an irate glance at me. "Both of you. This way." He spun and headed for the far corner along the back row of offices, veering to avoid direct sunlight. Camille followed almost precisely in his footsteps.

He led us to a huge windowless office lit by recessed lights, filled with art, splashy fabrics, sleek furniture and a teak aircraft carrier desk holding an insanely thin laptop. But the desk was strewn with papers and notes, and the matching credenza was stacked with equipment and models. Image was important but this was a working office too.

He shut the door.

Camille sauntered to a guest sofa, plopped her tiny tight butt into it, patted the cushion next to her and grinned at Ric. My fingers curled.

Ric ignored her. He strode behind his desk and adopted a power stance, the "I'm more fucking dangerous than a hungry cheetah" kind. "All right, Camille. I'll consider your proposal."

I drew an outraged breath. "You can't give her—"

"I'll consider yours too, Synnove." The frigid anger in his tone cut me off quicker than a raised voice would have. "Here's what will happen. You each have one week to put together your vision for Meiers Corners. I'll gather a team of my best—account and production managers, copywriter and art director. If you convince them to take you on, I'll do it."

Camille's green eyes narrowed. "You'll come to Meiers Corners?"

"Yes. On behalf of whichever campaign is chosen. Ladies." He strode to the door and opened it. "You have what you want. Good day."

Camille rose, tossed him a pert smile and sashayed out. Without a word to me, Ric left too.

I stood there, strangely deflated. I had what I wanted? Then why did it feel like a disaster?

Chapter Eight

I dawdled leaving so I wouldn't run into Camille—or Ric. Surprisingly, given the regular pantsing that fate had been handing out, I didn't encounter either of them. *See*, I argued with myself as I pushed out of Holiday Buzz's glass door. *Not everything ends in disaster.* Surely I was just on edge because of the past week, with The Incident and then Twyla dressing me in spiral cut hams and sending me into the lion's den.

Starring tawny, muscular Ric as the powerful lion.

My thoughts shifted. Powerful, yes, but when Camille threatened him with Nosferatu, Ric had jumped like he'd been stabbed. What was up with that? Nosferatu was a harmless old businessman. And when she suggested taking me to meet Nosferatu, well, Ric had gotten downright feral.

I jabbed the elevator's down button. CIC Mutual was one of the big insurance companies, based in Chicago. The very city Ric avoided. There had to be a connection. Ric, Camille, Nosferatu...was Nosferatu a vampire too?

Yikes. I was seeing fangs everywhere. Yet it went *kerchunk* in my head, like a puzzle piece dropping into place.

I wondered when Scully would show up to whack me over the head with the meat cleaver of reality.

A ding startled me, the elevator arriving. I started forward before the doors cracked, anxious to get away from both my thoughts and dangerous men who might be more.

"Synnove, wait." Déjà vu barred my way in the form of a powerful, well-dressed arm. At least this time I didn't play bumper cars with my chest. I turned.

Ric Holiday in his full sizzling glory was *right on top of me.*

I stepped back, spine hitting the edge of the elevator shaft. My nipples reached out as if trying to stay in touch. *The erection of the mammary papilla is due to muscle contraction, like the pilomotor reflex which causes goose bumps*—Stupid nipples. "What do you want?" I spoke a bit sharply, but his heat and heady scent had goosed my frustration into borderline rudeness. I flushed but held my place. Well, fused against the corner of the shaft, I had to.

He stared down into my eyes, his own frustrated too. "I want to explain."

"You made it clear enough. Me and Camille at the O.K. Corral, one week from today." I looked away. The elevator was leaving.

"Synnove." He slid two strong fingers under my chin and urged my face back to him. The blue had softened. "I'm sorry."

"Why? There's worse?" I scowled, but I had to work at it. Why did he have to be so gorgeous? Why did his fingers have to be so gentle, so warm? "You're going to make us bikini mud wrestle?"

"Ouch." He smiled slightly. "I deserve that."

"No," I grumped. "You don't. But you're getting it anyway."

The grin slowly widened, making his whole face edible.

"The vaunted Byornsson honesty. I'm beginning to see the advantages."

And I was beginning to see the advantages of hot sexy sizzle. But no way I was admitting that to him. Not lying, just omission, which is not a lie. Mostly.

When my lips parted to say something that was not a lie and definitely wasn't about how sexy he was, his eyes darkened. "Shh."

He replaced the two fingers on my chin with two cupping hands, holding my face gently, like it was something precious. Like *I* was precious.

My lips stayed parted but no words came out.

In that moment of silence, he lowered his head. Slowly, so I could have stopped him.

Should have stopped him.

Did not want to.

He's nothing but image.

Image and intense pleasure.

The lips have one of the highest density of nerve endings in the body…

Argh. Shut up and kiss him.

While I was arguing with myself his warm mouth settled on mine, tongue sliding deftly between my lips. It rasped my sensitive skin, rubbing my lips awake like a thorough toweling. A steamed towel, hot and wet.

Confused feelings fled. I gave a little moan and opened wider.

He swept inside, all spice and heat. He groaned, a sound of masculine hunger. His questing mouth, his hot kiss, said lust plain and clear. Yet his hands were tender on my face, his sweet caress speaking of something beyond sex, a closeness that transcended the physical.

Happiness blossomed in my heart. Our groans were intertwined, mutual. For this one moment, the battle was suspended and we were on the same side.

His fingers tunneled into my hair, holding me firmly while his tongue drove deeper. He pressed closer yet, pinning me to the edge of the elevator shaft with his body, imprinting me with every muscle, every bulge, every place he was hard and primitive under his worsted.

I rippled against him and moaned softly in response. If he could generate this kind of pressure standing, how would the weight of his body feel, pressing me into a mattress?

At the thought I nearly exploded.

He shifted me, his powerful hands urging me away from where the corner of the elevator was digging into my spine and guiding me onto the wall. There he pressed me into vinyl wallpaper and kissed me like he was starving for me. The honest hunger in his kiss undid me. I grabbed his head and kissed him back with everything I had.

A big hand slid up my ribs, sparking a trail of heat, stopping under my breast. The mound throbbed, waiting, wanting, *yearning* for that hot hand to slide up the curve, to touch my delicate and private flesh. To brand it as his own. My soft moans shortened to whimpers, and I arched to thrust my breast more fully into his hand.

A deep rumbling started, a lion's purr. His hand moved, fingers barely brushing the bottom curve. I stopped breathing. His fingers skimmed higher, circling nearer, nearer to the hardening tip. I twitched in anticipation, greedy for his touch on sensitive flesh barely covered by a thin blouse and the wispiest scallop of lace. Bless Twyla's endless supply of sexy bras.

Finally, *finally* his thumb scraped my nipple. I shrieked into his mouth, jerking against him. My nipple furled instantly, wordlessly urging him again, more, *now.*

He opened his hand and covered my breast, his heat searing. Slotting the nipple between two fingers, he began to pump and tug gently, rhythmically squeezing, pulling. I thought I'd go insane from the sweet soft tugging.

Until he replaced the hand with his mouth.

His lips closed on my erect nipple through thin blouse and bra, breath wetting the material until he could have been sucking directly on flesh. It was the dream become real; it was better. More aroused than I'd been in my life, I grabbed his ears and beat my hips into him, not thinking at all, just moving. A pressure built between my legs, a hot, heavy throbbing that made me want him on his back and me naked and clamping him between my thighs.

A ding startled me; my eyes flew open. The elevator, which had gone and come back again, disgorged half a dozen professional-looking people.

Before I could even think about dying from embarrassment, Ric gently disengaged and palmed me behind him, shielding me completely with his body. I pressed my hot cheek between his broad shoulders, the fine wool of yet another tailored suit coat soft against my flushed skin.

"Mr. Holiday, sir. We've been looking for you." Feet exited the elevator, the expensive click of conservative heels, both male and female.

In a moment they'd see me. I glanced down. The thin material of blouse and bra clung wetly to my skin. I could see the color of my nipple through them. Too bad I'd left Ric's navy coat under Rosie's reception desk. No way to cover the very obvious fact of what I'd been doing with their boss, a man they knew and respected. I wasn't certain either of us would survive with that respect intact—although I'd probably care more than he would. I braced myself for discovery.

"*Stop.*"

Plastered against Ric like I was, the dark power in his voice vibrated my chest as well as my ears. Still, it seemed impossible that a single word could stop six people coming full tilt—when the feet stopped.

"Go into the office. Work on your most pressing projects. I will be with you after lunch."

There was silence. Again it seemed impossible that just ordering those bright, inquisitive people of his to go somewhere else would work.

The feet tromped away.

The final weirdness. Enemy action, Mr. Bond. I raised my cheek from Ric's back, fully convinced he was a vampire.

I should have been trembling in my shoes and running as fast as I could in the other direction. But Twyla was happy with her v-guy. And after that kiss…I was trembling in my shoes, but not because I was frightened.

So when he took my elbow and guided me into the still-open elevator, I went. It took longer for the doors to close than it took to drop one floor.

"Here we are. Thirty one: accounting, shipping, IT and account support." With a ding, the elevator opened. Ric shepherded me out. "This way."

"Why are we here?" Not more kissing, not with this unsexy blue-flecked beige carpet, utilitarian cubicles in navy and oatmeal, and office machinery that was merely current rather than next gen. If not for the silvery chrome and running water, I wouldn't have known it was the same company.

Typical, right? Working departments always seem to be shoved below execs and glitzy jobs, both in goodies and in actual positioning. It lends credence to the idea that oxygen is thin in the upper "adminisphere".

"We're here because I owe you, remember?" Ric glided through the cubicles, smiling at workers and greeting each by name. Thin air hadn't dimmed his brilliance. But that simply might have been because vampires didn't need to breathe.

"Owe me? For what…? Oh." I'd flung that at him after last night's kiss. With everything that had happened, I'd forgotten about it. "I didn't mean it. Mostly."

"I know. But I'll help you anyway." Ric led me to a small, windowless work room, like a music school's practice room with a plank table instead of a piano. He seated me at the table and took the chair next to me. We turned toward each other in a sort of V.

"First things first. Here's my personal cell phone number." He tapped a card onto the desk. "If you have any questions or concerns, call me. Day or night."

His eyes were sharply blue, as if he was trying to beam something unsaid directly into my brain. Questions or concerns? Like what to wear to the face-off? Or concerns of a more fangy nature?

I took the card and rubbed my thumb across thick linen paper with embossed print. I turned it over. He'd written his cell phone number on the back in slashing black ink. "Thanks. You're helping me, but to do what?"

"Fight Camille."

"Good. Um, how?" I admit I had visions of Camille and me squeezed into strips of spandex, knives strapped to our thighs, me with a bandoleer of stakes across my chest, battling with halberds and maces.

One corner of Ric's mouth turned up as if he saw the Xena images in my head. "I'll help you nail your presentation. If I'm travelling to Meiers Corners, I want to go in on the side of right."

"You're a businessman. Any side with enough money is the right side."

The other corner rose. "Winning against Camille isn't going to be easy."

"Of course it is. Meiers Corners as Vegas of the Midwest? Please. All I have to do is show pictures of showgirls in lederhosen. So wrong."

His lips twitched. "I know you want logical arguments to

win the day. But you'll be dealing with a committee."

"A committee is just people."

"People who have personal agendas. Camille will play to that. She knows how to work the system." He took my hands. "Despite her saucy siren act, she's ruthless. She fights dirty, and she likes it. She'll do whatever she has to. Lie, seduce, threaten. Schmooze. You won't. That's a handicap."

"Being honest isn't a handicap. Anyway, I'm not naive. I know how to schmooze."

"Really? What is schmoozing but little white lies?"

"It doesn't *require* lies." I paused. "Maybe a little spinning of truth."

His brows rose. "Isn't that still on the evil side of the Lie Line?"

"Lying for profit is bad. But telling the truth hurtfully is bad too. They're both on the same side of the Lie Line."

"The evil side?"

"The dick side."

He blinked. Then he laughed, a deep masculine chuckle that rippled inside me. The laughter lit his whole face, warming me, making me want to kiss his beautiful curved mouth. I leaned forward…he leaned forward…

We bumped heads. I sprang straight. "I never understand why people laugh when I'm just telling the truth."

"Maybe it's your delivery." He had such a powerfully attractive smile. "Synnove, I do trust you, and definitely respect you."

Happiness fizzed inside, like Synnove champagne. Then—"There's a 'but' coming, isn't there?"

"Now who's the mind reader?" He said it lightly, but his gaze was warm. His thumb began to caress the back of my hand. "I trust you as an expert in your field, in medicine. *My* area of expertise is making the right impression, the right way. I'm trying to give you the benefit of my knowledge."

"I can win without being another Dr. Bearsylls." I paused. "Why do we have to bid at all? If you know my side is 'the side of right', make an executive decision and go with me. I mean come with me. I mean..." I blushed. "Pick my side?"

"I can't." His lips twisted, his smile self-mocking. "There are circumstances you don't know about. Suffice it to say that for every nasty thing Camille can hand out, her boss can smack it down ten times harder. If I let this play out, there's a good chance he'll stay away. If not, we'll all suffer his temper. And that's vicious." He sounded like he knew firsthand.

"But what if I lose the bid?"

His expression went dark. "Then appearances be damned. I won't work for Nosferatu agai—I won't work for him." He cleared his throat, making what, for him, was a visible attempt to recover from that slip.

Work for Nosferatu *again*?

Ric's hands tightened on mine. "Bottom line, Nosferatu and Camille are serious bad news. A real attack would be devastating. Best to simply avoid it. So. Here's what you need to do to sell this. First you—"

"Wait." *Sales*. Horrors of school fundraisers, rapping on door after door, selling nothing while my friends made sale after sale—remember, I was the plain, unnoticeable one—made me hyperventilate. "Why start now? The presentation is a week away."

"The sooner you're armed, the better I'll feel. In case..." He stared past me at the blank wall, but the pain flickering in his eyes told me he was seeing something awful projected there. Maybe having to do with working for Nosferatu *again*.

I put a reassuring hand on his.

His eyes returned to me and the horrors faded. He gave me a small smile. "In case business calls me away."

"Business." I didn't like any of this, not his evasiveness, not the horror in his eyes, and especially not his trying to teach me about *sales*. He'd blocked the Nosferatu topic so I threw up my own block. "No sales. I've memorized countless Latin terms but sales is different. Sales is hard."

"Relax. Breathe normally." He took me by the shoulders. "I'll start with basics. Holiday Buzz has five departments." He released me slowly. "Just a handful. Easy peasy."

"*Easy peasy*?" I was panting, cold little puffs of air, my heart was thudding painfully, and worse, anatomical terms were starting to bubble up in my head. "My brain's been coated in industrial nonstick. Unless the departments have a mnemonic device, like the one for the cranial nerves—Ooh, Ooh, Ooh, Topless Tiffany and Fat Valerie Got Vaginitis And Hepatitis—"

"Memory aid?" Grinning, he grabbed my hand. "Five departments. First is account services."

He kissed my thumb, then flicked his tongue across the pad.

I stopped panting. Hell, I stopped breathing.

"Creative." He kissed the index finger, butterfly light. Then sucked delicately at the tip.

My heart's painful thudding stuttered. I swallowed, hard; hot liquid desire ran down my throat.

"Finance." He kissed the middle finger, then licked and nipped the tip with deliciously sharp teeth, leaving me wide-eyed and squirming in my chair, and I still had two more fingers to go.

"Media buying." He kissed my ring finger. Then, with a wicked glance, he ran his tongue from the base to the tip.

I jumped in my chair.

"And last but not least, production." He kissed my pinkie. Then he ran his tongue along my whole throbbing hand, from pinkie to thumb and back again.

I squeezed my eyes shut—clenching everywhere, jaw, thighs, sweet inner muscles. "I'm not sure I'll remember all that." I opened my eyes and held up my other hand. "Repeat it?"

His grin widened.

And he did, in such a scrumptious way that sweat broke out on my skin and I nearly slid out of my chair. Finishing, he gave me a hot smile that managed to be smug, amused, delighted and pure wicked sex. "Again?"

"Nope, got it," I said before my whole body went up in flames, *whoosh*. "What's left for you to do?"

"Set the tone. The direction for the company. I make sure the agency's thrust is positive. We only take on clients that have a definite favorable impact on humans and humankind."

Humans and humankind. Oddly, I wasn't finding phrases like that strange anymore.

He kissed and licked the inside of my wrist. I squealed. "Five departments, positive impact." Any terror I'd held over sales, Nosferatu or vampires in general, fled. "Stop that or I won't remember my name, much less what you're trying to teach me. So I convince five departments to take our account?"

"The departments are general umbrellas." He dropped a kiss on my palm, closed my fingers with his and held my hand to his chest. Like holding it to his heart.

Wished-for image?

Or reality?

Yikes. Fluttering heart, sweaty skin, everything tinted rose… I was falling in love, treacherous because Ric Holiday was dangerous, powerful, smart and not even human. Worse, I wasn't sure if I was falling in love with *him*, or who I wanted him to be.

I started to tug my hand away.

"Time to move on?" He gave my hand a regretful pat before releasing it. "All right. It's not the creatives I'm worried about. Your colorful folksy town of Meiers Corners is right up their alley. But the number crunchers' job is to keep things on time and under budget. And don't get me wrong, they do a wonderful job and I'm grateful. Without them Holiday Buzz would be Holiday's Bottomless Pit. But Camille will tailor her message to them, and she'll nail it. Casinos? Instant money."

"Lovely." My heart was starting to race again. "What do I do to compete?"

"That's what we're here to figure out."

For an hour Ric asked me detailed questions about Meiers Corners, some of which I knew, some of which I had to phone Twyla for. After she quit panting—did she and Nikos ever stop?—and no I wasn't jealous—all right, maybe a little—we ended up putting her on speaker and Ric quizzed her until she explained everything to his satisfaction. He was very picky and got quite detailed. I think she made some of it up.

Then he and I conferred for almost another two hours, heads together, working on the proper tack to take. He didn't kiss me again, but he sat close, his body heat and scent caressing me. In some ways the simple closeness was nicer.

Finally he sat back and considered me, his eyes a serious blue. "You're exhausted," he said flatly. "Your skin is gray, your eyes are bloodshot, and you're sagging."

"Thanks. You don't look so good yourself." Which was a real whopper. He looked delicious, like a chocolate sundae with whipped cream and cherries. Hmm, lunch time.

A fleeting smile twisted his lips. "This isn't my best time of day. I'm more of a…night person." He searched my eyes. "But perhaps you guessed that?"

I sucked in a breath. It seemed impossible. It sounded as though he was asking if I knew he was a vampire. "I might have guessed. I mean, my cousin's significant other might be a 'night person'."

"Yes." He was gazing over my shoulder again. "It can make for a difficult relationship." Something in his tone or eyes made me think he meant him and me. Like maybe he was contemplating a relationship with me.

I held my breath, waiting to see if he followed up on it, maybe with a kiss.

"Well." His gaze returned to mine. "I think we're done for today. You should head out while it's still daylight. Camille isn't the best person to have working against us. I don't think you're in any actual danger, but I'd feel better if you're safe with your cousin before the sun goes down."

"Okay." I rose, mind churning. He'd as good as said that not only did vampires exist, but both he and Camille were of the sharp-toothed persuasion. A truth, completely unasked for and totally unexpected. A secret not even my best friend had shared with me.

Ric trusted me more than Twyla. Zap me with a TENS. I shook my head, trying to clear it.

"Are you okay?" He was right on top of me. I sucked in air, got a noseful of hot spicy male and choked. He patted my back gently and I thought maybe here was the kiss coming, but after I was breathing more or less normally he stepped back and his hand dropped. He did look regretful. "You'd better go."

"Yeah, while it's still daylight, got it. Is the training all done, then?"

"Not really. We've made a good start but I'd like to do more. Tomorrow you could come to my penthouse..." His color rose and his canines got a bit longish. His fingers clenched. "No, better come here. First thing."

"Okay."

"Maybe not first thing." His expression was unusually troubled, doubting. "Maybe give yourself a few hours."

He was second-guessing himself for the sake of my safety.

He truly cared. It made me fizz again. "I should start out after sunrise?"

He smiled, his azure eyes lighting like a dawn sky. "Yes. I'm glad we understand each other."

When I left, I was smiling too.

I got back to the cabin plenty before sunset. But while I had avoided Camille, I walked straight into the Spanish Inquisition, and not the one with comfy chairs.

Not my fault. No one expects the Spanish Inquisition.

Well, except for the part where they gave thirty days notice.

But Twyla met me at the door of the cabin and dragged me in one handed. From the look on her face my secrets were grass and she was coming after them with a weed whacker.

Chapter Nine

"Holiday's working with you? I thought you were avoiding him." Twyla peppered me with questions as I stumbled into the cabin behind her. "What's going on? Did the bra help?"

The bra. Thoroughly wet by Ric's suckling outside the elevator. I glanced down. Thank goodness the blouse had dried without staining, or Twyla would have known how much the bra had helped.

"It's a long story." I caught sight of myself in the entryway mirror. Ric was right, my face was a bit gray. "How about another glass of that merlot?"

"And then you're telling me everything—and I do mean everything?"

"Yes, all right."

"Nikos!"

Soundlessly the second bedroom door opened. No noisy moans and creaking bedsprings came from behind the first. "Where are Elena and Bo?"

"Elena's swimming. Something about the water's buoyancy helping her relax. Bo's...resting." Her odd pause made more sense now that I knew Bo was probably a sun-shy vampire.

And there it was. The perfect opportunity to confirm what Ric had told me. Or not *told* me exactly, but implied really hard. "So about fangy vampi—"

"Your merlot."

I spun. Nikos was almost on top of me. I fell back a step, heart leaping into jackhammer mode. Nikos was as silent as Ric, and damn, the Greek was big, a dark mountain handing me a dinky little wine glass. Smiling, I took the glass, though both smile and hand were a mite shaky.

Twyla said, "Don't let him bother you. Where he comes from, that scary dominance and discipline is bred in. He doesn't really mean it."

"Maybe not with you." I eyed the Spartan. "But that's what I'm talking about. Vam—"

"Why was Holiday," she cut me off hurriedly, "asking me all those questions on the phone? Is he going to take us on? Drink your wine." She tipped my hand and I got a snout full of merlot. She was busy glaring at Nikos then glancing pointedly from me to the couch. She released me to go sit, then had the nerve to pat the cushion next to her genteelly.

I stayed put. "But what about vampir—"

Nikos snared me by the elbow, jarring me so I not only cut off the word, I nearly chomped off my tongue. He hustled me to the couch where he practically planted me beside my cousin. Then he topped off my glass.

What could I do? It was two against one, and their side held the wine hostage. I gave in and explained about the Advertising Bowl faceoff against Camille. "Since Holiday Buzz only takes on clients who have a positive impact on 'humans and humankind', Ric's helping me." I waggled my brows on the "humans and humankind", inviting her to broach the v-topic herself.

"He's helping you? You got friendly!" She beamed at me like a star pupil. "Told you the bra would work."

"We didn't get friendly *that* way!" I blushed. "Not exactly. Not intentionally. I mean, not today. Today was just business. Mostly."

"And yesterday?" Nikos rumbled.

He *would* have to hit on that.

I glared at him. "I liked you better when you never said anything." But two could play the evasion game. "Actually, Nikos, I'm glad you're here. Ric said something and I need to ask you both. About vam—"

"Drink your wine," Twyla said at the same time Nikos thrust a bag under my nose and said, "Chocolate?"

Enough was enough. I swiped the bag from him and yelled, "Vampires! Details. Juicy. *Now.*"

There was a shocked silence. Then Twyla said, "Ooh. You shouldn't have done that. Not with Bo in the next—"

The bedroom door slammed open. Limned by the sun striping through the bedroom's vertical window blinds was six-four, two hundred pounds of Viking.

He stalked into the living room. Thick wavy blond hair, frosty blue eyes, shoulders like a freeway, chest like a brick building and arms like tree trunks, he was tightly muscled and radiating intensity. He wasn't quite as big as Mt. Nikos but the sheer command in his stride said if there was a master vampire for the city of Meiers Corners, Bo Strongwell was it.

"Vampires don't exist." His dark rumble echoed weirdly in my head. "You will forget this conversation ever took place."

"Okay." I nodded pleasantly. "Whatever you say."

He stopped. Frowned at me. "What did I say to you?"

"You told me to forget this conversation ever took place. So I'm forgetting it, see?" I put down my glass—but held onto the chocolates—and spread my hands. "It's forgotten."

"Damn me," he said. "Not another one."

Nikos chuckled. When Bo skewered him with a nasty look, the chuckle subsided to a grin.

Twyla, to my surprise, was preening. "That's my cousin."

"What's the problem? I said I'd forgotten it."

Bo got all grumpy-faced. "If you'd really forgotten it, you wouldn't have remembered forgetting it."

"Sure." How had the people I loved and trusted gotten harder to understand than a sales guru? "Well, if I'm not forgetting it, can you tell me what you meant when you said 'Not another one'? That's what Camille said yesterday, and 'another one' meant me."

"Oh boy," Twyla said to no one in particular. "Here it comes." She poked me. "I'm gonna need chocolate for this."

I pulled one out of the bag I'd swiped from Nikos and unwrapped it before handing it to her. "Camille also asked where you Alliance boys find 'them', again meaning me. What's an Alliance boy?"

"Fuck." Bo ran a hand through his hair, rumpling it, paced away two steps, whirled back and glared at me like this was my fault. "*Jævla rasshøl.*" I didn't know what that meant but he said it like "fucking asshole". Hopefully not me.

He threw himself onto the other sofa. On him it looked like a big chair. Even though he was fuming, the boyishly mussed hair made him look good enough to eat. I was beginning to see all vampires were unnaturally attractive, maybe part of their predator kit.

He shot an aggrieved glance at Twyla. "How long has she known?"

"*She* is right here," I pointed out.

"This is the first I've heard about it." Twyla shrugged and nibbled her chocolate. "But I'd guess she's suspected for quite a while. It's impossible not to see if you're living right on top of it. I should know."

"Right here." I was starting to understand how Camille had felt last night, ignored by Ric. Without the, you know, kissing part.

The front door slammed open. "Wish you could stand sunlight, Bo. Did you know that if you float on your back the fishies will nibble your heels...whoa, a wine and chocolate party and you started without me?"

Striding into the living room was five-nine of lithe, deadly female, shaking out a wet mop of black hair so curly it could arrest criminals all on its own.

Detective Elena Strongwell.

Only to my shock she wasn't exactly striding so much as waddling. I hadn't seen Elena since high school. Wearing a bikini top, cutoff jeans and sandals, either she'd duct-taped a watermelon under her belly button or—

She was honking pregnant.

"Well." I unwrapped a chocolate of my own. "Good thing I've been through my obstetrics rotation. You're due when, two years ago?"

"Nah. Not 'til July fuck-me twenty-fifth." At a raised eyebrow from her husband she amended, "Pardon me, July fuzzy-bears-and-kittens twenty-fifth. Trying to dial back on the swearing in prep for the kid. A few weeks, but I've been ready for *months*." She tossed her beach bag onto the couch, flopped down next to Bo and levered her feet into his lap. "Rub."

"What's the magic word?" Aimed at her, his dark growl had softened to almost a purr.

"Now."

With a smile he slid off her sandals and began to knead the ball of one foot.

She moaned. "Ohhh, that is so fuh...fudgy delight good."

"As good as the rubbing you got this morning, Detective?"

One eye cracked. "Unfair. That's like comparing

chocolate and wine. They're both out of this world."

"Eww," I said. "I don't want to think of you two 'rubbing'." I pulled a couple chocolates out of the bag and tossed them to her. "Take those instead. There's a reason that kind of thing stays behind bedroom doors."

Twyla smirked. "Only because you're not getting any. Or at least not that way. Not intentionally. Only business." She added teeth in a shark's smile. "According to you."

My cheeks heated. Relatives are annoying. Rels with great memories are why wedgies were invented. "He kissed me, okay? Happy?"

"Exceedingly." She had the gall to smirk. If it hadn't been for Nikos's protective hovering, her thong would've been around her ears.

"You got kissed?" Elena opened both eyes—on me. Her stare was direct and piercing, her cop stare. "Who? Where? How was it? C'mon, I want details."

"Cops always want details," I grumbled.

"The 'who' is Ric Holiday." Twyla was gloating so hard I wanted to either crawl under the sofa or do her next gynecology exam with a speculum from the fridge. "*Where* is at the party. I knew the sexy pushup bra would do the trick."

"Still. Right. Here."

"The old lingerie trick." Elena pursed her lips. "Yeah, that's always a good one. Bo gave me a lavender set that rocks. Although my near-B bra wouldn't fit her." She looked down at herself. "Wouldn't fit me right now either, the tit fairy having finally visited, ten years late."

"I love you both ways, Detective." Bo started rubbing the other foot. She groaned and went flat on the couch.

"Look, enough." My face was hot. I unwrapped chocolate to give myself time to recover. "I kissed Ric but that's all I've done. And that's all I'm going to do." I popped the chocolate in my mouth and started chomping. "There's no future in it. He's an ad man, okay? All sizzle, no steak. He's lies and misdirection, not meaty facts."

"Meaty?" Twyla waggled her eyebrows.

My face flamed. I stopped chewing because the chocolate just melted. "I didn't mean it that way. Exactly." I swallowed. "Look, the point is, he told me something that might not be a lie. Might be true. Probably is true from the way you're all acting. About his being a vampire—"

Bo hissed. "Keep your voice down. This cabin is sturdy but not soundproof."

"I wasn't shouting," I said.

"We don't use the v-word except in private," Twyla said. "Very private, like our soundproofed households. Public cabins are…public."

"Oh, come on. The nearest occupied cabin is three doors down."

"We've learned the strangest things can hide electronic bugs." Twyla pointed at the bag of chocolates and then at herself. I tossed her one and she unwrapped it thoughtfully. "Holiday used the v-word?"

"Well, no, not the *word*. He said he was a 'night person', wink-wink nudge-nudge. And that Camille was a 'night person' too. Guys, enough with the secrecy." I crossed my arms. What had the world come to when the ad man was more truthful than my friends? "Since I'm battling Camille for the freedom of Meiers Corners, stop pussyfooting around and give me some useful *facts*. What did Bo mean, not another one? And what did Camille mean by Alliance boys?"

"Lotta questions in those questions." Twyla tossed the chocolate in her mouth. "You have the time?"

"No." Bo underscored the word with a jabbed finger. "The more people we tell, the more likely the secret will get out."

Nikos raised a brow. "Have we a choice?"

"I vote we tell her," Elena said.

"Me too," Twyla chimed in.

"This is not a republic." Bo's dentures were getting kinda pointy and his eyes glinted a peeved violet. "I said no. We're not telling her anything."

"Fine," I said. "I'll just phone Dolly Barton."

Silence. Four sets of eyes swung to me and glued, the mix of expressions from awed to annoyed to amused.

Dolly Barton wasn't a vampire, at least I didn't think so. But as the queen of gossip, she was a real threat. Nobody knew more about the lifeblood of Meiers Corners than Dolly.

Although to say Dolly was a gossip was like saying an MRI machine was a magnet with aspirations. Dolly knew everything that went on, sometimes even before it happened. Some people said Police Chief Dirkson got most of his arrest tips from Dolly during his weekly mustache wax.

Bo folded his arms, his gaze slashed to the side in disgust.

Elena gave the nod to Twyla. "Tell her."

"I wanted to explain long ago," Twyla said. "But if the secret gets out, the v-guys are as good as dead. In a manner of speaking."

"I'm not going to blab. I just want to know what's going on. What did Camille's 'not another one' mean?"

"That's the rare human who's immune to v-guy compulsion, which is a hypnotic combination of eyes and voice, though some older ones can do it by voice alone."

Elena said, "All of us spouses are mostly immune to it. Well, we'd have to be to have a chance of a true relationship with a particular v-guy."

"Okay." I didn't get the strange music in her voice when she said "a particular v-guy" but I was going for the executive summary right now. I'd get to the refinements later. "And the Alliance?"

"Bo can explain that one best." Elena struggled to sit up.

"I don't agree with this." He helped her up. "I'm not going to be an active part of it."

"You refuse to make me into a v-gal. The least you can do is give Synnove a few facts."

"That's different." He narrowed his eyes at her.

She snared a bottle of oil from her beach bag and held it out to him. "Isn't."

"Is." He held his scalding stare a moment longer before sighing and taking the oil. "It's too dangerous to turn you now. Hell, it's too dangerous, period."

"Language, Viking." She grinned and pointed to her swollen belly. He started rubbing oil onto her skin. A pleasant coconut odor filled the air.

"Heck, then." He turned to me but kept rubbing. "To make my wife happy, I'll tell you. But if you ever spill it—"

"I won't."

"You'd better not. The Alliance is the Iowa Alliance, a group of us who hold common ideals, the most important of which is that humans are our equals. I stand for the Alliance in Meiers Corners."

"Why the 'Iowa' Alliance?" Again, I'd get the humans-as-equals later.

"That's where Kai Elias, the Ancient One who leads the Alliance, lives."

"Okay. And everyone belongs?"

"No. Not everyone holds our ideals. The Chicago Coterie would treat humans like blood cattle. The Alliance stands against the Coterie."

"Great." I rolled my eyes. "V-guy politics."

"No." Nikos stirred. "Elias stands against Nosferatu. We follow."

Nosferatu? That shocked me straight. "What does Nosferatu have to do with…oh damn. Nosferatu leads this Chicago Coterie dealie?"

Twyla said, "Nikos thinks the dispute between Elias and Nosy is more personal than philosophical."

"Like the Trojan war," he agreed.

I wondered who starred as Helen. "Okay, it's Elias against Nosferatu. And only the Coterie v-guys suck blood? Or do you use us for food too?" I hoped that part wasn't true. Although the idea of Ric's hot mouth, sucking at my neck…I shivered.

"We do," Bo said. "But not for food. For our veins."

"Like humans who can't make their own blood," Twyla said. "They take transfusions."

"By mouth," Nikos said.

"Really? You can't make your own blood?" Now we were talking my field. "You guys don't drink daily, do you? You'd have to take, what—about three pints a month?"

At that, both Bo's and Nikos's heads snapped toward me, weirdly fluid. Creeped me out—although not as much as Camille. Everything is relative.

But for the first time they looked at *me*, really looked. Even Elena gaped as if seeing me for the first time.

Twyla only grinned. "Synnove's a doctor. Got her M.D. and everything."

Elena blinked. "A doctor, Bo. Like I'm police."

Bo frowned at her. Nikos cocked his head. She'd said something significant.

"Okay, I feel like there should be a *whuh-whuh*. What's so good about me being almost a doctor?"

Bo said, "We used to have problems keeping v-issues from the attention of law enforcement. Elena smoothed all that over. We've had questions about our physiology for a long time, but no one we trusted to ask."

"Until now," Nikos rumbled.

"What…wait. Me?" This called for fortification, and I dug out a chocolate. Immediately two other hands went out. I tossed Twyla and Elena their own fortifications as I considered it. "Like, I'd be a v-guy doctor? I don't think so. Research is all about sharing information. Just the opposite of v-guys and their big secret."

"Don't think of it as a secret," Twyla said. "Think of it as controlled information."

"Wiseguy." I threw another chocolate at her. She caught it one-handed, unwrapped it and popped it into her mouth with a smile. "I don't see why we can't say the word vampire though. It's not like anyone's listening—"

Bam-bam-bam.

We exchanged horrified looks. Someone was at our door.

Chapter Ten

Twyla was elected to handle things by the simple expedient of Elena and Bo nodding toward her and Nikos picking her up and depositing her in front of the kitchen door. I followed to rescue the purse I'd dropped at the door when Twyla pulled me inside.

Bam-bam-bam. Nikos growled. Whoever it was, was strong and persistent.

Cautiously, Twyla cracked the door. "Hello?"

A short, round woman with blonde hair lacquered into a beehive, a long nose, and sweeping fake eyelashes stood on the stoop. "Hello," she said brightly. "I'm town chairperson Michelle Llynn Tiyers, two Ls, two Ls, two Ns. Confidentially, my parents wanted a unique name for me."

Twyla smiled and nodded. I could almost hear her thoughts. Some names were unique, some parents wanted their children to grow up forever scarred.

The woman handed Twyla and me each a card. Under her name and title was a slogan that read, "Chipmunk Lake. We're better than you think we are."

I looked up from the card. "You look familiar."

"You must remember me from the Miss Wisconsin pageant in '70…I mean '80…I mean '92. I was Miss Up North." She pronounced it Oop Nort'. "Not to be confused with Miss Northwoods."

"No, I don't think so—"

"I won Preliminary Talent and Preliminary Swimsuit. The only thing I didn't get was Miss Congeniality, but isn't *that* the kiss of death."

Twyla said, "So why—"

"Of course, that self-important little cheerleader won the state pageant. But she's nothing now, and I'm chairperson of a whole *town*. And, mind you, a town that's *going places*. Well, it will be if I have anything to say about it."

"But why are you—"

"We've got our own Chipmunk Lake YouTube channel and everything. Why, our video of 'Best Billy Bass Impressions' got five hundred hits." She put her hands on her cheeks and waved them like fish gills. "Roll me over in the clover, roll me over, lay me down and swim upstream," she warbled. "Such fun. Confidentially, I think we're going to get picked up by *America's Got Talent*."

"Whyareyouhere?" Twyla yelled.

Michelle Llynn blinked. "Why, to welcome you big city folk to our little home. Here's a coupon for 25% off all fireworks and worms at Chipmunk Lake Supplies." She handed Twyla a paper. "Make sure Roy puts them in separate bags. Confidentially, some of the fireworks are hair-trigger. It can make a mess."

Inside my purse, my cell phone deedled. *Saved*. I fumbled getting the thing out and nearly missed the call. I'm not saying I carry a lot of junk in my day purse but in a pinch I can use it as a traction counterweight.

Walking away for privacy, I hit talk. "Hello?"

"I can't stop thinking about you." Ric's voice was deeper than I remembered, richer. "I need to see you. I'd like to take you to dinner. My treat."

I glanced at the living room where two sets of overly inquisitive eyes stared at me like cats or dogs waiting to get fed. I schooled my voice into nonchalance. "Twyla's planning dinner here."

"My treat," he said again. That deep, coaxing tone slid over my skin like silky lotion. "I have reservations for a private balcony at Rustermann's."

He'd named only the most expensive restaurant ever, the kind of place run by a rock-star chef where there are three menu choices, each a signature special, memorized by the waiter with prices that are never mentioned because if you have to ask, you can't afford it.

"I'm in," I said. "If only because my cuisine for the last eight years has been macaroni and cheese and vending machine pretzels. And with my student loans I won't have anything better for the next twenty."

"Excellent." Strangely he sounded, not triumphant but almost relieved. Like he expected me to say no.

Who said no to gorgeous Ric Holiday? Well, me. But the fact that he'd heard "no" more than once was another clue there was more to him than met the eye.

"I'll pick you up in half an hour."

"I have a better idea. I'll meet you there." I was staying with a couple of real live vampires. I had no idea what would happen if Ric came into their territory.

Really. It didn't have anything to do with the fact that Twyla would have been all over him, pumping him for embarrassing details.

"You're not driving alone. Camille—"

"Doesn't know where I'm coming from. And unless your phone is bugged, she won't know I'm coming into town at all."

"My phone isn't bugged. She could get wind of this in other ways though."

"Fine, then I'll get one of the guys here to accompany me, okay?"

"Guys?"

"Twyla's and Elena's. They're more than a match for Camille."

"Well—"

"I'll meet you there." To forestall any more arguments, I hung up. Then I went to rescue Twyla and Nikos.

"Roy is my second cousin twice removed," Michelle Llynn was saying. "His son by my third cousin's daughter Michelle Lluane—two Ls two Ls—is named Craigg—two Gs—and he minds the general store—"

"Sorry to interrupt." Mostly sorry. But from the glazed, slightly ill look—two Ls, two Os—on Twyla's face and the low, dangerous growl coming from Nikos, it was an emergency. Although now I knew why Michelle Lynn looked familiar. Everyone was related. "Our contact in Minneapolis wants to meet with me. Could I get a ride into the city?"

"Ooh, Minneapolis," Michelle Llynn said. "I could drive—"

"I need a few things," Twyla cut in quickly. "Nikos can take you."

"Right." Nikos hustled Michelle Llynn out the door.

"But I—"

"Thanks. Bye." He shut the door in her face. We all sagged in the silence.

Twyla said, "Nice save."

"Um, it wasn't a save. I'm having dinner with Holiday."

Her eyebrows shot into her hairline.

"I'm sure he only wants to cover more sales stuff."

"You keep telling yourself that, honey. I'll get my

shopping list. Nikos can drive you to Minneapolis, drop you off, do the shopping, then pick you up."

The nice thing about being tall was that the few chocolates I'd eaten hadn't made much of a dent in my appetite. I donned my business skirt but borrowed a soft lilac blouse from Twyla that gave the skirt an evening social cast.

And maybe I snatched a matching purple satin bikini underwear set while she wasn't looking.

Rustermann's sat atop a downtown skyscraper, a lush dining room with a large bank of windows overlooking the beauty of the city at night. But instead of one of the tables, the maitre d' led me along a back corridor and out a door.

I stepped onto a small balcony, open to the sweet summer air, with a single intimate table set for two.

Ric was waiting.

He smiled the moment he saw me, a complex mix of relief, boyish excitement, male interest and pure masculine sex appeal. He rose and pulled out the other chair for me. "I'm glad you made it here all right."

As I sat, he slid the chair smoothly under me. Very nice manners, this vampire had. "So, more coaching?"

"No. I wanted to spend time with you. Try the scallops. I've heard they're exquisite."

Then, to my utter shock, throughout a long, flawlessly served, superbly cooked meal, he set about *entertaining* me. He regaled me with humorous stories of the clients he'd snared, and strangely, also clients who got away. He told both with equal amusement, as if it wasn't the money that counted, but the game.

Food disappeared from his plate. When I asked him about it he simply smiled. I never saw him eating. The doctor in me wondered where, if he didn't eat, he got his energy.

He didn't try to seduce me overtly. But the entire meal was an exquisitely sensual experience, almost a seduction in itself. The thick silk napkin slid fluidly over my knees. The heavy brushed metal cutlery was cool to my heated touch. The scent of hothouse flowers, roses and orchids and freesia, came with each quickened breath. Wineglasses of thinnest crystal shivered against my lips. The wines—a different one with each course, from crisp white to full-bodied red with hints of oak and pepper—made me light-headed, almost giddy.

The food on the translucent china was a delight to both the eye and the mouth. I dined on everything from creamed spinach tortes to pan-seared scallops almost as big as my fist. The pièce de résistance was the ten-layer chocolate cake drizzled with raspberries and sin.

Gradually, under the spell of rich elegance and delightful company, I became so totally seduced that I forgot my troubles, forgot even The Incident.

Sipping a fruity dessert wine, I eyed Ric. It wasn't only the meal, I decided. It was the man who made the meal possible. Vampire. Whatever.

He'd somehow known I needed the luxury of time away from my issues, forgetting about my mental and emotional problems in sheer physical delight, and simply set about making it happen.

A bandage instead of a cure, the illusion of happiness, but still lovely.

If only illusion would hold up for a lifetime.

I was pleasantly sated and sporting a slight glow when I stood. "I have to go. It's been three hours and a guy like Nikos can only do so much shopping."

"Before you do." He came and took my face in his hands, as lightly as if I were precious. "May I kiss you?" I could only nod.

He dipped his head and brushed my lips, so softly, so tenderly, my insides melted. It was the perfect kiss to end the perfect date.

With the illusion of the perfect man.

He escorted me to the door. "You look delectable in purple, by the way."

"My blouse? It's lilac..." I looked down. The top buttons of the blouse had come undone, exposing a lot of me cupped in purple satin.

"Sorry." He grinned and rebuttoned my blouse. "Fingers slipped."

Okay, that made him more real. Somehow I liked it better.

Back at the cabin, Twyla tried to pry details of the dinner out of me and I parried with questions about v-guys. Now that the secret was broached, they told me some amazing, startling things...things that spoke directly to the physician in me.

It was after two a.m. when Nikos gathered Twyla for a walk around the lake and I finally crawled into bed. I'd just drifted off to sleep when a clank popped my eyes open. I lay in bed, listening to a few hoots, rustles and other non-city animal sounds.

Then a hissed swear.

More clanks, scrapes and swears. I kept absolutely still and tried to gauge where the noise was coming from. I couldn't quite tell.

But after another, louder swear, I could tell *who*. That was the troll who had tried to stop me on the bridge this morning. I got up, crept to the window and nudged open a peephole between the blinds—and got a great view of the log siding of cabin next door. I dropped the blinds and tiptoed out of the bedroom into the kitchen and peered out the back door.

The cabins had a central garbage and recycling area across the drive from cabin five. Sure enough, the troll crouched next to a bin, a lumpy black plastic bag lying on the gravel next to him. Just taking out the garbage, though it was rather late for that. I thought about asking him what he was doing, remembered his ominous shouting to stay out of the woods and decided not to go socialize.

I returned to bed but I was wide awake now and not going back to sleep any time soon. What made it worse was that Bo and Elena were at it *again*. Not only were they contributing to the noise keeping me awake, if a mugger or thief did break in, I wasn't so sure Mr. and Mrs. McMoany would hear my screams.

Not to mention all that giggling and bedspring creaking brought back images of Ric. The tactile memory of Ric. The smell of Ric, locked in my nose to stay.

Yeah, that was responsible for the most tossing and turning. I replayed every searing look, every soft caress, every masterful touch. Every kiss. Oh, that man…vampire… guy could kiss. I slid a hand where it would do the most good and replayed it all, with self-added moan track and tactile stimulation.

I got so hot I rolled off the bed.

Picking myself up, I went back to bed without finishing—fantasizing over a guy I barely knew only dug the infatuation pit deeper—and tried to get some rest. I was dozing when I caught a flash of light through the blinds. What…? I glanced at the clock. I must have fallen asleep because it was four in the morning.

I waited, growing chilled. If that flash of light was Nikos and Twyla, why hadn't they come inside yet? And what would anyone else be doing out this late, or this early? Anyone human, that was. All good little diurnal humans should be in bed. Unless the troll was taking out more garbage.

After a breathless few minutes, the light didn't come again. I'd probably imagined it. Gradually I relaxed enough to laugh at myself. All good little humans should be in bed, including me. I had a meeting with a hunky ad man in a few hours.

Which started me thinking of Ric again, and his touch. His kiss. His expensive, spicy scent…

I didn't sleep any more that night.

The next day I arrived at Holiday Buzz at nine sharp…or actually a bit groggy. All that wine, chocolate, and rich food topped off by night noises, not to mention my extracurricular activity fantasizing about Ric's incendiary kisses, had kept me from getting much restorative sleep.

So when I arrived and was sent by the uniformed guards directly to the windowless workroom, I threw open the door without caution.

Ric paced the small room with the fierce energy of a caged lion, his elegant hands folded behind his back, his tawny, exquisitely tailored suit intensifying the king of beasts image.

The minute he saw me he whipped around. His tense expression tightened to a scowl. "You look like shit."

"So sweet. Did you get me flowers and candy too? You don't look so hot yourself."

"I was worried about you. I *am* worried about you. You need to take better care of yourself."

He cared. I suddenly looked more kindly upon that scowl of his. "It's no biggie. I didn't sleep well."

"I didn't sleep at all. I thought about you the entire night." His voice was all sexy growl as he shut the door behind me.

"I did too. Thought about you. About us."

"*Synnove.* My sunshine." He pulled me into his arms.

Maybe if the last few days hadn't had a surreal, timeout-from-reality feel to them; maybe if that dream the night before hadn't knocked the camera completely out of focus; maybe if

I hadn't spent last night imagining exactly this, being in his embrace, smelling him, feeling him, I would have said no. Or at least I wouldn't have jumped into his arms like a treed cat.

But it had, and I had, and I jumped. "Kiss me."

His hand tangled in my hair and he pulled me into a wild kiss. He'd been drinking something sugary, fresh and hot, like tea with honey and lemon. His tongue thrust into my mouth. I wasn't small but he filled me with masculine fire.

All that fantasizing, the replay of tactile memories, the self-stimulation, was a fuse to the bomb of his hot, questing mouth. My passion unleashed. I grabbed his head and kissed him back like I'd crawl down his throat.

I ran my hands over him as I tasted him. Tactile memory became a tactile riot. His cheekbones and jaw were razor-sharp. His hair was silky soft. Scrubbing it released a scent fresh as an ocean breeze. Skimming his skin stirred the spice of his cologne, tangy with overtones of Oriental ginger and hot pepper, all of it heightened by pure male heat. The smell of him, the taste of him, the feel of him was complex and compelling.

He set me on my feet and slid hands down my back, stopping on either side of the small of it. He pulled me relentlessly into his hips, where the thrust of passion was starting. A sharp response lanced my belly.

Two could play at that game. I ground myself into him so hard he gasped.

His erection unfurled inside his slacks against me. He held my hips tighter and ground into me in return, a pelvic swirl so lithe that it conjured hot images of limber erotic strength, given the proper horizontal playground.

I nibbled his jawline, stretching myself along his chest to nip his tender ear. "Why don't we take this to a motel room?"

"Can't." He tongued the cord lying along my throat. "Sun's outside."

Grr. "Does the door at least lock?"

"Oh yes." Keeping me firmly curled in one arm, he twisted to spin the thumb lock. It gave a comfortingly secure snick. He regained his two-handed grip on my hips, ground into me with another athletic swirl. "The room's soundproofed, in case you're worried about that."

"Good to know." I twined arms around his neck and offered my lips.

He took my mouth with satisfying swiftness, kissing me greedily. His mouth ravaged mine, tongue plunging, teeth tugging, sucking and nibbling. All the while he grew harder and bigger in the escalating heat between us.

But his hands stayed flat on my back and aside from the raging intimacy of his mouth and the insistent pulsing of his erection against my belly I'd have thought he had no intention of going further.

That was going to change.

I untwined my arms and slid a hand onto his pants. The fine wool was taut, leading me directly to his cock. I palmed it; it overflowed my hand.

"Mmm, Synnove. Do that again." He kissed hungrily across my cheek, my ear, to the tender skin below.

I curled my palm over the thrust of him under tented cloth, was rewarded with another, louder *mmm*, almost a purr. So I rubbed.

Teeth brushed my neck, edged, sharp. "*Yesss*."

I started a rhythm, rubbing and squeezing. His hands convulsed on my hips. I thought it was reaction until cool air brushed my thighs and I realized he was winching up my skirt.

Heh. He was in for a surprise.

His tongue glided along my neck as he worked my skirt up, warm licks soothing the skin scraped by sharp teeth. He kept rolling the skirt until it bunched around my waist.

Having exposed my panties and pantyhose, his fingers gently, delicately went exploring.

Except I wasn't wearing panties and pantyhose. I was wearing thigh-high silk stockings. And nothing else.

His fingers met bare skin. He hissed. His head dropped to the crook of my neck. There was the thinnest film of perspiration on his forehead. "You…" he breathed heavily, "…are a wonder. A paragon among women. May I?" His fingers curled and uncurled.

Hell yes. "Please." I squeezed his cock under the worsted of his pants. "If I may, in return."

His answer was to unzip himself so fast that sparks flew. A yank, his hips jerked, and then he was naked and warm and pulsing in my hand.

And huge. His cock, smooth and throbbing, filled my circling fingers.

While I was enjoying the feel of him he cupped my nape in one powerful hand, bent and kissed me, his mouth like drugged honey.

And he slid one finger onto my aching sex.

I nearly exploded. His touch, anticipated for hours, was even better than I'd dreamed. Strong, warm, confident. He began to stroke me with tongue and finger in rhythm. I melted against him. He was wonderful, this was wonderful. His cock bobbed gently in my hand like it agreed.

The firm thrust of his finger along my hood made me quiver. I wanted more. Harder. I moaned my needs, grateful for the soundproofing.

He began thrusting two, then three fingers along my groove. I dug a hand into his soft hair, thrust in counterpoint with my tongue in his mouth. He synched up, rubbing me at the pace I set. My hand on his cock squeezed automatically in the same rhythm.

Suddenly he caught my tongue with his lips, pulled

himself out of my hand. "Not yet." His voice was tight. He kept hold of my head, kept thrusting with his hand as his eyes, azure heated to violet, burned into mine. "You're so beautiful."

Beauty. Style over substance. My arousal started to turn off.

Until he added "—So beautiful like this, flushed from my kisses, enjoying yourself so honestly. You're a wonder, Sunshine."

His words rushed through me like a wildfire. I pressed into his thrusting hand, tilting my hips so the next thrust went *in*.

I gasped. He echoed it. "Damn me. You're so slick. More. I want more from you."

He drove two fingers into me, then thumbed my clit hard.

My whole body lit with pleasure. He began to thrust and rub rhythmically with the pressure of an earthmover. I clutched his neck with both arms, rocked against him. Need built deep in my pelvis, throbbing, heavy. I groaned louder.

"You're so lovely, moaning in my arms, slick under my hand. Come for me, my lovely sunshine." He kissed me deep.

Two days of attraction, a wet dream, a full night of fantasy and a hot expert touch came to a head. I exploded under his fingers. Sweet climax flooded my body, my brain. It washed me clean. When I came to, panting in his arms, I was at peace for the first time in months.

"There's my sunshine." He smiled down at me, eyes softened to the blue of a warm sea. With all the variations of his smile I'd seen in the past two days, from deadly to happy, this almost loving look was my favorite.

I smiled back. "What about you?"

The smile grew. "I am a bit tense. Think you can help with that?"

"I know I can." I straightened in his arms, not moving

away, simply freeing my hands. I got the feeling this would be a two-handed job and touching him, I was right. He was like a baseball bat in my hands.

I slicked my fists over him, watching his eyes fire from gentle blue to fiercely glowing violet. If I'd thought about finishing him with my mouth, that kept me from it. I wanted to see his face as he came apart.

His eyes closed. His hard jaw and thrusting cheekbones glistened with a fine sheen. His nostrils flared. Peeking from between his lips were two pointed teeth.

My hands faltered, seeing that. He opened his eyes, compassion warming them, and laid fingers over mine. "You don't have to."

That released me from my fears. "I want to." I regained my rhythm. He swelled even bigger in my fists. Good thing I hadn't gone for oral sex—I'd have choked.

He began to thrust his hips counter to my hands. A flush rose above his collar, impending orgasm. His eyes were closed and now his mouth opened, exposing long, lethal fangs. I wondered what they'd feel like, sinking into my flesh. Seeing him so beautifully aroused, the idea was strangely attractive.

He pulled the handkerchief from his suit pocket, wrapped us both in it. Then, with a shout, he came in my hands. Hot passion spilled into my palms, overflowed into the cloth. It went on and on.

Finally he straightened, opening his eyes. The blue was so startling that all the oxygen seemed sucked from the room. "Thank you, Synnove." His teeth were normal now, fangs gone.

"Sure." I felt oddly embarrassed. I'd had sex before, but usually the men muttered something about it being great before going comatose. No one had ever said thank you, certainly not with this apparently heartfelt gratitude. Me, or the quality of men I dated? It no longer seemed to matter. "Thank you too."

He smiled. "You're very welcome. Let's cuddle." Without releasing me he turned a chair out and sat us both in it, with me between his thighs. I relaxed into him as if it were the most natural thing in the world.

So caring. In a way, he knew me better than I knew myself. It was perfect.

He whispered into my hair, "You deserve happiness, Synnove. The forever kind, with someone special."

I absolutely glowed.

Until he added, "But not with me. You need to marry someone else."

Chapter Eleven

Chicago, 1816

Fourteen-year-old Ric's panting breaths stirred the dust on the sheet-covered couch hiding him. Aiden crouched nearby, prying the top off a crate. To Ric's hypersensitive ears, the boards' creaks of protest shrieked, "Here we are!"

The tiny female child huddled in Ric's arms didn't seem to hear a thing. But she was human.

Aiden finished prying off the top, revealing a painting. "Damn," he whispered. "I wouldn't have believed it."

"I told you," the girl piped, her voice unnaturally loud in the dark storeroom. "I watched from the window the whole time he posed for it. But you didn't trust me."

"We trusted you, Pumpkin." Ric stroked her silky hair.

"But you didn't believe me." The little girl's voice was pouty. "Now maybe you do. He doesn't want anyone to see that picture until he has the painter paint out the gun. If we take it, it'll keep him from following us."

"If we can steal it without his knowing. And if we can get

it out of here before he catches us."

"Lots of ifs." Aiden replaced the crate's top. "I have a bad feeling about this."

"You and your bad feelings," the little girl said. "You're trying to get out of doing your part. But I did my part and now you two have to do yours. Because that's how partners work, everybody doing their part."

"We will." Ric patted the top of her head. "We'll protect you."

"Silly Ric. Partners don't need protecting. I meant our escape. You take me along. I did my part," she repeated stubbornly.

"You have indeed." Aiden left the crate to drop a kiss on her head.

Her face cleared. "So now that you see the picture's real, when do we leave?"

"Tomorrow." Ric's heart beat with fierce excitement. It was finally here. After four years, their vague plans for escape from this hell hole had snapped into place with this last piece. "Tonight Aiden will sneak the painting out and hide it. When he has it secured, we'll be safe to go—"

Bam. The storeroom door slammed open. "You!"

At first all Ric could see were the glowing red eyes of a pissed-off vampire. But the dry, raspy voice shot acid arrows into the pit of his stomach.

It was Nosferatu himself.

"What are you trainees doing here?"

"Nothing, sir." Aiden unfolded to his full height, already tall for sixteen. He edged in front of the painting. "We were practicing our concealment skills."

"Don't try to bullshit me." Nosferatu stalked into the storeroom, face half-plated and fangs protruding from between fleshy lips. "Not with her here. You think you're the first assholes who've tried to escape? You'll never escape me.

I'll destroy you first."

Fine hair rose along Ric's spine. The vampire knew. Their plan was falling apart before it had begun.

But their training had been brutally effective; they had a fallback plan, even for what was only supposed to be a short exploratory trip. He glanced at Aiden. They had one shot to get out of this with their skins whole. He flicked eyes to one side, then to the girl, then to the other side of the room.

Barely, Aiden nodded.

Ric counted a mental one, two, three.

He picked up the girl. At the exact same moment, Aiden snatched up the crate. Aiden ran one way and Ric the other.

"Damn you," Nosferatu snarled. But giving chase was ingrained for a vampire. He flickered into the center of the room where the boys had been, then paused, head churning between them. Before he could choose, Ric and Aiden both spun for the doorway.

They were lucky. Nosferatu had come alone. The doorway was unblocked.

Aiden reached it first, Ric a split second later. They were through like bullets. Both headed left, into the maze of dimly lit underground passageways below the vampire's house.

Nosferatu sped out behind them.

"What are you doing?" The girl struggled in Ric's arms as he ran. "We don't need to run from him anymore! We have the picture."

"It's...not safe." He panted it, fear making his lungs into bellows.

"You're wrong." She wriggled out of his grasp.

He'd been running fast, fast enough that hitting the ground would hurt her badly. He spun on a dime and caught her by her waist, managing to keep her from completely cratering. But when he tried to lift her again, she shook him off to stand on her own.

Aiden disappeared around the corner. Nosferatu shimmered to a halt a few yards from the girl.

"You can't stop us," she flung at him. "We have the painting."

"*We* do, do we?" The vampire started moving again, stalking them slowly, his red eyes marking his advance along the corridor. Instilling fear. Even though Ric knew the technique, it was working, his heart hammering so hard it nearly cracked his ribs. Nosferatu went on, "Seems to me only one of you has the painting. If that's actually what was in that crate."

"You know it is," the girl said. "Or you wouldn't have stopped." Gloating triumph shone on her face. Ric felt slightly sick. The triumph was premature, the gloat ill-advised.

"I haven't stopped," Nosferatu said.

"Please. You're trying to bluff. But we have the power."

"Are you so sure about that?"

Ric heard the pair of assassin trainees behind him before he saw them. They herded Aiden around the far corner, his friend still grasping the picture crate. Ric didn't hold out any hope the pair would help him and Aiden. The training program was cruelly adversarial.

They blocked one end of the corridor. Nosferatu blocked the other. His smile wasn't pretty. "Who has the power now?" he asked the girl.

Aiden and Ric turned back to back, the girl between. So they were to die, Ric thought. But they'd go down fighting.

Aiden, facing the assassin trainees, snarled, "Don't be fools. Look at him. Nosferatu is scrawny! What kind of leader is that? We can beat him with ease. We can *all* be free."

"*Do not listen.*" Nosferatu's voice echoed like thunder in the narrow corridor. "You will remember only that I am tall and strong. Beautiful."

Behind Ric came two sing-song voices. "You are tall and

strong. Beautiful."

"He's lying, Ric," the girl said. "You trust me, you know he's lying."

Ric shook his head to clear it. Nosferatu was lying. That was why the picture was so vital. In person, Nosferatu could use vampire compulsion to overwrite reality with his own illusion. The picture, taken out of that sphere of influence, would convince others of his true nature. Ironic that an image was more true than the actual person.

It struck Ric hard—image was a powerful but double-edged sword.

"I have to admit, this was cleverer than most escape attempts," the master vampire said in a more normal tone. "I might let the pair of you live. You can go—if you leave the girl."

"Don't believe him," Aiden murmured. "He'll never let us go."

The girl elbowed out in front of Ric, hands challengingly on hips. "You want me? Why? You don't care about me."

"But I do, my dear." Nosferatu's smile, resting on the little human, was genuine. "I love you. More than you'll ever know."

"Is that why you locked me away? Wouldn't let me play with my friends?"

"Those scruffy boys? Come, my dear, they're hardly friends."

"Then what are they?"

Nosferatu paused. In a low snarl he said, "Tools."

Ric's fangs punched out of his gums. Aiden was right. Nosferatu had never cared about them. That tore it. Ric was fighting his way out, now, whether it destroyed him or not.

He reached out for the girl.

She wasn't there.

She'd run straight at Nosferatu and slammed into him,

human fingers clawing at his eyes. "Liar!"

The vampire held her away from himself while she shrieked and clawed.

"No!" Ric launched himself at Nosferatu, knocking the girl from the vampire's grip. She scrambled to her feet while Ric faced off against his maker.

Though no bigger than fourteen-year-old Ric himself, Nosferatu was far older. He grinned a mouthful of glinting fangs. Ric stared at the horror of those long, dripping monstrosities.

Nosferatu reached over his shoulder and drew a hidden sword.

Ric fell back a step. His heart was hammering and he knew he couldn't win, not with Nosferatu wielding sharp steel. But maybe his death could give Aiden time to grab the girl and escape.

Ric leaped for Nosferatu, brandishing a fledgling's fangs and claws.

The sword swung up, poised to impale him. Ric knew he was dead.

A hand seized him by the waist and hauled him back. The blade whistled inches from his nose.

"Time to go." Aiden shoved the picture into Ric's hands and pulled him in the other direction.

"We can't abandon her!"

"He won't let her go. Look."

Aiden was right. Nosferatu held the struggling girl securely under one arm, sword at a low angle in the other.

"There's no other way. I'm sorry, Ric. We'll return for her. Watch my back while I take care of these punks."

The trainees leaped.

Lunging forward on one leg, the black-haired sixteen-year-old dodged trainee blows, sweeping their knives out of their hands as they tried to stab him. Sliding back gracefully, he crossed the blades at one vampire trainee's neck; a muscular scissor action left the vampire without his head. A quick repeat took care of the other.

Then he seized Ric's shoulder. "Let's go."

"But what about Eloise?" Anguish tore Ric's throat as he looked back at the tiny girl.

"Assassins, attend me!" Nosferatu bellowed.

Aiden pulled Ric close and whispered fiercely in his ear, "I'm good, but even I can't stand against all Nosferatu's trainees, much less the trainers. We could die here and it still wouldn't win Eloise her freedom. We have to go."

"She's my partner!"

"I'm your partner too. We'll come back for her, I promise. But now we must hide. Grow in stealth and strength so we can rescue her. *Or her sacrifice will be for nothing.*"

Ric, eyes red with unshed tears, ran.

But by the time they were strong and smart enough to breach Nosferatu's lair again, Eloise was gone.

Chapter Twelve

"Marry someone else?" My heart dropped into my gut. I twisted in Ric's arms. My first reaction was: *totally out of the question.*

The problem wasn't the idea of traipsing down that lifelong aisle. The problem was that, standing at the end of my dream aisle, waiting to take my hand, was Ric Holiday.

My head spun like I'd sniffed ether. I wanted to marry Ric Holiday? No, no, no. We were total opposites. Image/substance, vampire/human, male/female… No future in it. He lived in Minneapolis and I…could live anywhere I wanted. But my family was in Meiers Corners, seven hours away…far enough for them not to show up daily yet conveniently close for the holidays.

Donate my brain to science because obviously I was done with it. What I wanted out of a marriage were not things Ric could give me. Honesty. Equality. Aging together. How could an ad man, a vampire, a creature of image in both aspects, give me those things?

I jumped to my feet, wrangling my bunched skirt into

place. All my thoughts collided in my head. What came out was, "I'm not…we can't—"

"I hear running." Ric stood and deftly put himself away and zipped up. He was helping me recombobulate when the frantic pounding on the door began.

"Mr. Holiday, please, come quick!" The high, tight voice was barely recognizable as Rosie, the Holiday Buzz employee at the reception desk. "The men say they won't hurt anyone, but only if you come right away."

"I don't like the sound of that." Ric reached for the door, stopped and glanced at me with a raised brow. I checked out my skirt and nodded. He unlocked the door and opened it to Rosie's white face.

"You have to come." She swallowed hard. "And you have to bring Dr. Byornsson."

"I like the sound of that even less. What's going on?"

"They're holding the employees hostage. They say they'll kill somebody unless you both come upstairs *right now*."

A muscle worked in Ric's jaw. "No. She's not—"

"I'll come." I started toward the door.

"Like hell." Barring the doorway with one arm, Ric switched his glare to me. "You will stay here until I figure out what's happening." He slipped out and shut the door in my face.

"Unless that door locks from the outside, you can't stop me." I didn't raise my voice but I didn't have to. V-guy. He'd hear.

He did. The door opened again, and if thunderclouds had faces they'd have been Ric. "Men violently invade my company the day after Camille shows up. I don't think it's coincidence."

"Neither do I. But how many people know the full implications of that?" The v-implications. "How many of those people up there can really help you?"

He chewed on that. "Half a dozen, including Rosie."

Not what I expected, but I had a trump. "Okay, but how many of those are doctors? Even if they haven't hurt anyone yet, you know I may be needed."

"*Fuck me.* Fine, come." He strode away, nodding to Rosie to fall into step. "But stay behind me. And no matter what they say, what they do, you *stay* behind me, do you hear?"

"I hear."

"You agreed to that much too fast." He pulled out his phone as he eyed me over his shoulder. "You're incredibly honest, which means…damn it, 'I hear' doesn't mean you agree. Lie by omission. You're getting sneaky, Byornsson. I like that."

I winced.

"But I won't tolerate it if it means you getting hurt. You hear and obey."

"Geez, what am I, a jinni? I obey, master?"

He whirled to take me by the shoulder, his eyes narrow blue fire. "Unless you agree, we're not going anywhere."

"Please don't argue." Rosie tugged at my sleeve. "Dr. Byornsson, the kidnappers won't wait long. Please agree with Mr. Holiday."

"Why are you pleading with me? Ric's the one who's being stubborn. Oh, okay. I'll stay behind him."

"Good." Ric strode off, hitting a speed dial on his phone as he went. He held a short conversation—Nikos short, only a few words—in a barely heard murmur, and snapped the phone away less than a minute later.

We used the stairs to go up the single flight. I got the feeling Ric could have gone faster without us, but he kept checking over his shoulder to make sure we were right behind him. Like he trusted me to be wise with Camille but not to keep my head in a crisis. Obey, sheesh. What did he think this was, the Regency?

On the way up, he quizzed Rosie. "How did they sneak by security?"

"They didn't. They hustled Ralph into the office at the point of his own gun. Then they shouted at us and herded us into the far corner of the floor."

I assumed Ralph was the security guard on thirty-two.

"How many?"

"Five. No, six. I think."

Ric grimaced. "And Ralph?"

"He's okay. They locked his wrists and ankles with those zip tie things, and packed him into your office."

"One good thing, at any rate. Anyone hurt?"

"No. But the men are seriously armed and on edge. Things could blow up any minute."

"We'll have to make sure that doesn't happen. Quiet now."

He cracked the stairwell door and edged into the lobby, hand raised to stop us. He scanned the lobby area with keen eyes, finally waving us forward. We approached the Holiday Buzz office cautiously.

No one was visible through the glass.

"Where are the hostages?" he murmured to Rosie.

"When I left they were right there, in that corner." She was nearly panting in fright. "I don't see them now. Maybe they're gone?"

"Rosie, it'll be all right." Ric spared time to lay a comforting hand on her arm and look her in the eye. His tone wasn't the weird hollow echo of vampire compulsion, but rather the simple deep timbre of reassurance and authority. "I'll make sure of it. You believe me, don't you?"

Her breathing eased. "Yes sir."

"Good. All right. I'm going in. You two stay here."

"No!" Her face went white. "They said you had to bring Dr. Byornsson or they'd shoot you on sight."

"That doesn't bother me nearly as much as the thought of them shooting Dr. Byornsson on sight."

I gave Rosie a quick hug. "Shh. It'll be all right." When her color returned I let go and asked Ric, "Why would they shoot me? I'm no threat to them."

"No." Ric's eyes were serious on me. "You're leverage."

"What? How?"

He raised one eyebrow.

I blushed. "They can't think that I mean anything to you. You barely know me. Why would they think threatening me would matter to you?"

He flashed a brittle smile. "Camille."

"Sure, she saw you and me and what we did at the party." I specifically avoided the word kiss. "But, well, you're a bit of a playboy, aren't you? She wouldn't think I'm anything special."

"Except she has a *nose*." He touched his own. "She'll have scented the nature and strength of my attraction to you. Trust me, you're very special."

While the implications were terrifying, a small part of me thrilled at that. I was special? So many men thought I was only a warm blow-up doll. I wanted so much to be taken seriously. And now Ric Holiday, rich, successful and smart, thought I was "very special".

No, Synnove, he just means you're sexually special. It's attraction based on superficial looks, like all the rest.

Arg. This is not the time to get in an argument over it.

Who's arguing?

You are. I mean, I am. I mean…crap.

Not important at that moment. Whether Ric's attraction was only physical or something more, it apparently could be used against him. *I* could be used against him. I shuddered.

At the shudder, Ric hugged me close. "I'll protect you. Rosie, you stay here."

"Please, I can't." She wrung her hands. "I promised I'd return with you and Dr. Byornsson. They're expecting me."

Ric swore again. "Fine. I'll simply have to protect you both."

He glided to the door, every inch the deadly predator. I took Rosie's hand and followed.

As we reached the door, Chicken Little barreled into view, rake of bangs and red wattle quivering as he ran. The door flew open with a crash. "The shit is falling!" Charles Little screamed.

Yeah. If fairy tales were coffee, I was *so* switching to decaf.

Little ran past us into the stairwell. The thunder of his feet tapered quickly into silence.

Ric glanced at the two of us. I shrugged. Rosie swallowed. Grim-faced, he nodded, turned and led us through the door.

Chapter Thirteen

The agency was nothing like yesterday. It was still, silent, and empty save for the scattered workstations and half-walls. Even the bank of windows to the left, which had streamed bright sunlight yesterday, was shadowed and blotchy.

I blinked to clear my eyes. The windows weren't dirty. Those shadows were *people*, stretched against the glass.

Men and women lined the whole length of the windows, palms flat against the panes—except for one bear of a man whose eyes burned angrily over his shoulder. He looked familiar. Harry, that was his name. He'd been protective of Rosie, and she'd dosed his headache with aspirin.

Behind the Holiday Buzz employees, half a dozen men clad in black from head to toe pointed lethal looking rifles. The ease with which they stood, the lithe economy as they checked their surroundings said they were serious trouble.

One good thing was their black masks. No faces meant maybe they planned to let the hostages live.

Another good thing, the men stood in the bright sunshine. So probably not vampires. Which meant Ric was faster than them.

Although the combination of so many men and the sunshine might make overcoming them impossible even for Ric.

Then I saw a seventh man standing apart from the rest, holding a flat, serious-looking handgun. The leader? He was taller than the others and heavier in a lumpy way. His chunky features were smashed flat by dark nylon.

He looked like an ogre.

Forget the decaf. From now on no more fairy tales, period. In fact, I was only reading Barbara Cartland.

Unless he really *was* an ogre. I'd thought vampires were fairy tales, after all. Maybe Ric would know. I caught his hand, pressed two fingernails into his palm, imitating fangs, and cast a significant glance at the seventh man.

Ric concentrated on the leader, nostrils flared. Then he twitched his head, left-right. The ogre-faced man was indeed human.

"Finally." The ogre's voice was a growl, not the kind I'd come to associate with vampires, but like Batman trying to disguise a high voice.

Ric eased in front of me. "Why have you taken my people hostage? What do you want?"

"Mr. Nosferatu wants to ask you some questions."

Nosferatu was behind this? Why? His emissary Camille had already strong-armed Ric into agreeing to listen to her.

"There's no need for this," Ric said. "I'm working with Camille—"

"I don't know nothin' about that. All I know is Mr. Nosferatu calls me in a couple nights ago and tells me bring in Ric fuckin' Holiday cuz he wants to talk."

Night before last? Was it possible Nosferatu didn't know about Camille's victory yesterday morning for team Nosy? Or had he sent these goons and simply not bothered to recall them?

"I got my team," the ogre said. "Last night we drove here and today you're gonna talk."

"Fine. I'll give you my phone number." Ric's stance was relaxed but I could see his hands clenching. "He can call."

"Funny guy. But you're in no position to be funny. Here's what you're going to do. You turn your girl over to us."

Ric's *girl*? I'd gone through fire to become a doctor. I was *nobody's* girl. I surged forward.

Ric palmed me back before I took a step. Damn, he was fast. "Then what?"

"We hold her while you get in our car for a visit to Mr. Nosferatu. Once he's satisfied, we let your girl go."

There it was again. Girl, indeed. Any fear I might have felt dissolved in the need to kick insulting black-clad butt.

Ric murmured over his shoulder, "I know something about hostage negotiations. We'll get through this." He turned front and, tone calm and professional, said, "And why should I do that? What are you offering me?"

"If you don't do what I say, asshole, we start killing your people. One every five minutes, until you decide to play nice. Put this on." Ogre Face tossed a white loop at Ric.

It sailed through the air like a Frisbee and landed near Ric's feet. Plastic zip tie handcuffs. He picked the loop up. "If I do, you will let my people go. Did you hear me? *Let them go.*" His voice echoed with vampire compulsion.

Several heads jerked toward Ric including a few masked ones, but Ogre Face laughed. "That won't work on me, Holiday. Mr. Nosferatu picked me special for my natural resistance."

Ric's hands clenched, but he only said, "Had to try. Still, you want something, you give something. Let my people go."

"Tell you what. I'll let *one* go." Ogre Face pointed to an older woman near the line's end. "That one. C'mon, get her out of here."

A black clad man latched onto the woman's elbow, jerked her out of line and pushed her toward the door. She looked around, head darting like a frightened doe. The man shoved her with the point of his rifle. Eyeing the man's gun, she took a stumbling step. He pushed again. She took an involuntary step toward the door, then another on her own, then another and another, gradually speeding up until she scampered across the floor and out the door.

"Your turn. The cuffs."

"Right." Ric slid his wrists into the loop. A snap of teeth pulled it tight. He held up his restrained hands with a challenging half-smile. "Now what?"

I'd encountered plastic cuffs during my ER rotation. On the negative side, if misapplied, they could cause nerve damage. On the plus side, unlike metal cuffs, they could be cut or melted. Or, rarely, broken. A doctor had related a story where a young man hyped on drugs had actually snapped the things. I didn't know how strong vampires were but from Ric's confident smile, he must have been more than strong enough to get out of these.

Ogre Face snorted. "Mr. Nosferatu's head of security designed those cuffs himself. Maybe you've heard of him—Giuseppe Marrone?"

Ric's smile disappeared and he actually got angry. "Fine. I've put on the cuffs. Now let another of my people go."

"Why not? That one, I think." He pointed to bearish Harry. "He looks like trouble. Might as well get rid of him."

Harry glared at Ogre Face then strode out of line. I was sorry to see him go. Ogre Face was right, Harry might have been helpful in a fight.

As he passed us he snagged Rosie and dragged her along with him.

"Hey," Ogre Face shrieked, forgetting to disguise his thin

voice. "Stop!"

Harry turned. "If I leave, she leaves too." He squared his shoulders into a bulldog stance. "Unless you want me to stay."

"No." Again the little-girl voice. Ogre Face scowled, dropped into his motor-oil growl. "Fine. Go."

As Harry made double-time for the door, dragging Rosie behind, it struck me how he'd make a dandy bear prince, like the story of Rose-Red and Snow-White. Not Grimm's *Sneewittchen*, but *Schneeweisschen*, where Rose-Red befriends a bear and also tries to help a dwarf. The bear is grateful but the dwarf is nasty. Eventually the bear kills the dwarf and turns into a handsome prince.

Substitute ogre for dwarf, and Harry had rescued Rosie like the bear rescues Rose-Red.

Aw, that was sweet.

Smack me sideways. If I was going to see fairy tales everywhere, it would've been handy if Harry had killed the ogre first. Or at least mauled him a little.

As the door swung closed behind Harry and Rosie, a dark patch, barely a shadow, seemed to filter through.

I blinked.

Nothing there now. Must have been seeing things.

"Time to go," Ogre Face said. "Come on, Blondie, get your gorgeous heinie over here. I think, to be sure everyone cooperates, we'll take you along."

"No." Ric's shoulders tensed in front of me. "I'll go with you. But Dr. Byornsson stays here."

"Forget it. We'll take her with us—in a different car, so you don't get any funny ideas."

A shadow darted between wavelike partitions and silk screens. I blinked a couple times. Nothing again.

"I'll agree to play nice," Ric said. "If she stays here."

"Tell you what. We'll play nice." Ogre Face's smashed leer made me shudder. "With your girlfriend."

"Unless she's safe, deal's off." Ric's growl was menacing.

"Then one of your people gets it." Ogre Face pointed at a woman near his end of the line. "Her. Bring her here."

The biggest of the men, a black mountain, grabbed the woman's wrist and yanked her away from the window. She stumbled and nearly fell, awkward with a distended belly.

I covered my mouth. "Oh my God."

She was as pregnant as Elena.

"I'll come," I said. "Don't hurt her."

No one heard me. The big man brought his gun up. The woman screamed.

"No!" Ric leaped forward.

"*Stop*." The mountain's gun snapped to the woman's head. Her scream cut.

Ric reined himself in with obvious difficulty. "All right. You hold all the cards. Synnove?" He turned to me, his eyes so blue I nearly drowned. "Go ahead. Go to them."

I warmed. Ric respected me enough to handle myself with the bad guys. "First he has to let her go."

There was a pause and for a second I wondered if I'd pressed too hard.

Then the ogre said, "Let her go."

The mountain released the pregnant woman. She wept in relief and staggered back to the window.

I expelled a breath I hadn't known I was holding.

The mountain extended a sausage finger at me. Curled it.

My mouth dried. My heart tripped then started hammering. Moment of truth. Sure, I had martial arts and self-defense training. But my particular martial art was for distance fighting, and self-defense was only useful when you could strike your assailant and run away. The mountain wanted me to come grabbing-close. My martial arts wouldn't help, and I couldn't do a self-defense move and run away, not when my fleeing would trigger the pregnant woman's slaughter.

I was stuck.

Ric nodded me forward. Maybe he had a plan.

Okay. If he could trust me, I could trust him.

Slowly, I went, practically inching. Even so the trip across the wide agency floor took maybe ten seconds. They were the longest seconds of my life.

The instant I got within reach, the big man seized my wrist and yanked me into him. He had a grip like a nut crusher. I twisted against the pain.

"You're a looker." The mountain grabbed my hip and pulled me flush with his oversized body. "Give us a kiss, baby." He pronounced it bay-bee.

First Chicken Little and now this monstrosity. I was beginning to hate the term *baby*. Sugar Babe and Apple Bottom seemed almost charming in comparison.

He lifted the bottom of his mask and puckered up. I jerked my face away. He caught my chin and tugged back. Automatically I went with him—until I faced his cauliflower lips. Yuck. *Pass*. I kept going, turning away before he could plant one on me.

My view wheeled to six black-clad bad guys watching avidly. In an odd coincidence, they were lined up in reverse order of size, the biggest at the far end and a short skinny dude nearest me.

Whoa, wait. Shouldn't it have been *five* black-clad guys? I blinked.

Still six.

A shadow had crept up behind the last raider in the row. Unfolded to its full height, it became a tall man.

Whip-fast, the shadowman raised his arm and struck, chopping a sharp, silent blow to the tallest masked hostile's head. The bad guy collapsed without a sound. The shadow caught him as he fell and eased him to the floor.

None of the other bad guys seemed to notice.

Shock rushed cold through my veins, freezing my limbs. Six to one weren't great odds, even vampire versus human. Unless I could keep the men's attention off the shadow. Surprise could better those odds. Especially if I could distract the mountain with the dick-crushing grip.

Before the yuck factor could stop me, I swiveled back to center and planted one on cauliflower. For the team.

They say all true heroes endure suffering. Kissing that asswipe, I sure did. His lips were wet foam rubber and his tongue was stale garlic with a garnish of cat litter. But I mashed sour lips for all I was worth.

Yuck yuck yuck...a throttled cry snagged my attention. I cut eyes to my left. Two more bad guys were down but the penultimate had screamed a warning before a smack across the face sent him crumpling.

Worse, the shadow's blow was much slower than that first neat karate chop. And wisps of smoke rose from him.

My scalp prickled. Sunlight lanced through the gaps between hostages and the shadowman was smoldering, and fading fast.

"Stop him," Ogre Face shouted.

The mountain smooching me raised his head.

Time to change distracting tactics. I unpuckered. Cleared my throat.

And head-butted him.

He made a pained *gah*. Mission accomplished but I'd gone forehead to chin. While skull trumps jaw they're both still bone. Pain burst in my forehead and for an instant I lost track of my surroundings.

"Stop! I'll kill her." Not the mountain or the ogre.

I blinked. The scene resolved slowly. The shadow had taken out all but the leader, the mountain and the last of the lined-up bad guys. Good news, he was the skinniest of the bunch. Bad news, he'd had time to wrap an arm around a gray-haired grandma's neck. Silent tears trickled down her wrinkled cheeks.

He swung his gun up to her skull. It made an audible thud. "One more step and I'll shoot her."

The shadow froze. The lancing sun revealed a tall, lean man with broad shoulders, powerful arms and long-fingered hands, in a black hoodie and jeans. Barely visible through the puckered hoodie were black slash brows and glittering black eyes. He held himself like a ninja, with a dangerous ease.

He glanced at me, and for the merest sliver of time, I was staring into death's dark abyss.

Then those death-dealing eyes shifted to the skinny dude. The bad guy startled visibly.

"Y...you. Stay there." Chest pumping, he inched his hostage closer to where I stood in the grip of Mt. Nut Crusher; scared, even though he held the gun. Having met that black gaze, I couldn't blame him. He stopped a foot away from me, gun jammed against his captive's head. "One step closer and I'll kill her."

Grandma whimpered.

The shadow glanced again at me. Enigmatic eyes considered me like a man weighing his tools. He seemed to decide something because he twitched a significant glance at the punk's gun hand. I followed his gaze. The dude's finger rested *outside* the trigger guard. I cut wide eyes back to the shadow and raised a brow. The shadow glanced at my feet, then at the skinny punk, who was standing with legs braced apart, then again to me.

Oh. Obvious.

I drew back my foot. Kicking from the hip, I connected with punk stones, hard enough that my toes penetrated body cavity. His eyes popped, his breath expelling on a whoosh. Yeah, Mr. Miyagi taught his grasshoppers well.

Even before I pulled my foot back, the shadow launched. I'd never learned to hide my telegraph. First time that was a good thing.

As my foot connected, the shadow snared goon wrist and shoved the gun from grandma's head, simultaneously pulling his trigger finger the other way. It broke with a snap. The goon screamed. Automatically his arms constricted, yanking the gun inward. The shadow went with the motion, using the punk's momentum to haul him away from the woman entirely.

Whereupon the shadow yo-yo'ed the punk by his gun wrist, tossing him out one handed, then reeling him back—into the shadow's waiting fist. Several times, like a paddle ball, whack, whack, whack.

It was all fun and games until the gun hit my skull.

Thud. A bright pain cracked in my brain, telling me the mountain had brought his own weapon to bear.

Almost immediately something heavy plowed into us, spinning me away from the gun. I staggered to a stop.

My sight cleared to Ric, wrestling the mountain.

The big goon seized Ric with one arm, hugging him close like he was going to give him noogies. But the gun in his noogie hand made reality more chilling.

Ric shimmered, and suddenly the mountain was holding a cloud of mist. Vampire fighting technique? I cheered before it occurred to me to wonder why Ric hadn't used it before and why the shadow hadn't used it at all.

The edge of Ric's mist caught a stray beam of sunlight. It instantly combusted—poof. My elation turned to horror.

Ric snapped back into being like a rubber band. His cheek was seared open, exposing red muscle surrounded by blackened, bubbling skin. But he lost no time raising his bound hands, swinging, and whacked the bad guy's head with fists like a mallet.

The mountain swayed but didn't go down. Ric spun, once, twice, winding up his whole body behind it, and whacked him again.

Still the guy didn't go down. My heart tripped double time. The mountain swept his gun toward Ric.

I leaped at them. Went *oof* when I hit the shadow's arm, stuck out like a bar. I folded over it like a cheap towel and staggered back.

Ric slid *into* the rifle.

The mountainous goon opened fire as Ric knocked the gun to the side—the ogre's side.

Ogre Face ducked and covered. A spray of bullets rat-a-tat-tatted a line where his head had been.

Ric chopped his forearms across the mountain's right wrist. The mountain howled, both arms flying up in defense, right hand dangling with a protruding lump at the wrist presenting as broken. The gun fell to hang from its clip. The mountain groped for it with his left hand.

Ric grabbed the big man's balls.

The guy shrieked. Ric wrenched. The mountain dropped, curling on the floor like a shrimp. Apparently Ric also had a grip like a nut crusher.

"Stop!"

I whipped around. Ogre Face pointed his gun at my head. He rasped, "You're dead."

Terror burned that instant into my head like a snapshot. I stood facing the ogre. About ten feet separated us. Behind me was the hostage-lined bank of windows, the shadowman already running toward them. A few feet to my right, the mountain goon curled on the floor, Ric breathing deeply over him.

Both Ric and I were too far away to stop the ogre from shooting.

"Down!" The shadowman pushed hostages to the floor,

starting with the ones in Ogre Face's direct line of fire. Well, if you didn't count me.

Ric leaped.

My knees started to bend.

Ogre Face pulled the trigger.

Ric wouldn't hit him in time, even though he'd leaped before the ogre pulled the trigger.

The gun went off.

Chapter Fourteen

But Ric wasn't leaping for Ogre Face. He plowed into me. I went down, Ric's heavy body covering mine.

Warmth trickled down my neck. Shock hit me. Had I been shot?

My ears rang. Concussive sound. I blinked. I was in a place where all time was compressed into one point. A lifetime went by in a flash.

A second report. Shock but no pain. But there wouldn't be, not until later.

And then, between one breath and the next, time uncoiled and ran normally. Ric's harsh breath was in my ear. The warmth on my neck was cooling.

"It's safe." The shadowman's shoes were to my left. When he wasn't shouting, his voice was as deep as Ric's but cooler, more rigidly controlled.

"Stay down." Ric rose to his knees over me. His eyes, intense violet, seared me. "I need to check things out."

Stay down? Ha. I flipped my Crisis Time switch. First, triage.

Me, still no pain. Ric? Facial burn gone. How...? Irrelevant now. The shadowman slicing the cuffs, good. Dark hole, suit coat, breast pocket.

Red bloomed.

The bullet had *hit him*. It knocked me out of Crisis Mode. "Wait."

He sprang to his feet. "No time."

"Damn it, Holiday, you're not indestructible!"

He shot me a small, warm smile. "Almost."

Then he spun, sweeping the floor with his own triage scrutiny as I levered myself to my feet. His people, near the windows, were starting to move, none bent in pain or injury although the floor was cluttered with moaning black-clad men.

Ric's expression changed to grim satisfaction. "Aiden. Your timing is impeccable, as always."

He addressed the shadowman, who held a subdued Ogre Face by the scruff of the neck. Ogre Face's gun was tucked under the shadowman's arm, and two goons' rifles were slung over his shoulders, crisscross like a pair of bandoleers. Despite the violence and being armed to the teeth, he looked slightly bored, cool. Well, except for the bits of smoke still rising from him.

His black eyes went to Ric's chest, where the flower had spread to more of a lake. "You need to get that hole patched."

"He's right," I said. "I have my kit in the car—"

"What I need," Ric said viciously, "is to make sure this never happens again."

Aiden started, "Our plan—"

"Fuck the plan," Ric said. "I want this over now. We need a bigger gun against Nosferatu. We need to get the item."

Ogre Face's head swiveled to Ric, ears practically quivering.

Aiden's black brows rose. "Is that such a good idea?"

"It's the only idea." Ric slashed the air. "We screwed up, not foreseeing this."

"We can't plan for every eventuality—"

"I don't care. I won't have Synnove or any of my people threatened again."

Aiden raised a palm. "It's your call."

"Damn right it is. John!" He waved a man over. "Cancel my appointments for today and tomorrow. Make sure the VPs know."

"What are you doing?" I asked.

In two strides Ric was hugging me. Abruptly he released me and stepped away. "I'm going out of town. Stay with your cousin. Do not come here."

"Why? Where are you going?"

"To make sure you're never attacked again."

That evening Ric glided, vampire-fast, along the dark Wisconsin country road. He moved in absolute silence, a creature of the night and one with it.

As good as he was, the merest shadow glided next to him, indiscernible to the human eye. Ric was one of the best, but Aiden was beyond even that. Normally Ric would have enjoyed flexing his abilities with his best friend.

He missed Synnove.

Which was sharply unexpected. Since his parents' death, he'd gone it strictly alone, accepting even Aiden's help reluctantly and only when absolutely needed.

Yet when they'd needed to distract the guards from Aiden, she'd simply done it. Ric knew if any of his people were injured, she'd help.

How had he come to rely on her—to lean on her—so quickly?

As he had another young, beloved human female.

Damn. He shoved the thought away.

Before he left, Synnove insisted on attending to his wound. The bullet had already pushed out of his body, the crater almost completely healed. She'd been amazed and, unless he missed his guess, intrigued. That was his Dr. Sunshine.

He really missed her.

"Thinking about Beautiful?" Aiden said over the wind they stirred.

Ric raised a brow. "You sure you're not omniscient?"

"Please. Your face gives you away. You look like a big dreamy goof."

"And you look like an asshole in need of a wasabi suppository. Did we have to park so far away?" Five hours to drive here; at nearly two in the morning, he chafed to get back to Synnove. "July nights are short. We have little time as it is."

"We had to make absolutely sure Nosferatu's henchvamps hadn't followed us. Or even Nosferatu himself." Aiden slowed to a human walk in front of a round building. He stopped out of range of the night lights near a sign announcing, "The Cave of the Mounds".

Ric stopped beside him. "What's wrong?"

Voice barely above the summer breeze, Aiden said, "I'm still not sure."

"How could he have followed? No one was driving behind us. No one loped alongside us here." Ric raised his head and tested the air. "I detect no scent."

"He could be downwind." Aiden's nostrils flared. "He's old, Ric. And even though he looks like a mummified weasel, he's sly. He can shape shift."

Ric scowled. "That's a vampire legend."

"No. I was in Iowa recently and saw…or perhaps was *allowed* to see…things that made me revise my opinion of what's fact and what's fantasy."

"Okay, Nosferatu can shape shift. No wolves following us either."

"You ass." Aiden dropped his hunting animal routine to give Ric a disgusted glare. "You're being deliberately obtuse. What about birds? Insects?" He waved his arm around, a gesture of unbridled passion for him. "You're sure all these creatures are natural? Absolutely positive that none of them are the same owls or crickets or nighthawks that were hooting or chirping in Minnesota?"

Ric rolled his eyes. "Nosferatu's no nighthawk. Maybe a goatsucker."

"A nighthawk is a goatsucker, you turd." The ghost of a smile played across Aiden's lips. "But you knew that."

Ric smiled slightly in return. It didn't count toward the tally, but even a partial smile was a win tonight. "What choice do we have? We need to make Nosferatu back off. Which means having the leverage in hand."

"I still say it's premature." Aiden eyed Ric coolly. "We've been courting Nosferatu's attack for two years, with a solid plan. The leverage was our emergency backup. Now he attacks, according to plan, yet instead of following protocol you leap directly to the emergency backup. Why?"

"You know why." Because even now Ric's heart thudded when he thought of how close it had come. If he hadn't shielded Synnove, if that bullet had pierced her human body... "Because the plan didn't work. Camille got in. That immune human got in with his goons. We had the place fortified against normal vampires and humans. But Nosferatu's hitting us faster and harder than we ever imagined, with agents who are battle-ready, trained and ruthless. We're off script. That's why we're going after the insurance."

"And that's your only reason, hmm?" Aiden was silent for a beat. "Nosferatu's looking for her again. He's got people searching all over."

They weren't talking about Synnove now. Ric's brows rose. "He's revealed her existence to others?"

"No, not that way. She's too vulnerable." The black-haired vampire was still looking off into the night. "He's only asking humans to look for a female, with a vague description."

Ric snorted. "Good luck with that."

"And your heartbeat has slowed."

This time Ric didn't follow the shift in conversation. "So?"

"So your problem isn't Nosferatu, or even Nosferatu plus a vulnerable woman. Know what I think? I think your problem is medical."

"Fuck." The first change of subject had been a trap. Proving yet again that Nosferatu's goons weren't the only ruthless, sly, battle-hardened warriors around, or even the best.

Ric met his friend's eyes and finally let Aiden see the fear he'd barely admitted to himself. "That muscle-bound ass wasn't holding Synnove accidentally. Nosferatu's gang asked for her by name. They were holding her as hostage against my good behavior."

"Ah." The black eyes shifted away, staring into the distance. When they returned to Ric, they were burning. "All right then. Let's get this done."

Ric's smile was fierce. Here was another reason why he rarely asked for Aiden's help. He rarely had to. Aiden gave him what he needed without asking. Like Synnove.

Partners, both of them.

The chime of memory. Again he shoved it away. He only had one partner, the vampire beside him.

Aiden paced off an exact number of steps onto privately owned land. At a certain location, they dissolved into mist, the vampire ability that came at a hundred years dead, and dropped together through the earth.

They materialized in a small cavern about thirty-five yards below the surface. Although researchers had completely explored the Cave of the Mounds itself, the nearby sinkholes on private land had not been investigated thoroughly. Small, unknown caverns often existed adjacent to known caves. This was one.

"Damn, it's dark." Aiden's eyes glowed in the blackness. "I keep forgetting what real dark is like."

"I keep forgetting how weird our eyes get." Living as a civilized human for so long, Ric found Aiden's red charcoal eyes a bit unnerving, though his own would be as eerily luminous. In the complete absence of light, their vampire eyes made their own, bioluminescent, like fireflies and deep ocean fish.

"And I keep forgetting what *he* looks like." Aiden pointed.

A headless body rested on a translucent plastic bier in the middle of the cavern. The still figure's arms were folded over its chest, a mockery of peace, since the hands inadequately covered a gaping hole where the heart used to be.

Ric shuddered. "Stuff a heart in him, and he's fine. That's scary."

"Or wait a century and he'll grow a new one. But he's not touching earth, so he can't suck energy and rise. I still can't believe that's really *the* Dracula." A growl roughened Aiden's voice.

"He is." Ric consciously suppressed his own growl. "I researched him when we decided to move the item here. That is pure vampire. Even the brain. Especially the brain. That's why he's the only vamp who doesn't die if you destroy the head."

"No humanity at all? Nasty."

"Pure vampire instinct. Monstrous," Ric agreed.

"So why not burn him? Get rid of him permanently."

"There's a legend that it would unloose pure evil on the world, but it's probably hokum. Still, the Ancient One must have some reason not to."

"Makes this the perfect hiding place from Nosferatu though." Aiden walked slowly around the small cave. "Since the Ancient One has secured the area."

The Cave of the Mounds, undiscovered by humans until 1939, along with its nearby hidden caverns, had been in use by vampires for at least fifty years previous. Or rather, one specific vampire, who'd originally captured and incarcerated Dracula. The Ancient One living in Iowa, Nosferatu's mortal enemy, Kai Elias.

"How is dear Kai?" Ric asked. "I assume that's why you were in Iowa."

"Enigmatic as always. I still haven't gotten a good look at him."

Which, for Aiden, was saying something.

As Nosferatu's enemy, it would have made sense for Ric and Aiden to seek Elias out decades ago, when they'd first run. After all, the enemy of an enemy is supposedly a friend. As mere boys, they certainly could have used the help. But they hadn't even known about Elias's existence until several years into hiding and Nosferatu's training made them mistrustful, Aiden even more than Ric. They'd hidden from everyone, including Elias.

Later, they'd grown to enjoy the independence. The freedom. No master, no factions. Didn't mean they didn't know about the ancient vampire and his deadly reputation.

"I, for one, was grateful when the Alliance set this place up," Aiden said. "Sure beats having to move the item every six months."

"No one's here. You can call the painting what it is." Ric tore his eyes away from the headless body. "Are you certain the Ancient One doesn't know we've invaded his hiding place?"

"Elias?" Aiden snorted. "I'm sure he *does* know. He's got techie gurus up the ass." He looked around at the cavern walls. "Elias probably has real time ears and eyes on this place by now." He waved at a particularly knobby stalagmite.

"Fuck," Ric sputtered. "He'll have stolen it!"

"Chill. For all his vaunted omniscience, Elias keeps his nose out of other people's affairs. He won't have touched the painting unless he had good reason."

"Well, he'd better not have," Ric said grimly. "Or we're as good as dead."

"We could bluff."

"We tried bluffing and barely got away with our asses intact."

"Fine. Get it then."

Ric examined the cavern ceiling to find the guide stalactite while Aiden got the shovel they'd left here. The stalactite pointed to an area choked with debris. Ric grabbed the shovel from Aiden and dug. His heart beat faster than the simple exertion demanded. When he and Aiden buried the crate, their lives were on the line. Now so much more was at stake. More than even the lives of his household. If Elias had taken it… To Ric's relief, he hit something solid. "It's still here."

"Pull it out and let's get out of here. I have a bad feeling."

"Shit. Now?" Ric shoveled faster, heart beginning to pound. He wished he knew what caused Aiden's bad feelings, sensing a change in air pressure or smelling the faintest of scents or even simple intuition. Then he'd know from which direction danger was coming. A scritch-scritch made him whirl. Nothing was there. He shrugged it off as nerves and returned to digging. The crate was big enough that it took a long time, too long. He was sweating cold buckets by the time he finally freed the crate and lifted it from the cave floor, debris trickling like pellets. "Got it. Let's go."

Aiden didn't move. "Check that the picture's still inside."

Ric was chafing now—Aiden's feelings were never wrong—but he knelt to open the crate.

Revealing the portrait of Nosferatu.

It had been painted in the early 1800s by an unknown pupil of John Singleton Copley. Like Copley, the unknown portraitist included ordinary items in his pictures. In this case he'd painted a blunderbuss braced against Nosferatu's foot. A wooden house, a mansion for the times, was in the background. The second floor window was clearly visible.

Aiden, looking over Ric's shoulder, grunted. "Once he finds out you've retrieved this, he'll attempt to steal it back—after which he'll try to kill us."

"I know." And if Nosferatu killed them, he'd be free to attack Ric's humans, including Synnove. *Especially* Synnove. Ric didn't know when she'd become the most important person to him, but there it was. "But I've had it. Enough with image and smoke. Synnove is too important for tricks. It's time for me to stop faking it and just deal with the bastard."

"Using the picture as a deterrent isn't actually dealing with him. Not like walking up to him and punching him in the face."

"Satisfying, but it didn't go so well last time we tried." Ric closed the crate, gathered it up and stood. "This is the best we've got."

Holding the crate to his chest, Ric dissolved into mist and filtered up through the soil, easier than hiding it here a hundred years ago. Then, they'd been too young to mist. They'd had to dig a hole to get down.

He'd calmed somewhat by the time he snapped solid on the surface. Misting was a strange process, when he thought about it. The first few times his clothes had dropped through, and he'd snapped back naked. It took him painstaking years to learn to mist his clothes along. "Carrying" the clothes, but he didn't know what the actual process was or where they went. Even after he'd learned to carry his clothes, small items dropped through his misted pockets, thumping uselessly to the floor. The day he'd first carried his knife he'd danced like an idiot for ten triumphant minutes.

Now it was automatic to carry anything light attached to his skin. Which had actually backfired with the zip cuffs. He could have dropped them through his mist and fought two handed. Unless Nosferatu's pet scientist had not only made them stronger but mist-proof as well. Thank goodness that had eventually worked out all right.

Aiden emerged from the cavern beside him. Ric set off at a glide, streaking along at nearly forty miles per hour. He hugged the picture to his chest and didn't slow until they were in the car and squealing off into the night. Ric drove so Aiden could protect their insurance.

"What's wrong with you?" Aiden leaned back in the passenger's seat, hands negligently behind his head. "You're as jumpy as a chicken in a hatchet store."

Ric scowled. "May I remind you that your bad feelings are never wrong?"

"Relax. We got back to the car just fine. Apparently this time I was off."

"'Never wrong' means you're never off. Something is going to happen. Damn, I wish the digging hadn't taken so long. Are you sure we can't get back to Minneapolis before dawn?"

Aiden gave him the dead black glare he'd perfected.

Ric glared back, but then his shoulders slumped. Another delay seeing Synnove. He'd have to call her when he got settled. No, no good. She'd be asleep. He mustn't wake her. Except he needed to make sure she was okay. That was a much better reason than the simple churning in his gut, the yearning need to talk to her. "You reset the booby traps at the office, right? Checked the safeguards at the condo complex?"

"Yes, dear." Aiden rolled his eyes.

Ric's foot pressed harder on the accelerator. He should have made sure Synnove knew how to check for tails. Camille couldn't have followed her in daylight, but the vampire woman could have a shielded car driven by a human minion. Or even another of Nosferatu's human goons could have tailed her.

No, Synnove was staying with her cousin, whose lover was a very old vampire. He had to believe she was safe enough where she was while he and Aiden were stuck in a motel, hundreds of miles away.

He had to believe it, or he'd go insane.

Early the next morning—as in five-crack-my-eyes-with-a-pry-bar-thirty—Rosie called me.

I'd been dreaming about Ric.

He laid me naked in bed, his eyes burning violet. His long fingers trailed sparkles along my skin. I sighed happily. He kissed down my chin and along my throat to lave my collar bones. I threaded fingers through his spiky hair as he sprinkled butterfly kisses along my breasts, then licked down my belly…all the way down…and *just* as he'd extended his tongue to flick the "go" button—

The phone rang. I snatched it off the night stand where I'd put it. *Dreamus interruptus* made me bark, "Hello."

"I would have called sooner, Dr. Byornsson." Rosie was almost panting in her anxiety. "But I didn't know myself until Ms. Park phoned me, and that was an hour ago which was so early I thought I should wait rather than wake you…" She was talking so fast she was stumbling over herself.

"Slow down, Rosie. Deep breath. It'll be okay. Start from the beginning."

"The beginning." She sucked air audibly, whistled it out. "Last night, late, after everybody got done with the trauma counselor, Mr. Little called me. He wanted Ms. Park's cell phone number. She's one of our top account reps."

"Why did he call you for Ms. Park's phone number?"

"I was her secretary. Now she's mentoring me. We're both in Mr. Holiday's 'condo group'." The emphasis made me think vampire household. "Mr. Little sometimes does things behind Mr. Holiday's back. So I called Ms. Park to find out what was going on. But she didn't answer so I left a message to ask her to call me about Mr. Little, but Ms. Park didn't get back to me until after the meeting or I would have called sooner—"

"Breathe," I repeated, wishing I was there with her to give her a hug. "What is Little doing?"

"The client presentation. The Meiers Corners comparison? Mr. Little moved up the scheduling, Dr. Byornsson. He's set it for ten thirty *today*."

Charles called my meeting days early? I dragged a hand through my hair. "I thought Ric had to be there. He's out of town."

"Sure, the person who sets up a comparison presentation usually runs it. But there are precedents. Mr. Little has taken Mr. Holiday's daytime meetings before. And as I said, it isn't the first time Mr. Little has gone behind Mr. Holiday's back." She added in a low undertone, "But it's probably the last."

The faceoff with Camille, this morning? I wasn't ready. I swallowed past a suddenly tight throat.

But when Ric returned he could reject the results, right? I started to relax.

Except Ric had allowed the competition in the first place because he was trying to avoid a costly confrontation with

Nosferatu. Charles Little was Ric's legitimate representative. Ric couldn't countermand the chicken without breaking some major eggs.

"There's more."

I threw my legs over the edge of the bed, sat up and scrubbed my face with a hand. "Of course there is."

"Last night's meeting was to schedule who'll be there today. Besides Mr. Little and Ms. Park, it was only Mr. Riley from Finance and Ms. Dullea, a media buyer." She paused for me to get it. It was too early. She had to spell it out. "Dr. Byornsson, there was no one from creative at all!"

Hippocrates on a pogo stick. Without creatives at the meeting, the number crunchers would favor Camille.

I was well and truly screwed. It wasn't quite Crisis Time but I flipped my switch and shut off the panic. "It's okay, Mr. Holiday briefed me before he left. I'll make sure Camille has some real competition."

"But, well...Mr. Little shouldn't get away with this. I'd like to help you." She took a deep breath, then said in a rush, "I can call some creatives, get them to come. Mr. Little won't like it but...well. I know a copywriter and a couple photographers who will help if I ask them. And Ms. Park can call in a few favors...well, she *can*, but I don't know if she will. Oh, and I'm secretly dating a production artist. I'm sure he'd help."

"You mean Harry?"

A little gasp. "Nobody's supposed to know that."

"I guessed." Why let her know it was painfully obvious? And why let her know I heard every cell in her body screaming against going behind Little's back as he'd gone behind Ric's, even for a good cause? "That's awfully nice of you. But unless I win this on my own, Little will continue to think he can screw with me." Not a very solid reason, but I needed to reassure her fast.

"Well…if you need me to I will." The relief in her voice was palpable. "Whatever happens, know I'm rooting for you."

"Thanks, Rosie. That means a lot."

I'd managed to lock away the panic for Rosie's sake, but as soon as I hung up it surged back, worse than ever.

I'd counted on Ric's being there, not only to nudge me from any black pits of infinite mistake, but for simple moral support. Now it would be just me and Camille and the numbers.

And Chicken Little, who hated me.

Chapter Fifteen

I dug in my purse for Ric's business card, the one with his cell phone number. Not to ask him to come rescue me, but for some long-distance moral support. Or maybe last rites.

I released a pent-up breath when I found the card, and thumbed the number into my phone.

He picked up on the first ring. "Sunshine." His voice was warm. "I was thinking about you."

"And I was dreaming about you." Until Rosie splashed me with cold water. I gave him a quick sketch of what had happened.

"Damn. This is Aiden's bad feeling."

No, it isn't, I heard from the phone.

"Shut up," Ric said. "Not you, Synnove. Just an attack of the interfering stupids here. Don't go, please? Stay safe at your cousin's cabin for me."

"Ric, I can't *not* go. Little's your legitimate rep. I don't think I'll be in danger. I had a talk with the gang here last night. They think Nosy sent that wave of goons because you said no to Camille at the party."

"Nosy?"

"That's what my cousin calls Nosferatu. Dunno why. Camille phoned Nosy after you said no—she told us that the next morning, remember? He probably sent the goons before he got word that she has another chance. Now that she does, Nosy will hold off. Ric, you don't want an escalation. Let me handle it."

He made a frustrated noise. "I don't have a lot of choice, with the sun up and me stuck in Ma…stuck here. But I should be *there*, with you."

More vampires secrets. But the yearning in his voice spoke directly to my heart. "I understand. Your nature means you'll be unavailable at times."

"My sunshine." A pause. Even in the silence, Ric was so very present. "Some day I'll tell you everything. But one hurdle at a time."

"I'll hold you to that 'some day'." I shivered, realizing I'd just made a date with Ric Holiday. "I have to go now, to prepare. I've got a proposal to win."

"Wait! Please don't go. I don't care if it escalates. I can deal with anything, as long as you're safe."

"You can, but what about your employees? Your condo group? This meeting is bogus, but if we back out now, Camille will say you bargained in bad faith and Nosy starts a war."

He chuffed a laugh. "When did you get so business savvy?"

"It's not business, it's the nature of bullies. I have to play their game while they hold the cards."

He made an angry sound. "It started out as *my* game but they've changed the rules." A snap of fingers. "I'll simply reverse any bad decisions when I get back."

"You can't," I said. "Same problem with backing out."

He blew a sharp, disgruntled breath. "They won't play fair."

"I know. But I have to do this, Ric. *Trust* me to do it."

"I trust you. I don't agree…but I do trust you. Don't underestimate Charles."

"I'm not worried. He's not the sharpest scalpel on the tray."

"No. But he's willing to fight dirty. Both he and Camille are." Silence, but Ric hadn't hung up. "Synnove…I'm in Madison. Near Cave of the Mounds."

My secretive vampire had shared something of himself. I was deeply touched. "Thanks. And thanks for what training you were able to give me. I won't let you down."

"You could never let me down, Sunshine."

I smiled as I ended the call.

All right then. Time to not let Ric down. Time to *fight*. Cue the warrior music.

Camille and Little are willing to fight dirty. When sparring an opponent who has the upper hand, Mr. Miyagi taught us that the trick is to overwhelm them from the start. So knock 'em dead with my infallible arguments and reasoning.

But it wouldn't hurt to add a bit of sizzle in the form of starching the hell out of my white cotton blouse. Good thing I'd packed for an extended soul-searching.

Twyla pleaded with me the whole time I ironed. "You're not wearing that, are you? Don't you want to dazzle them?"

"With my wit, not my clothes. This gives my arguments the right backdrop."

"That gray thing? They'll yawn to death. At least take one of my bras. I know thirty-two D is too small—"

"Thirty-six, Twyla." I sprayed more starch and finished up the collar. "You haven't been a thirty-two since freshman year in high school."

"Whatever. Just try my Stealth Top." She held up a skimpy knit. A line of tiny snaps marched down the front. "It starts off at Nun and unsnaps to Wink, Gasp, Slaver and Kill

Me Now."

I clicked off the iron. "Even at Wink, I'd look like an inflatable rubber raft with more cleavage than a plumber's trousers."

"But if Little is going to fight dirty—"

"I'm not stooping to his level. I'm going to win this battle on my own merits." Rosie's reluctance had rung a chord in me.

Twyla muttered something about leaving the gun holstered to shoot it. "Fine. I'll put it in your dresser, in case you change your mind."

Ten-twenty sharp I waited for the elevator in the Holiday Buzz main lobby, armored in the starched blouse, stiff tailored suit—and Twyla's best ivory underwear set. She'd forced it on me at the last second, maybe hoping my blouse would get torn again. The lacy bikini thong with the tiny red bow fit but the bra's band was two inches less than I was used to, and I couldn't take a full breath.

So I was shifting foot to foot, nervous and uncomfortable too. This was it. The confrontation between me and Camille. Crisis Time. I reached for my emotional "off" switch—

My cell phone rang. I pulled it out and saw *Hospital*. "Byornsson."

"Dr. Synnove?" Teddy's thin voice greeted me. "He's doing it again. Dr. Bearsylls is threatening you."

"I'm sure Dr. Bearsylls doesn't mean it." I kept my own voice level. Teddy had had a very difficult surgery and didn't need to be upset on top of everything. I mentally burned Bearsylls for scaring the boy.

"But he's so angry. He's saying it's your fault that I can't walk."

Yes. The final piece of The Incident that I hadn't told Ric. Teddy was the patient. That botched surgery had happened to a *child*.

Routine surgery to correct the leftover effects of a clubfoot had turned nightmare; Teddy could no longer use that foot and might never walk or run again. I couldn't make up for the damage, but I did everything I could to balance it, visiting him daily and reading him stories to keep his spirits up.

And what about the surgeon, the one who actually did the damage? Was he in the least remorseful? Well, he was behind on his malpractice insurance premiums and his two sets of alimony. He simply took out more advertising to offset the "incorrect impressions".

So no. No remorse at all.

This was the full horror of The Incident. A maimed child—and the guy who'd maimed him dismissed it as a cost of doing business.

"Why is he saying that, Dr. Synnove? Why is he so mean?"

My fingers tightened on the phone. Poor Teddy sounded really afraid. I was scared too, but Teddy needed to be reassured. I put aside my own feelings. "It's an adult thing, sweetie. Some people deal with their anger and fear by taking it out on others. It's not very constructive, but it's nothing to worry about."

"I know he's wrong. You've been nice to me. I know you couldn't have done anything bad."

"Thanks, Teddy. That means a lot to me." Unfortunately it wouldn't mean anything to a judge, if it came to that. The boy had been under anesthetic at the time. And as far as support from the rest of the surgical team...well, not only Teddy was afraid of Dr. Bearsylls.

There was a short silence. Then he said timidly, "He talked my mom into it."

I chilled.

"She says we can't afford my treatment unless we sue somebody. Dr. Bearsylls said that Dr. Bearsylls Cares and everybody knows it. That she'd never win against him. He said she should sue the hospital instead. And you."

That was a blow. But unfortunately, the way of the litigious world. "Your mom is doing what's best for you, Teddy. Don't worry about me."

"But Dr. Synnove—"

"You concentrate on getting well. And the minute I get back into town I'll visit, okay?" When he didn't answer I prompted again. "Okay?"

"Well…will you show me that neat card game again? Sheep guts?"

I laughed in spite of everything. "Sheepshead." The card game learned by all good little Meiers Corners *kindern* while they were still in diapers. "You bet. But you'll have to promise to practice for me in the meantime."

"I'll get right on it!" The sound of ruffling cards underscored the last words.

I hung up, glad to hear life come back to Teddy's voice, glad I'd distracted him from worrying. Talking him down had worked, at least for now. Next time, who knew? I'd try my best.

The fact that I was scared too? Wasn't Teddy's problem, nor even his mother's, who worked two jobs just to pay the insurance deductibles for the surgeries. She needed money to help her boy. It wasn't her fault a malpractice suit was the only way to get it. Unfortunately, that meant she'd sue everybody from the hospital to the PG4s, that is, me.

One person was at fault, but we'd all pay.

And unless I got into the right mindset to take on Camille and Chicken Little, a whole city would pay another price.

The elevator had come and gone while I'd been on the phone. It was now ten thirty and my meeting was about to begin without me.

I tried to flip my Crisis Time switch but I was either too

distracted or needed the smell of disinfectant as a cue—nothing happened.

Damn. I pushed the elevator button, chafing. I heard a distant ringing—the elevator was on hold. Being late wouldn't strengthen my position. If they listened at all. No, I was a doctor by training. They'd respect that. And maybe they'd understand if I explained I was late because I took Teddy's phone call.

Unless they didn't wait for me. Unless they decided that, because I wasn't there at 10:30 sharp, Camille won by default. I pushed the button and held it. An extended ring told me it was still stuck. I waited. Pushed again. The shrill ring had a faintly mocking tone to it. Whoever was holding it wasn't letting go.

My nerves, already frayed, pushed me away from the elevator to run up the stairs.

I promptly got new respect for Rapunzel's prince, clambering up a towerful of hair. Even a workout with Mr. Miyagi's head teacher Thorvald, a grueling mix of running, agonizingly slow kicks and mountain climbers, culminating in a duck walk around a city block—affectionately known as "Thor's Hammering"—didn't prepare me for running up the side of a football field-size mountain. I was gasping for breath, rumpled and sweaty by the time I made it to thirty-two.

Rosie, at the front desk, leaped up the moment she saw me come through the agency door. "They've already started." She grabbed my hand and led me toward the offices. "They're in the big conference room. Do you want coffee?"

"Water," I croaked.

"It's on the table." She studied me, biting her lower lip. "Good luck, Dr. Byornsson."

From that look, I'd probably need it. I nodded my thanks, and stumbled in.

The big conference room next to Ric's corner office

ran half the building's length. It was dominated by a long hardwood table circled by twelve black captain's chairs. Four chairs were occupied, by Camille, two women, and a man; Little was standing. The man must be Mr. Riley from Finance. I guessed the neat Asian woman with the short glossy black bob was Ms. Park, which left the painfully thin brunette as Ms. Dullea, the media buyer.

Charles Little strutted at the head of the table, arms behind his back. He was obviously trying to give the impression of a captain pacing his ship's deck but to me that strut said rooster. When he saw me he stopped. "*Miz* Byornsson. Finally deciding to grace us with your presence, I see. Sit. There."

I'm not naive. I try to play fair, but I'm perfectly aware of how the game goes. That introduction was one of the most damaging blows Little could have dealt me. I lost points for being late. I'd been stripped of my title's respect, and asking for it now would make me look petty. Explaining why I was late would look like I was currying pity points.

Without a word, I sat. My lips were as tight as rubber bands and my nerves were singing like horror movie violins.

Charles began strutting again, his wattle jiggling importantly. "I am often called on in Mr. Holiday's absence to step in and keep Holiday Buzz running smoothly. Such is the case with this Meiers Corners competitive presentation. For both our efficiency and the client's best results, it is imperative to move on this in a timely fashion. Thus, I've decided to hold the meeting today. In deciding which client to take on, my sole objective is to be fair." He smiled sappily at Camille.

Well, that answered who he was rooting for, as if I hadn't known. I hoped the entire vote wasn't stacked against me.

I checked out the room. Tailored suits, crisp shirts and power ties. It didn't mean their minds were made up but I certainly had an uphill battle. Even my professional togs were a point against me, as rumpled as they now were.

Chicken Little turned from Camille to me and his simper clicked off like a light. "Ms. Byornsson, if you're ready...?" He sounded like he doubted it.

"Of course." As I got up I kept in mind that I was pitching to people like me—realists. Interested in results, not feel-good empty talk. Like a doctor who, after surgery, requires not flatulence but results... Okay, bottom line, Meiers Corners's folksy message might connect better to the creatives, but these were *my* equals.

"Meiers Corners is positioned for enormous tourist growth. Let me tell you why." I'd carried in a manila folder and now I opened it on the table so everyone could see it. "We've already taken steps to make the city more attractive to tourists." I tapped the graph on the top sheet. "Here's tourist volume before and during the run of *Oz, Wonderful Oz*—which is now on Broadway, a great selling point, I'm sure you'll agree."

From their stony faces, they didn't. I swallowed my disappointment—a mistake because I hadn't had time to pour myself water, my throat was extremely dry, and the swallow took half my tongue with it. "Uth ook aa..." Damn it. I bit the inside of my cheek, which relieved some of the dryness, and tried again. "Just look at the numbers."

The facts were solid. I pointed to the first bar, then the second, which was five times taller. We'd already quintupled our tourism, proving our work ethic. Surely that was impressive.

Little smiled like a razorblade. "So you went from one tourist to five?"

Dullea tittered.

"No, it's five times as many—"

"Oh! From two to ten?"

Riley snorted.

I clenched my eyes briefly. "The point is, we attracted hundreds of tourists to our city. *New* tourists."

"You've forgotten something." Camille smiled slyly. "Many of those tourists actually came because of *my* club."

"Is that true, Ms. Byornsson?" Little's shocked expression was *way* overdone. I wanted to smack him. Come on. Even image should have an element of taste.

But because of who I am, I had to admit the truth. "It is my understanding that *some* of them came because of your club, but—"

"You do know you're making Ms. Lebeau's case for her?"

The whole room laughed at that.

"But they stayed because of the musical—"

"I promise I didn't pay her." Camille's eyeteeth got pointy as she went for the kill. "Synnove is giving me an *honest, truthful* evaluation."

The words hit like hammers between my shoulder blades. How could honest and truthful be so awful?

"I think that's enough from Ms. Byornsson. Let's hear from Ms. Lebeau."

My mouth worked but no more words came out. A slow, awful cold invaded my body, taking the strength from my legs.

I sat down. I'd lost, and more than the pitch.

Camille rose, her lush form poured into a red bandage minidress, and swayed around the room on platform spikes. "Let me stress how much *money* my casinos will make."

The room was so quiet you could hear my ego drop. Ding.

As she went over her cash figures, heads nodded. She passed out slick packets of glossy pie charts, stepped back and let them absorb the numbers, her lips curled in a small, smug smile.

That smile cankered. I found my voice for one last

try. "What about the Holiday Buzz mission? Where's the favorable impact on humanity? My plan—"

"History-book charm? Please. Hoary and irrelevant." Camille braced her hands on the table and leaned forward until her cleavage popped, completely reclaiming their attention, even the women. "*My* plan brings Meiers Corners into the twenty-first century. Your plan? As helpful in this economy as a liberal arts degree or educational television. Mine is a high tech degree; a blockbuster movie. *My* plan generates the kind of jobs that'll last through whatever turns our modern age hands out. Real jobs for real people."

"Real jobs," Riley murmured. "Real benefit."

My chest ached as I sat there, not quite hearing because my ears were stuffed with cotton. I started shivering. Maybe I was coming down with a cold. That would explain my prickly nose and my gummy eyelids.

With all my heart, I wished Ric were with me. Not so he could help me as I floundered against Camille and Chicken Little.

But so that he could hold me in his arms when, in a vote of three to one, Holiday Buzz decided to take Camille as client.

Chapter Sixteen

I don't remember leaving. My mind was blank as I emerged into July's bright sunshine. I blinked rapidly. How odd. All that sun, when it felt so cold and rainy.

I'd tried my best, but my well-reasoned arguments had failed. The side of right had failed.

No. Truth, Synnove. *I'd* failed.

My breath hitched, watery. I'd worked for years making life fair for people less fortunate than me. In fact, I'd spent so long at it that I did it automatically. And yes, sometimes I handicapped myself in order to level the playing field.

But Camille and Charles weren't less fortunate. Well, maybe Chicken Little was. Though I'd been warned they'd cheat, I'd held myself above all that and played fair.

Fairness didn't stop Camille and Charles from steamrolling over me.

I fumbled my reality picture out of my purse. Stared at it. Me with scrawny limbs, hair like straw. I hadn't known a thing then, smiling like an idiot, my teeth too big for my face. Crooked too. That was before braces.

I'd been an ugly girl—but I hadn't felt ugly. I was beautiful now, but I didn't feel beautiful.

I felt stupid.

Charles and Camille had hit me where I was most vulnerable. I'd never been so humiliated in my life, not when I'd found the semen in my unknown, not when I was a gawkward preteen ridiculed by the pompom squad at tryouts thanks to a stupid cartwheel. On another note, before you put on your tighty whities, always check them for holes.

If only I'd listened to Rosie, to Twyla, to Ric...

No. I'd played the game my way and I'd lost. No more self-pity. I jammed the picture back in my purse and stomped off, searching for my car. Where was that damned car? I circled the whole block before I remembered I'd left it in the underground parking.

I stomped back into the lobby and hit the garage elevator down button like it was Little's wattled face. They'd ridiculed and rejected me, so what? The game was rigged, I'd known that from my ugly duckling childhood and learned how to live with it. In the parking structure, my heels rang on the clean concrete surface. My childhood drove me to play fair, to make the game fairer for others.

Playing fair had lost me the account.

My stride faltered. Twyla had counted on me, Meiers Corners had counted on me—*Ric* had counted on me.

I stood outside my car, wiping annoyingly wet eyes. Damn it, I hated this emotional roller coaster. No more playing fair. From now on I was playing to *win*.

I would be the Beast.

I tried to build some rage as I unlocked my car, got in, started the engine and drove away, but only squeezed out a tear. It trickled down my cheek.

I made an annoyingly poor Beast.

I drove and drove. I nearly missed the turnoff for the

cabin. Instinctively I headed south. Not to go home. To find Ric and apologize for not listening to him.

To hear his deep voice soothe me, feel his arms around me.

Last minute I managed to steer off the freeway, jerking the wheel and bumping over rumble strip and grass. Horns snarled at me from behind. I snarled back.

Yeah. That was better Beasting.

I didn't need Ric. Reality was, we'd only known each other a few days. We had no past, no future. Nothing real tied us together—except my stupid heart, which seemed to be having trouble beating as I tried to head north.

I slammed to a stop at the bottom of the exit ramp. What the hell did I want Ric for? What did he have going for him aside from being exciting and handsome and protective and smart?

Fuck.

Even if there was a Prince under *his* Beast, what made me think a few days qualified him as my Happily-Ever-After? He'd given me the best orgasm of my life then as good as said we'd never be together.

My inner beastie died. I snatched a paper napkin out of the glove box and wiped my eyes. The paper smeared with wet mascara.

I buzzed down the window to get fresh air. Ric Holiday was an ad man—and a vampire. Not quite real in either respect. A vacation romance; an exciting story I'd tell my grandchildren.

Ric was a fairy tale.

Pain hit me so hard I doubled over the steering wheel. I breathed through it. Thank you, obstetrics rotation.

I reached for my purse and pulled my crumpled picture out. Staring at it, I faced facts. I'd been badly hurt by The Incident, so badly I was thrown from my path. I'd lost my way.

No wonder I thought I'd found the answer in Ric. I would have grabbed anything, anybody.

No more fairy tales.

I fed gas and headed for the cabin. The wind slapped my face through the open window, but I needed it. Kicking a drug addiction can result in shakes to seizures, anxiety to rage. Kicking the Holiday fantasy made me a little insane.

As I crunched up the gravel drive to the cabin, the first thing I saw was the one-lane bridge, blocked by the troll, another big guy shaved bald and a third carpeted in wall-to-wall hair.

Sure, that bedpan had spilled long ago, and they weren't intentionally blocking the bridge, just smoking and tossing their butts in the crick. But as I said, slightly crazy. My gaze narrowed dangerously, my fingers tightened on the wheel. "Get out of my way."

Two guys scowled but stumped off the bridge.

The troll gave me the finger.

My beastie came roaring out from her cave. Yeah, the Beast was bad but he also protected Beauty and didn't take any shit.

I narrowed my eyes and gunned it.

A hybrid doesn't make that much noise. But the troll must have seen the *I've fucking had it up to my fucking eyeteeth* on my face because he jumped aside with satisfying haste, teetering on the edge of the bridge before falling into the crick.

I should have been appalled. Definitely that was not playing fair. But I'd won against a rude troll. Not fair, maybe, but *right*.

Yeah.

Twyla opened the cabin door as I cut the engine. "You're back early." She paused, frowning. "It's not good news, is it?"

"No." I slammed out of the car and stalked toward the

cabin. "Inside. Merlot, stat."

"Ooo-kay." She walked open the screen door and held it. "After you."

"You're so reasonable. I forgot how annoying that is." But as I sank into a living room chair, my tension drained. With Twyla, I was safe. With Twyla, I didn't need my Beast.

She lifted down a bottle from the cabinets. "Good thing Elena's pregnant, or we'd be running low."

I frowned at her. "I just realized something. Elena's pregnant."

"You missed that? Hon, you'd better get your eyes checked." She uncorked the bottle. "If you're asking if Elena's baby is also Bo's, the answer is yes. If you're asking out of general doctorly curiosity, only the males seem to be fertile, and then only with their mates."

"That's odd."

"Yeah." She brought bottle and glasses to me. "They don't eat, either."

"Then how do they get their energy… Hey." I realized she'd distracted me from the horror of that meeting. Not long, but enough that I felt slightly better. "You're sneaky."

"Yup." She gave me a quick sparkle of teeth as she poured.

"I like that about you, Tafel." I took my glass and drank off half in one long swallow. "As long as you've brought up v-guys…you're all so happy with yours. But Ric…he's like trying to catch smoke."

She snorted as she sat. "*All* v-guys are smoke and secrets. They have to be to survive in a world that fears them—and also outnumbers them a bazillion to one. Especially when the more numerous side has armies, and ordnance." She sipped her wine, silent until I'd finished my first glass. "Better?" she said.

"A bit."

"Go change while I pour another round. Then you can tell me what happened at the pitch session."

"Do I have to?"

"No. But you'll feel better."

In my room I peeled down to Twyla's silky ivory bra and bikini thong with the cute bow, then tossed on tank top, shorts and flip-flops. It was amazing how much lighter I felt just getting out of the business armor.

As I swung into the living room, Twyla handed me a full glass. Okay, I could do this. I sank into a chair next to hers, curled my feet under me and gave her the blow-by-blow reenactment, which took us through half the bottle.

Though her face was smooth, I saw my own disappointment mirrored there. The fate of Meiers Corners had rested on this ad campaign. I'd let us all down.

Sure enough, when I was done, she wordlessly gathered our wine glasses, rinsed them out, got down an amber bottle of Irish cream and poured the thick liquid until both glasses were almost full. Irish cream is my favorite. No secret would be safe after a glass or three of that.

"So." She handed me a glass and sat. "Where was Ric in all this? I thought he was helping you."

I blinked at her. And here I'd thought her long face was because she was disappointed in me. She'd hit bang on the one topic I was trying to avoid.

Pretending she hadn't scored a direct hit, I took a nonchalant first swallow of Irish cream. Spoiled it by gasping when the alcohol hit my palate like I'd inhaled a match strike. Yeah, good stuff. I coughed, swallowed several times and ignored her smirk. When I got my voice back I said, "Ric? Oh, he had to go out of town last night, that's all."

"Oh?" She stared, her eyes like brown needles poking into my secrets.

I tippled more cream to gain some time. This time it slid

down smoothly. The alcoholic heat unfurling in my belly and brain gave me false confidence. I began to embellish. "My meeting came up last minute. I almost didn't find out myself. I called Ric but he couldn't get back today, emphasis on to-daylight."

Then something struck me, and I set down my glass with a thud. "You knew all along that Ric's a v-guy, didn't you? Before you even sent me, you knew."

She sighed. "That's why it's so important that he take us on personally. Meiers Corners needs max exposure, but our v-guys need max privacy. Only Holiday can do both."

"This goes beyond a cute prank. You sent me *alone* into the lair of a bloodsucker. He could have drunk me dry!"

"Don't get your undies in a bundle." She topped off my Irish cream. "I did my research. Holiday's got a human household, and a reputation to protect. I knew you were safe. Believe me, if he were a killer, he'd be dead. Exsanguination raises big red flags to some pretty dangerous people."

"Unless he used compulsion on me to make me forget. You didn't know I was immune."

"If he did that regularly, we'd have heard in the couple hundred years he's been around."

"Couple hundred…?" My eyes widened.

"Bottom line, Meiers Corners has special needs when it comes to advertising. Holiday understands those needs." She sipped from her own glass. "Okay, Camille as client means he's coming to our fair city. When he does, you can talk him away from her side and onto ours. I think he likes you. You can use that."

"No, I can't. Even though I'm beasting now, I won't manipulate him emotionally. It's not fair. Besides, it's only in fairy tales that the prince risks confronting the wicked queen one-on-one."

Fairy tales. Not fair. Fairest. Amazing I'd never noticed

that before.

Yeah, liquor makes everything into Great Philosophy.

"Beasting? Fairy tales? Wicked queen?" Faint lines appeared on Twyla's smooth brow. "What are you talking about?"

"Um...only that more is at stake than Meiers Corners getting gobbled up by generica."

"Hon." Twyla put down her liqueur to gather my hands in hers over the end table. "I want to see us win, but that's not the only thing prompting me to push you at Holiday. Not anymore."

"It isn't?"

"When you left the hospital last week, you were so angry. So heartbreakingly sad. I never thought I'd see you smile again. Yet two hours after you met Holiday, you were bright eyed and excited. Happy in a way I hadn't seen you since childhood. Ric Holiday is the first guy who's had that effect on you."

I was trying to exorcise him and she wasn't helping. "It's not like that."

"What is it like, then?"

"I'm not sure this will make any sense but..." Haltingly, I told her about my fairy tale idea. "His 'listening' to me, his 'respecting' me... I want it to be real so badly I've convinced myself it is. But he probably doesn't care about me any more than any guy who wants to get in my size sixes." I squeezed her hands before releasing them. "The saddest part? I'm the one selling myself the fiction."

She was silent, expression thoughtful. Finally she asked, "Are you sure?"

"Absolutely." Mostly.

"I hope you're right." She smiled sadly at me. "Because it's taken you twenty-six years to find one guy to smile over. I'd hate for you to have to wait twenty-six more to find the next."

Anesthetize me with a mallet. She was only helping me push the fantasy deeper. I had to escape. I jumped to my feet. "Ric Holiday is not The One. Look, I'm sorry I didn't win us the campaign, but I've done what I can."

"You haven't—"

"I have. I'm done. And in the morning I'm heading home."

Chapter Seventeen

Twyla watched me with big, dark, concerned eyes. Those eyes guilted me harder than a verbal scolding. She'd learned too much from her silent significant other Nikos.

It didn't help that my heart was on her side.

Needing to be away from those *eyes*, I headed into my bedroom and shut the door. Spent some time with my ereader, scanning words without really absorbing. Gradually my Irish cream buzz wore off and I realized what an ass I'd been. Twyla was only trying to help. In a codependent, not very helpful way.

A little after sunset the scuff of movement and murmur of deep voices said the guys were up. A little later sizzling sounded faintly through the door, and the stinging waft of frying onion. Safety in numbers coupled with my growling stomach convinced me to swallow my idiotic exit lines and join them.

Elena was making dinner, something with tomatoes and tangy spices. Bo worked a whetstone along the edge of a wicked-looking switchblade. I scanned the area for Twyla but she was nowhere in sight. Nikos wasn't either. All the bedroom doors were open.

I gave up and asked. "Where are Twyla and Nikos?"

"Taking a 'walk'." Elena raised her eyebrows significantly. It was a euphemism for something, but she didn't say, and with that scary grind-grind going on, I didn't ask.

Instead I got out a bowl, found leaf lettuce, tomatoes, green and red peppers, and a can of black olives, and tossed together a salad.

Supper was on the table when Twyla and Nikos got back. She greeted me like our heated discussion had never happened—thank God for lasting friendships—and sat down to eat while Nikos built a fire.

After dinner, the five of us sat around the crackling logs, roasting marshmallows and playing Sheepshead for a nickel a point. My head wasn't in it so Twyla cleaned up.

It was after midnight when Bo and Elena disappeared out the lakeside door. Nikos, Twyla and I sat silently in front of the fireplace. I brooded, Twyla shot concerned little glances at me, and Nikos was just Nikos, big, silent and still. We sat that way for over an hour, until sometime after one in the morning.

Suddenly Nikos leaped to his feet, a dormant volcano erupting. His skin hardened like concrete, tusk-sized fangs exploded from his mouth, and his eyes boiled blood red.

My heart kicked into my throat at the sight.

"What?" Twyla was on her feet too.

"Vampire," he snarled. "Coming—"

The lakeside door slammed open, but it wasn't Bo. An unknown vampire filled the opening, chest pumping like bellows, face plated. Firelight glinted off shining fangs. Red eyes burned above them, eyes which flew immediately to me.

"Sshynnoffa—"

Nikos blurred. He snapped solid at the door with huge

talons and slashed the vampire.

The vampire's jacketed arm shot up in a block. Nikos's talons tore through black leather, skin and meat. With a twist of the arm, the vampire snared Nikos's claws in the material of the jacket and jerked down. Nikos tipped forward. The vampire launched an uppercut at his jaw.

Nikos simultaneously stepped forward to catch his balance and snatched the vampire's wrist before the punch could land. Fluidly, the vampire ripped his jacket loose and turned Nikos's hold to seize his forearm. Tugging sharply down, the vampire fired a knee into Nikos's solar plexus. Only a lightning twist kept Nikos from a goring.

All this happened in a split second. The vampires' battle was almost too fast to see.

My heart knew the new vampire's identity before my brain recognized the face under the plating. "Ric!" I ran forward.

Twyla grabbed for me. I dodged and ran for Ric.

Ric and Nikos's fight had turned them and brought them slightly into the room. My leap sent me right in the middle of them.

I plowed into grappling vampires, my brain sending me frantic signals—many, many vampire ends are dangerously pointy. Sure enough, Nikos speared huge talons toward Ric as I hit between them.

"Sshynnoffa, no!" Ric snatched me, wrapped himself around me and whirled.

Pain skewered my back. Damn, Nikos's sharp claws had nearly broken skin, and definitely had bruised me.

Ric pushed me away. I spun to yell at everyone and anyone.

White claws protruded from Ric's belly.

Nikos had impaled him. Only the tips of those lethal talons had reached me.

I covered my mouth with both hands. "Oh, no. No, no."

Nikos ignored me, growling like a really pissed lion. He raised his other hand high, talons glinting like knives, aimed at Ric's vulnerable neck.

"No!" I ran two steps and hit Nikos's shoulder with everything I had.

Maybe he let me shove him off, but all I remember is the sound. Nikos's talons came out of Ric's flesh with an unnerving set of *thwucks*.

Ric groaned.

Crisis Time. I clicked off my emotion and ejected my nausea to spin toward Ric and shove his jacket off his shoulders. Holes in his black T-shirt were seeping blood. "I need to pack those wounds. Then we have to get you to a hospital."

"No hospitals," Twyla said.

Nikos was still growling.

"I'm...I'm all right." Ric's fangs were gone. His eyes were no longer red but a dulled gray, his face was drawn, and he was panting. "The big guy...is strong. One of yours?"

"My cousin's. Don't be a testosterone ass, Ric. A hospital is—"

"Not...necessary." He raised his shirt.

My eyes were drawn to his rapidly rising and falling six-pack. He'd stopped bleeding. And if I wasn't mistaken, the holes were already closing.

In fact, before my very eyes, they closed entirely. They even began to lose their pinkness. I stared in amazement. Sure, his burned face and bullet wound had healed quickly day before yesterday, but this was the first time I *saw* it, watched the miracle real-time.

"Sorry for the scare." His voice was stronger now, and steadier. "I smelled you with a vampire and just reacted." He lowered his shirt and turned to Nikos. "I'm Ric Holiday."

Twyla answered because Nikos was still growling. "Nice to meet you in person. I'm Twyla Tafel." She elbowed Nikos hard in the ribs. The growling cut, though he didn't budge a millimeter. "This is Nikos." Twyla held out her hand. "Synnove has told us so much about you."

"Any of it good?" Ric glanced at Nikos before taking Twyla's hand.

"Nope." Twyla grinned.

Ric's eyebrow rose, and his eyes shuttled between Twyla and me. "You're Synnove's cousin, aren't you?"

Both of us stiffened. Now he'd ask if one of us was adopted. Unintentionally hurtful, but it would bite anyway. So much for my fairy tale prince.

Ric smiled, a child-like grin of discovery. "So Synnove is African as well as Scandinavian, how fascinating. Who else is in your family tree?"

Something inside me eased. "I'm German," I admitted. "Mom was a Brandt."

He nodded. "I don't know what I am. Some woodpile combination of French and English, I think. I take it the meeting didn't go well."

Well, hell. I thought I'd imagined his whole knowing-me-better-than-I-knew-myself thing, but here he was doing it again. I gaped at him. "How did you—?"

"You glow when you're happy. You're distinctly not glowing."

My stomach flipped. For a story I'd imagined, for a relationship that didn't exist, it felt pretty damn real. "It could have gone better."

"I'm sorry. Normally I'd have stepped in right away. But with Camille in the picture it will take more subtle handling—"

Bang.

A sharp report from outside stopped him. Fireworks.

Or a gun.

It was followed by a shout, far off. The voice was dark with pain, guttural and deep.

And definitely female.

"*Elena.*" Nikos spun, swept Twyla into his arms and dashed out the door.

"Elena?" I started to follow. "She must be having her baby—"

My voice jarred as Ric swept me up and followed them. He said, "That's not childbirth pain."

"It isn't?"

"No. That dark? That's something worse."

I've studied medicine for years. I've dissected cadavers. I've watched surgeries on living humans, and later assisted.

But what happened next was so horrific that I wouldn't blame you if you skipped it. I would have myself, except I didn't know what we'd find when we dashed out of that cabin. I went through that hell because I had to.

Ric ran so fast the wind beat my face and tangled my hair as if I were in a sports car. What I could see of the trees in the near dark blurred by. If I hadn't been worried about Elena, it would have been exhilarating.

Nikos ran abreast of us with Twyla in his arms, although at first all I could see were the red lights of his eyes. As my own sight adjusted, it was evident his face was bladed again.

"How can you tell it isn't childbirth?" I shouted over the wind at Ric. "Elena's due."

"Blood." Ric slurred it, his fangs lengthening.

"Blood is part of the process. That's normal."

Elena's shout, dark with agony, came again.

"Just labor," I repeated. My reassurances sounded

desperate even to my own ears. "It hurts like hell, but it's not deadly. Mostly." But now even I could smell the metallic tang.

If it was labor, it wasn't going well.

"No," Nikos said. "There."

A shaft of moonlight cut through the trees like a spotlight.

She lay on the ground of a small clearing, clutching her belly with one hand while she stabbed repeatedly with a knife at a sack scarecrow.

No. Not a scarecrow. A vampire in tattered clothes. He curled over her like a python, mouth wide and fangs dripping red blood.

A shriek stuck in my throat.

Elena's knife hit home. The vampire flinched. It struck again and he batted ineffectually at it, a confused look on his face.

Nikos transferred Twyla into his left arm, leaped forward and slugged the creature.

The vampire, bare feet and arms trailing, flew into a tree, hitting bark with a sharp crack.

Nikos gently deposited Twyla on her feet. He thrust a hand into his back pocket and drew out a flat black case the size and shape of a bundle of dollar bills. A flick of his thumb and a half-foot leaf-shaped blade shot out, glinting sharply silver on both edges. It looked like a Spartan sword, if they were miniaturized into switchblades.

The vampire pushed erect. Nikos decapitated the monster with a single mighty whack. He swung so hard the blade embedded in the tree trunk behind the vamp like a headman's axe into a stump.

The head tumbled to the forest floor, hitting with a sound like a watermelon thudding onto a cutting board. My stomach heaved. I'd never seen someone killed before, and the violence shocked me.

Elena moaned, her fingers stiffening over her belly.

Crisis Time. I flipped my switch to lock shock away. This one was personal; I'd have to deal with it later, but for now, I was a doctor. "Ric. Put me down."

"No." His arms tightened. "I smell—"

"Elena!" Bo shot into the clearing, naked, dripping dirt. "What the hell happened to my wife?"

"It's Bo, Ric. Put me down."

Bo's red eyes widened. "My God. Elena!" He dropped to his knees next to her and started to grab her. "The blood... so much." He turned to us. He looked lost and confused and scared, which frightened me. Bo Strongwell doesn't confuse or scare easily.

"Ric. *Now.*" I struggled. Ric finally set me down. I ran to Elena and squatted on her other side. "There was a vampire..." I turned her chin. Scanned her neck. Not a mass of blood. A couple pinpricks, already closing.

But I smelled blood. Was it the baby coming? I checked her pants. Dry. Not the baby. What was causing that smell...?

She groaned again. Her hand clutched above the mound of her stomach.

Rivulets of blood ran from between her fingers.

I raised her hand.

Elena's belly had been slit with a knife.

The laceration was deep enough to see into. Bad. But it was bleeding freely with no embedded objects. Good.

Immediately I put my hands on the wound and pressed. First step, stop the bleeding. Pack the wound and apply pressure. Infection was the least of my worries just then. "Ric—no, Nikos." He had the blade. "Cut up your shirt. Several strips. Twyla. Call 911."

I glanced at Elena's face. Her eyes were glassy with shock.

I didn't have much time.

Twyla pulled her cell from her pants pocket. Her voice murmured in the background.

"I need to heal her." Bo's eyes were brimming red liquid. "But I need to be clean first, right? An open wound risks infection?" He was seriously frazzled, the master out of his element.

His form blurred, like Ric when he'd escaped the mountainous goon…was it only two days ago? For a moment I lost my focus as Bo became fuzzy, almost misty, with a sound like the wind stirring a thousand tiny leaves. The dirt coating him dropped to the ground with pellet-like smacks. A moment later he solidified in a snap, his naked skin completely clean.

Nikos pressed strips of shirt into my hand. I snapped back into doctor mode and packed the strips into Elena's wound.

Bo's head dropped, and he began *licking* around my hands.

"What the fuck…?" I kept packing. Used my elbow to shove him away. "What are you doing?" I got the wound packed and applied pressure. He tried to shift my hands. "Stop that!"

"It's okay," Twyla said. "Their saliva heals."

"You're kidding." I glanced at her. She was serious.

I didn't like it. But vampires existed. What was a miracle or two besides? I slid my hands to one side so Bo could try his vampire therapy. As he began to lick vigorously I asked, "The baby?"

"I can hear its heart beat," Ric said. "It's fine."

I relaxed somewhat. Babies in the womb are incredibly well-protected, packed in fluid-filled human bubble wrap, thick muscular sheeting and a sturdy bone box. Still, good to know.

"*Herregud*. It's not working." Bo's voice cracked as he raised his head. Blood trickled from Elena's ruined abdomen. "The wound…it's too deep."

No vampire miracle. Not good. I readjusted the packing

and pressed down.

Elena's brown eyes were going in and out of focus. Definitely not good. Her breathing was labored. I touched her skin. It was cool despite the July heat.

"She needs warmth." I pointed at Bo. "Lie next to her." It would give him something useful to do. Especially helpful if later…

No, that was later. Now was for doing everything I could.

Bo stretched out next to his wife. He kissed her forehead tenderly. "Stay with me, Detective. We made it through Dracula, we'll make it through this."

"This…hurts more." She coughed. "Chilly…" Her eyes closed.

"More heat," I said. "Her other side."

"On it." Ric lay down next to her.

Shivering, Elena's eyes closed.

"Please, Detective." Bo's voice broke. "Stay with me. I need you."

"The ambulance is coming," Twyla said.

"Good." I kept my tone brisk, despite my hammering heart and clammy hands. "Twyla, come here. Keep this in place." I put her hands on the shirt-bandage. "Keep the pressure up." When I was satisfied she was holding steady, I moved to take Elena's wrist.

No pulse. Her extremities were closing down. I went immediately to the carotid in her neck.

A pulse, good. But far too rapid, bad. Her heart beat like a hummingbird, trying desperately to pump blood that wasn't there. "How long until that damned ambulance gets here?"

"Ten minutes," Twyla said. "Will that be enough time to—oh."

My face must have said what I would not put into words. Elena didn't have ten minutes.

"Maybe the bleeding has stopped," she said tentatively.

"Let's peek under the bandage—"

"No." I cut her off. "Keep the pressure up."

"Synnove." Bo's cheeks were running red tears. "You're a doctor. Can't you do something? Sew it closed?"

"It's packed. The best thing is to keep the pressure up and wait for the ambulance—"

"No," Nikos said. "Call the Ancient One."

"What can he do?" Ric demanded. "He's no human doctor."

"He knows things," Bo said. "Call him, Nikos."

"I have no phone."

"Use mine." Twyla raised her hands to reach for her back pocket.

"Pressure," I snapped.

Startled, Twyla pressed her hands back.

Elena started gasping for breath.

I barked, "Whatever we do, do it now!"

"*Theos*." Nikos grabbed the phone out of Twyla's jeans. It looked like a toy in his big hand. He hit a speed dial and put it gingerly to his ear. There were no introductions. The instant the line connected he said, "Sir, Elena's dying."

The pulse under my fingers weakened. I gritted my teeth. Even unconscious, hearing "dying" was bad.

"Yes, sir. Right away." Nikos stowed the phone, then knelt next to me, took out his leaf-bladed knife and raised his arm over Elena. "Do not stop me."

I glanced at him. Then stared. In the wash of moonlight, the stoic Nikos looked absolutely sick. "Nikos, what are you planning?"

He hadn't had time to get more than a few words of instruction. I didn't see how he could save Elena's life with a few words.

"I give her my blood."

"Your *blood*? You mean, like make her into a vampire?"

It kicked me out of my knowledge zone. All the doubt and fear that I'd switched off came flooding back. "No. No way. I know she wants to, but we don't know what it will do to the baby."

"No time." He raised his blade. "Remove the packing."

"Mine," Bo snarled, rearing up. "My wife, my blood."

"It must be the oldest blood," Nikos said. "That's mine."

"Lover. Do you have to?" Twyla's eyes glistened with tears. Whatever Nikos was preparing to do, the act was significant.

"Yes, love."

"No." I barred Elena's body with both arms. "At least let me deliver the baby first—"

"I heal her." Nikos grabbed my wrists in one hand and gently moved me out of his way. Arm directly above Elena's belly, he slit his wrist without a flinch. The first rivulet hit Twyla's hands as she pulled strips of shirt from the wound.

The gash exposed the liver's purplish brown, almost black in the moonlight. How did Nikos think he'd heal that? The wound was fatal. "But vampire blood turns humans." I was panting but I couldn't hear it as my vision narrowed on Nikos's arm and Elena's mutilated belly. A thin stream of blood ran between, as slender as an IV line. I couldn't hear anyone breathing. Maybe they'd all stopped.

Nothing happened.

It wasn't working. Well, how could it? How could dead vampire blood heal a live human being? Bo and Nikos hadn't known about it. Probably the Ancient One had made it up.

"Blood turns the dead," Twyla said. "As long as she's alive, this'll heal her."

Elena's harsh breathing and her stuttering pulse said the end was near. Hoping for a miracle but knowing it was too late, yet I begged for one, with all my might, as Nikos poured out his blood.

Still nothing happened.

In the near-silence, a rustle from the bushes crackled clearly.

Ric jerked up. "Who's there?"

Branches snapped. The thud of running feet went off into the underbrush.

Someone had been watching us.

Ric started to get up. I caught at him. "Keep her warm." He sank back down.

"It's not working." Bo, voicing my fears, made them coldly real. His face was stark white, red tears brimming dark in contrast. "Oh God, it's not working."

The thread of blood had become a rivulet. Nikos hadn't stopped cutting. I'm not squeamish when it comes to blood, but he sliced until the rivulet became a river, sawed until dark sheets were pouring into Elena's wound. Until his own skin was pale and translucent.

It was unspeakably messy. The blood splashed like rainwater from a gutter, pouring onto the forest floor.

Still nothing happened.

Nikos wavered on his knees. My stomach lurched. It was a horrific sight, Nikos pouring his lifeblood onto Elena's violated belly. I nearly shouted *Stop*. Stop the horror. Let her die with dignity.

But then…Elena's gash…heaved. Red flesh started bubbling up like foam, filling the wound. Bit by bit the liver and other exposed organs were covered. Skin rolled out over the gash like tawny masking tape. The gash narrowed to a cut, then a line…and then disappeared completely.

Just as Elena expelled air with a rattle and went still.

I lost her pulse. I pressed harder, rolled my fingers for it, but it was gone. "Fuck. Nikos. Move. I have to start CPR."

"No pressure." Nikos's words were slurred.

No blood pressure, he meant. If Elena's arteries had

collapsed, chest compressions would be useless. Breathing in oxygen wouldn't do any good without circulation.

"I don't care." I tried to shove him aside.

He didn't move. He was pale and swaying on his knees and his teeth were chattering, but with fierce concentration he stared at his raised hand. It blurred.

He thrust the blurred hand into Elena's body.

Suddenly he went white, as if he had lost all his blood all at once.

He yanked his hand back, barely in time to keel over.

Chapter Eighteen

Things happened pretty fast after that. I remember them in flashes. The EMTs arrived. The defibrillator shock restarted Elena's heart. Nikos had apparently gotten enough blood into her to inflate her blood vessels.

Then, the moment the EMTs stabilized her and announced her pulse and blood pressure were strong, Bo hypnotized them into walking away.

"She needs to be in the hospital!" I got in his face. She'd brushed too near death. "She needs to be under medical supervision."

"No." The Viking scooped her into his arms. "She's full of Nikos's blood. We can't be sure what the doctors will find. She and the baby are fine; I hear both heartbeats. No hospital."

"But—"

"I said no." Then he took the whole thing out of my hands by disappearing with her in the direction of the cabin.

I ground out a string of curses and started after him.

"Wait." Twyla's hand, touching my shoulder, trembled. I

turned to see her eyes glistening with tears in the moonlight. "Nikos…he won't wake up. Can you look at him?"

"Elena should be in a damned hospital." But I glanced at Nikos's mountainous body…which didn't seem quite so mountainous.

Other things were off as well. His eyes looked sunken, his mouth was bracketed by lines and his hair was frosted silver in the moonlight. Apparently the shock and stress were making me see things. "They *both* need a hospital. Why doesn't Bo get that?"

"It's the Big Secret," she said tiredly. "Human authorities ask too many questions. Could you…could you please take care of Nikos?"

"I can try." I knelt next to him. Nikos was sheet white. He wasn't breathing. In fact, he looked dead. I touched his skin. It was cool. "Is this normal for a vampire?"

"I don't know." Twyla knelt beside me. "I mean, sometimes he doesn't breathe. But I've never seen him like this before."

I glanced over my shoulder at Ric.

He shook his head, expression grim. He didn't know either, which worried me.

"Let's get him back to the cabin. Maybe we can tell more in better light." And then I could check on Elena too. She and the baby were still my primary concern.

Ric got the task of lugging Nikos's heavy body while Twyla and I walked behind him. I chafed to go faster but I could barely see as it was.

The instant we got back to the cabin I ordered, "Put him on the couch. I'll be back." I got my kit out of my car, threw open the first bedroom door and walked smack into six plus of angry Viking.

Bo snarled. "She needs rest, not more poking."

"After I see her."

"Not. Happening."

I don't know what would have happened if Twyla hadn't shouted, "Strongwell! Get out here this instant and give Nikos blood."

He didn't want to go but I could snarl too. "You said she didn't need a hospital. Prove it. Go help Nikos."

Bo gave me a final snarl and spun out.

With him out of my hair, I hurried to where Elena rested on the bed. Bo had removed her dirty, torn clothes and dressed her in a man's white T-shirt. I lifted it gently. He'd washed her too. Her belly wound was clean and closed. In fact, I couldn't tell where it had been. I took her blood pressure and listened to both her and the baby's heart. They were strong. I'd barely satisfied myself that she was recovering when Bo appeared, rushed me and my bag out of the bedroom and firmly shut and locked the door. But I'd seen enough to know she and the baby were in good hands.

Twyla was alone in the living room. Next to her on the end table sat a full glass of wine, the wine bottle, an empty glass and the Irish cream.

I went to her and hugged her, and kept hugging until her trembling slowed. When she straightened away, I said, "Where are the guys?"

She blinked glossy eyes. "Ric and Bo did what they could for Nikos. He's resting. Recovering. I hope." She took a deep, shuddering breath, which seemed to calm her somewhat. She poured me Irish cream and handed me the glass.

I took the bottle with me when I sat down. "And Ric?"

"He said he was going back to the clearing to look for clues. And to dispose of the rogue vampire."

I shivered and belted Irish cream without any regard for its price, just because it was booze. "So Nikos is resting. Will he be okay?"

"Yes. I'm pretty sure." She took another breath. "No.

I'm not sure at all. He didn't wake up, not even after Bo and Ric gave him blood. Neither of them has seen anything like this. And lying there on the couch…he looked frail, Synnove. Almost…old."

"Oh, hon. Trauma and shock can cause temporary aging and make hair go gray." Not waking up wasn't good, though. "What about that Ancient One, Elias? Can't you ask him? His advice saved Elena."

"We're only supposed to call him in emergencies." She breathed again, heavily, like it took an effort. "But after Ric left, well, I called. I had to. That's part of the problem."

I clenched the glass. "Did that asshole brush you off? I'll kick his testicles into next week if he even dared—"

"Synnove, no." She choked on something that might have been a horrified laugh. "He said a couple nights buried in the soil would bring Nikos back. The problem is he also said Nikos won't be the same. He may not ever be the same." She shuddered.

That was good for another round of hugging. "What does that mean?"

"Even after Nikos wakes, he'll need a long time to recover."

"Months?"

"Years." She blinked. "If he weren't as old as he is, he'd be permanently dead."

I nearly didn't ask the next question. I wanted to ignore what had happened; I wanted it to just go away.

Classic avoidance behavior. I closed my eyes and gathered my strength. I'd been through dozens of crises as a doctor-in-training, but this was *personal*. We needed to talk this out, both of us, or risk post-traumatic stress disorder.

I opened my eyes, sat back down and cautiously peeled back the lid on the emotional can of worms. "You trust this Elias?" I watched her closely.

Twyla bit her lip. "Mostly. I've never met him and he's secretive as hell, but the guys trust him—Bo and Nikos and the rest. He did give us the information to save Elena's life." She met my eyes and hers were as dark and serious as I'd ever seen them. "I'd heard that v-guys could heal humans, even aging. I was thrilled. But the cost… No wonder it's not something they do casually."

She drank off her glass. Filled it again.

Yeah, this could turn into PTSD way too easily. Best thing for her was to keep talking, but we needed to start easy. "Look, I need more info. Take me back to the beginning. Why did Ric and Nikos fight?"

She gave me a watery smile. Twyla's hella smart; she knew what I was doing. Wouldn't stop it from being effective. She said, "They're vampires. Highly territorial. Fiercely protective, especially of their humans. Enemies until proven otherwise."

"Okay, but what was with the googly faces?"

That almost made her smile for real. "The battle mask? When they call on their natures their eyes go red and their fangs elongate. When they fight, their skin additionally hardens and their claws extend. The older they are, the longer the claws, among other things." She managed a wink.

"You don't mean…of course you do." I sighed theatrically, fiercely relieved she was able to tease even a little. "Too much info. I don't want to know how long Nikos's 'claws' are." I emphasized the present tense. "So Nikos attacked Ric because he thought he was a threat?"

"Yes. Because he smelled an unknown vampire."

"I thought we couldn't use the v-word."

She set down her glass. "At this point I don't care. You need to know, without the euphemisms. Just keep your voice down. Bo will scent any eavesdroppers."

"Bo didn't smell the eavesdropper in the clearing."

"He was distracted."

"Why was Elena alone to be attacked by that rogue vampire in the first place? Where was he?"

"The guys have to recharge their batteries. A couple hours of skin to soil. Elena doesn't take sitting around too well, so I'd guess she went off exploring."

Skin to soil, and Bo's hair and face had been dirty.

And though Nikos was supposed to be resting, the door to their bedroom was open and he wasn't on the bed.

I swallowed hard. "You mean like…a burial?"

She'd seen my glance. "They sleep in bedrooms with normal beds, not graves. Recharging is separate from sleeping."

"Oh. Good deal. And the vampire biting Elena…you called him a rogue? What's that?"

"Rogues are vampires who drink humans to death."

"They're evil?"

"Evil." She blinked. "I'm so angry. Furious at what happened to Elena. To Nikos." She curled her arms around herself. "But no, they're not evil. Most are newbies who don't know any better, and are too young to control the thirst."

I got up, put my hands on her shoulders and looked her straight in the eye. "Twyla, Nikos will be all right."

She hesitated, then nodded once. "I know." She breathed again, a sigh. "I know he will."

"Believe it. Your belief will help him heal." Time to inject some normalcy. "Hey, I'm hungry. I'm going to see what's to eat." I went to the kitchen. "So when Ric picked me up he really zoomed. Can all vampires run that fast?"

"It's not exactly running, but yes. They all can go much faster than humans, some as fast as forty to fifty miles an hour, depending on age and training."

"So they can't outrun a car?" I rummaged in the cupboards, found boxes of woven whole grain crackers—

rosemary and olive oil, and oregano with chive.

"When they're old enough to mist, they can zap places with that. It's almost instantaneous but they can only go short distances before collapsing back into their natural form."

"That explains Bo's fuzzy act." I checked the refrigerator, found some tubs of spreadable cheese—Swiss almond and wine-swirled cheddar. "How about cheese and crackers? Wisconsin does good cheese."

"I suppose."

That was better than a flat refusal. I put tubs and boxes on a tray and added a couple knives. "Can they do the bat thing as well?"

"Not all of them, at least not right away." Her eyes followed me as I carried the tray into the living room. "At a thousand years old they can shape shift. Bats, birds, you name it."

"A thousand years? Holy needleroni, that's old."

"Age is a good thing in a vampire." She watched me open the tub of creamy Swiss. "Makes them stronger and smarter. And bigger." She tried an eyebrow waggle and almost pulled it off.

"TMI. I don't need to know how 'big' your boy toy is." I spread the Swiss on a woven cracker and offered it to her.

"I'm not hungry...oh, all right." She took the cracker and nibbled off a corner. "I meant height and weight. This is good." She smiled slightly. "We don't know why, but the older the vampire, the more massive. Unless they get majorly damaged somehow. Hit by lightning or too long in the sun, that sort of thing." Her smile faded. "That's why Nikos looked smaller. After."

"He'll be all right," I repeated. Vampire physiology. If not for my need to keep Twyla talking, it would be a fascinating field to discuss.

Twyla blinked. She looked at the cracker in her hand,

then me, then put the rest of the cracker in her mouth and chewed, idly dusting her fingers on her pants. "I can almost believe that now." She washed down the cracker with a sip of wine. Food and talk, the great healers. Thank goodness.

I spread another cracker with cheddar. "Something I don't understand. If Elena was attacked by a vampire, why did it look like a knife wound? I'd think a claw or fang would tear or puncture." I bit the cracker in half. *Mmm*, tangy.

She frowned. "Maybe the rogue didn't do that. A newbie isn't savvy enough to carry a knife." At my raised eyebrow she added, "To destroy a vampire you have to burn him, but to stop him you only have to cut off the head or dig out the heart. Which means a knife, unless you're the Ancient One, who reportedly has talons like switchblades."

"And this keeps getting yuckier." I set aside my half-eaten cracker. "So you're saying it wasn't the vampire who knifed Elena?"

Her expression was troubled. "Probably not."

We were both silent a moment, wondering, if not the rogue, then who. Finally I said, "Three sets of bad guys, then? Elena's attacker, the vampire and the Peeping Tom?"

"Maybe. That's what your guy is trying to find out."

"Ric is not my guy."

"Deny it if you have to." Twyla was silent for a long time, sipping wine as food and company seeped through and the shudders ebbed from both of us. Though the shock had gone, something was obviously eating at her.

I waited, heart aching for her, hoping whatever was bothering her worked its way out.

Finally she said, "Everybody's so big on Happily Ever After. But I've only ever wanted Happily For Now. Because you can't count on HEA, you know?"

"I know your arguments." We'd discussed this before. "Things happen, like falling out of love or accidents or just plain death."

"Exactly. No such thing as Happily Ever." She took a deep breath. "But."

"But?"

"Elena was dying. She could have died." Twyla shook her head. "She and Bo have only been married nine months. Only nine months of HEA. But Synnove—" her eyes met mine, "—that's nine months more than Nikos and I have had, with me insisting on Happily For Now. I've been fooling myself."

"Oh hon, you're being hard on yourself—"

"No, don't you see? It could have been me on that forest floor." She thumped her breastbone. "Even Happily For Now isn't for sure."

"Nothing is for sure."

"One thing is. Real love." She set down her glass firmly and stood. "There's only one way to get Happily For Any-Time-At-All. *Grab* it. Grab real love, right now, and enjoy it for as long as you can."

Thinking of Ric, I shook my head. "But what is real love?"

She leaned a hand on my chair's arm. Searched my eyes with hers. "The kind of love that commits itself to forever, and keeps on committing to forever, moment after moment after moment. Whether you and Ric have a shot at that or not, I want it with Nikos." She stood, a bit unsteadily. "And I'm going to get it."

I put down my glass, narrowly missing setting it on the table's edge. When I stood, I swayed too. "You going to make an honest man of him? Er, honest vampire?"

"Damn skippy I am."

"Well, hell." I grabbed her in a quick bear hug, blinking suddenly moist eyes. "Only if I get to be maid of honor."

Her smile was brilliant. "You may have to fight Nixie for that," she said, referring to her five-foot zilch, hundred pound punk rock musician best friend.

"Bring it," I said. "I'll hold her by the forehead and let her swing."

"She trained with Mr. Miyagi too. And she doesn't always fight fair, so be careful. She'll kick you in the nether puffies. Lots of blood down there."

"Don't I know it." We both collapsed in a fit of giggles on the couch.

Which was where Ric found us when he returned half an hour later. We were misty-eyed with wine and Irish cream bottles nearly empty.

I jumped to my feet, wanting to run into his embrace to feel his arms around me and hang on forever.

How could I have become so attached in such a short time?

I probably couldn't. Even love at first sight takes months of relationship-building to confirm. *Needy hormones and danger's adrenaline rush can mimic love...* Still, the simple sight of him made me tingle from my head to my toes. To avoid something neither of us could live down, I only said, "Glad you made it back. Are you okay?"

"Yes. I'll take some of that wine though."

I handed him my glass. He poured from Twyla's bottle, draining it.

Twyla said, "Did you find them?"

"I found the eavesdropper. Caught him, questioned him and then wiped his mind. Then I called the sheriff's department and had him carted off to jail."

"And Elena's attacker?" I asked.

Ric shook his head. "The tracks were confused. I'll try again tomorrow, after some rest."

"Too bad." Twyla yawned.

But Ric's eyes silently let me know he hadn't told the whole truth. I flicked a glance at my bedroom. We needed to talk privately. And maybe more. A delicate shiver woke every cell of my body.

He tipped his head once in agreement. Tossing off his wine, he said, "Synnove, if I can borrow your floor, I'll go lie down."

"Sure." I turned to Twyla. "You should get some rest too."

"I don't think I can sleep." She stifled another yawn.

"I can help," Ric said.

Twyla shook her head, her eyelids flagging. "I'm immune to mind control."

"I meant a shoulder rub."

"Oh." She yawned so hard she shuddered with it. "Okay."

Ric stood behind her chair and kneaded her neck and shoulders. Twyla groaned. "I didn't know I was hurting until you made it stop."

"Shh. Close your eyes."

While Ric worked, he exchanged a word-filled gaze with me. *She's exhausted.*

She's worried about Nikos.

He'll be fine. "Relax, Twyla." As he deepened his massage, he started humming, a soft, sweet tune, almost a lullaby. He had a lovely rich baritone. *She'll feel better after a good sleep.*

Yes. And as Twyla nodded off, I pointed toward her bedroom.

Ric slipped hands under her knees and shoulders, lifted her effortlessly, carried her into her darkened bedroom and laid her gently on the bed.

"Mmm?" She stirred.

"Shh," he said. "It's all right. Synnove's here. Rest now."

She snuggled into the bed with a sigh. I slipped off her shoes and covered her with a spare blanket.

When she was settled, Ric motioned me out of the room.

He followed, flicking off the light and shutting the door behind him.

What he'd done for her was lovely and sweet, and coming on top of the horrors, made me long for some comfort of my own. Yes, I'd declared Ric wasn't my guy but that seemed hollow and cold when right now all I craved was his solid warmth.

So when he opened his arms to me, I went into them gladly, leaning into him with a sigh. "So what actually happened?"

"Something that would have had her out for blood. Let's talk in your room."

I took his big hand and led him to my bedroom, shutting the door after us. I sat on the bed and glanced at the spot next to me, hoping for hot, sweaty things I shouldn't have, but what the hell.

Ric leaned against the wall, a sort of self-deprecating quirk to his lips. "I would, but I need to use my mouth for talking right now. This is important."

Ooh, his mouth, and what he could do with his very clever tongue… With a sigh, I settled back on my elbows. "What did you find?"

"A set of tracks, made by waffle stompers, in the bushes where we'd heard the eavesdropper."

"Waffle stompers?"

"Big boot print." He held his hands about a foot apart. "Grid tread pattern. Deep, meaning a heavy guy. Waffle stompers."

"How colorful you ad men are."

"Wait until you hear what else I found. Waffle Stomper was our eavesdropper, but his weren't the only tracks. Two more sets, a ferret and a clown, led *toward* the clearing."

"A real ferret?"

"No." He grinned. "Pointy-toed boots, you know, the

kind made of lizard skin and ego?"

"Right. And the clown?"

"Fucking dinner plates. Clomp-clomp clown shoes."

"I will never get those images out of my head. That goes beyond colorful. I can see why you do well in advertising."

His grin broadened. "The woman understands me."

I grinned back.

Somehow we were smiling into each other's eyes. Everything melted away but a feeling of profound connection.

Our smiles died. I looked away first.

I cleared my throat. "You're rather good at the tracking stuff for a civilized ad man, aren't you?"

"I've had diverse training," he said neutrally.

"And the wall goes up. Okay, another secret. So what did you find that you thought Twyla would be out for blood?"

"The scuffling obscured most of it, but I found signs that all three tromped *into* that clearing. And Ferret's and Clown's tracks were deeper than they should have been. As if they were weighed down by something heavy."

"Heavy? Like what?" I swallowed hard. "Were they carrying the vampire?"

"No. His scent and spoor tell me he was watching on one side of the clearing. I think he capitalized on Elena's situation but didn't cause it."

"So what were they carrying?"

"I'll get to that. The three, Waffle Stomper, Ferret and Clown tracked into the clearing. Elena's hiking shoes followed their tracks, and had been for some time."

"How can you tell she was following?"

"Her tracks overlay theirs. She marched into the clearing and there was a confrontation and scuffle."

I sat up straight. "They attacked Elena? Why?"

"I'll get to that too. The men's tracks run off, Ferret and Clown deeper again, while Waffle Stomper went into hiding behind those bushes. And here's the significant thing—after we heard him and he ran away, his tracks came back. When I questioned him I found out he saw Elena's miraculous healing."

"That's not good."

"It's okay. As I said in the living room, I wiped his mind. But I'm getting ahead of myself. After he left again his tracks joined up with Ferret and Clown, who were significantly unburdened this time."

"So spill! What was the burden?"

"A dead body. Human. I didn't even have to dig it up." His nose wrinkled. "I thought about getting Bo, but the day I can't handle a few humans...well. I followed the trio of tracks back to their lair. Guess where they led?"

"I'm afraid to. It didn't take you long, so it must be nearby. The other occupied cabin?"

"You're so smart." He grinned with pride. "Exactly right. I questioned them, and they told me everything." He polished nails on his chest. "I have a certain facility at suggestion."

"So who are they? Why were they carting a dead body around?"

"They're enforcers for a Minneapolis gang. Apparently they do this sort of thing fairly often—cross the state line, take a cabin, then wait until night to bury the bodies. Backwoods and secluded lakes make great dumping grounds."

"And Elena...?"

"Elena tried to arrest them."

I winced. "She would. That's why they attacked her so brutally."

"Yes. They were trying to kill her."

"Frankly, they would have, if Nikos hadn't pulled off a miracle."

He shook his head. "That thing Nikos did, healing Elena—it really took a toll on him. It's a mark of the depth of his love that he would even consider doing what he did."

"Is he really smaller? Older? I thought Twyla and I were seeing things."

"Yes." He closed his eyes and grimaced, and I thought he was disgusted at the horrors Nikos had endured for the sake of a mere human until he said, "Strongwell too. The way he acts around Elena…I'm beginning to understand some of the things I feel for you."

"Feelings? For me?" My body heated, my lips throbbed, and I started to hope for things I shouldn't have. "Good feelings?"

"*Strong* feelings." He opened his eyes directly on mine and they were a hot, piercing violet. "I want you in the worst way."

I shivered. "Oh. Well, my feelings are strong too." My nipples hardened and something farther south put out a welcome mat and started fanning herself coyly. I shushed her. "The problem is, we're so different." And wasn't that an understatement? "But…"

"But?" His gaze never wavered, now so hot I was about to burst into flames.

"For a little simple sex, I might not care. Since you were so brilliant tracking, then questioning the bad guys. We could try it, find out." I patted the bed again. Both my lips and my sex smiled hopefully.

"Oh God. I want to. But…"

I suddenly wanted to set fire to that word.

"I donated to Nikos and now I'm…thirsty." Sticking his hands deep in his pockets, he pushed away from the wall to pace the narrow room.

"Thirsty?"

He stopped. Looked at me. His eyes flared a hungry red. "Really thirsty."

Maybe I should have been scared at the eyes and the glint

of fang. But I trusted him. No matter how thirsty he was, if I said no, I trusted him not to bite me. If I said yes and he bit me, I trusted him not to take too much. Weird.

"I *should* go." His tongue touched the tip of a slightly elongated fang. "But…"

Okay, I wasn't setting fire to that word.

"But with the big guy in the ground and Bo fixated on his wife, that would leave you unprotected."

"Okay. Good." I twiddled my thumbs, so I wouldn't grab him by the ears and kiss him. "How much blood did Nikos lose? It seemed like he was pouring out everything he had, but I know better. The heart stops pumping long before the last pint."

"True, except for us. We can expel nearly all our blood, even without a beating heart."

I blinked. "Wow. That's…incomprehensible. How low are you now? A quart, two? More?"

"I don't know." He jerked one shoulder, an irritated shrug. "I only know that I'm thirsty." He stared at the door, jaw working. "I should head out. Visit my donor humans before sunrise."

Neither of us wanted that. I had a brainstorm. "How about you satisfy my doctorly curiosity, and I'll donate to you in return?"

He turned fiery eyes on me. "Synnove. I'm not going to stop at a standard donation. Not with you."

"You mean you'll take more than a pint?"

"I mean I'll throw you on that bed and pound into you until you're screaming for mercy."

"Oh. Well." I paused to fan myself. "Bonus." I grinned.

His eyes narrowed, red lances. "I thought you distrusted advertising men. You and I, we're not compatible, according to you."

"According to you too, Mr. Marry-Someone-Else. But

that doesn't stop me from being curious." Not the total truth. I owed him better. I met his eyes. "You don't lie because it's good for business. You're secretive because you have to be. Twyla's always talking about happily for now, and she's got a point. I'd like to be happy. How about you?"

He continued to stare with those bright red eyes. Apparently he needed convincing. I stood, snared the hem of my tank top and pulled up, revealing Twyla's ivory silk bra crammed with my bouncy DDs.

His eyes ignited. He swallowed heavily. "How can I satisfy your curiosity?"

I tossed the top and unsnapped my shorts, flashing a peek of crimson bow. "You'll need to get my blood pressure cuff." Most doctors didn't carry a medical bag these days, but I packed a few things for emergencies—mouth-to-mouth masks, bandages, foam disinfectant and the like. My stethoscope and a blood pressure cuff were also inside.

"Cuff, okay." His gaze riveted to that wisp of silk. "Where?"

I unzipped the shorts and peeled them midway down my hips. Enough that, when I did a flirty twist, it showed that I was wearing, not panties, but a thong.

He made a strangled sound. When I peeked back his eyes were soldered to my ass.

"*Where?*"

I smiled. "I left it in the living—"

He poofed. Literally, mist shooting under the door.

I stripped off the shorts and stood in only ivory underwear.

So when the bedroom door opened and he walked in carrying my kit bag, he stopped like he'd been felled. The bag dropped from his twitching hand.

Well. I'd never *wanted* to be beautiful. But with Ric, I was loving it.

"I'll get that." I sauntered over to him, *reeeal* close, and bent to pick up the bag. I did it from the waist, not the knees, kicking my butt in the air.

Yes. I was abandoning my need to be taken seriously, throwing away my desire to be wanted for my mind rather than my body—at least for a while. What had being serious gotten me anyway but bitterness and disappointment?

Besides, his throttled groans made it so much fun. Go Beast.

"I've been meaning to ask." With a wiggle I picked up the bag and sauntered back to the bed. "Do vampires feel pain?"

"Oh yes." His groans emerged. I peeked. His eyes, soldered to my butt again, were a bright shade of red that made me wriggle. "More than humans. Pleasure too. Everything…more."

"Good to know. Why don't you close the door?" I set the bag on my bed, opened it and found my blood pressure cuff. "Then take off your jacket." I cleared off the bag, sat on the bed, and as he shut the door, patted the space next to me. He nearly ripped the jacket, getting it off. When he lurched over, his gait was gratifyingly stiff.

"What…" His voice was raspy. He stood over me, hands clenching and unclenching. Long claws curled into his palms. Verrrry long. Looked like Twyla was right. He said, "What are you doing?"

"You've lost blood. Either your blood pressure will be low, or your system will compensate and it'll be normal. Either will tell me something about vampires that no one has ever known before. Sit." I patted the bed again. "I want to see if you're your basic 120/80."

"Synnove. Your scent…" The tips of his fangs glinted as he spoke. "I can't. I want you too much."

"Which is why we're doing my part of the agreement first. Come on, you have to sit for me to do this."

He swallowed hard. His eyes were actually glowing. "All

right, then. Talk to me. Take my mind off..." He waved at his lower body.

"Okay." I held up the cuff and made my voice cool and professional. "This measures blood pressure. It works by cutting off the blood flow in your arm."

Gingerly he sat. Closed his eyes. Sucked in a deep breath. Choked. "Your scent. Pure sunshine."

"Sunshine has a scent?" I was absurdly pleased, more than if he'd eloquently recited a dozen sonnets. I fastened the cuff around his arm. "I pump air into the cuff until it cuts off the blood flow. I release the air pressure gradually. At some point your pressure equals the cuff pressure, and the blood starts flowing again. I can hear when that happens through the stethoscope." I stopped talking to listen. His pulse beat like a bass drum underwater. "There. It started. The number on the gauge is the pressure reading."

He opened his eyes. They were a stunning violet, no longer red, and his fangs were gone. "Why two numbers then?"

"The higher number matches your heart filling your arteries. I continue releasing the pressure until there's no sound." Slowly, I let more air out. "There. The lower number is the pressure between beats, when the heart rests." I frowned as I released the cuff. "You're at 80/50. You should be fainting." This was amazing. "Something must be keeping you going. Maybe your capillaries are all constricted. Or maybe there's some pseudo air pressure thing going on. Maybe your blood vessels or heart aren't constructed like humans. Maybe—"

"Maybe I'm desperate for you." He grabbed me and yanked me into his rock-solid torso.

Chapter Nineteen

"Maybe I'm desperate for you." Ric Holiday, desperate for me? My mouth was already gaping open in astonishment, so when he kissed me it was easy for him to drive his tongue deep into my mouth.

His lips were burning hot. His taste was darkly male. The cuff dropped from my nerveless hands.

He planted palms on the mattress behind me and leaned forward, pressing me onto the bed. As I flattened beneath him he climbed over me, tongue still deep in my mouth. He wedged his thigh into the crease between mine and thrust insistently. My legs parted. Immediately his thigh filled the gap, nestling tight. Both of us could feel the moist heat of me. He groaned.

He began flexing his thigh, pressing my mons in rhythm with the thrust of his tongue in my mouth. His hand found my breast, cupped it. Hefted its weight. His hot palm felt so good. I curled my legs around his thigh and rocked my hips in counterpoint to his flexing rhythm. That made us both groan.

His thumb found my nipple, already half-peaked under the thin silk. He flicked it. I yelped. He seized the stiff peak between thumb and forefinger and *pinched*.

I shot straight into the cage of his heavy body. I moved maybe half an inch, rippling into his strength like a little bird. I gasped into his open mouth. He took my panting breath, gave it back with masculine fire.

His leg between mine was driving me insane. I'd never fired so hot or so fast. I wanted more. I rubbed my hands over his arms, his back. More, much more—all of him, hot, sweaty and naked. I tried to say that with my petting hands. He only flexed his thigh between my legs and thrust his hot tongue into my mouth and tweaked my nipple until I thought I would explode. Frustrated, I snatched his shirt and yanked it out of his pants so hard it tore.

He swore and released me to rear back on his knees. Strip-strip and the shirt was gone. I was confronted by a tautly muscled, bronzed god.

Desire flooded me at the sight of so much bulging male strength, an elemental *mine* seizing me. My hands grabbed whatever they could. With one hand I clutched an incredibly sculpted external oblique—damn, could have used him to practice my anatomy—and with the other I caught his belt.

Belt. A good idea is a good idea whether you've actually thought of it or not. I whipsawed the end until the buckle loosened, then came undone. It took me forever and I was relieved when he pushed my hands aside to unsnap and unzip. He was a whole lot more autocratic in bed and I was liking it.

Until he stopped. I reached for his pants with a whimper. Again he pushed my hands away; this time I was a lot less pleased. "More," I demanded, waving at the luscious abs, the line of hair rippling down into happy land.

"Too soon." His voice was a deep, feral growl and the tips of fangs flashed as he spoke. I shivered. I'd unleashed something very beastly in the urbane Ric Holiday.

And I loved it.

"*More*." I didn't think it was too soon at all, but apparently I needed to convince him of that.

He had uncaged me when he stripped his shirt and unfastened his pants. I did a half sit-up and reached behind me to flick open the hooks of Twyla's bra. Tearing it off, I tossed it to the floor.

That convinced him pronto.

He roared, circled my ribcage with one arm and hauled me to him. Opening his mouth he latched onto one breast and suckled like a mad man. I gasped at his hot, questing lips, the suction of his mouth, the spike of fang grazing my skin. He wrapped me entirely in that muscled arm, and thrust his free hand between my legs. His fingers dove under the thong so aggressively it tore. Warm, rough skin skidded on my moisture and slipped deep into my body.

I shrieked. One of his fingers began to plunge in concert with his suckling mouth. I clutched brawny back, muscles hard and defined under my fingers. My hands began to rove the wonder of him of their own accord, not subtle or caressing at all but feeling him up like a sexual beast. In my defense, he was attacking my body with the same mindless fever.

He released me to press me back into the bed, licking my breast until it bobbled, hand riding me between the legs. I arched in pleasure so intense it was like tightening a screw. He licked lava trails from one breast to the other, latched on and suckled me brainless. I was mewing and arching and wanting even more when he sank the fingers of his free hand into my DD globe.

Sensation flashed through me, bright and almost painful. I howled. I wasn't sure who was the beast any more. My thighs clenched in reaction, grabbing his riding hand. If I'd thought that would stop him I didn't know him very well. He simply doubled his efforts, shaking my whole bottom until my hips bounced into the mattress. My fever climbed. I was naked and close to orgasm, just from a hand job, and he was still half-dressed. Although if the bulge ballooning against my leg was any indication, he wasn't unaffected.

"You're so beautiful. So hot and wet and lovely." He returned to my mouth, kissing me while his hand squeezed my breast and his other hand rode my pussy so insistently it drove me up the slope of no return. I moaned, long and low.

A rumble started, vibrating where our bodies pressed together, a deep roll of thunder like a lion's purr. "I love your smell." His words were ruffled by the purr. "I love your taste. I want more. I'm starving for you, Synnove."

"You're starving for blood," I gasped.

"No, not blood. For you." He kissed down my jaw, hot open-mouthed kisses, sharpened by the nick of fang. "Only you. Let me bite you." Two fingers thrust into me, sudden, burning. I cried out. He purred louder.

I panted, almost mindless with need. But I managed, "Does it hurt?"

"Mmm. It's exquisite." His tongue traced along the tendon of my neck.

"That doesn't answer—"

"Please, Synnove." He nuzzled my throat. His breath billowed hot on my skin. His fingers drove into me repeatedly. I built higher, higher still. "I'm desperate for you. Say yes." His thumb rasped over my clit, sending waves of need crashing into me. "Say it." His fangs pressed into the sensitive flesh of my throat, not breaking skin but sharply pregnant with sensation. His thumb flicked, hard, sending me so close to the edge I could see the canyon dropping into the warm lagoon below. "Say it *now*."

I launched myself over the edge, flying like a cliff diver.

"Yes!"

Midair, lightning skewered my throat. Twin bolts spiked through my body straight to my groin where his fingers had thrust practically to my eyeballs. They met in an explosion.

I screamed. I didn't fall over the edge of orgasm, I shot straight up into the stratosphere. Climax didn't ripple, it sheared, a jagged bolt of lightning that tore through the night sky. I came so hard my brain lit up, my ears rang and my body wrenched apart.

Slowly, relaxation enveloped me like freshly laundered sheets. When I finally recovered enough to open my eyes, Ric was licking my neck and purring madly. His eyes were closed and his expression was blissful.

I could imagine what he'd look like if he'd bitten me during actual intercourse.

I yawned. I felt fresh, new, sleepy. My mind wandered. For not having gotten any, he certainly looked satisfied. Maybe with vampire physiology, he'd orgasmed from biting.

I yawned again and roused myself enough to tap his forehead. "Hey. You. Did you want something other than my blood?"

"I want…" He placed a final broad swipe on my neck and sat up. His chest was flushed and his nipples were so tight they were pinpricks. The top of a sizeable erection jutted from his gaping fly. "I want everything."

Or actually, it came out "I wan' e'ery'ing," because his fangs dented his lower lip. His eyes glowed bright red.

Again, maybe I should have been scared but I was only intrigued. Because this was Ric. I wanted this from him. Needed it. My own Happily-For-Now.

"Everything, hmm?" I waved a hand at my thighs, parted in utter relaxation, glistening with my climax. "In case you hadn't noticed, I'm sort of ready for everything." My wave dislodged air scented with my satisfaction.

He choked—and fell to his knees with his head between my legs.

His first long lick popped my eyes open, revved me higher than ever. His tongue dug deep between my swollen labia, caught on my rising red clit. I gasped, automatically trying to close my legs. His palms stopped me, firmly asking me to keep my thighs where they were. When I did, he really got to work.

He lapped hard, branding me with hot breath and fiery tongue. It got rougher as he licked, until he was toweling me with his lapping. When my mouth opened on a moan, he thrust a finger into me, then two. I groaned. His purr started again, rumbling low, pausing as he swallowed. He beat against me rhythmically, thrusting and driving with fingers and tongue. My breasts bobbled with the force of his laps. My body started jerking from the power of his.

He opened his mouth on my sex, fangs pressing the length of my labia.

I whimpered at the volcanic heat. "Don't…don't bite there."

His eyes flashed up at me, red and hungry, but somehow I knew he was trying to reassure me. He pressed his tongue against my rigid clit, then sealed his lips on my pussy and sucked.

I came so fast I jerked against his hard hold. He thrust his fingers and slapped clit and sucked right through it, spiraling me into another buildup before I could even shout. He thrust and sucked until I writhed on the bed, until I thought my skin would turn inside out.

When he'd driven me to the peak of insanity yet again—he stopped.

I throttled a scream of frustration. He rose between my legs, all that beautiful sleek musculature, rose to his knees, set a foot on the floor and spun off the bed. I cried out in disappointment—

Just as he shucked his pants.

My cry cut off. I gaped. His erection thrust huge and smooth from his hips. The claws predictor was right on. If six inches was average, Ric was two men.

I came to my knees on the mattress. My hand reached out automatically, stopping just before I took him. My eyes sought his, asking permission. His burned dark red. With careful fingers he led my hand to his cock. I took him in my hand.

He throbbed, smooth and warm. His purr was practically deafening now. So I had to. Really I did.

I opened my mouth and sucked him deep.

And choked. I didn't have much gag reflex but I'd never experienced that much man. Ric's cock filled my mouth and throat and then some.

"Synnove." Ric groaned, but his hands caressed my hair, reassuring, warm. "You don't have to."

I looked up at him with one eye. "Is that a challenge?"

"No, it's—gah!"

I opened my throat and thrust my mouth over him as far as I could. Concentrating, I managed to stuff him down until my nose bumped the incredible muscles of his abdomen.

He throttled a long groan. His hands clenched in my hair, and his cock went rigid in my mouth and I knew I'd rung his bell like he'd rung mine.

And then, as a pièce de résistance, I drew slowly off him, letting him feel each ripple of cartilage, each rasp of tongue, all polished off with a knife-fine scrape of my teeth.

He threw back his head, gritting his own teeth against a roar of pleasure, perspiration glistening along his fine torso.

Still in control. So not happening.

I grabbed his hips for purchase, clamped my lips tight around his cock and bobbed along his length. He gasped. I lapped and swirled as I rode him with my mouth. He howled. I drove and tongued until he was trembling.

Then I took him down my throat, to the hilt—and swallowed.

He came, great hard contractions of his balls I could feel on my chin. The roar that he'd been throttling erupted full-voiced.

It went on and on. I lost control and ended up wearing some. But it was entirely worth it to see the extreme pleasure on his face, and then see him relax into bliss.

He collapsed to his hands on the mattress, head down, panting. I started to roll off the bed to get a towel. He snared his shirt, more agile than I would have expected given his state. Gently, he used his own shirt to wipe me.

Then he laid me on the bed and slicked his tongue along my swollen sex. The orgasm delayed by his shucking his pants rolled through me, a thundershower power-washing away every tension, every obstacle.

After, we lay together on the narrow bed. It felt less tight than close. Comfortable. Right.

It felt right.

Me and Ric Holiday, vampire and ad man, felt right. That should have scared me almost as much as what had happened in the woods.

But I try not to lie to myself, and I wasn't going to start now. It felt right—maybe because it *was* right? I didn't like the idea, but in all honesty I had to consider it.

I put aside thoughts of getting rid of him and considered lasting happiness instead. A relationship.

A fairy tale come true.

Not. Possible.

I was missing something. Couples adjust to each other but we were far too different. Dissimilar at a basic level. Different to the point of being discordant.

But what if, despite that, we were meant for each other?

That did scare me. If, despite being true opposites, we were stuck with each other anyway, we'd rub each other raw. Which, considering the last half hour, wasn't unpleasant…

Smack me with a *lutfisk*. Emotional fire in the bedroom most often translated to bloody strife outside it. Like social, vivacious Twyla and her self-contained, masterful Spartan. Like brash, confident Elena and her householder Bo…

No, they all seemed pretty happy, now that I thought about it.

So why couldn't I have that? Why couldn't I find happiness with Ric?

My stomach swooped. Why not?

Warmth filled me, surprising with its strength. I'd always pictured myself as a doctor, smiling at patients, discussing treatments. But even more clearly I could see a future with Ric—us sitting together reading, doing dishes, discussing our work over a cup of tea.

Maybe we could try it. Try…a relationship. I turned to Ric, opened my mouth to tell him my thoughts.

He was on his back, snoring softly, out like a light.

Dammit, this was important. I put my hand on his shoulder to shake him awake. Got distracted by velvety skin over rock. Mmm, nice. I forgot to shake, caressed instead—

A shadow filtered into the edge of my vision. I sucked in air. I swear I did not scream.

I did squeak a little.

Ric's eyes flew open. He sat up so fast the covers flew. "What the hell? Aiden?"

The shadow inside the room was a *man*. I shrieked at that, a little girly yip, and grasped covers to my chest. Shrinking violet modesty and shrieking at shadows. Damn it, if this was what having a steady guy made of me, I'd have to rethink my relationship decision.

Beyond Ric, the shadow solidified. "Sorry to interrupt." The laconic voice had a pained amusement in it. "But this couldn't wait."

"What's so fucking important—?"

"The painting is gone."

Chapter Twenty

"*What*?" Ric shot to his feet. "When? Where? How?"

The shadowman Aiden was wearing a black leather coat and looking bulkier than I remembered. "When, about an hour ago. Where, from where you told me to put it, the safe in your office. And how? It was an inside job. No new scents."

"Damn. We need to find it." Ric started throwing on clothes, boxers, torn shirt and one sock. "Let's get back to the office—"

"Problem. Sunrise is minutes away. I'm surprised you didn't notice."

Ric collapsed, half-dressed, on the bed. He closed his eyes and shook his head. "I was distracted."

"I can tell." Aiden's eyebrows waggled suggestively.

"You." Ric cracked an eye. "You're cruising for a fist to the jaw."

"You can try." Then black eyebrows lowered and Aiden's lips compressed. "Although it's no more than I deserve for losing the painting."

"Don't. You didn't lose it, it was stolen from us. The

question is, by who?"

"Someone better than us."

"Aiden, stop it. There's no one better than you, not at tracking, not at intelligence gathering. So, an inside job?"

"No break-in, the safe wasn't blown and then there's the timing—almost the minute I returned. Someone was waiting at Holiday Buzz. Watching."

"Someone we trusted has betrayed us." Ric made a low, terrible sound.

A cell phone rang, muffled. I startled.

"It's mine." Ric snatched up his pants and extracted his phone. "Holiday."

The voice on the other end sounded tinny, mechanical. Ric's jaw worked hard; he didn't like what the caller was saying at all.

I exchanged a glance with Aiden. Any softness had gone from his face, leaving only the cool ruthless shadowman.

Ric's jaw abruptly stopped working. His eyes flicked to me.

Suddenly his face drained of color. He snapped, "Out of the question. This conversation is over." He ended the call with an abrupt clip of his thumb.

"The thief?" Aiden asked.

"Yes. Using a voice disguiser, unfortunately." Ric put on the pants then thrust the phone into his pocket.

"What did he want?" Wrapping myself in the sheet, I stood to put a hand on Ric's arm. He was trembling with rage.

"Money. And other considerations to be named. Delivered at three this afternoon." Ric's nostrils were white and the tips of his canines protruded. "Whoever this asshole is, he's got some nerve."

"Steady, Ric." Aiden slid away from the window, where dawn was creeping through the cracks between the vertical blinds. "At least we know the painting is safe. The question is, what do we do now?"

"I can go out in the sun," I said. "Maybe I can deliver the money."

Ric spun on me. "Not. Happening."

I stepped back at his vehemence. "But I thought this painting is important. That it's some sort of leverage against Nosferatu."

"You figured that out? You're quick. Most of the time I like that." He ran a hand through his hair.

"Which is his way of saying yes," Aiden drawled. He leaned, arms crossed, against the door. "The portrait is…*was* his insurance that Nosferatu won't attack his household or Holiday Buzz. We have to get it back."

"But not by paying any damned ransom at three in the damned afternoon." Ric glared—at me.

"*Sorry.* Only trying to help."

"Help." Ric whipped toward Aiden. "Can you trace that phone call?"

"Not from here."

"Damn it."

"Ric, what's really wrong?" I touched his shoulder. His muscles were as tense as steel cables. "Is it the sunlight? Do you need to, um, go to ground or something?"

"No." He made an obvious effort to relax. "I just hate feeling this exposed and not being able to do something about it."

"Maybe we're asking the wrong question." Aiden started pacing, lean, springy. "Not who stole the painting, but who could get into the safe?"

"That's good," Ric said. "Nosferatu. He has some East European techies on his team."

"His lieutenant Giuseppe Marrone," Aiden said. "Marrone's a tech."

"Unless it's that Ancient One guy," I said.

Sudden, horrified silence.

"What?" I said. "He's got techies on his team too, doesn't he? And he knows everything, from what I can tell."

Ric shuddered. "If the Ancient One is against us, we're as good as dead."

"Oh. Okay." I held up one placating hand. "Not Elias."

"Camille," Aiden said. "She doesn't have technical skills of her own, but she could seduce someone to crack the safe."

"Seduce...?" I snapped my fingers. "And an inside job. Chicken Little."

"Who?" Ric said.

"Sorry, I meant Charles Little. That cock's comb hairstyle and red wattle neck remind me of a chicken... Ric, the point is, he looked awfully taken with Camille at yesterday's meeting."

"Little wants Holiday Buzz," Aiden said. "He's made no secret of that."

Ric's face hardened. "And he knows the combination to the safe."

Aiden nodded. "That's it, then. The instant the sun goes down, I'm going after the bastard."

"We go together," Ric growled.

"You're forgetting something," I said. "He wants the money at three p.m.. If he doesn't get it, he might destroy the picture, and there goes your leverage."

Ric glared—again, at *me*. "I won't let him back me into a corner."

I didn't understand the glare. I was only trying to help, and it was a reasonable solution. "Why are you so stubborn about this? If it's the money—"

"It's not the money."

"But—"

"Synnove, that's enough!"

I drew myself up to my full height and glared coldly.

"May I remind you, you can't stop me?"

He stepped in until we were toe to toe. "Oh, can't I?"

"Yikes," Aiden said. "Get a room."

I jerked away from Ric, my face hot but I couldn't help smiling a little at him. "We're a pair, aren't we?"

"Yes. We are." Ric's tense expression eased. "Synnove, I'm sorry. I'm worried, but I shouldn't have taken it out on you."

"Me too."

"Still here," Aiden said. "And gooey making-up eyes are as bad as frustrated sex yelling. Can we nip all of this in the bud? Why don't you call Little? Let him know we're on to him."

I got the impression that Aiden knew what really had Ric going nuclear. That with his vampire hearing, he'd heard what Little had said in that first phone call.

Ric smiled down at me. "Good idea."

He dug in his pocket for his phone, thumbed up a number and pressed it to his ear. "Charles. I know you have the portrait. I want it back. Let's talk terms."

"It doesn't matter that you know," Charles Little said into Ric's ear after a shocked pause. "I still want Synnove Byornsson here at three."

Ric clutched the phone so hard the plastic *cricked*. When, as a child, he'd sneaked into that wagon headed east, he'd been trying for a better life. Now he was rich and successful. But his life really hadn't been better, not until an aggravating, luscious female had walked into it.

A few hundred years of sex with both human and vampire females had given him a fine taste for it. He'd thought the body rush of pleasure it gave him was the epitome of delight.

Delight, ha. Even kissing Synnove went far beyond mere delight. Orgasms with her made his whole brain detonate with sunshine and his blood fizz with joy.

In two sentences, all of that was threatened.

"No." Ric snarled the word. That a man he'd trusted would betray him this way—especially for mere greed—made him shake with anger. "Not negotiable."

"Every time you say that, the price goes up," Little said. "I want a half million dollars—and control of Holiday Buzz. Majority stock transferred to me at three p.m.. Today. And Synnove will deliver the authorizations in person."

Ric's chest tightened. All the times Nosferatu and his sadistic trainers had threatened Ric's life, he hadn't felt this desperate.

"Is she there with you now?" Charles said, softly menacing. "Let's hear what she has to say. Why don't you put her on the line?"

"*No.*" Icicles stabbed Ric's heart. Charles Little had just made himself Enemy Number One. And this had ramped up to war.

Ric summoned his predator's instincts and his businessman's brain, neither far from him. The ice burned away in a tumult of angry fire. "You're not talking to her. And she's not going anywhere."

"That's too bad," Little said. "Because if I don't get what I want, I have another interested party. Mr. Nosferatu."

That cracked Ric's anger. "Damn it, I can't believe you're doing this to me."

"And I can't believe it took me so long." He cackled. Chicken Little indeed.

"I'll get you your stock," Ric spat. "Hell, you can have the company. But you may not have—" he cut a glance at his beautiful blonde with the too-sharp eyes, "—any person under my protection."

Now to move the sale along. "I'll set up the stock transfer and the cash." There. That would remind Little what he wanted that Ric would give. "Electronic, contingent on my ratification. We'll meet at the office, tonight at nine. You bring the portrait and the receiving account numbers. When I get the picture, I'll complete the transfers."

"Do you think I'm an idiot? Camille told me what you are, Holiday—well, I knew your looks couldn't be natural. I'm not insane enough to meet you after dark. The girl is not a negotiable item, nor is the time. I'll have to contact my other interested party."

"Little, wait—" The connection cut. Ric felt like he was breathing fire. "He hung up on me." He stared at his phone. He'd lost control of the situation, like the time he'd had to abandon Eloise.

His anger chilled, leaving him scared.

"What did he want?" Synnove asked.

He fell into her clear blue eyes. Reaching out with a thumb to caress her healthy pink skin he breathed in her light clean scent. She had outer beauty, yes. But it was a reflection of her inner beauty, her inner strength.

His heart rate slowed. She was a strong, beautiful woman, not a helpless little girl. "He wanted what we figured. Money. Stock. Control of the company."

"There's more," she said. "What else?"

She was with him and almost ahead of him. He'd have his work cut out for him, keeping up with her. He wanted a lifetime of it. "He wants it through an agent." He bit off the words in a way that hopefully made her see the topic was closed. But to be sure he followed up with something to distract her. "I need access to a computer to set up the transfers. Do you have one here at the cabin?"

"No." Her tone was suspicious and her beautiful blue eyes were sharply narrowed. "What about your phone?"

"Normally, but I'm out range for my network."

"Except you just took a phone call."

Shit. "I don't have the right app. Don't you have *anything*?"

Aiden raised a black brow at him. He knew both their phones could tap dance and lip sync the "Star Spangled Banner" if they needed them to. Ric shook his head. Distracting Synnove was more important.

Synnove grimaced. "Twyla might have a 4G tablet. She's plugged in."

He curved his lips in his best coaxing smile. "Could you go ask her for me?"

A beat, the longest of his life. Then she said, "All right." She snatched a long T-shirt and a pair of jeans from a drawer. Pointed at Aiden. "You. Turn around."

"I'd rather not."

Ric could have cheerfully used a cherry pitter on his friend's crotch.

She smiled sweetly. "You want me to cath you with a silver needle—and a mallet?"

Aiden's lips quirked. "Okay, okay, I'm turning."

She slipped out of the sheet and into the tee and jeans, sliding her phone into a pocket. "This may take a bit. Twyla was bushed after last night."

"Take your time," Ric said.

After Synnove had gone, Aiden raised both brows. "You've only delayed the inevitable. She knows the original three p.m. delivery time means Charles intends a human to bring the ransom. It's only a small hop to figuring out the human is her."

"I know." Ric's gums were itching around his fangs.

"What if it doesn't work?"

"Then I keep her here by bodily force."

"Good luck with that." Aiden leaned his long body

against the wall. "If she doesn't go, Little will sell the picture to Nosferatu."

"Can't be helped. We'll have to appeal to the Ancient One in Iowa. His Alliance can protect my humans."

A low *brrr* of displeasure sounded from Aiden. Even his quirk of a smile had disappeared. "I did not run from one superpower to get trapped by another."

Ric's hands shot out. "What do you suggest? I must protect my humans. I'll do what I have to."

"By giving up our precious freedom? Which, may I remind you, we nearly died to win?" Aiden's only sign of anger was the slight lengthening of his fangs and an edge to his words. "We said we'd never break neutrality. *Never.*"

"I don't like it any more than you do. But principles don't mean squat when lives are on the line."

"I disagree. That's exactly when they matter most."

"I will not sentence my humans to torture and worse at our enemy's hands, not when a simple phone call can do something about it."

Aiden's fangs receded. "Ric, please. I can't live with another overlord. Not even one as supposedly benign as Elias. There have to be other options."

"There may be. But I don't know what they are, and it's too late. We're a couple of small fish caught between two fighting dogs. I'm picking Elias as ally. In fact, I'd better start negotiations now, while Synnove's out." He pulled his phone and dialed a number he'd known forever but thought he'd never need.

Just as Synnove walked back into the room.

I left the bedroom on Ric's quest, shutting the door behind me. I was about to knock on Twyla's door when my phone rang.

I didn't recognize the number. "Hello?"

"Synnove. It's Charles Little."

"Hello, Charles." The weasel. "How did you get my number?"

"Please. I have connections."

"Or you looked it up in my client file. Give the portrait back."

"I want to. Your lover won't cooperate."

"What?"

"Oh, didn't he tell you? Why am I not surprised? I offered to return it."

"Sure, for ownership of Holiday Buzz."

"At first it was only money. I raised the price when Holiday wouldn't cooperate. It's a controlling interest now. I might rename it Little Buzz."

"You're kidding, right?" Might as well call it the Sky-Is-Falling-Don't-Use-Us Buzz. I switched ears. "Doesn't matter. Holiday's cooperating now. Why are you calling me?"

"To see if he's also honoring my other request. I'd hate to have to raise the price again—or sell to Nosferatu."

My spine iced. "What other request?"

"That you bring it. In person."

Well crap. That explained Ric's chest-beating. "Sure. Three p.m., right?"

"Right." Little's tone was smug. "Don't be late."

I leaned my head against the wall outside Twyla's bedroom. Great. I had to meet Chicken Little. Ric would try to stop me. But Ric needed that painting, so I'd have to escape somehow.

Worse, Charles specifically asked for *me*, which had a distinct odor of trap. While I wanted to help Ric and get his picture, I needed to do it *without* Lois Laning it and getting captured or worse. I mean, I wanted to help, not end up being rescue bait. I needed backup.

Immediately I thought of Twyla. Not only could she help me with Little's stock and cash transfer—she could make any business system sit up and beg—it would solve the heroine-goes-alone-because-she's-too-stupid-to-live angle. Twyla could call the cops. And she has a mean right hook.

Okay, one thing solved. But what about the meet itself? Because, while Twyla and I could take out Mr. Scrawny Chicken Little, if he had sublet any black-clad muscle from Nosferatu, we'd be in serious trouble.

Except wouldn't I have a crowbar advantage? Little would want his cash and stock options. As long as I held onto that, I had room to maneuver.

So. If Little was alone, I'd negotiate for the picture. If he wasn't, I'd remind him I had the transfer and when he hesitated, run like hell.

Okay, another thing solved. Now I had to figure out how to get to my car without Ric following.

Vampires were lightning fast. Daylight slowed Aiden fighting the six goons, but not until he was directly exposed.

Well, hopefully Twyla could help with that problem too, since she knew more about v-guys than me.

Okay. What did I do when petty and mean Little double-crossed me like yesterday? Because going head-to-head, he couldn't outsmart me.

Head to head. Dammit.

Little had outmaneuvered me, Camille had outmaneuvered me, exactly because, in trying to be fair, *I'd gone in with my head.* Little had gone in with Camille, and she went in with everything she had. Head, heart and body.

Their side had won because *I'd held back*, and she hadn't.

It rocked me to my soul. In some ways, she'd deserved the win. I'd held myself above all that, and it lost me the account.

Now Ric's people were at stake. And from the tension

in both Ric's and Aiden's reaction, something even more personal was on the line if Nosferatu got his hands on the portrait. Maybe their freedom, or their lives.

That hit me with absolute, awful clarity. *Ric's life,* at stake. Not if I could do something about it.

"No holding back. Not this time." This time I *had* to win. I jammed my phone into my pocket and jacked my spine straight.

A soft snore leaked through Twyla's door. Okay, I'd wake her, but not yet. I sneaked into her room and opened her racy underwear drawer. One of the bras was a black push-up that would plump my tits into my chin. Its matching thong was faced with a heart so tiny I'd have to shave everything but a sliver to make it work.

Yes. I'd do *anything* to get the job done.

Including flashing my boobs at Chicken Little.

Part of me was appalled. Another was curiously set free. *Time for beastie to play.*

I grabbed Twyla's tablet and headed back to my room.

But when I slipped in with my black lace weapons and decoy tablet, Ric was on speaker phone. "Mr. Elias, you don't know me, but…"

He flashed me a glance and a grimace. Obviously he hadn't wanted me to hear this. Which of course made me determined to stay. He saw it in my eyes, sighed and started again. "I'm—"

"Ric Holiday." The answering voice was from the depths of hell.

I clutched Twyla's underwear and tablet to my chest, my heart suddenly thudding like a parade bass drum. That *voice*…even on speaker phone, it was as deep and timbral as if a giant California redwood were speaking.

Ric's head jerked back in astonishment. "You know me?"

"Of course. Who is with you?" A pause. "I hear a

human. I assume it is Dr. Synnove Byornsson. And…Aiden Blackthorne, I believe."

Aiden stiffened, his expression so horrified it was almost funny. "You *heard* me?"

"No. But the way sound is folding, a third person was in the room. You're one of the few of our kind clever enough to be truly noiseless."

"Not clever." Aiden shook his head and leaned again against the wall, seemingly relaxed but his biceps were twitching. "Or I would have made a counterfeit noise, pretending to be someone else."

Elias chuckled at that, a sound so rich and masculine that my nipples peaked just having it ruffle over my skin. "That might have worked. Shall we try next time?"

"Well, now you'll be expecting it." Aiden almost smiled.

"Mr. Elias," Ric said. "I don't have a great deal of time. I'm calling because I hope you can help me. An article of leverage to keep Nosferatu away from my humans has been stolen. I'm going to try to get it back but if I don't… My humans need protection."

"I assume you mean my protection. What are you prepared to do in exchange?"

Ric took a deep breath. He flicked apologetic eyes at Aiden, who glared black daggers at him. "I'll join the Iowa Alliance. I'll fight for you."

"Hmm. While the idea is intriguing, and you and Mr. Blackthorne have certain unique talents I'd be interested in, I have to say no."

"No?" Ric stared at the phone. "*No*? But why?"

"It's simply not in your best interests to ally with me at this time."

"Not in *my* best interests?" Ric's fangs flashed as he spoke, and his tendons on the hand holding the phone had gone rigid. "What the hell does that mean?"

"Mr. Holiday. What do you know about the situation between Nosferatu and me? Not between the Alliance and the Coterie, but between us as individuals—"

"He hates you." Ric's tone was flat with anger.

A pause. Obviously Elias wasn't interrupted often. But when his cave-deep voice came again it was mild. "Hates, yes. Do you know why?"

Ric opened his mouth to snap something, but Elias's words must have penetrated because he slowly closed his mouth and frowned. When he spoke again his fangs were gone. "No."

"Does Mr. Blackthorne have an idea?"

Aiden cocked one black brow. "If Nosferatu only opposed you, he would simply attack. But he goes out of his way to appear reasonable."

Ric snapped his fingers. "He doesn't want to give you reason to attack him in return. He's *afraid* you."

"Yes."

"But why?"

"Let's just say Nosferatu and I have a past."

I'd taken patient histories from corpses who were more forthcoming. This Elias might have taught Nikos how to be taciturn.

"I don't see how that affects my joining the Alliance." Ric's fangs started to emerge again.

"Nosferatu is angry because you and Mr. Blackthorne escaped him. He'd like to make an example of you."

My breath caught. Ric and Aiden had escaped Nosferatu? When had they been in the bad guy's clutches?

"So what else is new?" Ric started pacing, short, jerky turns around the bedroom. "He already sent a goon squad. Without the threat of the picture, he'll do worse. Which is why I'm asking for your help."

"But you've only made him angry. He doesn't hate you."

"He doesn't fear us," Aiden said.

"Exactly. Remember, the threat the portrait represents is useful but it's not the only leverage you have."

Ric spun, lips tight over extended fangs. "Which means *what*?"

"Mr. Holiday, listen to me carefully. You have a previous connection with Nosferatu. You might reinstate that connection...with the right persuader. As long as he doesn't hate you, that is."

"The right *persuader*? What, a battering ram?"

"Don't be obtuse," Elias snapped. "You're letting your emotions block your brain. Stop it."

"You're not helping—"

"I am, if you listen. Your job is advertising, correct? You know what will make a person buy a product. You're good at it. Pretend Nosferatu's another client. What would he buy from you?"

"That's ridiculous." Ric stalked the room in even more of a frenzy. "Nosferatu won't buy *anything* from me."

A breath of air over the phone might have been a deep sigh. "I'm sorry you feel that way."

This was going nowhere fast. While I didn't have Ric's ability to sell sand in the Sahara, I *had* learned how to coax patient details. "Mr. Elias, please. We don't have your wealth of knowledge and experience. Can you tell us what Ric can do to protect his people? What would you do in his place?"

A pause. I held my breath. If Elias wanted to help, this would hopefully start him. If not, nothing would.

Finally the deep voice came again. "Very well. Mr. Holiday. You know about Nosferatu's daughter? Eloise?"

I gasped. Big Bad had a daughter?

But Ric only nodded impatiently. "Yes."

"What do you know about her mother?"

"She died soon after they came to Nosferatu's compound

to live with us."

The air I'd sucked in exploded out of my lungs. Ric and Aiden had *lived* with the wicked old vampire?

"How old was she at the time?"

"Six. Look, what will going over ancient history do to protect my people?"

"Ancient doesn't begin to apply until before the tenth century. Think. Where were Eloise and her mother before coming to Chicago?"

Ric stopped pacing. He exchanged a thunderstruck glance with Aiden. "I don't know."

"They lived with me. As did Nosferatu, for a time."

"*What*?"

"He was my lieutenant. Until 1806, when he made a human member of my household, a young woman, pregnant. Rather than admitting his culpability in the matter, he silenced her through intimidation and pain. To make matters worse, when she began to show, he drove her out of my home. Do you know the fate of a young pregnant woman alone in the early 1800s? It wasn't pretty.

"I found out and immediately returned her to my care. I would have ripped off Nosferatu's head."

I would have ripped off anything I could reach.

"But she begged me to spare the father of her child. Begged me so strenuously that she went into premature labor. She was having hysterics, endangering both the child's life and her own. I had to agree. I couldn't harm him, but I could and did expel him from my home, and my life.

"Nosferatu hated that I cast him out, and hated even more that I did so for the female he had discarded, a mere human. He was furious that I favored her over him.

"I believe he left the country for a time, fleeing to Europe. He met Dracula in London—this was before I had captured and interred the count permanently. Nosferatu became enamored of that one's power—you may not know this, Dr. Byornsson, but Dracula is pure vampire. Nosferatu sought that purity himself, thinking it would give him power, and purged himself of all he could that made him human. By the time he returned, he was as you knew him, Mr. Holiday. Spindly and mean."

"Smaller?" I said without thinking. "Like Nikos?"

"Not like Nikos. Nosferatu lost much of what made him human. Nikos lost much of what makes him vampire. Which reminds me. While Nikos will continue to need donations of human blood three times a month, more will not help him heal faster. Only vampire blood will restore his vampire nature. That, and time. Please tell Ms. Tafel that, would you, Dr. Byornsson?"

"Um…okay."

"Good. Nosferatu settled in Chicago—near enough to me to test his new abilities, but far enough that he could hide if needed—and proved to himself he was the victor by seducing Eloise's mother back to him. The rest is as you know."

"So why didn't you rip his head off when he returned?" Aiden spat. "Would have saved us a lot of grief."

"Mr. Blackthorne. I gave my word to the mother."

"Under duress," Ric said. "That doesn't count."

"Perhaps not for you. Your mate might disagree."

Ric jerked as if he'd been jabbed by a fat G needle. "I'm not mated."

"Of course not," the dark voice said smoothly. "Simply put, I do not break my word except *in extremis*."

"Not even for a greater good?" Aiden asked.

"What is the greater good, Mr. Blackthorne? Tethering a scapegoat might save some, but it's never good for the goat. Mr. Holiday. You have all the information you need to protect your humans, and I have talked long enough. Goodbye."

Chapter Twenty-One

"Wait," Ric said. "I—damn. The cocky bastard hung up."

While he was still staring at the phone in his hand, I stuffed Twyla's underwear into my cleavage to hide it. It was so fine it fit with room to spare. I set the tablet down.

"That was *not* helpful." Ric ran an agitated hand through his hair. "I don't have any other ideas. Do you?"

"Kill the whole lot of them?" Aiden said. "Starting with Elias?"

"I'm considering it." Ric slid his phone into his pants pocket.

I put a palm up. "Killing later, guys. Explanations now. First tell me about this painting."

They stared at me. Finally Ric blew air and nodded at Aiden. "Show her. She deserves to know, since she's the one who got Elias to open up for us."

As Aiden extracted his phone I mused. "Eloise, Elias. Hey, you don't suppose Eloise's mother named her after Elias?"

Aiden gave a startled laugh. "Wouldn't that chap

Nosferatu's ass?" He thumbed up a picture on the phone. "This is double-whammy blackmail."

A portrait filled the small screen of a man standing outside a wooden two-story house wearing a brown cutaway coat with high collar, elaborate cravat and waistcoat, tight tan trousers and high black boots.

Aiden pointed at the man's hand. "Note the gun."

The man held a typical first-Thanksgiving turkey blaster braced against his foot. "Nice," I said. "Is it extremely valuable? Or is there a problem with it?"

"There's a problem, but not with the gun," Ric said. "That's a blunderbuss. Identified by the flared barrel."

"They're short," Aiden said. "Especially compared to muskets. The barrel of a blunderbuss is usually under two feet long, the whole thing three feet or less."

I stared closer. "Wouldn't a three-foot gun hit mid-hip or thigh on a man? This one is chest high."

"That's the point," Aiden said. "It's not a long gun. It's a stunted vampire."

"Okay. So he's stunted, so what? He's still nasty, isn't he? A menace?"

"Yes. But you have to consider vampire psychology."

I slewed a glance at him. "Vampires have shrinks?"

"I mean we play a lot of mind games—and dominance games. This picture is evidence that Nosferatu is spindly. He might as well have saplings for legs and twigs for arms."

"Pinched," Ric said. "His body, his face, his guts, hell, his whole personality."

"And that's bad, why?" I asked.

"You know other vampires," Ric said. "Me, Bo, Nikos. What's the first thing you notice about us?"

"Well, I hate to be shallow, but you're all tall."

"Exactly. I'm the youngest at a couple hundred years and I'm six two. The Viking is taller than me and eight hundred years older; and the Spartan, who's several millenniums old, is a mountain." Ric frowned. "*Was* a mountain."

I reeled at Nikos's age. "Several…thousand…?"

"The point is," Aiden said, "size means age, and age means power. If Nosferatu's followers saw this, his size would make them question his power. His right to rule."

I shook away the implications of *several thousand years* to concentrate. "Doesn't everyone already know that?"

"No. He compels them to remember him as bigger than he is. Which is why the picture's so important. It's evidence, and away from his mental influence."

"But this is the Pinterest and instant video age. Aren't there other pictures?"

"He's scrawny but he's not dumb," Aiden said. "He's careful to stand against false measures—a couple steps up or in diffuse lighting."

"Okay. But didn't Elias say the reason Nosferatu is scrawny is because he's more like Dracula? Purer vampire, which is actually scarier."

"Won't make a difference to his followers," Ric said. "Like the Nixon/Kennedy televised debate, we've got some pretty serious caveman biases toward the taller, more relaxed guy as the better leader. Besides, there's a second, more important feature on this particular painting. Show her his face."

Aiden clicked zoom. A small black mark marred Nosferatu's cheek, a double wave, like a line drawing of a bird or bat. "All the vampires I've seen have flawless skin. Is that what I think it is?"

"A birthmark, yes. Tattoos and scars disappear when we turn. But some birthmarks survive the change."

My brain clicked. The body's original DNA encoding…

"Nosferatu sees it as a sign of his destiny," Aiden said, and my thought disappeared. He pointed to a small window in the house behind Nosferatu. "She has it too."

I took the phone from him and stared. "I see a smudge."

"It's a face at the window. The resolution isn't good enough to capture what the artist's eye—and brush—did on the original portrait."

I handed the phone back. "Nosferatu's daughter?"

"He never claimed Eloise as his daughter," Ric said. "But even before Elias's story, we suspected. She has the same birthmark."

"Which, once we pointed it out to her, very suspiciously started getting covered with dirt and paint," Aiden said.

I said, "And you all lived together—at Nosferatu's. What's that all about?"

Ric and Aiden exchanged a glance. Aiden's tiny shake of his head said *Don't say anything. It's secret.* Ric's eyes flicked to me and I could practically hear his *Tell her. She'll figure it out anyway.*

I added my own *Bet your sweet ass I will.*

Aiden sighed. "Are all immune females this irritating?"

"There are two more in this cabin," I said. "Want to find out?"

"Nope. In the early 1800s, Nosferatu built an army of assassins loyal only to him. He did it by turning boys who had no parents, no homes, into vampires."

"Us," Ric said.

I filed that away. "So the wicked leader of bad-guy vamps raised a gang of assassins—and brought his sweet little daughter to live in their midst?"

"We weren't assassins then," Aiden said. "More like trainees."

"He tried to keep her away from us," Ric said. "But Aiden was sort of our resident adviser and he had special privileges and freedom of movement. We heard her sobs one day and followed them. We found her in a back room with a princess bed and silken clothes and royal food—and nothing else."

"No toys?" I asked. "No teddy bears or books or anything for comfort?"

"Poor little kid," Aiden said. "We broke in the first time but after that she welcomed us. We played with her when we could."

"We tried to shield her," Ric said. "But we weren't that much older. And we tried to take her with us when we escaped. But we failed."

"No. She refused to leave." Aiden's tone made it plain they'd been over this many times before. "She'd developed an attachment to him. She *wanted* to stay."

"Stockholm Syndrome," Ric snarled.

"Maybe. But I think he honestly loves her, in his own warped way."

"Poor, sweet little thing, it's impossible not to love her."

Aiden shook his head. "She was a sweet child then, but we have no idea what she's turned into by now."

"Turned into *now*?" I asked.

"She's still alive." Aiden thumbed up another picture. "Or at least she was fifty years ago."

A young woman, her ironed-straight hair flowing past her waist, marched amid a crowd outside the Chicago International Amphitheatre. The '68 Democratic Convention protest? She carried a poster decorated with flowers and peace signs. "How do you know that's Eloise? Her cheeks are flawless—no birthmark."

"I was there," Aiden said flatly. "She covered the birthmark with makeup, but it was her."

"So you talked with her?"

"No." Aiden's mouth thinned. "She was wearing pink."

"Ah." I nodded knowingly. "Such a fashion faux-pas. I wouldn't be seen with her either."

Ric said, "That was our signal to be left alone. Like a sock on the doorknob to roommates."

I shook my head. "Even if it was Eloise, it was fifty years ago. You don't know she's alive now."

"The fact that she was marching around a century and a half after she was born means she was turned. Chances are excellent she's still alive."

"Whatever alive means to a vampire," I murmured. "What good does this do us? You have a picture that shows Nosy's size, and his daughter. That doesn't seem like enough to stop him if he's really determined to hurt you."

"He loves her," Aiden said. "And my intel says that he still isn't admitting she's his daughter. That's a secret he's gone to a great deal of trouble to protect."

"He's kept her a secret because she's helpless," Ric said. "Innocent. Couldn't save herself if you put an UZI in her hands. The only thing keeping her alive is that no one knows he has a daughter. Except us."

"She *was* innocent," Aiden repeated. "Either way, she's his Achilles' heel."

"So your only protection is the sole extant picture of Nosferatu's daughter proving she's his daughter?"

"Since Elias turned us down," Ric said. "Yes."

"We used to have distance and secrecy going for us," Aiden said. "But the world is shrinking. Secrets are a thing of the past."

I took the phone from his hand and considered the picture. "You could probably get the photo enhanced. Wouldn't that work as proof?"

Aiden shook his head. "Digital pics are too easy to photoshop. Even vampires know that."

"Right," I said. "But paintings are just as easy to alter."

"Except we can get an expert to analyze a painting. Authenticate that it's early nineteenth century, and hasn't been altered."

"Antique road show, huh?"

Aiden took the phone back with a twinkle in his eye.

"Bottom line," Ric said. "We know the painting's real and Nosferatu knows it's real. That would have been enough of a threat to keep him at bay. The operative terms being 'would have'."

I nibbled my lip. "What about other allies? You're a successful businessman. You have clout."

"None who will stand against Nosferatu, especially when they hear I let one of my own trick me."

Now I had another beef against Little. "Okay, what about you, Aiden? You're…whatever you are. You taught Chuck Norris to be awesome."

Aiden's thin, sexy mouth quirked. "I have certain abilities. We both do. But we're like Europe, sitting between the United States and the U.S.S.R."

"Rich countries caught between superpowers," Ric added.

"I had some history," I said. "Even I get the cold war reference. Okay then. No other pry bars or coshes to use on Nosferatu, at least not any we can think of in the next six hours. That just means we'll have to get the picture back."

"Not we," Ric said. "Me."

"And me," Aiden said.

I put hands on hips. "But not me. Because I'm a girl?"

"Because you're human."

"So is Little!"

"Little is in touch with Nosferatu, who has a vampire army behind him."

"Fine. Then if you'll excuse me, I'm going to dress for a day of doing absolutely nothing but creaming my complexion and eating bonbons. Whatever the hell they are." Keeping my face turned because I couldn't lie very well, I manufactured a stomp and went to my dresser to sneak out Twyla's special Stealth Top, 80% spandex and 110% hot.

And then I went to plan my getaway with Twyla.

But when I knocked on Twyla's door, she didn't answer.

I knocked again, harder. Nothing. Worried, I knocked hard enough to make the door rattle.

From next door came a distinctly grouchy Bo-like growl. "Hold it down out there. Elena's resting."

That finally roused Twyla. "Go 'way. I'm sleeping."

"I need you. Open up or I'll huff and puff and blow your door in!" Actually I'd probably huff and puff and turn blue in the face, but that wasn't as dramatic.

Or effective. She opened the door, wearing a surly expression, which frankly was better than scared and lost like last night. "What the fuck do you want?"

"You, Grumpy." I laughed. "Hey, we're the dwarves."

"What?"

"As in Snow White's Seven. You're Grumpy and I'm Doc. Heh."

"There are only six of us, doofus." Her face got long. "Five, without Nikos."

"He's recovering. He'll be with us again in no time. Remember that; hold onto it. We're definitely six."

She shook her head. "Don't lie to me. My guy poured out all his blood and I don't know when I'll see him again… if ever."

"Dearest." I took her hands. "Recovery is at least fifty percent incentive and Nikos has something to come back for. You."

She blinked. "I hope you're right."

"I'm a doctor. Of course I'm right."

"A doctor?" A ghost of a smile wavered on her lips. "I wondered if you'd call yourself that again. Okay, what do you want?"

"Where can we talk without the guys overhearing?"

"We'll need to go outside. Give me five to get dressed."

She emerged four minutes later. "This had better be good." She preceded me through the lakeside front door.

From here I could see the water, sparkling blue between gaps in the trees, and relaxed in spite of everything. "We can talk?"

"We'll still need to keep our voices down. What do you need?"

When I told her what was going on, and what I wanted her to do, all grumbles dropped away. I searched her intelligent brown eyes. "You understand what I'm up against?"

"Not what *you're* up against. It's Ric's battle, and I really think you ought to let him fight it."

"I'm not going to stand by while he risks everything—"

"Got it." She held up her hand. "But you should think about what Elias said. He's got the lock on Annoyingly Enigmatic, but he's usually not talking out his ass."

"I *have* been thinking about it. I even have an idea or two. But there's this little deadline to meet first. I'm the only one who can field that."

"Since Little asked for you specifically, yes. But I don't want to leave Nikos."

"I understand. I'd hoped, but...no, you stay here. Help me escape?"

"Maybe. Who'll watch out for your skinny ass in Minneapolis?"

"I don't need anyone—"

"You're kidding. Did some beer help you decide that?"

I snapped my fingers. "I'll call Rosie. She and her boyfriend live in Ric's quote-condo community-unquote. They'll guard my back."

"Huh." Twyla considered me. "You're actually not too stupid to live."

"We're the same gene pool, doughhead. You're only insulting yourself."

We planned my escape for right after lunch, including Twyla disabling Bo's shielded car and the sedan Aiden had arrived in so the guys couldn't follow. Then I clasped her hands briefly before heading off to shower and shave.

Yes, shave, and not my chinny chin chin. Remember Twyla's black heart thong? After drying off, I slipped into it and her push-up bra, throwing on jeans and the tight sleeveless Stealth Top over them. Not only did the skinny knit make my bosom stand out like twin basketballs, the snaps down the front, while now closed to the neck, later…well, let's just say we'd start showing off the bra's pretty lace and work down from there.

While Twyla made chicken noodle soup and grilled cheese sandwiches with fried onions, I went outside again to phone Rosie who agreed to gather Harry and meet me at three. At the smell of food, Elena woke. We took her a small portion of soup and some gelatin on a tray and ate with her in her room.

Bo was hovering. He kept touching his wife with feather-light strokes, caressing her hair, her face, her hand, syrupy if I hadn't known what they'd been through. But I understood, only too well. He'd almost lost her.

It really didn't bear thinking about. If he'd been a normal human being, if his friend Nikos hadn't been a two-thousand-year-old vampire willing to sacrifice everything for her, she'd be dead, and possibly her baby with her.

Twyla had the right idea. Life was too short to love with anything less than full speed ahead.

If the person was right for you.

As Elena ate, she told us what had happened. I knew most of it from Ric's investigation but let her talk. Twyla and I weren't the only ones at risk for PTSD. It was important for

Elena to work out her traumatic experience at her own pace.

"After Bo dug in, I went to check the trolls. They'd been acting strange." She spooned up some gelatin. "Hey, this is good for congealed horse hooves."

"Eat your soup too, Detective." Bo picked up a spoon and dipped up a bit, making sure to capture a cube of chicken meat, and held it to her lips. "Chicken noodle. Vitamin C. Good protein."

"Yes dear." She gave him a slight smile and sipped. "Anyway, I'd barely gotten to the cabin when out they came, carrying what looked suspiciously like a body wrapped in a black tarp. So I followed. They got to a clearing in the woods, set it down and started arguing about where to dig the hole. While they were distracted, I checked the tarp out. Sure enough, it was a guy, hands and feet tied, shot through the head. Suspicious death, burial in the woods. Well, I had to act."

"You didn't have to, Detective." Bo's voice and face were stern but his hand, feeding her more soup, was slow and gentle.

"Of course I did. I'm a cop."

"Off duty."

"We're never off duty." She pointed to the gelatin cup. He spooned a bite for her. After she ate it she went on. "I drew my gun and told them they were under arrest. They jumped me. I got a shot off but, well, there's him." She nodded down at her raised belly. "My body's kinda unwieldy. I fought back but not very effectively. They disarmed me."

She set down her cup. "Then they slashed me." Her hand reached for Bo's. She swallowed hard as her husband's strong fingers circled hers and squeezed gently. "I was so worried. They ran off with the body, the proof, but for the first time I wasn't thinking about the criminals getting away. I was worried about my baby. Whether he was okay. Oh God." She stared at the wall but the sheen of her eyes said she was seeing a more horrific scene. "I would have done anything to make sure he was okay."

I put a hand on her arm. "The baby's fine. I checked myself. He's fine."

"Yes." She drew a deep breath through her nostrils, let it out slowly. Her eyes came back to us, but she didn't release her husband's hand. "While I lay there, the blood must have drawn the rogue. A fledgling, barely turned." She glanced at Bo. "We have to look into that. Whether he simply wandered into the area, or if there's someone turning vampires here." Releasing his hand, she picked up her spoon and started eating with more vigor. "The last thing I remember is you all showing up and telling me the baby was okay. That was what I was waiting for, hanging on for. Once I knew he was okay, I let go."

Battle-ready Elena, more concerned for her child. That told me how much she loved her baby, her husband. Made me think maybe, if I got out of this alive, there were worse things on the planet than making a life with Ric.

And if I didn't get out alive, I'd at least make sure the picture—and thus Ric—was safe.

We ate the rest of our lunch in silence. I was thinking about Chicken Little and the painting; Twyla, from her sad face, was thinking about Nikos; and Elena was just eating, pragmatically going about the job of regaining her strength.

But when she finished, she set one hand on her distended belly and touched Bo with the other. He put both hands over hers; over their child.

I knew then that I was doing the right thing. Even if I had to throw away fairness and self-respect.

When Twyla and I emerged from Elena's room, the living room shades were drawn and Ric was sitting in a chair. His eyes followed me as I took the dishes to the sink. I'd been hoping I could just walk out, but from his narrowed gaze, that wasn't happening. Ric suspected I was going to try something—which I was, but I wished I didn't have to.

I wished I could stay snuggled up in bed with him all day. Nibbling his jaw, licking the curve of his chest, testing the weight of him in my hand—maybe making a few dreams come true.

Instead I nodded at Twyla as I set our stuff in the sink. Twyla pretended to notice the full kitchen garbage—the one she'd filled up earlier with every bit of trash she could find. She pulled the plastic liner out and tied it off, then lugged it to the back door.

Where she stopped, seemingly stymied. "Hey, Synnove. Can you open the door for me?"

She could have opened it herself—Twyla is nothing if not resourceful—but that was our ruse. "Sure," I said brightly, too brightly. I winced and had to bite my cheek not to glance at Ric to see if he was buying it.

"What's going on?" Suspicion edged his words.

That answered that. Never try to sell a salesperson.

"Nothing." Suppressing the urge to whistle tunelessly, I sauntered to the kitchen door, a combination main door and screen door. I opened the first inward, then took the handle of the screen and walked it open, pretending I needed to do that to get out of Twyla's way.

Which put me *out*side.

Twyla lugged the trash out toward the garbage and recycling. I let the screen go and started casually toward the car, pulling my keys from my pants pocket.

Ric's face slammed into the screen. "What are you doing?"

I jumped. My keys jangled and my heart goosed into my throat. "Just forgot my purse…in the car." Actually Twyla had put it there earlier when she'd stowed her 4G tablet that Ric had preset with Little's transfers and reparked the car front end out for a fast getaway. I grinned at him, trying for unconcerned and, from his snarl, failing miserably. I backed nervously toward my sedan.

The screen door clicked open.

Damn it, it was a bright, sunny day. From what Twyla had told me and from what I'd seen of vampires smoked by the sun, Ric would burn up soon after he hit that sunlight. I'd had coffee spilled on me once and burns are painful with a capital P, as in Picture-getting-your-face-ripped-off. My skin screamed at me for days—and since the skin is the largest organ in the body, that's a mess of screaming. I didn't want that for Ric.

My nonchalance broke and I ran for the driver's door, frantically hitting the unlock button on the way. I yanked the door open and leaped in. Twyla dropped the trash and spun for the cabin. She made it two steps.

Ric's roar, and the *bang* of the door thrown wide with such force that it shattered into a pile of kindling, are sounds that will remain with me for the rest of my life. I fumbled the key into the ignition and cranked the engine.

Just as Ric thudded against the car frame.

Chapter Twenty-Two

I stomped the accelerator. Tires spun, kicking up grass and dirt. Ric got his hand on the driver's door handle…just as the tires caught purchase.

I sped out of there. Ric shouted but I ignored him to blast toward the bridge. I glanced in the rearview. Ric wasn't there. I slowed to take the bridge.

A spume of dirt kicked up into the air behind me, Ric pursuing at jet speed. I jumped so hard I nearly smacked my head on the roof.

Ric slammed into the trunk. "Synnove!" His roar was full of pain. "What. The. Fuck?"

Hitting the accelerator, I drove my foot through the floor and tore over the bridge, my heart hammering so hard it rattled my ribcage. My lungs were heaving like organ bellows. I never drove so fast. I took the hook by the main house at thirty, spitting gravel, and hit blacktop going forty.

I dared a glance in the rearview.

Nothing there.

As I drove, the rearview stayed empty. My heart

decelerated from sheer panic to merely scared bunny, but it took a while. It wasn't until I got to the Interstate that I felt safe enough to stop and fasten my seatbelt. But then it hit me. I'd done it. I'd gotten out of there without my vampire.

Without my protection. I could only hope humans were as capable as I thought we were.

When I got to Holiday Buzz I parked in the underground lot. Rosie and Harry were waiting for me. Holding hands. When Rosie saw me she blushed and slid her hand from his paw. With a growl, he snatched it back.

"It's okay," I said. "In fact, I think it's kinda sweet."

Rosie's cheeks turned bright red. Oddly, so did Harry's.

In the lobby, the guard waved us over. "Mr. Little asked me to tell you he's waiting around the corner at the Buzz Annex for you." He pointed to the right.

Rosie and I exchanged a look. I said, "Thanks. We'll head over."

We went out the front door, silent. On the sidewalk, Rosie said, "This doesn't feel right. Dr. Byornsson, I think you should reconsider."

"I can't. It's already three o'clock."

Harry grimaced. "I hope you know what you're doing."

"Sure. Meet Chicken Little. Negotiate." A.k.a flash some cleavage. "Take the painting. Simple."

"What could possibly go wrong?" Rosie said brightly.

Harry growled. "Now it's a trap for sure."

"Yeah," I said. "Doesn't matter. I have to do this, or at least try." I passed under a sign reading Buzz Annex and pushed through the door.

We entered a pleasant pub restaurant with a large bar, wood floors and plenty of table seating, much of it already filled. "Maybe this won't be so bad. At least there are a lot of witnesses."

To my right, a neat young man stood at the host station.

"Ms. Byornsson? Your party is upstairs in our private dining area. I'm to take you." He paused and eyed Rosie and Harry. "Only you, Ms. Byornsson."

The fine hair on my neck rose. "I need them with me."

"One moment." The young man clicked an earbud. "I've been instructed that if anyone comes up but you, your meeting is cancelled. Next, please."

"Damn it, wait. Give me a minute." I glanced at the pair. "I'm going up."

Rosie's worried eyes searched mine. "Dr. Byornsson, you can't."

"I don't see much choice." I handed Rosie the 4G tablet. "This will give me a reason to call you up. If I'm not back in half an hour, send out the troops."

"Right," Harry said. "The Troops." His disgust was plain.

I nodded at the young man and smiled. "Okay, take me up."

"You've made the right choice." The young man smiled back. Tiny fangs flashed.

Yup. It was a trap.

Still, Little wanted the money and stock, so I had some leverage. Backup was a mere floor away. I had the Stealth Top. Conditions would never get better. I followed the young man/vampire up a return style staircase to the second floor.

It was cooler here in the hushed hallway lined with springy red paisley carpet, muted red wallpaper and wall lights with glass chimneys meant to look like oil lamps. Despite that, my skin tingled with perspiration.

Four doors lined the hallway, all to the left, and all closed. He opened the first. "Your party."

I entered. No lights in here so I only got a few steps in before I faltered.

"Well finally."

A light clicked on. Charles Little lounged behind a

white linen covered banquet table, smirking at me. The little electric table lamp gave the small chamber a romantic glow. I wasn't feeling it.

Image, Synnove. I strolled toward him. "Here I am."

Little's face flushed with victory. "Here we are. Just you and me." He giggled.

I'd heard that sound once before, on my psych ward rotation. My shoulders tightened at that mindless giggle. Maybe Camille had done more than seduce him at the meeting. Maybe she'd done some vampire mind control thing that mushified his brain.

And wouldn't that make a dandy medical specialty practice?

No, no. I was reconsidering medicine, and life in general. Assuming I had a life after this, because the bad feeling of Trap had escalated through nerve-jangling TRAP to *You idiot what part of TRAP don't you get, the big teeth or the bone crunching when it snaps?*

But I kept my limbs relaxed and my attitude casual. "Yep." I started whistling, tunelessly, while surreptitiously checking out the area. "Just you and me. Noooo surprises."

"It's a good thing you left your friends downstairs. If you hadn't, I'd have had to—*take care of them.*" His voice turned ugly, brutal.

I suppressed a shiver. As casually as I could I said, "One problem. I left the tablet to transfer your stock and money with my friends. I need to bring them up."

"No."

"Yes." For Ric. With a deep breath I popped the top snap. "Bring them up."

"Maybe." Little's eyes riveted to my hands.

I thumbed open another couple snaps, then played with the neckline until his eyes glazed a bit. "At least bring Rosie up to transfer your stock and money." I unsnapped another two snaps, exposing a frill of black lace—and a whole lot of cleavage. "As soon as I have the painting, that is."

"Well…I don't know. I'm not supposed to." His eyes narrowed and some intelligence crept back in.

Time to bring out bigger guns. I gritted my teeth and shimmied. My breasts wiggled like mounds of gelatin. "Bring Rosie up and we'll trade. After which, well. *Two women.* Maybe you know what to do with us." Bay-bee.

His mouth fell open. His gaze reglazed.

"But first, the painting." I popped another two snaps, exposing bra cups. The bra's tiny front clasp was conveniently nestled between. "You're going to give me that portrait. *Now.*" I fingered the closure, contemplating the horrors of total exposure to Chicken Little.

"Well…maybe…"

I closed my eyes and thought of England. Or in this case, Ric. I twisted the bra open.

His eyes fell out of his head. "W…wow!"

The top was too tight and I hadn't actually revealed nipples but my cleavage surged and he was totally concentrating on me. "The picture. *Now.*"

"*Okay.*"

And I suddenly understood the power some women get from the act of stripping. Triumph made me glow. I'd been limiting myself to other people's notions of respect. Trashing my doctorly dignity liberated me from caring about what faceless "other people" thought. I knew the human body more thoroughly than most people know their neighbors—and breasts, frankly, are cool.

Fuck Beauty. The Beast had all the fun. I shimmied again. "Where is it?"

"It's in one of the other—huh?"

Little's shirt went taut, as if yanked from below. His gaze slid down his body. He swallowed hard. "No. Money and stock first."

Damn. I grabbed material to peel back to ground zero. Time to let my inner beastie *roar*. "Painting first. Non-negotiable."

"It's a stupid picture."

My hands stilled. He wasn't talking to me.

In fact the direction of both Chicken Little's gaze and his comments were directed to his, um, Little Chicken. "Why the fuss over a stupid ugly dwarf—*ouch*!" He leaped to his feet, chair tumbling. His shirt tail hung over naked hairy legs. "You bit me!"

My neck iced and my scalp prickled. Little was not alone.

She rose from beneath the table, licking fangs, like a blood-sucking Venus.

Camille.

"Darling. You can't insult my boss that way." She twisted Little's tie playfully—until he went *ack-ack-ack*. Transferring her smile to me, she looked me up and down. "Hello, bitch. You can put those away." She pointed at my black-lace cupped breasts. "They're not as impressive as you think."

Ouch. So much for letting my inner beast play. Although why believe Camille, such a pack of total honking lies? Ric liked 'em. "Hello, asswipe."

Her face darkened. "You'll pay for that."

"Talk about hoary and irrelevant." I rolled my eyes. "That smarmy dialogue went out in the nineteen fifties. You're the real picture thief, aren't you?"

"Naturally. This minion—" her smile curled cruelly as she twisted Little's tie so tight he rose to his toes, "—didn't have the brains to steal it by himself."

Little's face darkened and choking sounds started coming from his throat.

He was a dick, but I didn't want him dead. I measured my chances of leaping over the table and taking her out before she throttled him completely. Not close enough. I needed to keep her talking while I edged nearer. "So why the exercise in humiliation yesterday?"

"Well I didn't have the portrait then, did I? Besides, it was such fun crushing you." She smirked.

I inched closer. "Yeah, you're top dog. How did you manage to break into the company safe?"

"This one has his uses. He knew the combination." She yanked the tie like a leash and dragged him from the table just as I got within striking distance.

Little's lips turned blue.

My hands tightened into fists. "If he's useful, don't you think you should let him go before he keels?"

"Well…" She gave a final yank to the tie. Little's eyes rolled back into his head and he went limp. She released the tie and he dropped with a *whump*. "I'm done with him anyway." She sauntered off.

I skirted the table. Little was sprawled on the floor, breath rasping. I knelt and loosened his tie. His breathing eased and his color flooded back. Tension in my shoulders relaxed slightly.

I stood and shot Camille a glare. "Where's the portrait?"

A sly smile crossed her face. "I'm so glad you asked. There are four private rooms on this floor, connected by a public hallway in the front and a serviceway in the rear." She pointed back to a second darkened doorway I hadn't seen. "The painting is in one of those rooms."

"Thanks." It couldn't be that easy, but nothing ventured, so I started for the service door.

She caught my arm, vamp-fast even in her Prada knockoffs, and pulled me in reverse so hard she nearly yanked my arm out of its socket. I did drop my purse. I will say this for her; the girl's strong.

"Hey!" I rubbed my shoulder.

She gave me a fanged grin as she tightened her grip on me. "I forgot to tell you. All the other rooms' doors are locked. You've been outsmarted and outmaneuvered, bitch."

"Yeah, you've been ahead of me the whole time, I get it. Go Team Edward." Sheesh. Apparently some people's egos were based totally on image. "Wait. Locked doors, which you *know* I can't get through… You expected Ric. This is an ambush of some kind for him. One problem, though. Ric isn't here."

"Are you sure?" Camille raised her voice. "Come out now, darling. But be careful. I've rigged a nice little trap for you."

"He's not here," I repeated, although there was a buzz in the air, raising bumps on my skin.

No, I'd left him at the cabin. Proof was the empty rearview mirror. Ric couldn't be here.

Could he?

"See this?" Camille held up a small box, her thumb on its red button. "It's armed now. The trap is rigged to go off when I take my hand off this button."

Damn, a dead man's switch.

"It's courtesy of some of my more technically capable allies. A bit repetitive, as they did the same trick for my predecessor, and a tad cliché, but they're only tech, you know. Not as creative as Yoo-oo." She sang the last to an unseen party.

Another chill fluttered across my arms. "No," I whispered. "I left him behind."

"Did you, now?" Her body quivered with a *heh-heh*, laughter that, pressed up against her, I felt to my marrow. "Your little human is here, Ric, where it seems all you have to do is wrestle her from my grasp. But your precious painting is in one of three locked rooms. And to make things more interesting—I've rigged a vat of acid above both your human and your painting. They're welded directly to the ceiling sprinklers, and trust me, you can't unhook or destroy them quick enough to save both human and painting. If I release this switch..." She laughed out loud, villain's cackle number three. "Your pretty little human gets ugly real fast. Or your precious picture is destroyed, but I think I know which you'll choose. Come out now, darling. Slowly. Or I release the corrosive." She waggled the dead man's switch. "*Now*, darling. Hmm. Well, I guess I get to destroy both your portrait and your whore. Ah. At last."

Mist trickled through the open doorway. It solidified into a very pumped, very angry Ric. In jeans and tee he was a lean, prime male, more dangerous than ever. "What the fuck do you think you're doing, Camille?"

"*Exactly* the fuck." Camille grinned. "Because I like to fuck. Cocks, mouths, minds. Hello, Ric. Took you long enough."

My heart yearned at the sight of his beautiful face, his azure eyes shading toward a stormy violet, his fingers clenching, claws sharpening the tips. I was stupidly glad to see him.

I was also pissed as hell. "I left you at the cabin!"

"I got into your car's trunk before you peeled out." He glanced at me, then returned his glare to Camille. "Burned half my face off, misting, but I recovered on the drive. Good thing it wasn't a hatchback."

"How resourceful," Camille said. "But I knew you'd manage if I got my hands on your plaything. Which of course is why I told Little to make the meet for daylight hours. I knew she'd come, I knew you'd follow, and I knew she'd make a perfect hostage to your good behavior."

Hearing it spelled out, I wanted to punch something—the wall, the table, or better yet her. She was using me against Ric. My Plucky Girl Heroine was all empty image. "Why,

Camille? What more do you want?"

"Ric, of course," she purred. "On his back, in my bed. In chains."

My vision exploded red, my pulse whooshed in my ears. One word rang in my head. *Mine*. "Not. Happening."

"That's not your call, whore."

"Watch your mouth." Ric, his eyes burning violet-red, started for her.

"You, stop!" Camille levered my wrist between my shoulder blades and jerked up. I stifled a squeak of pain.

Ric froze.

"You have a choice. Your 'lady love'—" she sneered it, "—is here. The painting is nearby. *If* I release the switch, the acid will fall. You have time to rescue one."

I snorted. "You've been watching too many *Batman* reruns. Not the movies, the sixties show."

"What?"

"Convoluted Traps 'R Us."

"Hey. Who holds who hostage?"

"It's a complex plan." Ric held up conciliatory hand. "Multifaceted."

"There. You see?" Camille sniffed. "I'm glad someone appreciates it."

"Right," I said. "Why? Why so"—needlessly—"complex?"

"Not that it's any of your business, but Nosferatu likes us to show some intelligence and advanced planning. He is like my dear Loo-ee." Her voice got dreamy on the name.

"Who?"

"Louis XIV, you stupid girl. King of France in the 1600s. That was a century."

"Oh, sure." My other history class. "He employed massively convoluted…excuse me, *complex* court protocol to keep his nobles too busy to rebel. Or, like a harried parent, out of his hair."

There was a silence. Then she yanked up on my wrist again. "Enough! Ric, what's it going to be? Miss Mouthy here, or your household?" She waved the switch box. "Your fuck or your feed?"

Ric snarled.

"Go for the painting, Ric," I said. "Your people's lives are at stake." All this time, I'd thought it was me versus Ric, sizzle versus steak. Sizzle wasn't the enemy. *Camille* was. "Remember Rosie and Harry. Camille will have to release me to escape the acid herself. I'll run for the door. A splash won't kill me."

"Think again, pretty girl. I'll maneuver you so your face gets it." Camille's breath was warm in my ear and smelled faintly of whiskey—maybe after a nibble of Little she'd needed a palate-cleanser. "You'll be scarred. How will you feel when Ric rejects your ugly ass? Not dead, but you'll wish you were."

Anger flooded me at her words, and I wished I could splash *her* with hazardous chemicals too...like my pepper spray.

My heart sped up at the thought.

"You win, Camille." Ric's fangs receded and his eyes banked to a careful blue. "You've been so clever. How did you know about the painting in the first place?"

"Finally. You noticed my brilliance." She cooed it. "How? I pay attention. After you beat Nosferatu's tactical team, you said you were going to retrieve 'the item'. The team leader reported that to Nosferatu. He figured out it was that portrait of him."

"He's smart." He edged nearer.

"There's a reason he's head of the Chicago vampires," she agreed. "You really ought to join us."

"Maybe I will. But how did you know about the painting?"

"Nosferatu called me. He said you were going out of town to collect a crate of his."

With one ear on her monologing I scanned for my purse. It lay four feet away on the floor, dropped when Camille grabbed me. Too far, with her attached to me like a lamprey.

"I seduced Little to watch for your return, to pump you for information. But since you were away, I also told him to make the Meiers Corners presentation happen. Until I got my hands on the crate, that was my ticket to first lieutenant. It was the perfect day—that morning I crushed your plaything; that night Little saw the crate go into your safe and we stole it. A doubleheader."

Ric took another step. "But how did you know about the portrait?"

"I peeked into the crate." She simpered. "When I asked Nosferatu about it he went apeshit, and I realized I might have even better leverage." She paused. "I really want that promotion."

"So is there something I can do to help you get it?" Ric slid closer to the kill zone.

"I only want a little information." Camille's mouth lifted from my ear, her tone girlish, almost coaxing. She must have finally seen Ric's advance because she stiffened. "Hey. Back off, buddy."

He froze, hands up. "Sure." He backed a step.

"More."

He backed another two. "Information?"

"Well…yes. Tell me why that picture is so important. A weapon? Blackmail? Nosferatu's a little scrawny, so what? He doesn't need to be big to be physically powerful. Well, some Lestats would care. But that's not all there is to it, is there?"

Maybe Ric could get my spray. I caught his eyes then flicked my gaze to the purse. Then I squinched my eyes and pulled back my upper lip and made an I-got-shot-with-pepper-spray face.

He blinked at me in a horrified way. "Um, *no*. Camille." It was clear from his expression the "no" was for me. "Nosferatu's size wouldn't stop him from being *really fast* and evading attack. Not to mention *misting*."

Damn, I'd forgotten that. She'd see Ric coming, mist to compensate, and I'd probably be the one to get a faceful of pain. I'd have to figure out some way she didn't see coming.

"Exactly," she said. "Besides, Nosferatu has me, and Giuseppe."

I couldn't retrieve the purse. Ric couldn't. Could I get word to Rosie or Harry downstairs? Somehow call up one of the serving folk—if there were any of them not under Camille's power?

Phooey. Talk about needlessly complex. I took a breath and centered myself. Forgot image to look at the facts. And knew who had to get the purse, and how.

"So tell me, Ric," Camille purred. "Why?"

"Don't tell her," I said. "Camille can deluge me with acid, make me a beast. *I've been ugly before*. I don't care."

"*Pfft*," Camille said. "You care. You're not as gorgeous as me, but you're nice enough for a human."

"Nope, I was ugly. And I can prove it. There's a picture of me in my purse. It shows what a scrawny kid I was."

"You expect me to fall for that? There's also a weapon in that purse, which you'll pull on me the instant you get your hands on it."

"Then get it yourself. The picture is in there, you'll see."

"Synnove." Ric raised both brows. "You were ugly? Why haven't I seen this picture?" He leaked just enough resentfulness into his tone to sell it. There was a reason Holiday was the best.

Camille tapped a foot. "All right, I'm curious. Ric, kick the purse over here."

He growled irritably, and did. I relaxed my muscles to the ready, alert for a moment of distraction in which I could escape.

But she kept me yanked tight while she picked up the purse one-handed. "Where is it?"

"In my wallet. You may have to dig."

She set the purse on the table and fingered through. "What's this?" She pulled out the small black canister. "Pepper spray?" She laughed and threw it out the service doorway, a tiny black missile. "Nice try, human."

"For heaven's sake. Do you have a Y chromosome? There's the wallet, right under the sunscreen. The picture's in it."

"No need to get insulting," she huffed. Extracting the wallet, she opened it to my pictures. The real me was on top, smiling like the naive idiot I was.

Camille started laughing. She laughed and laughed, to the point that it was almost offensive. "What a freak. Here, Ric." She crumpled the picture and tossed it at him. "Take a look at who your lover really is."

Ric caught the picture, smoothed it out and stared at it for the longest time.

His face was unreadable.

"Isn't that the ugliest kid you've ever seen?" Camille sneered.

"Physically, perhaps."

He wasn't pretending.

My insides crumpled worse than the photo. Had I counted on him seeing the Prince—Princess—inside the Beast? To love me anyway?

But men wanted beauty. Why would Ric be any different, simply because I *needed* him to be?

He looked up. "Is this really you, Synnove?"

"Yes. That's my reality." My heart was breaking. Might

as well spill it all. "Not only who I was, *but who I still am*."

"No." He stared at me, his eyes saying…something. "It's just a picture."

"A picture of *me*." Didn't he get it?

"My sunshine. You're not looking at it right." Ric turned the picture so I could see it, the spotted face and haystack hair I'd seen a thousand times. He said gently, "This is an image—and *it was only ever an image*."

I blinked at the crinkly photo in his powerful fingers. My fourteen-year-old face. *My reality check.*

Wasn't *real*.

I'd been so caught in the image of me as ugly duckling become gorgeous swan—add another fairy tale—that I'd never grown beyond it.

It was only a picture. It wasn't real.

It never had been.

I'd created an image of myself, a mask, and put it on. An image of me as a doctor who always told the truth and made life fair for others and who telegraphed her kicks. Then I'd made myself over in the image, rather than letting my full underlying reality express itself.

It had taken Ric Holiday, the king of appearances, to see the truth.

"Since it's not you…" He smiled at me—and tossed the picture away.

Lightning struck, and with it, understanding so powerful I staggered. About me, about Camille…about our way out of this mess.

Ric had thrown away my picture.

Camille would *never* throw away an advantage. She'd cheat first. The portrait wasn't here.

Ric had thrown away my picture.

Now I threw away the image of myself that I'd clung to all those years, free to claim the reality of who I truly was.

Strong, fast, smart and determined, with strengths and flaws, but most of all, a healer. I could switch to Crisis Time mode in an instant, triage like a goddess, and spontaneously spout *Gray's*.

Crisis Time. *Click*.

Triage. Camille first. Acid and fairness could wait.

And now for *Gray's*. I grabbed for the dead man's switch. My telegraph and her vampire reflexes ensured that I missed and she pulled the box out of reach.

But when I "missed", I smacked her forearm…and simultaneously set the edge of my foot against her shinbone.

"You want this, human?" She raised her arm overhead, waving the box tauntingly. "Try to get it."

"Camille." My voice was strong and calm. "Did you know the metatarsus is especially sensitive to shock? Vampires even more than humans, if I understand the physiology. Which, because *I'm a doctor*, I do."

"What the hell are you talking about?"

"This."

She might have felt my hit on her leg and, being faster than me, might have avoided what happened next. But her attention was on my hit to her arm and my attempt to get the box.

So she didn't stop me when, using her tibia as a guide, I stomped the hell out of her instep.

She yowled. Ric was right—vampires felt pain more than humans. Her hand sprang open, releasing me.

I ran toward Ric, both hands raised. If my wrists were unusually flat and my fingers clenched, that might have been my terror. I'd telegraphed my intent again. I hadn't even gone a step when she snared me by the wrist.

"No, you don't!" She hauled me back with an extra-vicious yank, rewinding me like a yo-yo.

Yep. I spun into her—like Aiden.

Fist first.

My entire hundred forty-five pounds slammed into her jaw. My shoulder was behind it.

She staggered back, swaying on her feet.

Damn. I needed her unconscious and unable to mist away. I pulled my arm back for another punch.

The electric shock of delayed pain cracked up my fist and arm. I howled. Vampire bone was like hitting a cliff. I wasn't using those fingers any time soon.

But without follow up all this would be for nothing. I bent over and head-butted her in the solar plexus.

With a soft *woof*, Camille collapsed. *Yay!* I thought.

Until the dead man's switch popped into the air.

Chapter Twenty-Three

Time clarified. *Moment.* Ric, caught mid-step, coming at us. *Moment.* The switch, button still flat, arching gracefully into the air. *Moment.* The button starting to rise, the red edge peeking up. *Moment.* Ric completing his step.

He'd never make it in time.

Acid was about to splash everywhere. I didn't care about my looks, but my eyes and hands were another story if I ever wanted to sew another kid's boo-boo. I tucked both hands in my belly, curled over and braced for an acid bath.

In a repeat of the Ogre shooting, Ric hit me with all his weight. I went down. He extended himself, covering my body. "I've got you, Synnove," he panted into my ear. "I'm here. I'll protect you, Sunshine. Forever, if you'll let me."

Amazement bubbled through me. He thought the painting was here. Yet he'd chosen me. My eyes and nose prickled with emotion.

"Very nice tackle," a dry voice drawled. "But not really necessary."

Ric's weight shifted. "*Aiden*?"

I lifted my head. The black-haired vampire leaned against the wall, dead man's switch in hand, thumb firmly on the button. He still wore that bulky black leather jacket, zipped shut despite the day's heat.

"Aiden, you fuck." Ric glared red daggers. "How dare you risk Synnove by trying to get the switch? We had a plan. I was supposed to distract Camille so you could rescue Synnove."

"Hey," I said. "I didn't need rescuing."

To my astonishment Ric turned his glare on me. "You. If you *ever* risk your life like that again—"

"I didn't *try* to get the switch, I got it," Aiden said. "Now I'm going to get the painting." He tossed me a grin over his shoulder. "Nice right cross, by the way."

"Wait," I said. "We need to restrain Camille somehow."

Ric began, "The painting—"

"Isn't here," I said. "If she'd been telling the truth and the painting were here, you could have saved it."

"I'd never have—"

"Yes, yes, but if you *had*, while I'd be scarred for life, she'd be out the painting. If you chose me, I'd keep my face but the painting would be given an acid bath. *And she'd still be out the painting.*"

Ric gaped down at me.

"Hell." Aiden turned back. "Camille had no intention of letting that portrait out of her grabby little mitts. She tricked us both."

"My household is screwed." Ric rolled off me, landing heavily on the floor.

"No, don't you see?" I said. "She keeps winning because we've let her set the goals. The fight for Meiers Corners, possession of the picture. They're all *her* images. To win, we change what we're after. Change it to *our* picture."

"I know what I'm picturing." Aiden's eyes were diamond hard. "Cutting off her head."

"Nosferatu would get another lieutenant," Ric said. "We need the picture."

"No," I repeated. "Think bigger. The picture is a tactic, not a goal."

A plan had solidified in that lightning strike of understanding, one so outrageous and audacious I couldn't even admit to myself I was thinking it. Elias had given me the clue. If I could pull it off, Ric wouldn't have to fear Nosferatu.

Camille groaned, reminding me there was a time limit on this offer.

"Can you restrain her? So we can travel with her but she can't mist?" I pushed to sit and winced when my sore arm complained loudly.

Ric leaped to his feet and offered me his hand.

I could have stood myself, but it was a sweet gesture. I raised my left arm and found myself flying onto my feet and into a hug that squeezed the breath out of me. Okay. One moment to rest secure in Ric's arms.

Camille groaned again and started to move.

"Restraints, now." Or this would all be for nothing.

"Got it." Aiden reached into his coat and brought out a dangling set of metal handcuffs. "Electrified. Key's in the lock." He tossed them to Ric. "Told you they'd come in handy."

Ric caught the cuffs one handed, his other arm still wrapped around me. "Sometimes you're damned annoying." He released me, bent over Camille and cuffed her wrists together. Then he removed the key and slipped it in his pocket. "No, wait. Scratch the sometimes."

Aiden gave a theatrical sigh. "This is the thanks I get for suffering being stuffed in a car trunk with you."

"*You* suffered?" Ric pressed something on the cuff and it lit up briefly. "You kept punching me."

"Not my fault." Aiden crossed arms. "You kept kicking."

"Because *you* were making snide remarks about how I smelled."

"Boys." I clapped my hands. "You guys bicker like Statler and Waldorf. Sorry to interrupt this male bonding ritual, but we have work to do."

"*Boys*?" Ric *hmphed*. "We're rough and ready vampire assassins. 'Boys', indeed. Who are Statler and Waldorf?"

"The grumpy old hecklers in the Muppets."

"Muppets." A choked laugh came from Aiden.

"Oh, that's just not fair." Ric's expression was adorably pained. "I work my ass off for decades to make him smile and you get a laugh for Muppets? Lame."

"Life isn't fair. Sorry." And I was, and I'd continue to fight for the less fortunate, but I was done hobbling myself for assholes like Camille. "I have a proposal for Nosferatu. I'd tell you, but I don't want her to hear."

"We're going to Chicago?" Ric asked. "How do you expect to get past all Nosferatu's guards to see the little Gollum himself?"

"Camille's our security. How long will those cuffs hold her?"

Her eyes slit open, a line of emerald green. We all looked at Aiden.

His smile sharpened. "Days. They're low level, annoying, unless she tries to mist. Then they'll zap her, and she'll collapse back into her natural form."

"What if she tries to mist repeatedly? Won't the battery wear out?"

Aiden unzipped a couple inches of jacket. "Then I have this." He reached into the breast pocket and pulled out a blunt-muzzled gun.

"Whoa." I held up palms. "I thought bullets were only effective on regular humans. Around here, that's me. And Chicken Little, if he counts."

"This is a stun gun." Aiden indicated the end, where a probe cartridge was already loaded. "If she gets feisty, I'll zap her." His grin was kinda pointy.

Camille checked out the cuffs, then looked from Aiden to Ric to me, and back to Aiden. Her lips curled and her eyes opened fully. "Nice try, darlings. But I have quick reflexes."

She leaped to her feet and ran.

But before she'd moved Aiden hit the trigger. Two probes shot out, trailing long wires. They were slower than her but they'd had a head start. With a crack, they hit her square in the back. She stiffened abruptly and fell to the floor.

"You have quick reflexes, I have a nasty disposition. Guess which is faster." Aiden's thin lips quirked as he ejected the cartridge. "If she even looks at me funny, I'll zap her again." He loaded another cartridge, then put the stun gun in a jacket pocket. "And I'll enjoy it too. Let's go."

We called 911 for Charles and headed out. As we came down the stairs Rosie threw open the Annex door. Harry ran ahead. We dashed along the sidewalk.

It was only the next building over, but by the time we hustled inside the three vampires were starting to smoke. The guard on duty looked the other way; another member of Ric's condo group, apparently.

In the parking elevator I pulled out my cell phone to call Twyla.

"You're alive," were the first words out of her mouth.

"Surprise. And I'd like to stay that way. I'm with Ric and Aiden. We're going to Chicago to offer a proposal to Nosferatu—"

"That's suicide!"

"Not entirely. We've got Camille as insurance against his good behavior. But if something happens, I want you to call the Ancient One. If we haven't reported in by dawn, I'm trusting you to make him protect Ric's household." We exited into the garage.

I could practically hear Twyla's slim eyebrows sweeping into her hairline. "Do I have a choice?"

"Nope. One more thing." I'd remembered what Elias said about Nikos needing vampire blood and related it to her.

"Thanks." Her voice hitched. "I can almost believe he'll be okay now. All right, if I don't hear from you by dawn, I'll make the call. Good luck."

"You too."

Ric led us to the corner where the firm's fleet was parked, including a smoky sedan and a luxury curtained limo. Rosie and Harry waved goodbye, Harry climbing into the sedan while Rosie took off in my little hybrid to return it to the cabin.

Aiden shoveled Camille into the back of the limo, climbed in after her and shut the curtains. The days were getting shorter, but sunset was still well past eight, so I'd be driving. But to my surprise, Ric took shotgun. When we hit the street he turned a little red, but the passenger side windows must have been treated because he didn't smoke. There was a medical experiment I'd love to try. The effects of various wavelengths of electromagnetic radiation on vampire physiology—how much sun before they went *whoosh*?

Once I hit the freeway, I had nothing to do but think. Or actually, rethink. My plan had flaws—we were headed into the opposition's maw without immediate backup. Problem was, bringing in Bo or his gang would have screwed the one advantage we had.

"So this proposal you have for Nosferatu." Ric echoed my thoughts. "You're not entirely sure he'll agree to it, are you?"

"What makes you say that?"

"Your last-will instructions to Twyla, bequeathing my household to Elias."

"No! That's not…I'm not… That's only for if we're injured."

His silence spoke louder than words. I chilled. I was naive thinking in terms of "dangerous". Nosferatu was deadly.

No, we held Camille hostage, and Ric and Aiden were the best. That wasn't wishful thinking or conjuring images—I'd seen them in action, and Nosferatu's team too. I'd take Ric and Aiden any day. But still…

Warm fingers nuzzling under my top's hemline derailed my worrying. "What…?"

"Shh." Ric slid his hand onto the small of my back and rubbed in tiny circles.

Tension released. I throttled a tiny moan of pleasure.

Ric's eyes crinkled, and he slipped his fingers lower to tickle the downy hairs at the base of my spine.

I yipped. Ric's smile grew.

"What's going on up there?" Aiden said.

"Nothing," we said together, then exchanged a warm, intimate smile. Ric's fingers delved lower and began to pet my tailbone. Little shocks of delight wowed me.

"Right," Aiden said. "Well, while nothing's going on, make sure one of you keeps her eyes on the road."

I did, though Ric's caresses made my lids heavy with pleasure. As a distraction from worry, it was wonderful; as a reminder of what I had to live for it was awesome. My entire spine tingled and I'd developed a permanent grin when he removed his hand.

And drove it down the front of my pants, directly onto my clit.

I shrieked, goosed the accelerator and nearly merged with the car in front.

"Hey," Aiden yowled. "Do I need to come up there and separate you kids?"

With a smile, Ric removed his hand. But the aftershocks

kept my mind off all things Nosy until we hit the Illinois border.

We made one stop for gas. Camille got unruly, but Aiden made good on his promise to zap her. He also had a few techniques for making vampires squeal. Not just Camille, either. Ric pulled me into the gas station bathroom for a quickie and...well, not going into details, but I'm sure as hell nailing tap cleats on Aiden's shoes and buying Ric unwedgiable underwear.

A little over seven hours later, we arrived at Nosferatu's lakeside mansion.

Lakeside mansion. Talk about conjuring images. I'd pictured a vast estate with green lawns, long curved driveway and huge wrought iron gates, the lake with pier and boat a picturesque backdrop.

Actually it was a five-story brownstone a few blocks west of Lake Michigan dwarfed by surrounding high rises. On the plus side it had beautiful narrow windows, arched entrances, lots of carved detail and a wrought iron fence.

But hemmed in by city streets, parking was a bitch.

I finally found a space between an Audi and a Beemer and we walked through the quaint spindled gate, Aiden hustling Camille. A set of concrete steps led up to the front door. I'd put my foot on the first when Ric caught my elbow and guided me onto the set next to it leading down.

"Is this like mansion flats in London?" I asked. "We're the help so we enter below stairs?"

Ric's smile held equal parts tension and love. "No, we're the vampires and there's as much mansion underground as above. Are you sure about this?"

I hadn't explained my proposal for Nosy to Ric, wanting to strike hard and fast without Camille having time to cook up a counter. I'd have left her behind, but we needed her as a hostage to make it inside.

Yet Ric was ready to back me up, only asking if I was sure. I glowed at his trust in me. "I'm sure. Mostly. You sure about going in through the front door?"

"Vampires respect a show of strength." Ric rapped sharply at the lower door. "Even when it's suicidal."

"Especially then." Aiden grinned, all fang.

A woman in apron and cap answered. "Yes?"

Wordlessly Ric brushed by her and hit the stairs going down. Ready or not, we were doing this. I trotted after him. Aiden followed with Camille.

"Stop," the woman called. "You can't go in there. Guards!"

The short entryway stairs gave onto a large, empty room with bare walls and smooth hardwood floor. "Booby trapped?" Ric asked.

"No," Aiden said from behind. "Those come later."

The thud of running feet shivered the floor and suddenly several rough-looking vampires filled the opposite doorway. The biggest of them muscled through. His jaw jutted as he glared, red-eyed, at Ric. "Who are you?"

"*Listen to me.*" Ric's voice rang with vampire compulsion. "*Let us pass.*"

"We…" The leader's eyes cooled to a dull blue. "We're letting them pass."

The vampires parted. The doorway was clear.

"Wow." I stared at blank-eyed vampires as Ric pulled me past them. "I didn't know you could do that to other vampires."

"They're n…newbs." Camille stuttered a bit as Aiden stumbled her along. "I keep telling Nosferatu to use seasoned warriors, but does he listen? No-ooo."

"Watch it," Aiden said. "We're coming to the tunnels. The traps are there."

The rich scent of damp earth underscored his words. It

reminded me uncomfortably of a freshly dug grave, all too possible with vampires. Were we headed into a cemetery?

Ahead, flooring gave way to an unlit tunnel of packed dirt. A second wave of guards confronted us at the mouth, five big vampires with bladed faces, long fangs and eyes that glittered ruby in the dim light. The pair in front were a tank with fangs and a male so muscular he looked like a golem made of car tires. They were so big I could barely see the three behind.

Tire Guy held up his hand. "I don't know how you got this far, but this is the end of the line. The tunnel's electrified."

Aiden shoved Camille forward and held up his stunner. "So's this." He slapped the business end to her temple. He'd run out of cartridges long ago.

Tire Guy gaped. "Hey. Those are illegal in Chicago."

"You think I care?"

The tank said, "It's Camille. We gotta stand down." The three in back exchanged confused glances.

"No." Tire Guy gathered himself. "She doesn't change things."

Aiden smiled, with a menace that made all the hair on my body stand straight up. He purred, "I was so hoping you'd say that."

"Caligula, you shit," Camille said. "I'm not going to forget thi—"

Aiden pulled the trigger. Camille convulsed and fell to the floor, twitching.

Ric leaped past Aiden, swinging open a bone-handled folding knife with a hard flick. The slim blade glinted wickedly in the low light. A muscular stroke cut tire-thick throat. A second and third slice decapitated the vampire.

Aiden reached into his bulky jacket and pulled out a long, curved butcher's knife. He sprang into the gap next to Ric and hacked at the tank.

I turned away, not because there was blood, although there was, but because I was watching our backs. Really. I only heaved a little.

The shouts died. I chanced a peek back. Ric was wiping his blade on one of the bodies. Its head lay a few inches away, staring at me.

I swallowed hard. "Is he…?"

"No." Ric straightened, folding away his knife. He nudged the head with his toe. "It'll rejoin his body, but not before we reach Nosferatu. Did you get the juice turned off?" The last was to Aiden.

"Of course." His knife disappeared into his jacket.

"Then grab her and let's go." Ric nodded toward the vampire woman.

Camille was already rousing. Aiden jerked her to her feet and we entered a warren of tunnels. I would have gotten lost, but Ric and Aiden led as if they could see a dashed trail pointing directly to Nosferatu. And maybe they could; I remembered Nosferatu had trained them both as trackers.

I was counting on Nosferatu remembering that too.

The deeper we penetrated into Nosferatu's lair, the more stagnant the air became. The less light. My breath came shallower, faster. My heart started to hammer. Aiden's and Camille's eyes glowed red, bumping the creepy factor into hard swallows and shaky legs.

Then Ric took my hand. His eyes were red too, but they crinkled in one of his many variations on a warm smile. My tension eased and my heart slowed.

The last light disappeared. Ric guided my steps. I clasped his forearm, briefly closing my useless eyes.

We stopped. My eyes flew open. I blinked into the pit of black.

Darkness resolved into a fourth set of red eyes.

Chapter Twenty-Four

I jumped. Hot adrenaline spurted into my veins, turbo-boosting my heart.

"Well, well." The voice was a dry rasp in the dark, as if dead moths were coming out of the mouth with the words. "The prodigal sons."

"Nosferatu." Ric's red eyes dipped in a nod.

I couldn't see a thing besides bloody eyes and the only air that moved was my panted little breaths; I was muffled in stifling darkness. My heart thudded and my ears began to ring. Or maybe that was the sound of my own nerves shrieking.

A rasping chuckle. "At last, you've realized the enormity of your sins and turned yourselves in. How nice. I'll make your deaths quick."

Ric's hand dropped from my arm. To have two hands to defend us, but now I felt even more alone, more isolated and helpless. My heart hammered in my chest, as if trying to escape. My feet turned with the same idea.

"And a sacrificial human for me to sup on." He made a

slurping sound, like Anthony Hopkins's Hannibal. I nearly cried out, *I'm not an entrée to be served with fava beans.* I did whimper. Nosferatu cackled. "You've earned a boon for bringing her. I'll kill you a little less painfully."

"We're not here to turn ourselves in," Ric said.

"I'll have to capture you? How tedious."

"You try," Aiden said, "and Camille dies." The dangerous click of his blade underscored the last word.

A rustle of rich cloth, as if Nosferatu was shrugging. "Then she dies."

"Hey," Camille said. "I'm your lieutenant. You need me."

"Second lieutenant, my dear." He laughed in a way that left no doubt—he didn't need any of them. "Plenty more where you come from."

"Giuseppe won't like that." Her eyes were frightened stoplights.

"Giuseppe is not your Master, bitch." His words struck like sledgehammers. "You'd do well to remember that."

Her eyes flinched. "I'm your lieutenant, deserving of respect—"

"Respect is earned. You've allowed yourself to be captured and brought traitors into my home."

"They forced me," she squeaked. "But…but they made a mistake, bringing me here. Let me at them, Master, I'll show them what it means to cross you."

"Bring it," Aiden said.

"A duel?" Nosferatu's red eyes narrowed. "I like that. Kill them, then."

I'd been waiting for an opening to make my pitch. But the way things were flushing, no pauses were on the menu… *Menu.* Me, with Chianti. *Brrrr.*

I shook it off. I'd have to make my own opening, quick, despite being fava beans in the dark.

"Wait!" I took a bold step forward, secretly praying I

wouldn't crash into a chair or table and fall on my face. For a change, my little bit of sizzle worked. Heartened, I planted fists on hips. "This ends, and it ends now."

"Silence, food."

"Nice try, Hemoglobin Breath. But you don't scare me."

"I ought to. I ought to scare you to *death,*" snarled his voice *right in my ear.*

Yipes. I crossed my arms, playing casual but really to keep my heart from leaping out of my chest. My bowels were quietly shedding their lining. "Nice trick. I bet you're great fun at parties." Happily, my voice didn't squeak.

"Bah. I've had enough." His footsteps stomped away. "You are all dead."

"Then kiss goodbye to what you want most in the world."

Dead silence.

I mean absolute silence.

Nosferatu's eyes reappeared, tilted, as if he'd turned back to consider me. "Very well. You have exactly thirty seconds to interest me. Talk."

Wow. Sizzle really was important. It had gotten my foot in the door.

But now I had to deliver. I had to convince this refugee from a grade B Dracula movie that my idea was worth his while. Which actually might take even more razzle-dazzle than getting my foot in the door.

My heart bumped unevenly, *ba-lump dum dum.* Could I do it? I'd long denied, even hated, that part of me that was sizzle. Maybe it had atrophied or even died.

Maybe I shouldn't attempt this. Or fall back on logic. That was a skill I knew I still had...no, I'd cratered at the presentation with Camille and Chicken Little.

Argh. If not sizzle and not skill, then what?

Then I remembered Elena. Hopeless. Dying. Yet she'd hung on for her baby's sake, long enough for Nikos and the

Ancient One to save her.

Sometimes skill doesn't do it. Sometimes logic fails. Then all you have is friends, and hope.

And being damned obstinate.

Ric's hand found mine and squeezed. The pulse conveyed his love and confidence in me.

The best sizzle of all. Love.

I talked.

"Here's the thing, Nosy. If you kill me, if you destroy Ric and Aiden, you'll be throwing away your only chance *to find Eloise*." I put a deliberate emphasis on her name, not to manipulate him emotionally but so that he'd know exactly how high the stakes were. "Unless you *want* the wrong people to find her."

"What are you talking about?" He blustered it.

I wished I could see his face, but still having my viscera on the inside was a good sign. "The world is shrinking. Someone will figure it out. How many people know about your bat birthmark? You used to boast about it so I'd guess quite a few. Are you sure she's still hiding hers?"

Silence.

I pressed my point. "You need to find Eloise before they do. You need to find her *now*."

"Who's Eloise?" Camille asked brightly.

I had a brief irrational urge to hug her. Even though she often played the sex pot card, she wasn't stupid. Nosferatu would hear the eager interest in her voice. He'd know the clock was ticking on his secret. On his daughter.

Click. A flood of golden light came from a small desk lamp. I blinked. After the total darkness even the mellow light was harsh.

Flocked wallpaper, overstuffed leather furniture and a wet bar padded with quilted leather were revealed. It was a study like Ric's but bloated—a handsome face gone puffy with overindulgence.

Nosferatu stood at the bar, pouring himself a drink. He was taller than in his portrait, and slender instead of spindly. Another facet of vampire physiology, maybe. He'd purged himself of his humanity, but in two hundred years something had made up for part of it. Damn, I really hoped I lived long enough to study all of that. Like, longer than the next ten minutes.

With his neatly barbered silver hair, suit and sweater vest, Nosferatu was almost dapper. But while his form was elegant, his features were coarse and bold, bushy black eyebrows and eyes now snapping black.

Sure enough, there was that small bat birthmark on his cheek.

Drink in hand, he sauntered toward us. Aiden gripped Camille more tightly. Ric stepped in front of me. I had to work not to back up, but Nosferatu only stopped beside Camille to pat her shoulder. "Time for you to leave, my dear."

She smiled coyly. "But Master—"

"Now."

Her eyes closed and I could see her seethe. When her eyes opened again they were blood red. "Yes, Master." Her voice was cold enough to freeze helium.

She turned her frigid glare on Aiden. "Well?"

He cocked his head, considering Nosferatu, then nodded and released her.

"Oh, Camille," Nosferatu said. "*You will return my portrait and forget you ever heard the name Eloise.*"

She jerked. Shook her head as if trying to clear it. After a few blinks she held her arms out to Ric, stiffly. He tossed her the key to the handcuffs.

She snatched it midair and swept out without another word.

"Now," Nosferatu said. "Come to the point, puny human."

Chapter Twenty-Five

Puny human, indeed. "You can't scare me with verbal jabs."

His brow rose in mock surprise. "Yet you try to manipulate me with fear."

"No. You have a problem, I have a solution."

"That benefits you, no doubt."

"Just listen, okay? You want to find Eloise. You can't risk lieutenants or minions finding her; they might see her birthmark and figure out why she's so important to you. Besides, they're not as good as Ric and Aiden, are they? I'd guess these two are among the best trackers in the world."

He sniffed. "I don't know about the best in the world—"

"Certainly they're the very best *outside the Iowa Alliance*."

"So?" Nosferatu drawled, but his eyes sharpened on me. I'd hit a bull's eye with that one.

"So, bring them in as consultants, to find your daughter. In exchange, you promise to drop your vendetta against them and stay away from their humans and their territory. Simple." Eloise, by her pink signal, didn't want to be found.

But we needed breathing space. We'd figure something out. "Remember, it'll take time, even for them."

"Naturally." Sarcasm dripped from Nosferatu's tones. "Years will go by while you pretend to seek her, in reality fortifying your position."

"*You* haven't found her in decades. Give them a couple months at least." Not as much as I'd hoped for. I cut eyes to Ric. *You onboard with this?*

Yes. His azure gaze twinkled. *You're better at sizzle than you think*.

My face heated.

"Interesting offer." Nosferatu tossed off his drink. "But why should I? Now that Holiday's within reach of my voice, I can compel him to find her."

"Except *I'm* immune," I said. "I'll remind him of the truth."

The vampire's eyes narrowed at me. "Then I will simply invade Holiday's territory and command him that way."

"If you even try, I'll destroy you." Ric's voice was low, angry.

"Don't be absurd." Nosferatu returned to the bar, pulled the stopper out of a cut crystal whiskey decanter and waved it at Ric. "You're nothing but smoke and mirrors. I have spies of my own. I know your numbers. Your traps are not real."

"Real enough to take out dozens of your Lestats."

"But not Camille."

"We weren't expecting her. Now we are. And may I remind you, all your earlier minions failed miserably."

Nosferatu set down the stopper, picked up the decanter and poured more whiskey, all seemingly nonchalant but his cheeks were stained dark. "I sent a few expendables to test your boundaries. I could have sent hundreds more. Could *still* send them." He corked the decanter and turned. "You and Aiden are good, but not good enough to stop hundreds of vampires. No, I can destroy you and yours. Maybe I'll start right here, right now. I'll call my entire household down on you and kill your plaything. You couldn't stop me."

"Aiden," Ric snarled.

With a deadly grin, the assassin unzipped his jacket to reveal a miniature flamethrower, fuel canisters strapped to his waist. That explained the bulk.

"Maybe I'm smoke but Aiden is *fire*," Ric said. "Are you absolutely certain you could take Synnove before he killed you where you stand?"

Nosferatu cleared his throat. But no words came out.

"Know this too. An agent is in place. If we haven't reported in by dawn, the agent will call the Ancient One. If any harm comes to my humans—including and especially Synnove—Elias will assume command of my territory." Ric took one lethal step toward Nosferatu. "I'm not just smoke any more, Nosy. Haven't been since I stepped into Synnove's sunshine."

"How cloyingly sweet." The words were brave but Nosferatu set down his glass with a trembling hand. "Even if I do hire you, I'll look like a fool when you join Elias's merry band."

"No," Aiden said. "You cut a deal with us, we abide by it."

Nosferatu snorted. "And I should simply take your word on that?"

"Not our word," Ric said. "Our actions. In nearly two centuries we haven't joined any alliance. We don't bow to any master. Not you and not Elias."

"They'll be nonaligned." I watched Nosferatu's eyes. "Independence is part of the deal."

His gaze narrowed, thoughtful. He was starting to buy it.

I hammered our advantage home. "Who else is there besides Ric and Aiden? You'd need to give your minions or lieutenants a real description. How many of them do you trust that much? Can you trust *any* of them not to kidnap Eloise, or worse? But—" my pause gave emphasis to my final selling point, "—*Ric and Aiden already know about her.* They care about her like you do."

"She was such a sweet child," he said slowly. "A sweeter woman. Then with the change... She disappeared and I haven't seen her. I do not know what kind of vampire she has become, but I assume she is as innocent. As helpless." His voice cracked and for one instant pity stirred.

Then I remembered who this vampire was, and what he'd done to Ric and Aiden. Life wasn't fair. Some tried to make it more so. But some made it even meaner and uglier than it was.

Pity was wasted on Nosferatu.

Confirmed a moment later when he strode to place hands on Ric's and Aiden's shoulders. "You two are my best. Do this and all will be forgiven."

Smarmy bastard.

As we left the mansion, vampire guards glowered but no one attacked or tried to stop us. Word must have gotten out.

Still, we were cautious as I drove away, Ric and Aiden free to defend us if needed. Ric instructed me through sharp turns and double-backs designed to suss out tails while Aiden watched the streets like a hawk. Even after we'd determined no physical tail existed, we stopped just over the state border so Aiden could scan every inch of the limo for electronic beacons. He found one and flicked it into the bushes with disgust.

Driving off again, I called Twyla to let her know we were safely away. She let out a breath and said she'd see us at the cabin.

"Are we really going to do it?" Aiden said. "Find Eloise when she doesn't want to be found?"

"She'll find us," Ric said.

"What?" I squawked in duet with Aiden.

Ric smiled. "Remember the signals? Pink for *stay away*. Green for *find me*. I'll just leak my picture to the press on St. Patrick's day."

"Sneaky bastard." Aiden was smiling too. "And once she finds us, together we figure out a way we can all be free from Nosferatu. I like."

We returned to the cabin moments before sunrise. Twyla was cleaning up the kitchen. Elena was resting on the couch. Bo had built a fire in the fieldstone fireplace and kept tucking in the afghan covering her. She grumbled but didn't look too put out with his fussing. Although once the day heated up I'd imagine either the fire or covers would go.

It was less morning and more the end of a very long night. Bo poured libations and the six of us sat before the fire, celebratory drinks in our hands: me and Twyla with Irish cream; Ric, Aiden and Bo with good brown ale; and Elena making faces at her carrot juice.

We updated the three Alliance members. "Of course," I said, "after Eloise comes out of hiding, there's no saying that Nosferatu won't attack Ric. But we'll deal with that then."

"Nosferatu with a daughter." Bo was shaking his head. "I can't believe old fart face has a weakness."

"*Bo*. I swore you to secrecy," I said fiercely. "You can't tell *anyone*."

"Don't fail us." Ric's eyes flashed red. "I *will* protect my people."

"Yes, yes. Of course." Bo's expression sucked straight lemon juice. "I promise not to tell anyone about her and never to interfere with your nonaligned status. I like a bit of independence myself."

Then he held out a hand. "But if there's anything we can do, call. *Anything*."

Ric stared at Bo's hand. My heart thumped.

Then Ric clasped wrists with Bo, and all was right with my world again.

Suddenly the door slammed open. We all looked up.

Nikos, his chest pumping like bellows, stood in the doorway, no longer filling it. "Twyla. *O Theos mou,* you're safe."

Twyla leaped to her feet—and nearly fell over. Not the Irish cream. Lack of sleep and worry had finally caught up to her.

Nikos tried to mist—I could see his edges blur—but stayed solid. He shook his head as if to clear it, then kicked into a run and barely caught her before she took a header into the fireplace. His dark eyes roved over her face. She grabbed his shoulders and devoured him with her gaze.

As they clung to each other, we stared with shock.

His gray-streaked hair, grizzled face, hunched shoulders and bent spine were an old man's. His mountain of muscles had melted and he was almost gaunt. He looked like a man just out of intensive care.

Or one who should still be in the ICU.

I glanced at Ric. He shook his head slightly. In my periphery, Elena and Bo exchanged a worried look.

"You're all right?" Twyla didn't seem to notice as she petted Nikos's scalp. "Tell me you're all right."

"Yes." His voice rumbled as deep as before, which was frankly a relief. It seemed that was all he was going to say, with his mouth at any rate.

But their eyes met, searched, communicated. Twyla's glittered with unshed tears. "You need to sit. I've got something to say."

She led him to a chair. He followed docilely, his black eyebrows raised. It was obvious he was expecting the worst as he sat.

"It's a question. For you." She went down on one knee in front of him. "A very important question that I want you to think over carefully." She paused. "Not too carefully, though. It'd bruise my ego. You wouldn't want to hurt my ego, would you?"

Even Nikos seemed to know words were necessary to answer that leading question. "No, love."

"Good." Her face cleared and she took one of his hands in both hers. "I, Twyla Tafel, ask you, Nikos…" She frowned. "Nikos—" Her frown deepened. "Do you have a last name?"

One corner of his mouth crooked. His version of a smile was even more restrained than Aiden's. "I've had many."

"What was your original last name?"

"We took names of place." He covered her hands with one of his. "Nikos of Sparta."

"Your last name is 'Of Sparta'? How the hell will that look on the paperwork?"

"Paperwork?" Nikos rumbled.

"How about Nikos Tafel," I suggested.

She snorted. "It'd serve him right. But the minister might raise consanguinity issues."

"Minister?" Nikos's rumble was more urgent.

"Nikos Sparta then," I said.

"Or O'Sparta," Elena put in.

"Is that a real last name?" I asked.

"If it isn't, it should be."

"Minister?" Nikos repeated. "What—"

Two of Twyla's fingers to his lips halted him. Or didn't halt him exactly. His eyes lit up and his tongue slid out to slick her fingers.

"Stop that." Her voice had suddenly gone breathy. "I

have to get this said first."

"Mmm." His eyes closed and he continued to lick.

"Nikos..." Her voice cracked.

"Keep going, big fella." Ric leaned casually against the arm of his chair. "I'm finding this quite interesting."

Nikos continued to lick, but a growl emerged, low and threatening. Another, higher pitch growl, joined in, from Twyla.

Ric laughed. It was a full, deep chuckle, appealing to my ears—and other parts of me, tingling all the way through my body, shimmering with hope.

I got up and settled on his lap, hanging my arms around his neck. "We'd better let Twyla finish what she has to say. I want to be a bridesmaid."

Nikos stopped licking. His eyes snapped open and they were very dark.

Twyla opened her own eyes. She and Nikos locked gazes, and I saw the meeting of two souls. "Nikos Sparta. Will you marry me?"

His face lit like a nova and for a moment his wrinkles disappeared. "Twyla. My love. I thought this day would never come. Yes, yes, a thousand times yes." He stood, catching her hips and fusing her to him. "And will you marry me?"

"Oh yes!" She laughed and they kissed.

It was beautiful and poignant, and coming on top of the roller coaster of the past few days, made me long for my own taste of Happily-Ever-After.

I tugged on Ric's arm. "Maybe we should give them a little space." I tipped my head toward my bedroom.

Complex emotions passed over his face, pain and joy intermingled. Then it resolved into yet another smile, this one intimate and only for me. "Good idea. I have one more thing to discuss with the Viking—go ahead and wait for me?" When I hesitated he added, "I'll tell you all about it when I come to you."

"Okay." Sure, I was curious. But as much as Ric was a male of image and sizzle, I'd learned to trust that what he said to me was the truth. He'd explain. I got up to head for my bedroom.

Bo slid his arms under his wife and lifted her. "If you have questions for me, I'll put Elena to bed first."

"Hey," she said. "I'm not a child. I don't need putting to bed."

He looked down at her, and all the love in the world lit his eyes. "And did you get any sleep last night, worried about your friends?"

"Well, no."

"Exactly. You need to rest now, for the baby's sake as much as your own." He strode off to their bedroom.

"That looks like fun. Shall we?" Ric scooped me up in his arms.

My stomach swooped, making me laugh. "Yes. Definitely."

Nikos nuzzled Twyla's neck and started purring.

"Fine," Aiden said mournfully. "Leave me alone in the living room. I'll just stuff cotton in my ears and plug my nose."

Nikos ignored him. His purr grew louder and his fangs flashed against Twyla's dark skin.

"Hey." Aiden's head swiveled toward them. "Aren't you…?" He nodded at their bedroom. "Where I can't see?"

Twyla grabbed Nikos's belt and undid it with a quick saw. A zip later his pants fell to the floor. His erection strained for her.

Aiden slapped a hand over his eyes. "While that was slick, I'd rather not have seen how hairy Spartans aren't." He stood and started toward the lakeside door. "I'm going to go try to burn that image off my retinas."

"Don't go outside," I said. "The sun's up."

"That's the idea." He strode for the front door without uncovering and only barely managed not to smack into a wall.

I laughed as Ric carried me across the threshold.

Inside the bedroom he set me gently on my feet. "I'll be right back."

"I know." I stripped off my tight top and was pleased to see his eyes fall out of his head. "I'll be waiting."

By the time Ric tore his eyes away from Synnove's beautiful breasts…and it was a measure of how important what he had to discuss was that he did…Nikos and Twyla had thankfully vacated the living room and the Viking had returned.

"So what is it?" Bo asked. "Questions about the Iowa Alliance? More intel on Nosferatu?"

"More personal than that, I'm afraid." Ric picked up the bottle of wine, shook it to judge its fullness, or rather lack because it was nearly empty, tilted the bottle to his mouth and drank off the rest. "How do you do it?"

Bo raised one brow and sat on the couch's arm. "Do what?"

"How do you let Elena go out and risk her life night after night and stay sane?"

"Oh. That." Bo grabbed another bottle and had his own slug. "I don't. Stay sane, that is. But it's not like I have a hell of a lot of choice. Being a detective isn't just Elena's job. It's who she is."

"I understand letting her go up against humans. But does she ever face off against vampires?" Ric shuddered at the memory of Synnove with Nosferatu at her throat.

"All the time. It's not a question of 'letting her'. Wish it were." Bo took another slug. "She wants to be a vampire, you know. Sometimes I think that would make it easier on me.

But the chances that she'll end up dead instead of turning…I can't take the risk."

Ric frowned at the other vampire. "You risk her dying on the streets, or in a vampire fight, but you won't risk trying to turn her?"

"I can protect her on the streets. Watch out for her in a vampire fight. We don't know what makes a successful turning. I can't protect her from something I can't see, don't understand. But that's not why you're asking, is it?"

"No." Ric took a deep breath. "When I was a young vampire there was another girl…not like Synnove, but still, I loved her like a sister. And I was forced to abandon her. For nearly two hundred years I've felt guilty over that, and worse. I'm scared shitless I'm going to fuck it up again. I don't just love Synnove. She's my heart, my life."

"Short answer? You do it because you have to. You let her be an adult and take her own risks because anything less is damaging to her."

"But I don't let the humans in my household take half the risks she does!"

"Because the rules are different for a partner," Bo said patiently. "For all that individual humans may be friends, you and your household are more like employer and employees. There's equal commitment and an equality of tasks but there's *not* equal responsibility. You protect them, end of story. If they choose to, they can leave your protection, but then they're no longer part of your household. It's not that way with a partner and a mate. A partner is your equal in responsibility. And a mate is forever."

"Shit." Ric snatched another bottle.

"Agreed."

The two males sat in silence, drinking occasionally from their bottles.

Then Ric said, "Why can't I protect Synnove like I do my

household?"

"Because if the shit's flying you can compel a human in your household. Even the immune ones, you can command and they have to obey—or leave your protection. You have final say. You try that with your mate and I guarantee you'll be ball-less within a week."

"But when I see her walk into danger…I want to grab her, cart her away and lock her up forever."

"Can't. She's her own person, Holiday. You can watch out for her but you can't smother her. Honor that."

"But what if it turns out like Eloise?" Ric's voice cracked, his veins freezing at the thought of Synnove in Nosferatu's clutches.

Bo met his eyes. "Your best friend is one of the world's top assassins. Your lady is connected by blood to the Iowa Alliance. You have resources you didn't have then. But there's more."

"More?"

"Thor's hammer, Holiday. You were a kid then, right? Your only weapons were masks and tricks. You've emerged from behind the mask now. Synnove helped. She's strong, and you're stronger because of her. Trust her."

"But—"

"No. I've got to get back to my wife. And you…well, just go to your mate. Join with her. Wonderful things await you if you accept her as your partner."

The bedroom door clicked open. I shifted nervously on the bed. Before, one thing had led to another. This was the first time I'd be seducing him from scratch.

Well, not counting the dreams.

Ric came in. The instant he saw me in the black lace lying

on the bed, his eyes heated to violet.

My smile was as hot.

Maybe it was the beauty of seeing Twyla and Nikos finally joining as they were meant to be, two parts of the same whole. But when Ric came to me and kissed me so sweetly that it was like drinking honey, it drove everything from my head but *me want*. I tore at his shirt.

He stood at the side of the bed and misted naked, his muscular body reappearing in an ephemeral swirl, his form a galaxy of stars.

Then he was solid and stretching his long muscled body out next to me. His hand ran like sweet oil along my arm, my breast, my thigh. I dewed everywhere he touched.

We came together in gentle sighs, drinking each other's breath, fingers brushing damp skin. His tender touch loved me. The sensitive pads of my fingers found roped buttocks.

And once I was aroused everywhere but the tiny patches covering my nipples and mound, he smiled at me with masculine knowing, warmly intimate, and opened my bra with one flick.

His mouth closed over my nipple like a prayer. He suckled, lightly, but the corresponding sensations rode me deep. The heat of lust was no less for being kindled slowly. I wanted him with everything I was.

So when he spread my legs, muscular shoulders filling the gap, I stopped him. "I'm ready for the next step."

His eyes, rising from between my thighs, searched mine. He didn't pretend to misunderstand. "Sunshine, I don't have protection."

"So? Twyla said v-guys aren't fertile. Well, except with their mates."

"Yes, exactly." His gorgeous azure eyes were so serious.

I blinked. "Wait, no, what?" Heat of a different kind rose in me. "No, you can't mean…I'm not your mate. We've only known each other a few days."

"Synnove." He sat and took my hands in his. "We don't know each other yet, not the kind of knowing it takes a lifetime to achieve. But you're immune to compulsion, and you smell and taste like mine. My mate."

I blurted, "Then why did you tell me to marry someone else?"

He sighed. "That was what Bo and I discussed. I want so much to do right by you, but it kills me to stand by and let you put yourself in danger. And I don't have the best track record. That's why I pushed you away. But I knew it even then, I think. From the top of your brilliant blonde head to the ends of your elegant toes, from the beauty of your honest mouth to the tips of your strong, clever fingers, you're my match." He sighed again. "Bo calls it being a partner. Whatever it is, I want it with you. I may screw up, but I trust you to help straighten me out. We have several lifetimes for potential to become fact. I want to spend those lifetimes with you."

My eyes prickled at the heartfelt truth in his words. I sat up too, and clasped his hands in return. "You know, I came here because I was at a crossroads in my life. Medicine, the thing that had once saved me, had failed me. I'd always thought only content is important. You showed me I was hanging onto an image of myself that never really existed. I was never simply a plain girl. Real life is always more complex. Messy. Real life is always *lived*. Sizzle, steak, isn't what's important. What's important is going after what you want the most with everything you have." I paused, searched his eyes. "Even if you have to give something up."

His smile twisted. "Are you trying to let me down easy? You're giving me up to go after medicine?"

"No. I want you *and* medicine. And I'm willing to give up my old ways to do it. I used to believe only brains mattered. But this matters." I kissed him. "And this." I freed my hands to clasp his head and kiss him, longer. "But most of all, this." I dropped one hand to his lap, to grasp his pulsing erection. It leaped in my hand as if overjoyed. "I'm ready to make this connection with you."

"No matter the results?" His breathing was unsteady, and he seized my arms as if he were in danger of falling.

"Well..." I smiled against his mouth, "...I'll just have to take a break nine months into my residency."

"Sunshine." He pulled me into his arms and kissed me so deeply I thought he'd crawl into my mouth. "I'll watch our baby while you finish your training."

He laid me back on the bed and slowly released his weight onto me. I rejoiced in his heavy body imprinting mine, hard muscles claiming their place on the softness of my breasts and belly. Pressing most insistently was his long, thick cock, pulsing eagerly against my leg.

I opened to him, mouth and arms and thighs. He fitted me even closer, his tongue inside my mouth, his chest and ribcage filling my arms, his erection nestling snug against my vulva.

He rolled his hips, thrusting the smooth length of his cock along the groove of my sex. It caught my clit and sent shock waves through me. He did it again. Little wows of aftershock throbbed.

His dark purr vibrated against my ribs. He rolled back to thrust again. The head popped between my slick lips and lodged, a promise of fullness.

I tightened everywhere, breasts, belly, thighs. I grabbed his lats, fingers digging into hard muscle. My legs curled, my feet scrubbing the backs of his thighs. I wiggled under his weight, trying to settle him more firmly inside.

He groaned. "Synnove." He raised his mouth from mine.

I opened my eyes. He braced on his forearms over me, breathing hard.

His eyes met mine. "I love you. I want to bask in your sunshine, forever. Be mine, and I will be yours, now and always."

The image imprinted on my heart, and it was no illusion. "Now and always. I love you too." I paused. "But I'd love you even more if you were *inside me*."

He smiled, and this smile was male satisfaction and trembling anticipation, overlaid with joy. "As you wish."

His first thrust possessed me utterly. His second rocked me into the mattress.

He set up a regular rhythm, hard, insistent thrusts that demanded I rise into joy with him. Sweet tension built in me as heat slicked the skin between us. His hands framed my face not my breasts, his fingers twined in my hair; his washboard abdomen and his powerful pecs abraded my nipples with delicious friction. My hands slid down his lats onto his buttocks and I urged him deeper, telling him without words that his pleasure didn't have to wait. His thumbs smoothed my cheeks and his gaze was totally on my face, telling me that he'd wait for me to come first. And that he'd wait as long as it took.

That unspoken testament of his love shook me and broke my hold on control. I held his hips for my own pummeling, churning against him until I was ready to shatter.

And then I did. Pleasure crested over me, around me. Through me. Waves of pleasure beat like heat on a summer's day.

Ric rolled faster into me, a locomotive gearing up for its final run. "Sunshine. The feel of you, slick, hot, is enough to destroy me. May I?"

He could have been asking anything but his tongue ran the length of one fang and I knew he wanted to bite. I lifted my chin to expose my throat.

Hands in my hair, hips hammering mine, he pressed the

tips of his fangs into the tender flesh of my neck. His cock swelled with release. As the last twangs of my orgasm shivered through me I began to throb with renewed anticipation, on the cusp of something even more shattering.

He bit down. His fangs pierced my skin like live wires. My blood ignited.

He thrust his cock to the hilt. I opened to him, taking every inch of him, sucking him in even deeper. He roared and began to come.

A second climax burst through me, brain and body shaking with it. His body quaked with mine.

He began to lap at my neck, tongue rough and hot. My blood sang, claiming him. Feeling him claim me.

He wrapped me in his arms, rolling his hips to draw out our pleasure. His tongue pressed against my neck. Gradually the hammering of my heart in my ears gave way to his more gentle purr.

Wrapped in each other, we relaxed into sleep.

As dusk darkened the sky, I awoke to a feeling of wellbeing I hadn't experienced since The Incident. Maybe not ever. Wrapped in Ric's powerful arms, the scent of his warm skin in my nose, the sound of his heartbeat under one ear and the lake's far-off gentle lapping against the pier in the other, it was one of the most peaceful and contented moments of my life.

But peace only lasts so long before necessity takes over. I rolled off him. "Be right back."

"Where are you going? Oh."

I slipped on his shirt to visit the bathroom.

Elena met me as I was coming out. "My turn. Then I have some news that may affect all of us. Go get Twyla, would you?

She's not answering my knock. Well, not with anything but moans."

I glanced into the living room. Bo was pacing. Aiden watched him with dark eyes, expression blank but I got the impression he was worried. Seeing Bo's hunched shoulders I got worried too. I went to get Ric.

Twyla didn't answer my knock so I pounded on the door with an empty bottle of merlot for nearly a minute. Then she opened, looking like someone had slugged her stupid with a happy bat.

Made me rethink my whole relationship thing with Ric. I'm not vain, but I *never* wanted to look that idiotic. But I was happy for her.

I went to sit next to Ric on one of the couches, tucking my legs under me. Twyla emerged with Nikos and they snuggled on the other side of the couch. It was still shocking how gaunt he was, how old he looked. But Twyla didn't seem to care and nobody said a word.

Elena came out of the bathroom, and got right down to business. "I just took a phone call from my counterpart in the sheriff's department. You remember the trolls? There was an irregularity with one of their phones. A file the size of a video was sent to an unknown party. To an untraceable number."

"A video of what?" Hairs rose on my nape as I remembered the eavesdropper, who'd returned to see Nikos's vampire blood pull Elena from the brink of death.

The confirmation was in her eyes. "The video itself was erased from the phone so we don't know for certain. But yeah. I think we can be pretty sure it was the recording of the forest incident."

"What do we do?" Twyla asked.

"I called the Ancient One," Bo said. "Asked him if any of his techies can trace the call. He's putting Steel himself on it."

Twyla nodded. "If anyone can pull a miracle out of his

ass, Logan can."

"Until then," Elena said, "we can only keep our eyes open. And wait."

That was the only dark spot on a wonderful, triumphant day. After a hearty dinner, Ric drove the two of us to Chicago.

"Where are we going?" I asked.

"You'll see."

He pulled into the parking lot of the hospital complex where I'd done my surgical rotation.

I stared out the window at the red brick and concrete children's wing where The Incident had started the whole sequence of events. Had it only been a little over a week? "Teddy is here."

"Yes."

I turned to Ric with a confused smile. "You knew?"

"I found out. He's being released tomorrow." He swung into a spot.

"I didn't bring any books to read to him."

"I've got something else in mind."

We got out, my brain churning on the question of why Ric had brought me here, and why now. But when we entered the hospital's cool quiet halls, even after everything, the slight medicinal smell comforted me. "It's well after visiting hours," I said to Ric. "The nurses will know I'm no longer attached to Teddy's case. We may not be able to see him."

"We'll see him." Ric's eyes flashed violet.

"Oh. Right."

At the nurses' station, one of the third shift nurses was standing, reading a chart. She had a short brown bob and blue scrubs. I thought about sneaking past her, remembered the v-eyes and cleared my throat. She raised her head and smiled. "Dr. Byornsson, good to see you again." Seeing Ric, her smile brightened ten watts or so. "Who's your friend?"

"Hi, Betty. This is Ric. We were in the neighborhood and I'd told him so much about the hospital he wanted to see it for himself. So since we were in the neighborhood, I thought, well why not stop by…"

I trailed off, because I'd been babbling, but also because Betty wasn't paying attention. Her smile faded and her face went blank.

I switched my gaze to Ric. His eyes burned almost red. He said, "*You haven't seen us.*" His voice echoed as if in a crypt.

Slowly, Betty turned away.

"What was that?" I whispered. "What are we going to do that you don't even want anyone to remember we were *here*?"

Ric took my arm and led me toward Teddy's room. "What you've trained half your life to do. Heal."

All the patient rooms were singles, so at least Ric wouldn't have to compel some poor child too. As he ushered me into Teddy's room I heard *brrrt, brrrt.*

Despite the late hour, Teddy was awake, shuffling a deck of cards the fancy way I'd taught him, ruffling deck halves together then settling them with a back arch. He was small for his age but happy and eager, with the curly hair of a spaniel puppy. His large dark eyes lifted the moment I entered. "Dr. Synnove!"

"Hello, Teddy. How's it going? That shuffle's looking pretty good."

His hands were barely big enough to contain the deck, but he must have been practicing steadily since our last phone conversation. Bright, determined, focused. I wished with all my heart I really could heal him completely. But the nerve damage was too extensive for anything but a miracle.

I stopped abruptly. A miracle. Like the one Nikos had

given Elena. I suddenly knew what Ric intended. I turned to him. "You can't—"

"It's all right." Ric's smile was gentle, reassuring. "I want to."

"But you're not millenniums old, and Bo's not here to replenish you after, and the *cost*..."

He laid his hand on my shoulder, his warmth radiating through me. "If it's any help, I don't think it will take as much as Nikos."

"Dr. Synnove?" Teddy sat still and small in the bed, his face puckered in a slightly worried frown. "What's wrong?"

Poor Teddy. He'd already gone through so much. Did I want Ric to suffer? No. But did I want to heal Teddy? Emphatically yes.

And, from the nova in his eyes, Ric wanted to heal Teddy too.

I clicked off my fears and doubts, not Crisis Time but simple belief in Ric. "Nothing's wrong, sweetheart." I went to Teddy, gathered his small hands in mine and smiled. "In fact, everything is all right. This is Dr. Ric. He's a specialist. He's here to try to heal your leg."

"Hello, Teddy." Ric's voice was deep and resonant. "We're going to get you all better."

Teddy's worried eyes turned to Ric. "More needles? More peppermint air?"

"No needles." Ric came to stand next to me. "No anesthetic. Just listen to my voice. Listen and let yourself float. Picture your favorite place. A warm, sandy beach, or a field, thick with golden summer grass."

As Ric spoke, Teddy's face, instead of the blank, slightly frightening mask that Betty's had become, simply relaxed into a small smile. His eyes fluttered closed and he gave a contented sigh, as if snuggling up for a nice sleep.

Ric's voice tapered off. I moved the tray out of the way.

"Now what?"

"You open the skin to each area of damage. I'll apply blood a little at a time until that area heals."

Much better than the wholesale bloodletting in the north woods. "I'll get his records to pinpoint the damaged areas. And an instrument tray to open. We'll need to move him into the OR, and we'll have to scrub." I started for the door.

Ric stopped me with a touch. "I think he'll be more comfortable here."

"What about infection?"

"Not a problem, with my blood. Blood…" His eyes turned inward, then snapped back to me. "And you may not need the charts." He spun toward Teddy and strode to the foot of the bed. Gently he lifted the covers from the boy's legs. He rested his large hand on the boy's right ankle and closed his eyes. "Yes. I can sense the problem areas."

"How?"

"Blood flow. The capillaries are behaving differently around the damaged tissue." He pointed. "Here."

"All right. Let me get a tray."

The surgical tools were counted and stored in a locked area but I knew the keycode. I set a basic open tray on a cart and wheeled it back to Teddy's room. Leaving it near the bed's foot, I checked the boy's pulse, and pulled back his lids to check his pupils. Everything was normal.

Then I went to the sink and scrubbed. Maybe there was no risk of infection with vampire blood, but my hands were human. They were covered in germs.

"I found all the areas while you were gone," Ric said. "This won't take long."

"Good." I gloved, then uncovered the tray and picked up two scalpels, handed him one. "Where first?"

"Here." Ric pointed.

I swabbed the area with disinfectant then made a tiny

incision in the boy's leg. Ric thankfully did not slice his wrist for blood. He cut his finger with the scalpel and squeezed a few red drops into the opening on Teddy's leg.

It wasn't as dramatic as with Elena, but it was still pretty impressive. The small incision immediately closed, neatly, like an invisible thumb smoothing a clay seam. The skin flushed, then puckered before settling back to healthy skin.

"Amazing," I breathed. "Did you see that? The puckers?"

Ric had gone pale. "Synnove, I'm sorry. I thought it would work—"

"It *did* work. You know how your skin wrinkles from a long bath? Skin with nerve damage doesn't."

"Oh." He smiled tentatively. Poor dear. He'd been crushed at the possibility that his healing hadn't worked. It made me love him all the more. "Next spot?"

As I opened each small area, Ric released a few drops of his blood. Concentrated on those tiny areas, it took much less to heal Teddy's leg than Nikos used to save Elena.

But even that little exhausted Ric. He collapsed in a chair while I cleaned up and removed the cart. Yet when it was time, he rose to hold one of the boy's hands while I held the other, and said softly, "Wake up, Teddy." I couldn't help thinking that he would make a wonderful father some day.

Teddy's lids fluttered open. "Dr. Synnove? Is it over?"

I was relieved to see clarity in his dark eyes. "All done. How do you feel?"

"Good." He sat up. A slow smile lit his face and eyes. "Really good." He flexed his right knee, then raised his leg. "It's like I can talk to my leg again. Like maybe I can walk again."

"I'm so glad you feel better," I said cautiously. "But we should go slow—"

"I can feel my leg, Dr. Synnove." He swung both feet off the bed. "I can stand, I know I can."

"Wait...Ric!" I grasped the boy's arm firmly. He was coming down off the bed, *now*, and I couldn't stop him. I could only cushion the fall.

But he didn't fall. He landed on both feet, wobbled between Ric and me, and straightened. Then he took one step from the bed. And another. Ric let go. And another. I let go. Teddy took another step, gaining confidence. He turned, then skipped a small step. "I can walk, Dr. Synnove. Dr. Ric, look! Look at me walk."

Dr. Ric. Image, but also true. Not because he had the medical degree, but because he'd healed the boy.

And in healing Teddy, Ric had healed the worst of damage The Incident had done to me. Dr. Ric, because he'd healed my heart.

Suddenly Ric leaned against the bed, eyes closed, breathing shallowly. I put my hand on Teddy's shoulder. "Sweetheart, I'll be back to check on you. But you need to go to bed now and get some sleep. Your mother's coming in the morning."

"Won't she be surprised! Now she won't have to do what Dr. Bearsylls said." He gave me a quick, hard boy's hug. "Thank you, Dr. Synnove."

"Well...your mom still has to pay for the surgery somehow."

"Teddy's healed," Ric said softly, opening his eyes on me. "Holiday Buzz will cover the medical bills. I think we can safely say you won't be subjected to further harassment."

Blinking, I met Ric's tired but steady gaze. How had I ever thought this male was image only? "Thank you."

Teddy hugged Ric's waist. "Thank you, Dr. Ric." Then he jumped into bed.

"Good night, Teddy." I took Ric's hand, led him shuffling to the doorway, and shut off the light.

But the moment we got out of earshot I said, "You need

blood. Take mine."

"I can't, not without endangering you." He gave me a wan smile. "I told you I wanted you too much."

My cheeks heated. He'd said that before giving me that first orgasmic bite. A glass of juice had taken care of any light-headedness, and I hadn't thought anything more of it. And then he'd bitten me again this morning…okay, maybe I was a couple pints down. "Then you should rest."

"One more thing to do first. I'll be all right."

But when I insisted on driving he didn't argue. Even that little bit of blood had taken a lot out of him. If it hadn't been so worrisome, it would've been fascinating.

He asked me to drive to Meiers Corners where he directed me to Julian and Nixie's townhouses. Twyla had moved there in January but I'd been busy with clinical and hadn't seen the place yet.

"What are we here for?"

"You'll see."

I parked the car on the street, and we approached the nearest townhouse. Ric's fangs peeked out from between his lips. Stress or caution or both had brought his vampire nature to the fore.

And then, between one breath and the next, a mist streamed before us and snapped into six-plus of black-haired, red-eyed and long-fanged lawyer.

"Who are you and what do you want?" Julian Emerson snarled.

"Pax." Ric held up a palm. "I'm Ric Holiday."

"Holiday?" Julian's fangs slowly receded and his eyes cooled to blue. "The Ric Holiday who wouldn't even speak to me?"

"Things change. I'm here to map out an advertising campaign for you. It'll take several nights. Got a place Synnove and I can stay?"

"Maybe." Julian frowned. "Let me get this straight. You're going to do an ad campaign for Meiers Corners as quaint and local, not the New Sin City?"

"Well, I've got some ideas for you. But someone else will have to implement them. It's vital I maintain my independence from your Alliance."

"But what about Camille?" I said. "The competitive presentation?"

"I can reverse it now. Discredited, she won't have Nosferatu to back her up."

"I'm onboard," Julian said. "Anything that vexes Camille gets my vote. But what changed your mind?"

Ric looked at me and smiled.

"Oh." Julian sniffed delicately. "Ohhh."

We returned to the Chipmunk Lake cabin complex a week later—Julian had gone ahead with the purchase—with half Julian's household. On the way we stopped at Chipmunk Lake Supplies to get sunscreen and beach toys.

As Roy the Friendly swiped my card he said, "D'ya went wirms wih dat?"

I nodded. "Why not? And you might as well add a couple fishing poles too."

And so it was that evening that Ric and I finally relaxed together on the pier in front of our cabin, worms bobbing in the moon-speckled water. For the first time since Bearsylls had botched Teddy's surgery I was completely at peace.

I smiled. "Wirms. Fer feeshin'. I get it now."

The next Match Day wasn't until March, so I had a wait before I could start a new residency in Minneapolis. Ric and

Aiden pretended to look for Eloise but Ric's real first move, allowing himself to be photographed in kelly green, wouldn't happen until then either. In the meantime, I volunteered at a local children's hospital. Rosie and Harry, who, after a whirlwind courtship, had gotten married, asked if they could volunteer too.

I got them a gig reading fairy tales to sick kids.

One evening I leaned against the doorway in my hospital scrubs, listening to Harry's deep voice as he read "The Beauty and the Beast". Rosie's eyes on him were lit with love.

Ric materialized silently beside me and dropped a kiss on my neck. "Harry does a nice job reading."

"That he does."

"That's my favorite story."

"Mine too. I used to think it meant 'Don't judge by image'. But these days I have a new moral for 'The Beauty and the Beast'." I smiled into his azure eyes, silently telling him how much he'd come to mean to me. "Love unlocked the real me."

His gaze told me I was loved in return. "I have one too. Love freed the Beast, and Beauty too. Love freed us both."

About the Author

I write steamy paranormal romances and wickedly fun romantic adventures, stories that crackle with action and love. Challenging, smart alpha men—and women not afraid of a challenge. And oh, do the sparks fly when he meets THE woman guaranteed to infuriate and inflame him most.

In real life I'm an author, a spouse and mother, a flutist, a computer geek, and a binge-TV-watcher of *The Flash*, *Elementary*, *NCIS*, and *Wynonna Earp*.

Discover the* Biting Love *series…

Bite My Fire

Biting Nixie

The Bite of Silence

Biting Me Softly

Biting Oz

Downbeat

Assassin's Bite

Passion Bites

Discover more Entangled Select Otherworld titles...

The Hunt

a *Shifter Origins* novel by Harper A. Brooks

Prince Kael has just lost his father to an assassin, and he's the next target. A murderer is on the loose, the kingdom is in disarray, and Kael is determined to make the person responsible for killing his father pay. But falling for the beautiful Cara, panther-shifter assassin and main suspect his father's murder, wasn't part of the plan. He's not at all sure she did it, and he finds himself going against everything he's ever known just to claim her.

The Queen's Wings

an *Emerging Queens* novel by Jaime Schmidt

FBI dragon Reed's disdain for humans can't mask the magnetic attraction he has for Carolyn, but when she tells him she's going to shift into a dragon he thinks she's crazy. A female hasn't been hatched, or shape shifted, in over a thousand years. He's proven wrong after Carolyn shifts and is named the new Queen on the block. When the Cult of Humanity kidnaps Carolyn to sacrifice her, Reed must face his fears—and feelings, racing to save the woman he realizes he can't live without.

Printed in Great Britain
by Amazon

49073375R00192